Bombay Blues

Tanuja Desai Hidier

PUSH

SCHOLASTIC INC.

For my parents,
Shashikala Karnik Desai
and
Dhiroobhai Chhotubhai Desai,
with utmost love, respect, and gratitude

Library of Congress Control Number: 2014906335

ISBN 978-0-545-38478-0

10 9 8 7 6 5 4 3 2 1   14 15 16 17 18

Printed in the U.S.A.   23
First edition, September 2014

The text was set in Electra LH Regular.
Book design by Whitney Lyle

I lost my heart under the bridge.
—PJ Harvey, "Down by the Water"

Put on your red shoes and dance the blues.
—David Bowie, "Let's Dance"

Prologue

The night before I left for Bombay, I had a dream. Heartbreath, scuba deep. Diving into that seventeenth summer, and my headfirst spill into Mirror Lake, Karsh above, ashore. As the waters closed over my head: panic. Then a vision of my grandfather, long passed on, now a kind of merman, fingers coaxing a glimmer of spiraling pink dusk from sea floor, his amber eyes turned away from me.

I was torn. Should I sink or swim?

A jittery jugalbandi, the only submerged sound. An ultrasound horseshoe heartbeat, a foal-like doublethump skittering across it.

I strained with fast-draining breath, trying to reach my Dadaji. But despite my efforts to drown down to him, I felt myself beginning to rise, into what seemed a boundless liquid universe.

There was no way to yell, to catch his attention. I imagined the current tiding me away, lost to my home and family forever.

An upwards magnetic gust and train-track onslaught of sound . . .

Seized with fear, I emerged.

* CHAPTER 1 *

A Tale of Two Cities

I woke up in my NYU dorm room. My heart thudded and I heard the sound of sobbing. And at first I thought it was me, waking, tremulous. But it was Karsh, scrunched up fetally beside me on the narrow mattress, shivering in the throes of his own dreaming. His tears; his heart. My hand a buoy on his wildly pulsing chest. A thin layer of sweat veiled his skin, and he was calling out again in that child voice — a choked melody, in Punjabi?

—Karsh, it's okay, I whispered, struggling to squeeze him, ease him out of his dark place. He seemed skinnier, shakier, since he'd returned from his San Francisco gigs, though from all accounts, everything had gone well. I'd seen him like this before. Since his father died, he'd grappled with these night terrors at least a couple times a week. This time was worse than the others.

He was shuddering. Ever so gently, I tried to peel his eyelids awake.

When they finally fluttered open, he stared right at me with no recognition.

It was like I was the ghost.

Finally, me stroking his hair, he anchored down into a deeper, silent slumber. But I was still shaken. I decided to get some air.

My bags were packed, set to the side of the room. My roommate had split for the weekend already, a steal of a deal back to London. I'd be missing nearly three weeks at NYU but figured it would fodder my final photography project, which had me stumped at the moment. On my desk, a voluptuous bouquet of swimming-pool blue gerberas that Karsh had picked up for me on Houston. Beside it, a brilliant blood orange Titwala Ganesha, god of new beginnings —

a gift from Dadaji after a long-ago pilgrimage. In Karsh's room was the dancing form of Shiva, god of destruction: Nataraj. Out of habit, I dusted off Ganesha's face with my right hand.

Campus was beginning to hustle-bustle, the up-all-nighters staggering around zombie-like with cavernous eyes, the bright-eyed early risers riptiding the air with an alert cheery smugness.

I figured I'd check my P.O. box before flying out, something I rarely did these days since pretty much everything went encrypted or attached, wirelessly uninked. The only other person in the mail-room was Death, a freshman so named because he donned black riding boots and matching cape every day, all year round. He gave me his strangely chipper smile as he exited, arms laden with letters like a stiff-finned catch.

I opened my own box, and discovered a sliver of acutely familiar foreign sky rippling in that slim grey space.

Pale blue airmail stationery, elephant-stamped from India, like my grandfather and I used to swap tidings upon. But he'd been gone nearly three years now.

Washed up on the envelope, indigo-inked in a script nearly identical to his, my name: *Dimple Rohitbhai Lala*. Untyped, it was as if it belonged to a forgotten time. To someone else.

I took the missive to Washington Square and found a seat beside a bench where an older couple sat feeding the pigeons.

I could just about smell the swells inside the sky letter, the salt scent nearly granular, a swift reminder of the Atlantic's proximity. I opened its triple folds and found a swirling fish sketched in my cousin-sister Sangita's artistic hand — and in the Additional Message area, a request to join her and Deepak for their nuptials in Bombay.

A twinvitation: from one city by the sea to another.

We already knew the date, just over a couple weeks from now. It had been postponed from the original one due to an astronomical astrological error by the chart reader in choosing a moment of great auspiciousness. Or, if you asked Sangita's peeved sister Kavita, more likely the groom had been delaying due to aesthetic concerns about his wife-to-be (too dark, too thin, specs).

Considering this, and the fact that it was to be an unusually tiny gathering of people already in the know, the invite was a formality, and as such was surprisingly informal.

No presents, only your presence.

It would not only be the first wedding of our generation in this family but also an arranged one, in a city and country I hadn't returned to since before my grandfather exited it in ashes. The event would last only one day instead of the traditional three (Sangita and Deepak had decided to skip the mehendi party and sangeet, limiting the festivities to the wedding and reception), and was to take place on the day commemorating Dadaji's passing. It was also the same month as my parents' silver anniversary. They were planning to celebrate while we were out there. (I was planning to secretly snap the sites of their courtship as a surprise gift.)

Karsh was going to DJ the reception. After a few gig commitments here in New York, he'd be joining me in Bombay in a few days. I was tasked with being the wedding photographer, and I was hoping that, after months of visual roadblocks, a change of scenery would help me reconnect to Chica Tikka, my third eye, who I pulled out now from my camera bag and examined. Though I'd supplemented my photo taking with my parental graduation gift of a digital, that apparatus seemed aimed firmly futureward, whereas this single-lens reflex was my direct portal to the past. The SLR had been my precious gift from my Dadaji. We'd used images to talk, to bridge the miles between us — a photographic dialogue that carried on for years, and one I still felt I was engaged in every time I lay eye to viewfinder.

Lately, all I seemed to be able to pull into frame were borders, dichotomies, black-and-whites, academic either/ors. I longed to crack open a kaleidoscope, to discover a new truth through a new hue.

To follow a color.

Something in me had grown numb the last year or so — which I only realized as the prospect of jetting off into the semi-known unknown approached. I knew I was young and that most of my life (hopefully) lay ahead of me. But I also felt that so much lay behind me . . . *really* behind me: an anterior past. In India — a world that meant so much to me and to those I held dearest . . .

All this studying I'd been doing, about "the gaze," Rilke, Baudrillard — sure, it was exciting, especially during the moments I'd slip into the cracks between the lines and feel that firefly of elucidation hovering close. But I didn't know how to apply any of it to my life. Sometimes I felt we were all talking in university code, our shiny (and pricey) new signifiers numbing us to — distancing us from — the neglected, moss-ridden signified itself. I'd often wonder: Was it possible, truly possible, to cut across Broadway for the infinitieth time, grab the same seat, with that invariable supergrande latte (skinny, with whipped), and have a no-catch deep thought?

I loved school. I loved sitting around and having a professor supply all the answers. But I also sometimes felt I already knew what I wanted to do . . . so why did I have to read so much about it?

When I was actually taking and developing pictures, that's when I felt pulse-quickeningly alive. Applying. Applied. My goal in India was to be as unacademically hands-on as possible. To live in the body — my own, as well as the city's.

And to live in Karsh's, too.

CHAPTER 2

Even Cowgirls Get the Browns

Karsh and me. We'd get through this, become one again. He was the ears, I was the eyes, after all — hearing the beauty, seeing the beat.

After class, my *Paris Spleen* tucked into camera bag (earmarked at "Loss of a Halo"), we met up at our usual Astor Place spot for a caffeine kick. He seemed back to normal, so I decided not to bring up the terrors; maybe anxiety and anticipation about the trip were keeping us both on edge.

It was to be my first visit back to India since I'd lost my Dadaji, and Karsh, his father. And though the idea of arriving there to no beloved grandfather filled me with trepidation, I hoped I'd be able to light upon some closure, a kind of peace, once I'd finally set foot on Bombay soil, and that Karsh would find the same.

Clutching our coffees — in blue paper cups with Greek Athens logos, bought from Mr. Hyun at Korean deli La Parisienne — we fell into stride, strolled into the East Village, turning into Tompkins Square. Karsh and I were always drawn to the semicircle of benches in the park's heart; we proprietarily claimed that one in particular, with a partially obscured plaque behind it, had our names on it. In the swelter of city summers, a loop of American elms there unfailingly offered their gemmed shade.

Now, under February's frostbitten branches, Karsh held out his half-cup.

—Well, rani. To our last day.

—No, Duggibug. To our first. And to finding what we're looking for.

The coffee splashed over the edge as we toasted, brown drops on blue jeans.

—Imagine. In twenty-four hours, you'll be wishing for this, Karsh laughed, noting my shiver. Wearing Birks at this time of year could do that to a girl, but I was a hot-footed thing. —Ninety degrees in Bombay about now, right?

Behind us, a fence split pavilion from parkland. Before us, upon a scant circling island, two particularly sublime elms swept up, sapling and veteran swooning towards each other. Through the gap between them, across the clearing, a busker busked the Taj Mahal blues, his guitar case scintillating with coins and picks, warm voice wavering up over the drenched chords of a twelve-string like a surfer.

Looks you ran to the ocean and the ocean runs to the sea. . . .

—I'll try to soak up twice as much sun for you till you get there, I vowed.

—Guess we didn't specify same flight when we sent out that message? he replied with a smile.

Last summer, at Long Beach, we'd come upon an iridescent high-and-dry bottle of Sam Adams — plugged and complete with paper scroll inside. The writing had been illegible, ink squid runny, but we'd written our own wish onto a Post-it I had in my knapsack: *D+K=B-Bay.* I'd chucked it off a pier into the Atlantic. And now, just a few months later, that wish was nearly granted.

—Break on through, I said.

—Our big break as well, Karsh added, referring most likely to the gig he had lined up at one of Bombay's hippest clubs. Then he turned serious. —I'm going to miss you, you know. We've barely been apart a day or two since . . .

—Our Indian summer.

The summer I was seventeen. Heartache had gone heartflame, misunderstandings had morphed into epiphanies . . . and we'd come together one starry-eyed, sweaty night at downtown hot spot HotPot, perhaps the most magical and brave night of my life.

Now, over two years later. I was nineteen, in the pith of college life. He was twenty-one, about to edge out into the adult world.

We blew steam off our coffee tops and sat in silence. Though I wouldn't trade the last couple years for anything, I had to admit our time together had not been entirely uncomplicated. It wasn't always easy being the DJ's girlfriend. That's how I was known in some circles: as Karsh's woman. Which — though thrilling at first (*yeehaw! everyone knows he picked me!*) — sometimes made my (ab)normally inactive feminist side rear its affronted frizzy head. Didn't my photos count for something? Why wasn't *he* the photographer's boyfriend? I supposed images weren't noisy enough to compete. Also, people didn't usually get as wasted for photo exhibitions, and thus were in a less embrace-the-world-and-artist state of being than they were at parties.

Mainly, though, I guess I hadn't quite "made it" to the same extent he had. I didn't know what making it even really meant for me, but a hunger was building in me to forge some kind of photographic mark, to sink my soul into the trays of darkroom liquid and unearth a truth. Though, or maybe because, I was the shutterbug of choice for any school event sponsored by a club beginning with the letters S and A (South Asian Student Association, South Asian Journalist Assembly, South Asian Women Unite Ignite, and so forth), I felt pigeonholed.

I felt especially awkward hanging out with the charity-supporting (i.e., rich) South Asian from South Asia contingent of NYU that flocked around Karsh. (The rest of us were mainly supporting the foundations of ourselves, if any, or pushing the limits of our families' charity with the surreal costs of a liberal arts education here.)

As Karsh and I sat on that bench and talked about who we might bump into in Bombay, I flashed back to a night out not too long ago, when I'd met up with him after a gig, just past the defunct CBGB and its pulsing back-alley secret, Extra Place.

The only person I'd known well at the Bleep on the Bowery table was Shailly, aka DJ Tamasha, back in town only briefly after a recce into the music scene in Bombay (two months between visits a stipulation on her visa); she was taking time off from NYU to explore it and had brought back a couple of I'd Rather Be In Bandra tees for me and Karsh, which I didn't totally get (at all) but still found cool and insidery even though I was outsidery. Shy was crammed in next to Karsh, slumping in a rakhi-sisterly manner on his shoulder and smiling beatifically into space. She was an elfin thing with green-blue eyes that everyone thought were fake. They weren't. Neither was the half-silver eyebrow over her left sea-hued iris. The jagged hot-pink buzzcut-gone-pixie (headbanded with a pair of swim goggles) was, though. I mean the hair itself was real, but the hue was that of the month, and matched the neon catsuit she wore under a pair of jean cutoffs. Shy may have been a good Indian electronica DJ girl from the burbs, but her inner punk had gone slightly outer, which made me like her even more.

There was nothing punk, however, about the Indian woman who seemed to be holding court over various hard alcohols and paper cones of fried calamari. Mallika Mulchandani, a brazen Bombayite grad student at NYU, was oozing enough sex appeal to warp the wooden banquette. As she leaned in, a little closer than strictly required, to Karsh with her laughter, I tried to remember that she was the one with the connection to the up-and-coming Bombay promoter who'd hooked Karsh up with the show. Her dad was some kind of real estate bigwig in India, and she had a Delhi boyfriend at Columbia Business School, Niket, who in fact had no need to go to business school as he was a sure shot for a job in his (or her) father's company. He did, however, evidentally require a dentally white Porsche, which resided in a midtown parking garage, only emerging to drop Mallika off at international relations classes five feet away from where she'd already been standing in her Jimmy Choos.

Mallika spotted me spotting Karsh, and guffawed (somehow elegantly):

—Ye aai Karshki bibi!

The table broke into uproarious laughter. I saluted them vaguely.

Karsh smiled, gesturing me over. Shailly peace-upped me and slid to the side to make room between them on the bench.

—This is Dimple, Karsh announced warmly. —Dimple Lala.

—Oh, *yes*, you're the famous Gujju . . . began Rohan (econ, specs, shipping industry dad; it was rumored his family, unimpressed with his dorm room, had simply bought him an apartment at 1 Astor Place his freshman year).

—Half Gujarati, half Marathi, I corrected. No one leaves Mom in a corner.

—I mean, the famous *ABCD* photographer, he said, not unkindly, though American Born Confused Desi couldn't exactly be said kindly, either. —You cover all those events, na? The desi clubs?

—You come to them? I asked, unconvinced.

—I went to one by mistake, he explained. —I thought it was a Student Association Against Student Associations meeting.

He laughed alone. I wondered if he was considered funny in India.

Save Shailly, who hailed via the US and UK, a little like Karsh, the entire table seemed to consist of Indians from India — which was not the same as a tableful of Indians from America. First of all, there was a bottle of surely requested Tabasco sauce on the blue-checked cloth, as well as packs of Classic Milds and weird Marlboros and Gold Flakes with an alarming black-lunged dude on the box, even though smoking wasn't allowed. And second, the punch line of every jokey anecdote, even if the rest was laid out in English, always seemed to involve some element of a South Asian language. (Distressingly, Patels were included in many of these punch lines, and I was related to a lot of them.)

But mainly, no one seemed to be having a discussion about the diaspora. Most of the American desis I knew at least hit on this issue at some point, usually with self-conscious self-importance.

Later, Karsh, who was learning Hindi in preparation for this trip, translated what Mallika had said when I'd entered: *Here comes Karsh's wife!*

I looked at my *husband* now: benchside, that beautiful burnished profile, long straight nose, tidy chin beard. His kind eyes were deeply shadowed. After he'd received the news of his father's death, Karsh had thrown himself into his work. He'd always been passionate about what he did, but something had shifted in that passion — a kind of desperation underlying what had once been pure joy.

For her part, Radha, Karsh's ob-gyn mom, delivered more and more babies oozing thickly into the world, a furrowed nostalgia already imbuing their expressions for that safe dark ocean now crossed and lost. The first diaspora.

She and Karsh's dad had been estranged for years. He'd been a compulsive gambler who'd nearly shuffled and staked away their very home. The pair had been friends with my own parents in med school in Bombay — in fact, my parents had tagged along on their first date to "chaperone" them (or, more likely, provide an escape route were it all to go pear-shaped). On that muggy night composed of sidelong glances and bashful laughter, it was my parents who fell in love.

Karsh never talked much about the years he'd lived with his father, before Radha had decamped them, leaving his dad to India. But I knew Karsh's love of music came from him — Pandit-ji Ravi

Shankar and Bollywood beats to the Stones, the Stone Roses, the blues, the Moody Blues. Zeppelin. Their home had been tipsy with spinning records, the hiss of needle touchdown synonymous with Daddy home: Boney M.'s "Brown Girl in the Rain" playing one blustery UK night, a very small Karsh half-dreaming on the sofa, his sleepy perspective aligned with his parents' jeaned-and-salwared hands-on-hips sway, his father singing along, his mother's hushed laughter and surely a kiss as the lyrics rose a notch higher off vinyl.

It was one of Karsh's earliest memories. The song was also actually "Brown Girl in the Ring," as he later discovered, but he could never hear it that way even after standing corrected.

A year after Karsh and I got together, the tragic tidings were conveyed: His father had toppled from the side of a train en route to Victoria Terminus (Bombay trains were notorious for being packed on both the inside and out with tenacious travelers), mowed down in commuter darklight.

The kindly landlord had gone through his father's spartan room in Mazagaon, found and mailed Karsh two items. Karsh conjectured that one was from their shared past, a silver baby anklet (Karsh's own?) that had trilled out of the pale pink envelope with its carefully scripted return address: *CHDB, Casa de Saudade*, in Matharpacady. The second item: a small gold cross on a chain, which had led him to speculate that perhaps his father had turned to another faith in his last days, as a last resort. The landlord's note stated simply: *He left these.*

I wondered where Karsh had cached away these keepsakes. He bumped his knee gently against mine now, gave me a querying look.

—Your father, I told him.

He was worrying that cuticle again, staring into his coffee cup as if seeking a fortune. But all he said, so softly, was:

—Oh.

—For whatever it's worth, Karsh, I think your dad would've been really happy to see you, hear you, play there.

—Who knows? he said. —I mean, he wasn't in my life all those years when he was around . . . so what's different now?

Now he never will be is what I thought.

—Maybe something about being in India will surprise you, I replied, trying to sound infectiously optimistic.

—I'm very scared, Dimple.

—About what you might find?

—About what I'm not going to find.

We fell into a synced silence. Dadaji had always offered words of comfort when it was time for us to separate after family visits, a Marathi message I'd learned to translate over the years.

—*Rani. Remember: We'll be watching the same moon. We are never so far as all that.*

And perhaps we still were, he from an angle I simply hadn't learned yet. I could feel a tingle climb my spine as fear flipped onto its belly, turned into anticipation.

* CHAPTER 3 *

Queens

As we made our way to Queens, my mother, clearly getting in the spirit, now informed us that this borough was basically invented in India: named for Catherine de Braganza, Infanta of Portugal, England's first and trendsetting tea-drinking queen, whose dowry to Charles II had been the islands of Bombay (though he'd believed them to be in Brazil at first). The two nations had apparently concluded that this relatively blind date would be the most beneficial of unions and, very greedaciously, had arranged their marriage.

—A statue was made of her, to be placed on the East River. But it was never cast in bronze, is just lying somewhere in an altoo faltoo upstate New York foundry, my mother rued with surprising emotion. —Demoted to a lady-in-waiting . . .

—Or promoted, I suggested. —Could be she's just bailing on her geographically challenged husband? I mean, I know guys hate checking maps, but this is a little much. . . .

My mother didn't laugh, but from his flinty jet-black rearview eyes, I was pretty sure our taxi driver, Mr. Abdul Ashraf (formerly of Detroit), did.

We arrived at JFK four hours before the recommended three hours ahead of flying time, as was to be expected when traveling with my mother.

—Twelve o'clock on the dot, my father said gently, with the closest thing to an eye roll he was capable of. (Basically, it was a little wink, accompanied by a very sweet smile in my direction.)

My mother intercepted the smile and grinned back triumphant.

—Yes, twelve o'clock. Better to be waiting at the airport than at home, and then hitting a blockage on the Turnpike and delays at the Verrazano, followed by a hopefully not too harmful accident on the Belt Parkway.

—We should've been just a few hours earlier than this, I remarked. —Then the time difference between our arrival at the airport and flight time would have been the same as in India, and we'd be over our jet lag as soon as we embark.

—Dimple, this is not very mathematical, my mother sighed. —In any case, it is important to be early.

Clearly, no one else heading to JFK got that memo, as we entered and walked straight up the non-line to the heavily lipsticked check-in lady: Shilpa Singh, as her name tag declared.

—My namesake! my mother, Shilpa Kulkarni Lala, exclaimed.

—Did you pack your bags yourself? Shilpa Singh replied in what I was pretty sure was a Brooklyn accent.

My mother always got slightly offended at this question. My father could see it coming, and gave me a look.

—It's a standard security question, he now pointed out in unison with Shilpa (Singh).

—Obviously! my mother huffed. —You think little elves come out at midnight and fold all my linens, too?

Shilpa just raised her better-than-Bloomies threaded brows, which made me suddenly wonder whether she was in fact from Jackson Heights.

After this assault on my mother's ability to function as an independent bag-packing liberated woman, we continued on to experience the joy of our first full-body scan at the airport.

I was already a little tense as I put my bags through. I had a couple items that I was *concerned* about. The first was Chica Tikka. I didn't like people manhandling her too much. And the second was . . . well . . . the Condomania pleasure pack tucked away in the inner pocket of my camera bag.

Though I had learned to live with and even embrace my boda-ciousness since high school, as we approached the teleporteresque booth for the scan, I started to get that old familiar feeling: a thighs-stuck-together baby-belly dressing-room-hell self-conscious sensation of being a chubster. My jeans suddenly tightened around the hips, my "I Wanna Be Your Dog" Iggy Pop tee tensing across the chest.

—Beta! my father said, alarmed. —You aren't looking so well. Why aren't you breathing?

—I'm trying to suck in my stomach.

—Dimple, he sighed. —This isn't a contest for most attractive full-body scan. It's a weapons check.

The TSA dude was gesturing my mother through, but she stopped dead in her tracks.

—Now, sir, I've read that I have the first option for the right of refusal as far as this full-body scanning business is concerned, she announced, rather grandly.

—Ma'am, with all due respect, this check is for national secu-rity. If we'd had this system in place back then, we could've even stopped that underwear bomber from boarding.

—Sir, do I look like I have explosives in my underwear?

He didn't really look like he knew how to answer that one.

—Well? my mother insisted.

—Ma'am, you can opt for a pat-down instead.

She stepped aside, considering it. I was left in front.

—Pat-down? TSA dude offered me now.

—I'm not really looking for anything serious right now, I said. —I'll just do the scan.

—Dimple! Are you sure? my mother cried.

I stepped past the magnetometer into the booth — lifting my

arms above my head like some time-traveling criminal. In the end, my mother went through as well.

After security, it was time for Mom's required round at Swarovski, where she scoped out some gifts for Sangita and Kavita (who was already out there from NYU) and Meera Maasi. I also knew she was mentally noting the designs on some of the other items as well, to order replicas for less in India.

—The fake ones are often the sparkliest, she commented as we exited and joined my father, who usually hovered at the entrances to stores such as these. I wondered whether our ladies of Andheri would prefer fake to diamonds, but I guessed we'd soon find out.

*　＊　*

After a few hours midair, my mind drifted from the ostensibly "rip-roaring" Bollywood comedy that was spectacularly (and surely exorbitantly) failing to make me laugh. I found myself thinking of my high school best friend, Gwyn, who'd often spoken to me about her yearning to go to India, her feeling she'd find home there at last. Lots of white people seemed to feel that way about my motherland, and I often wondered why for so many years I hadn't. When we were kids, Gwyn had considered our house a treasure trove, lingering over the cans of mango pulp, unconsciously crossing herself every time she passed the kitchen temple (in a doorless cupboard): an ivory Krishna, flanked by incense, Pier One candles, a silver pot of the kumkum my grandmother pressed between my mother's brows when she left India, the crisp Lotto ticket that was proof of my parents' eternal optimism (or perhaps pessimism) about the American Dream, and the black-and-white photograph of Dadaji. At her own single-and-hungover-mothered home, she'd confessed, she would pore over maps, hunch over the spinning globe, willing her finger to land on that elephant trunk triangle delving gently into the Arabian Sea, predicting her future sojourns there.

Me, I'd fled the other way. At that time, I'd wanted more than anything to have Gwyn's blue-eyed, blue-jeaned ease in the ways of all things American. But, though it was buried beneath my fruitless quest to blend in at Lenne Lenape High School, my gut was engaged in a constant tango with India.

Now I had Gwyn's yearning as well, a desire nearly hormonal in its potency. I wondered if it had anything to do with my being (at least lineally) from there, or was a more general phenomenon, as so many people seemed to long for something in the Indus Valley — an unnameable but poignant sense of connection and disconnection, to be embraced by something bigger than themselves, wrapped so closely in the foreign that the usual became unusual and the strange, natural. The stranger a friend. The dream an undream.

I'd voiced this sentiment to Gwyn once and she'd nodded pensively, then added, eyes reveried:

—Plus, they have such amazing fabrics and jewelry. And the *food* . . .

It made me smile now. This was typical Gwyn, operating on all levels — the most superficial as relevant as the spiritual.

It had been ages since I'd really hung out with her, and here, away from the distractions of street-level living, I felt both her acute presence and a spiked loss. We'd had our hard times but had always managed to work through them, most notably that seventeenth summer when she'd fallen hard for Karsh, and I had as well — a split second after her declaration. We'd spent that season, sticky with watermelon and jalebi, lip gloss and bindis, engaged in a tense *does he/doesn't he, loves you/loves me not*.

We'd fallen out then. Though superficially about Karsh, the fault had run deeper, all the way to our latent longings to swap places. But in the backyard playhouse where we'd passed child-hood afternoons dreaming a twin dream of sugar tea, pirates, queens, we'd laid it all out on the knee-hunching low table . . . and then, over the coming weeks, glued those broken bits together again.

We'd carried on all the way through our senior year, wrapping up our time at Lenne Lenape High as valedictorian (me) and not (her). I was with Karsh much of the time, either at NYU or back Jerseyside, when he'd drive his angel-winged beat-up blue Golf home to see me. We tried to include Gwyn, but mostly she elegantly stepped aside, said she had to find her own path.

Gwyn spent those next couple years boyfriendless — while I was pretty much glued at the hip to Karsh. My first day at NYU, I already knew my way around campus, thanks to my frequent visits to see him. Gwyn didn't get into NYU or anywhere else in New York City; instead, she deferred state college to take on a job assistant-managing this shoot-the-worm Tex-Mex joint by the mall cinema. She saved her pennies, deciding she wanted to educate herself by seeing the world someday, while my own family clanked so many of theirs into the university boar bank.

After all that work sealing our rift, we simply grew apart. And the most painful thing was how painlessly, how naturally, it happened.

I switched headphones from the movie to my music, Patti Smith mounting in my ears: *There's a mare black and shining with yellow hair . . .*

What ambled into mind as we soared through the ether, the visual counterpart of my burgeoning bursting aeronomic feeling about India, was not an image particularly Indian . . . but another kind of equine winging.

Horse in Motion.

In 1872, with a single photographic negative, Eadweard Muybridge proved a trotting horse was airborne at one point; many had thought this to be the case, but the human eye couldn't capture this fleeting, blink-quicker moment.

Until Muybridge, illustrators painted horses in motion with one foot always on the ground, and when they portrayed them airborne, in "unsupported transit," it was with front legs extended forward, rear to the rear. But the amazing thing was, it turned out that when a horse was in fact fully airborne, its four legs were all pull-pushingly bundled up beneath it.

Essentially, Muybridge stopped time. He split the second and proved a mare could fly. So maybe a cowgirl could, too?

When I first saw that image, I was filled with a corporeal conviction, that of the possibility of the impossible, that there was no dichotomy between them, in fact — rather, one was a bridge to the other.

Vision: Horse hues powered my mind's eye now. Dun, brown; chestnut, grey. Black. Roan. Roanoke — a part-mythical land, like the illusory sheen of the blue roans, the bay. The chimeric brindles.

Sound: In my ears, Patti's *horses, horses, horses* . . .

This split-second negative frame made you realize: If you could slow down — or speed up — time enough to see what was truly happening around you, you just might find that *everything* was happening.

As I drifted into a sky-deep siesta, it struck me:

With a little luck, light, and just the right timing, despite all the years I'd, we'd, been away, the mythical Bombay I'd always harbored in my deepest diasporic imagination could exist, too. My Bombay, where the impossible could occur as well, and I might find wings and fins and all manner of things, a kind of completion — fitting-ins; my own missing link. Or, even better, a leaping out of frame, labels, and borders, into the extraordinary.

CHAPTER 4

Customs

Woozy from precipitately interrupted sleep (and slightly redolent of eau de bug spray after a total bushwhacking cabin-dousing by the air hostesses), my parents and I worked our way through Chhatrapati Shivaji International Airport in a daze. During childhood trips to India, the daze had been fueled by the complete chaos found therein, but this time, it was due to a fatigued amazement at how ordered everything seemed.

—These people are really getting their act together, my mother commented as my father and I gathered our luggage with ease, and the three of us slipped into the nearly ruler-straight lines to exit.

—All over the world! my father agreed, smiling happily. —Even the obtaining of the visa was so much simpler this time. So very organized; the hours of opening on the sign actually corresponded to the hours of opening of the establishment, isn't it? Indians are really becoming professional in all areas!

He didn't usually say "isn't it?" but it seemed all those old habits were carouseling back with our arrival. Did I even detect an accent coming on? There was a slight *lilt.* . . .

—No *No Spitting* sign at the visa office this time either, my mother added, nodding her head . . . oh my gods . . . *side to side.* —How shameful I found that in earlier years!

—Um, the visa department's been outsourced, I pointed out, recalling the huge proportion of non–South Asians who'd been working the counters. Our own had been womanned by a genial African American with silver-hooped ears and no nose ring. —So

Indians are definitely getting the *outsourcing* act together. Anyway, why do you guys talk about *them* as if they're not *us*?

My mother gestured to the surrounding crowd, who, by and large, looked like our stunt doubles.

—All these people we left behind, my father said with emotion, taking them in with his loving gaze. —And now here we come, hoping they will accept us again after such desertion.

Thankfully, the headphoned, goateed South Asian twenty-something in a Jay-Z tee standing beside me, single-hand-texting on his iPhone, didn't look like he was holding anything against us. My father always viewed his and my mother's emigration as if they'd defected from the army. He'd always dreamed of returning to his homeland after a few years in America, to help the hard up and disheartened with his medical knowledge. But life had taken over, with its comforts and habits.

—I suppose we *ourselves* are outsourced, my father continued, smiling kindly at me. —But now we have returned to the source, isn't it?

I had to smile back. We had, and it seemed to be smooth sailing as first my mother, who made sure to use her Marathi with airport officials, and then my father were waved through the final doorway. But as I coasted along behind them, the very same airport official signaled me to the side for a baggage check. My mother, noting within eyes-in-the-back-of-her-head seconds that baby duck was not imprinting, whipped around with a violent look and began to storm the area.

—But she's with us! Maazi mulgi aahe!

—Madame, you cannot enter again the premises once you have gone through, Airport Official Two declared, barring her way with a burly arm. She and my father hovered there, like ill-dressed clubbers at the velvet rope.

A couple of other people had been pulled over for the check. I vaguely noted the goateed hip-hopster and a blue suede, brown-banded cowboy hat floating just beyond him, atop a tall man with robustly tanned arms.

Frisker Dude One unzipped my duffel and pulled out a few items, laying them bare before him. I was rather relieved my Condomania pleasure pack remained tucked away for the moment but a little alarmed when he rather cavalierly dumped my carefully wrapped SLR on the table.

—Any meat? he asked. I shook my head, tempted to inform him I'd already eaten. But apprehension took over. The pleasure pack winked a lascivious corner out of the camera bag's inner pocket. But he didn't seem to notice and was now unrolling my Patti Smith *Horses* (aka Robert Mapplethorpe) tee to reveal Chica Tikka in all her grand apertured glory.

—It was a gift from my grandfather many years ago, I explained. He nodded, *Aaachha.*

—My Dadaji, I added for bonus points.

—And a very fine specimen at that, a deep voice with twinkling accent of unknown origin commented. I looked up to see the cowboy peering over at me from below his brim. When our eyes met, my entire body swiveled towards him. He covered his own an instant, took a step back, then slowly lowered his hand.

We spoke simultaneously.

—. . . sorry, I . . .

—. . . thought I . . .

—. . . knew you . . .

—. . . were someone else . . .

—Maybe it was just the camera, he concluded finally.
—Canon AE-1?

—Yes! I smiled, pleased he recognized my hot-shoed relic. I could barely figure his eyes. They were a curious haze of . . .? Kind of a greyish bluish brownish . . . hazel? Khaki? He looked kind of old but young. Rugged? He was also really tall, but it didn't hurt my neck; it was more like looking at sky than skyscraper.

Frock. What was happening?

His own smile was warm and a touch mischievous as he nodded downward. I followed his gaze to find, laid out on the table before him, his equally chunky (by current standards) single-lens-reflex Sure Shot . . . beside a pack of condoms. I tried to fix my eyes on his SLR.

But I was mesmerized by the coincidence. The cameras, not the condoms. Sort of. It felt like it was a sign of amazing things to . . . come during this trip.

Had I just cackled aloud? Cowboy was grinning now.

—Who needs a hipstamatic? he said. —You know what the trouble with the modern-day hipster is?

—What's that?

—They don't know what's really cool.

I burst out laughing. Our airport official gave us the side-to-side head nod that indicated we were in the carry-on clear. Cowboy expertly packed up his camera and slung his bag over his shoulder. I smoothed my *Horses* tee out on the table and bundled up Chica Tikka.

He was off, but turned back for one last glance and three little words.

—Later, Indie Girl.

I looked up. He nodded down at my rolled-up-around-camera Patti, her minikin horse pin looking like a Lilliput plane on fabric.

—See you, Cowboy, I said with, for some reason, a goofy grin. As I started walking, it hit me: We were here! In India! Art! Life! Love! Biriyani!

Though I felt a budding desire to declare all of the above, my customs man cluelessly waved me towards the Nothing to Declare line. When I joined my parents, my mother peered into my eyes.

—Who was that Western Heston man you were chitchatting with for such an inappropriate amount of time?

—Another aficionado of film, not digital, I said.

—I do not know if you should be fraternizing with *aficionados*.

She said it like she was saying *mafiosos*. My father was more on my wavelength.

—Bacchoodi, it is a sign! he announced. —That you will take many, many wonderful photographs here!

—Yes! Thanks, Daddy! Anyway, all's swell with Chica Tikka, so why waste time?

I unzipped my camera bag. We were about to exit, but I stopped my parents at the threshold, signaling them to hold still.

My mother tilted her face at the Bollywood-influenced angle she always used for photos: slightly to the left, downcast head, up-peering eyes, tiny smile tugging one upper lip corner. My father gave an unabashed grin, concealing none of the boyish excitement he felt to be here again, nor his newly capped tooth. I snapped them there, flanked by Samsonites, and looking a little worn out but a lot happy.

As Chica Tikka sucked them in with her knowing wink, it struck me: Perhaps they'd looked then — the day they'd forsaken Bombay's potholed pavement for America's orthodontic disco-glow grin — just the way they did now (though back then, my mother's hair to hips, my father's a pure inky sea, no silver combers). There they'd been: quivery with optimism and even a sort of grief for discovering what lay ahead ... which maybe wasn't so different from the tremor of joy and longing now to find all that had been left behind.

—Welcome home, guys! I said, snapping. I packed up Chica Tikka. When I looked up from my camera bag, I was startled to be greeted by my father aiming his own digital cam at me.

—Don't move, beta! he said. —Candid, candid!

—Smile! my mother commanded, stretching her mouth ear to ear as if to demonstrate.

I was taken aback, and that same goofy grin deluged my face. I was hardly ever in the picture, but as my father clicked, he changed all that.

—This is your journey, too, my mother said softly.

—And your homecoming, my father added. He wrapped his arm around me as we three grouped together — not a line but a bundle — and continued on out into the blaring, bleating, bountiful Bombay late day.

⁕ CHAPTER 5 ⁕

Browntown

As soon as we exited, Bombay fell over us like a second, warming skin. Or perhaps our American scales shed, clattering childishly round our shadowed ankles, excavating an ancient underlayer.

Less than a second after we were out, a random brown guy ran over and picked up two of our suitcases. A second and third appeared and squabbled over the rest of our luggage. Numero uno triumphed. There would be many of these randoms; I'd forgotten that aspect of India, where the division of labor was so subsplit that myriads appeared at the whiff of any task, especially one that might result in US bucks for tips. My mother indicated the parking lot to the victor. We'd taken hardly a half dozen steps that way when I heard a joyful holler:

—Dimple! Shilpatai! Rohitbhai!

Materializing before us was my uncle, Dilip Kaka. I didn't recognize him at first; it had been a handful of years, but he seemed tinier, a scanter person than the last time around — or was it my chubby NR eyes playing tricks on me, the perspective of the NRI: Non Resident (Not Really) Indian?

A symphony of a smile lit his countenance; it was catching, and when I looked to my parents, I could see they, too, emitted this glow. Dilip Kaka's arms opened first for me.

—Beta! Home at last.

He pulled his face back, pinched both my cheeks with delight.

—You have all packed on! You look wonderful!

I'd forgotten *fat* was a compliment in our family.

—And Shilpatai, so well preserved! Come — we better get a move on or I'm in for quite a scolding. The girls are all anxious to see you.

It turned out that the first random guy wasn't random at all but Arvind, the family's occasional driver.

—How is Meeratai weathering all the premarital stress? my mother asked now about her sister.

—Let's just say it's been pleasant to get out of the house for a bit.

My mother and her sister had a checkered relationship. On some level, it felt Meera Maasi had never forgiven her for leaving India. In my childhood, my aunt had once chided me, in my OshKosh B'goshes, for not wearing a proper "frock," leading to my continued use of that F-word as an expletive. In fact, everything American about me — or perhaps it was America itself — seemed to irk her.

My impression of her narrow viewpoint only solidified when Kavita had confided to me in New York that she was queer, a fact she'd at the time felt she'd never be able to share at home, even though she was in love with her then-girlfriend, Sabina Patel. Though she and Sabz were now history, Kavita had made a vow to herself to fill her family in on her sexuality during this trip. *At least one positive thing should come of all we went through,* she'd told me.

As Kaka guided us towards the sky-blue car, my parents chattered with him animatedly in Marathi. I smiled at them blankly.

—Still no Marathi? No Hindi, beta? my uncle asked kindly, as if I were supposed to eventually grow into these lingos, like a bra. I shook my head, a little regretfully, decided not to mention I was, however, studying French. We got in the car, which played a stream of "Happy Birthday to You" during Arvind's brief reversing maneuver. —Well, no issues. Here, we speak Hindi English, Gujarati English, Marathi English, England English, and American English!

Exiting into the suburb of Andheri felt like catapulting into the dyspeptic but determined gut of a jeopardous roller coaster.

—Bahut busy flyover! my mother was exclaiming now, indicating an overpass whizzing above. —Baapray, so much construction? Still?

My uncle nodded.

—What is new in Bombay since you were last here? Well, that bridge across the ocean, linking Bandra to Worli, the suburbs to the south. They were building it last time you came, na? It is complete now, though unfinished. The Sea Link . . .

—Can we see it from here? I asked, intrigued.

—Aaray, no, beta. Not from Andheri.

—I guess not, I agreed (as an entire family, complete with side-saddling saried mother, zipped by on a single motorbike, helmetless). —Looks like in Andheri all you can see's cars and humans!

*   *   *

Out the window, everyone looked purposefully if precariously swept up on destiny's course. Lanes? A high-stakes exercise in the suspension of disbelief. Traffic appeared to obey only the rule of Who Honks Loudest Wins; pedestrians had no rights but seemed endowed with startling bravery, stepping nonchalantly between all manner of mad-dashing vehicles.

In *chappals*. Rickshaws rattled devil-may-care close, looking like endearing chunks of interplanetary auto shrapnel. A tuk-tuk seemed to be a hunk of a bigger, bolder gas guzzler that'd clunked off and managed to take steering wheel, three tires, and half the windshield with it (but somehow lose the doors, seat belts, and driver's shoes in the process); they yawed buggishly about, just missing toes, Tata trucks, cows, and each other by a hair.

In fact, other than the driver being on the right, it wasn't even so apparent we were driving on the other side of the road.

—There's a reason fatalism was invented in India, my mother commented now. My mother was convinced everything was invented in India, even the bagel (resembling the zero, which *had* been invented in India). But I could see her point, and even why reincarnation may have been as well (or you wouldn't dare cross the street!). She pressed her face to the pane. —Ah, Dimple. Out my window is the life I left behind. . . .

It didn't take long to see the India of childhood memory thrown into sharp relief against scaffolded sky: a side lane down which a throng of garlanded people song-and-danced, beating drums. A wedding? STD stands with old-style spiral-corded phones on rickety tabletops (Subscriber Trunk Dialing booths, not open-air help centers for those with the clap). Men walked arm in arm, even held hands. Women and girls also. Paanwallahs rolled thandak in betel pepper leaves at roadside stalls, phoolwallahs strung garlands, chaiwallahs pushed carts cut-glassed with steaming tea, and other inexplicablewallahs minded storefronts bursting a firework of saris, chunnis, bangles, spices, buckets, baskets, fruits, and veg.

And every wallah, voilà: brown! Whenever I was brown among the brown in New York I was at some kind of edgy desi underground event. Either that or in a Mexican cantina full of Dominicanas and Puerto Ricanos.

Or on the A train to 200th and Dyckman.

But for some reason being brown among the brown *here* . . . almost made me feel white.

Beige, at least.

I caught sight of something that seemed the nexus of all that glittered, all that golded: like a hallucination in the traffic's rotary heart, a saried creature, giddily swirling her own razored rainbow roundabout like some kind of Indo goddess Iris, mirrored fabric sending light spinning saber-like amidst the smoking, choking cars.

—Roll up your window! my mother cried urgently as the vision approached us, jangling earrings near audible. —Toh hijra aahe!

This I understood: a eunuch, a transvestite.

—She is here every day, my uncle said. —Our local hijra.

—They are very pushy about money, banging on the car, refusing to take no for an answer, my mother insisted. —I was terrified of them as a girl!

Too late. The roundabout hijra was plunging her palm into my cracked pane. I waited for the bossy begging to begin, but she simply laid her hand upon my own, gazing into my eyes.

I met her gaze. She grinned, withdrew her hand, did that side-to-side nod, and waved us on.

I grinned back; our eyes remained locked as the car moved away.

—It was as if she knew you? my father observed now. My mind turned to New York City, and how Zara Thrustra lit up the HotPot dance floor in much the same way this hijra seemed to be stopping Andheri traffic. Zara, whose photos I'd taken as she turned from man to woman — an act of creation, re-creation, reincarnation, that had intimated to me how much of one's identity is in one's own hands.

Was this her Bombay avatar?

We turned off and wound up the entryway of the Ramzarukha complex, exiting into the courtyard between buildings. Kids skittered about, playing kabbadi — a mythical sparrowlike sound I recalled from dozing off jet lag, head in Dadaji's lap, on childhood visits.

In a shaded area off the parking space, a small group of men and women in white sat in a circle, singing softly, hands bedded with flowers.

Dilip Kaka laid a hand gently on the shoulder of one of the older women, murmuring a few words to her before we continued on. In their midst, I caught a glimpse of a supine figure, cloaked in white as well.

—Someone has passed on, my uncle informed me quietly. Nearby, the watchman dozed in a plastic chair, as if he'd seen enough life and death to be saturated into a stupor. Asleep for the wake. —Last night. Raman-ji, one of the oldest tenants in the building.

My father nodded, moved, as we approached the elevator bank.

—The cycle of life. A funeral today. And in just over two weeks, Sangita's wedding.

—Yes. One must focus on the positive, my uncle agreed. —It's Shivratri soon, the festival of Lord Shiva, god of destruction. My heart goes out to those who are grieving. But fortunately, destruction is always followed by creation.

Above the elevator, a pulsing image of a cherubic Ganesha — remover of obstacles, son of this same Shiva — bloomed with the motto THE ONLY WAY IS UP.

I paused to photograph it. My uncle followed my eyes, smiling.

—See? The god of new beginnings.

Dadaji's favorite. *Here's to no end.* I took a breath, pulled open the grille.

—And so let us begin, I said.

CHAPTER 6

There's No Place Like Home

Although the only way was up, the ascent to the third floor was so
slow as to feel quite similar to going down. As my parents and uncle
chatted, I felt like a kid again, elders creating a protective halo. We
were such a tiny familial trio in America, it was reassuring to see a
larger context, clan, did exist, albeit eight thousand miles away.

I realized a part of my mounting excitement was to see my dear
Dadaji — and though my rational mind acknowledged the futility
of this, my emotional organs still couldn't quell the sense that this
was the closest I could get to him.

Memories flooded back now of exhilarated arrivals, after countless miles minutes years, finally gazing into the weathery face and
oceanic eyes of my grandfather, here in this very building. Irises that
made a seashell sound, sang of a faraway place he could make home
for me. The push-pull desire to lose myself in that most safe and
unconditional of embraces — but also to stand back and take in
that treasured visage, soak it up like a map sinking through skin,
my immersion in India entirely begotten through his eyes, nose,
smile.

We finally creaked to a halt and walked up to the front door
of the apartment. A marigold garland hung off the frame, fresh from
the phoolwallah no doubt, with a baby-blue image of Krishna poised
above it. To the right, on the corridor floor: a metal cage containing
a fledgling sparrow, a feathery flicker where surely her pindrop heart
was beating.

—Zepploo, our latest addition. Akasha saves birds, Kaka explained.

Akasha was the daughter of family friends, who was living with
my uncle and aunt while her parents tried to get a Häagen-Dazs

franchise off the ground in Atlanta — no easy feat with families skimping on luxury scoops during the economic bust.

—She is home today; it's an Islamic holiday.

—She's Islamic?

Kaka chuckled. —No. Not Mussulman. Her religion is just the holiday part.

The door was split in two, the top ajar. And then, like a magic trick, an avid face appeared.

—Akasha, my uncle announced.

She was a nine- or ten-year-old girl with eyes as piercing as the sparrow's, shining out through a bob of black hair spilling from spotty bandanna. She wore a *Loins of Punjab Presents* tee and cut-offs, inner pockets hanging lower than the hems, and fizzed with Thums Up energy.

—Dimple, the last time you saw Akasha, she was a baby, my mother enlightened me.

I had no recollection of this diminutive creature, but at the sight of me, the alert-eyed savior of winged things squawked with excitement:

—Dimple Maasi!

Although I wasn't, in fact, her mother's sister (or anyone's), I didn't mind simulating a blood tie to this perky little person.

Now both panels of the door flung wide, revealing my Meera Maasi and, close behind, two visages appearing perched on either of her shoulders like a maternal balancing act. Kavita and Sangita.

I'd never before noticed how much my aunt resembled my mother — they were like sketches of the same person, but whereas the artist had used an expert index to smudge soft the edges of my mother's features, Maasi's lines had been left untouched. Her face was a jumble of angles and points, but if you connected the dots, it was my mother's face. My heart seized: The tiny woman before me looked like she'd aged eons in the time since we'd last met — whether it was due to wedding stress, the loss of her father, or the way pictures froze a certain time in your head that fell out of sync with real time passing, I wasn't sure. Somehow it made my mother look older now, too.

I'd foreseen a feeling of emptiness here, but my heart was overfull. For the puzzle pieced together by these precise people, it struck me, was just about the exact shape of the space Dadaji had left behind.

—Shilpatai, said my aunt, almost shyly to my mom. —So much weight you have packed on!

—And too much you have lost, my mother said, a little shy as well. They stood staring at each other, perhaps accounting for the years, and pounds, between.

And then they hugged. A time-traveling, even time-effacing, hug.

—I can feel, I heard my aunt whisper. —He is happy. So happy we are together again.

My mother nodded, mute.

Oddly, considering that at NYU Kavita was always sporting a salwar kameez and, weather permitting (three months a year), chappals, Bombay Kavs was dressed in black skinny jeans stretched gloriously beyond their bounds on her generous hips and gravity-defying butt, and a ribbed rainbow tank under a plaid man's-style shirt.

Just behind her, a version more like the Kavita I knew from America: Sangita, the bangled and bindied bride to be, in long loose top over ankle-clinching pants. She stood anxiously twisting a string of mahogany beads around her neck.

—Sisters, unite! I declared, throwing an arm around each of them.

Kavita sighed with what seemed relief, squeezing me close. Sangita didn't move, but a little smile sparked her face and she actually clapped her hands, eeking out a suppressed squeal. Akasha even pummeled her way into the cuddle zone, then abruptly *be right back*'d, lifting Zepploo's cage and heading down the hall.

Now my aunt took my arm, ushering me farther in.

—Welcome, beta, she said warmly. —Welcome home.

I smiled back. —There's no place like it, Maasi.

*   *   *

Inside, we added our shoes to a sprightly jumble of chappals just past the threshold. I peered farther into the space, could almost see Dadaji coming down the hall, speechless with joy. . . .

A moment after we'd entered, the bell jingled, door opened, and Arvind deposited our luggage just inside without entering. He smiled, nodded at me, and disappeared.

My aunt now scurried her daughters off to the kitchen, while my uncle led the rest of us to the stripy sofas.

My nose ached: a familiar hot buttery scent with undertones of sandalwood and overtones of dust — a tickling sensation, a whiff of coconut-oiled hair fanned on pillows. Mosquito hum; the soothing whirr of a lazily spinning overhead fan. From the kitchen, a clanging concerto of stainless steel, intermittent sizzling, the soft scuff of bare feet on ceramic tiles — reverberating through the entire building, perhaps, as dinner was cooked in mustard-seed-popping pans throughout Ramzarukha.

It was as it had always been. At first. This front sitting room with the large grilled rectangle of window from which scads of buildings were visible, many under construction, some of the lower ones patched in blue. In the distance, something higher than a skyscraper: a brownish-black jut of a hill, turretingly atop which was a just-visible white edifice.

A strain of the muezzin uncoiled from somewhere in this landscape. My mother was close beside me now, gazing out the window. Her hand hovered over the arm of the cushioned chair there, still angled to face out the frame.

—Dadaji loved this hill, she said softly. —He often told me it was the one place you were guaranteed space, peace in Bombay.

I'd seen that hill on visits past, a fixture in this fenestra. As a child, I'd believed America lay just on its other side — as, in the

USA, I'd imagined India was a mere tobaggan ride beyond the early-snowed slopes of Rice's Fruit Farm.

My eyes began to note the present in the room: the plethora of cell phones, the thinner-than-air laptop by a Bhagavad Gita, a handful of magazines — *Vogue, Elle, People* — all with brown-skinned, brunette (and sometimes henna-highlighted) cover girls.

My aunt poked her head out of the kitchen.

—Dimple, why don't you freshen up if you like? Down the corridor to the left.

Not the first bathroom: That was just for bathing, entire space tiled, a smattering of pink and orange buckets, hand pitchers in one of which a splish of thick paintbrushes soaked. The intoxicating scent of Mysore sandalwood soap.

Nor the second small room over, with its Indian-style toilet: a hole in the ground, a hose for washing up. Sangita gently nodded me to door three: the Western-style toilet Maasi had installed for a past visit (my mother claimed she'd never heard the end of it though she'd been perfectly happy to squat). Just before I entered, my aunt hurried over and pressed a fluffy pink something in my hand.

—Especially for you, beta, she said.

A roll of Western-style toilet paper. My mother appeared behind her shoulder.

—Western Heston girls, she said with the barest wink. —Such trouble.

*   *   *

Bladders relieved and faces splashed, we found ourselves sofa'd once more, my cousins now bearing steaming cups of Maasi's famous chai our way.

Mugs, actually: ebullient with a rainbow pattern much like the one on Kavita's tank.

—I picked these up recently, Kavita explained too casually. —As a little gift for the family. The *chosen* family.

She gave me a significant look. I started. Was this her warm-up to letting them know?

—At Shoppers Stop? my uncle inquired.

—We went to Bandra. I took Sangita to Azaad Bazaar.

—Freedom bazaar? my mother asked . . . then nodded, comprehension dawning.

—Do they sell khadi? my father, though aware of Kavita's sexual orientation, now queried. —Gandhiji used this homespun cotton as a passive resistance protest against the British. The charkha.

—No resistance at all, Kaka! Sangita giggled. She smiled sweetly at Kavita. —Darling little shop! I made sure to pick one up for Deepak as well.

Kavita rolled her eyes at me. Clearly, her message had been missed. I downed my queer-friendly tea like a tequila shot, and in a blink it was refilled, my cousins serving us as if royalty had arrived. Any attempt on my part to lend a hand was shushed down as if I were an invalid, or a man.

—This is the best chai ever, Maasi, I declared, to show Maasi mercy. Then, to exhibit sisterly solidarity: —In . . . the best mug ever? The secret ingredient?

—Love, my father said with a smile, gently winking at my aunt.

—Love shove! Meera Maasi snorted, to his delight (and my shock). —Freshly grated ginger, lemongrass, a dash of clove powder, and a sprinkle of black pepper.

—Just like Mummy's, my mother observed wistfully.

My aunt nodded sympathetically . . . at my father.

—Only tea bags in America, I imagine, Rohitbhai? Or this ridiculous purported chai syrup concoction at the coffee bars?

—Shilpa Maasi's tea is exactly the same as yours, Kavita said now, staring defiantly at her mother. —You both had the same teacher, remember.

—We remember, my father said graciously. Sangita returned from the kitchen with roasted chana and chakri. He patted the seat beside him.

Sangita looked alarmed at the thought of respite, but caught between that or disrespecting an elder, she set down the tray and perched next to him.

—Too difficult to imagine our Sangita beta all grown-up and about to be wed! he said.

—Very difficult, ji, she replied quietly.

—Yes, commented Kavita. —*Very.*

She sounded so much like Sabz, now that they'd split.

—And where is the man of honor? my father inquired.

—He has been in Delhi for work, Kaka, Sangita filled us in. —His family business is there. Though there is a new office in the suburbs here. Santa Cruz. But he will be joining us for dinner tomorrow.

—I've booked a table at the Samudri Ghoda, my aunt divulged, excitedly. —The Seahorse. So you can properly meet him.

—He may be able to help you with any Delhi arrangements, Sangita offered, addressing my parents. —How wonderful you will be celebrating your anniversary in Agra . . . just as you did your honeymoon!

—But we will be here to help these few days, and back again before the festivities begin, my father now hurriedly said.

My mother took her time, however.

—Your mother *insisted* we go, she revealed now. —*We Americans would be of little help with an Indian wedding.* Isn't that right, Meera? In any case, you and Deepak are being very modern and organizing much of it yourselves, from what we gather?

Sangita looked at my mother, and her own, with sorrowful eyes.

I wasn't sure what she was lamenting, or if it was just the permanent state of her gaze. She had very soulful eyes, I realized now, an aurulent haze underlying the amber, just like Dadaji's. My mother noticed her expression as well and seemed to regret her words.

—Our anniversary is not the main event. You, my dear, will be the loveliest bride the world has seen.

—The world? my aunt scoffed. —How will the world see it? They are insisting on keeping it very small. Just us and a few of their friends.

—All the more beauty just for us to behold, then, I jumped in. —Sangita, you look . . . *different.* I mean, you always looked good, but . . .

—Pyaar ho gaya hain! my father clarified for everyone but me.

—She had her eyes lasered, my aunt announced proudly. —By that doctor in Breach Candy, no less. Courtesy of Deepak's generosity.

—Deepak didn't dig glasses, Kavita sneered.

—It is not that, Sangita protested mildly. —He just . . . it's better for my peripheral vision.

—Deepak is a highly educated man, my aunt added. Sangita nodded.

I scrutinized my cousin now, trying to draw the free-spirited girl I'd known as a kid from this demure creature before me. I recalled the story of how she and Deepak had met at a matchmaking event of the CKP, my mother's branch of the Kshatriya, or warrior, class. His parents initially had issues that Sangita wasn't fair enough. As in light-skinned, not justice-serving. I wasn't sure how sincerely glad I could be for my cousin, marrying into such a family. But what came out my mouth was:

—I'm really happy for you, Sangita.

Sangita nodded again. —Well. Thank you, Dimple. And, Maasi, Mummy, I don't think any brides could be as lovely as you both.

She swept aside the magazines and newspapers on the coffee (tea?) table, revealing a panorama of photographs under a transparent glass sheet.

The pictures were yellowed, furled — some Polaroids even. Two black-and-white wedding photos kitty-cornered the display: one of my parents, one of my uncle and aunt. From the way they were angled, it seemed my mother and aunt were gazing at each other diagonally across the table. A withheld goodbye on the very days of their newly wedded lives?

My eye moved to a honeymoon shot of my parents in that standard tourist pose, them "lifting" the Taj Mahal: my father grinning, airborne fingers pinching the air, creating the illusion of hefting up the sumptuous structure by its tip. My mother was by his side, simulating panic, arms outstretched as if to catch the swinging monument of Shah Jahan's love for Mumtaz before it crashed to the ground.

I was in nearly as many photos as Kavita and Sangita, an equal member of this household as far as the (grand)paparazzo was concerned. There was Kavita and Sangita and me dancing in torn sheets in a long-ago monsoon rain; in stitches in the shoe house at Hanging Gardens, perspective bottom-up as we chugged down in a three-child train. My high school yearbook wallet-size photo — eyelined and wild-haired — and many of my class pics from the years before, moving backwards through time to a childhood Halloween shot. In it, I was dressed up in a sari, anklets, bangles . . . as an Indian girl.

Sangita indicated a shot of me cross-legged poolside in my infamous OshKosh overalls.

—Magni*fish*ent, Dimple! I remember staring at this picture for hours — wondering about a world with such shades of blue. We have it here, too, of course, but not where you'd expect. Not always in the sea, the sky. It's my favorite color. Perhaps because it was the color of where you were.

—And I loved this one, I said, pointing to the monsoon shot, moved. —Do you remember? A second after, you were the first one to tear everything off, go running through the rain!

That same gleeful clap when I'd entered: She'd joined her hands that way on the day of this photograph, too. Only, back then, the squeal hadn't been suppressed but reeled out like a mighty kite in the inundating night sky. *Patanggg!*

—That's the Sangita I remember, Kavs said. —Running free.

My aunt pressed her lips together. My uncle quickly spoke up:

—Born blue. Perhaps this is why you love that photograph, Sangita, beta.

—What does that mean? I asked.

—Sangita was born blue, my uncle explained now. —Well, or so it appeared at first. Premature: a veiled birth.

—Veiled birth? I asked. I knew my cousin-sister had arrived ahead of her time but not this fact, nor what it meant.

—Born intact in the amniotic sac. Legend has it these babies can never drown.

—Doesn't always feel that way, Sangita said quietly.

—What altoo faltoo! my aunt cut in sharply. —Girls. Enough chitter-chatter. Let's get dinner on the table. The America-returneds must be famished!

It sounded like America hadn't been happy with us, had dug out its receipt and shipped us back. But Maasi looked my way, forced a smile.

CHAPTER 7

Food for Thought

They seated me first, with my father and uncle. My mother was about to pull up a chair as well, but noting the muttering maelstrom of my aunt in the kitchen, she cleared her throat, shrugged at me, and followed her sister to the hob. I couldn't resist, and followed, too, camera at the ready.

Sweat beaded my aunt's upper lip as she rushed back and forth, frying puris to popworthy proportions with a passive-aggressive panache.

A cupboard, partly open, revealed a top-row glim of amber jars. The dubba sat lidless on the counter, its stainless steel cups of dry spices creating a heady full-circle *arc en ciel*.

On the exposed shelf between condiments and chutneys, a temple like our own in Springfield — down to a framed black-and-white of Dadaji. It was a version of the one in our kitchen, taken by yours truly with Chica Tikka the last time I'd seen him. They'd been clicked a split second apart: In the USA print, his eyes were wide and all-seeing, and in this one, heavy-lidded, as if he were half dreaming. I must have caught him mid-blink.

My mother bowed her head before it. I squeezed her shoulder, and she immediately busied herself passing me the milk, still on the counter from our chai marathon. I moved to the fridge to stow it — noticing a large keyhole in its door.

—The kamwali was stealing from us, my aunt whispered, though I was pretty sure the maid in question wasn't around. —I looked the other way for months, but now with Sangita's upcoming nuptials, we cannot take a chance. I have made kanavla for this occasion, all of the last week.

—Kanavla! my mother sang. She'd sometimes crave this Marathi sweet back home: ghee-rolled dough stuffed with coconut, sesame, almonds, and, of course, a liberal dose of sugar. (This was India, after all, where even sugar was prepared with a liberal dose of sugar.)

—Four hours to make twenty-four pieces . . . with Sangita's help! my aunt nodded, expertly ladling the last puri onto plate. —Four hands!

—Where did you say you keep that key again?

—Don't even think about it, Tai! my aunt clucked. —The day will be here before you know it.

✳ ✳ ✳

Jingle of the magical mystery door and Akasha now appeared, setting Zepploo's cage by the grille and joining us at the table. My uncle raised his eyebrows questioningly at her.

She nodded in reply. —It's coming along. I can see he's considering it.

—Akasha takes the chaklee outside a few times a day to see other birds flying, my uncle explained to me. —To help him heal. A kind of exercise in sankalp. When your intention, focus, is so pure it manifests itself in the tangible world.

—So . . . like be careful what you wish for, you mean?

—More often, *who* you wish for, Akasha replied matter-of-factly. —But yes. In this case: the desire for flight. And safe landings. I like to position him in the window as well so he can aspire to greater heights.

—Ah, like the hill? I asked. Zepploo did indeed seem to be contemplating that humdinger of a highland in the distance.

—Um, excuse me, but it's in fact a sixty-five-million-year-old freestanding columnar basalt monolith, ya, Akasha gently pointed out. —Dimple Maasi, a simple sankalp exercise to demonstrate: Please concentrate on a number. It will appear in your eyes, and I shall focus my intention and tell it to you.

—You'll read my mind . . . in my eyes? I laughed.

—Where else? The brain is connected through nerves, and the nerves to the eyes, so the brain sends a signal through the network till you can see it on-screen. In fact, I can read your mind in any part of your physical being. But eyes are the easiest for a beginner like me.

My mind was teeming to the point I simply couldn't choose a number.

—Take your time, Akasha said kindly, nodding to my plate. —Go on. Eat.

Eat made me think of *ate. Eight.* The eight of us eating the bicultural meal awaiting us: Marathi-Gujarati. Maasi had prepared my and my mother's cravings — learned directly from my grandmother, who was a distant memory of a snug big-bellied embrace: mutton curry, cauliflower subzi, and puran puri. And my father's Gujarati roots were honored as well with a lavish spread of his childhood staples: limbdi-and-cumin-flecked bowls of kadhi, bhindi bhaji, kand puri, khichu and makhan (the creamy post-churning pre-butter that myth claimed Krishna was so fond of he'd steal it).

—Aaray waah, Meeratai! he rhapsodized, spreading the makhan onto a crunchy chunk of khicchoo. —You must have been Gujju in a past life.

—I remember all your favorites, my aunt replied. —It was I, after all, who assisted our mother in cooking for you whenever you came to visit my sister.

—And what was my dear wife doing in the kitchen during all those visits, then?

—Stirring where stirring was not required, lifting lids as if she knew what to look for, and mostly swooning.

—Meera! my mother scolded her. —I most certainly was not swooning! I was too tired from medical school to see straight in those days.

My aunt nodded. —Of course. You had loftier things to think about.

My mother rolled her eyes, but I noted she was taking seconds of the fried bob-gobble bread herself.

Me? Thirds. Of all. And much to my delight, spicy *was* spicy here! My eyes watered, sinuses cleared for life; it felt so good to . . . *feel*.

—Oh . . . my . . . *gods*! I cried passionately.

—Personally, I love Taco Bell, Akasha remarked. —I went there in Atlanta with my parents. And Subway.

—In Atlanta, too?

—No, ya. The Andheri branch. Quicker to get to when you need a fix.

She paused, pensively.

—You know, they say if you eat Mentos with Coke, you die. But I tried it and nothing really happened.

My aunt looked at her impatiently, my uncle fondly. Then he trained that fond regard on me.

—So, Dimple, what would you like to see — photograph — while you are in Bombay?

—I don't know, I said. —I guess . . . the real India?

—That you will not find in Bombay.

—Well. The real Bombay, then.

—*This*, said my aunt, gesturing to us, —is the real Bombay.

—Sitting in traffic trying to *get to* the real Bombay is the real Bombay, Kavita smirked.

—Crawford Market? my father joined in. —Dimple, remember we went together last time?

—I do. Loved it. But still, they were trying to sell me apples from Seattle.

—Sure bizarre, intoned Akasha dramatically.

—It wasn't bizarre, just . . .

—*Chor* Bazaar, Sangita translated. —It started as a place where stolen goods were sold. It means *thief's market* in Hindi.

—And Urdu, Akasha added, and then continued, perplexingly, in French. —A *marché aux puces, marché aux voleurs des antiquités.* Flea market. Antiques. You can get anything there!

Sangita nodded. —Mings, Muranos . . .

—Sleigh bells, barbells, phonographs, and clocks stuck back in time! Akasha raved. Then she leaned in and whispered, —There's a saying that whatever you lose, you find at Chor Bazaar.

This piqued my interest. There was this elusive track, a favorite of his father's, Karsh had been seeking. Might it be here?

—True, Sangita agreed. —Deepak's driver once bought back his cell phone from there. And got a much better deal than what he originally paid for it.

—You must let us know and we will organize with Arvind to drive you wherever you like, Dimple, my aunt proposed now.

—Thanks, Maasi. But I was kind of thinking of being more on the ground. I mean, in New York I always take the subway or walk. So I thought I'd — wander. Maybe try the train.

A collective gasp.

—Not the train! my aunt exclaimed.

—What happened to the train? I asked.

—It is too crowded, Dimple, Maasi explained. —And they are not in their proper mind-set, some of these people. They will sit on you.

Sangita edged in. —And if you are not in the ladies' compartment? Beware your backside.

—Or even *in* it, Kavita said mischievously. —Still . . . Victoria Terminus? Breathtaking.

I'd heard. I figured it would be a long shot to get Karsh to come along, given what had happened to his father, but you never knew. Perhaps it would afford a kind of closure?

—Take a car there, my uncle suggested.

—A car to the train? I laughed.

—Seriously, Dimple, Akasha said. —It is one of the busiest train stations in Asia, with three million commuters passing through daily. So I'd advise picking up some protective footwear on Linking Road. . . . And be sure you can do the Train Dance.

—Which is?

She jumped to action, engaging in a bout of odd but enthu choreography that involved jimmying forward, clucking like a spastic chicken, shooting both arms straight out stuck together, then apart and to her sides with military breaststroke precision.

—Shuffle, hen-bend, stroke, swipe; shuffle, hen-bend, stroke, swipe. Oh, and watch out for the thieves that slice off your back pockets whenever the train stops.

—Since when do you know so much about train travel, beta? Dilip Kaka inquired now.

—Everything, Akasha said very seriously, tapping her head, then indicating the room, the windows, the world, — is just . . . out there. It is a matter of having your antennae out.

She exited, still riding the poultry express. Moments later, I was pretty sure I heard a chord being strummed to the same rhythm.

—I was also thinking about going to . . . Lower Parel? I said now. One of Karsh's potential gigs was in that area, if his first went well. Plus, the name intrigued me.

—The defunct *mills*? That's very dangerous! my father cried, vehemently shaking his head.

—De*funked*, Kavita piped in, with a peculiar little dead-reckon chicken-head move that looked like it belonged to Akasha's transport jig.

—No worries, Kaka. These days, you can think of Lower Parel as Upper Worli, Sangita mysteriously reassured him now.

—How long does it take to get there? I asked tentatively. —Theoretically speaking . . .

—One to three hours, Kavita replied, —give or take.

—But if the traffic is on Tulsi Pipe Road, you may enjoy it, Sangita informed me. —The Wall Project is there; people have painted the entire thing. Like at Mahim station, and in Bandra, of course. But might be nice for your shooting.

My father spoke up now, looking a little worried at the concept of me outside of this apartment, ever.

—Would Arvind be available tomorrow? Before the dinner? I was thinking Dimple and I could take a stroll on Juhu Beach. She could start shooting . . . somewhere more familiar?

—We can most certainly arrange that, my aunt quickly assured him. —But of course the most important shooting of all, beta . . . You will of course do some photography at our Sangita's ceremony and reception?

I nodded enthusiastically. —I'd love to. In fact, was planning on it.

—Sangita is insisting on keeping everything in the family, my aunt sighed. —Sorry to put you to work, Dimple.

—Well, Sangita's been working hard as well, Kavita pointed out. —She's not treating everyone like lackeys. Dimple, Sangita here even made her own wedding outfit!

Sangita shrugged modestly. —I like to sew, she said. —I had a contact at a fabric store and thought it might also cut down on some of the costs.

—Model it for us now, beta! Maasi instructed her.

Sangita looked less than pleased.

—Isn't it bad luck for any men to see it before the wedding? I jumped in. My cousin seemed so shy, I wasn't sure she'd be able to handle such a spotlight on her. But ever the obedient daughter, she promptly rose and exited the room.

—This is India! Everyone sees everything before the wedding, my uncle laughed into the silence.

—There is no *before* a wedding, Kavita added drily. —There is *always* a wedding.

A little while later, a ponderous swoosh, and Sangita emerged donning a drop-dead gale of a sari, a heave and wooze of teal and turquoise, sunset-sea-streaked with violet and rose, with a pot-of-gold border.

—It's beautiful, Sangita, I whispered.

—Beta, I keep telling you to add something red, Meera Maasi berated her. Then, addressing my mother, as if she didn't know, —The traditional color.

—The red is ideologically mixed in, Mummy, Sangita offered. —In the purple. Pink. Blended with white, blue.

Before my aunt could groan on, Akasha swooped back into the room, a sizable guitar strapped across her tiny troubador chest. Her hands were poised over the frets . . . but froze there when her eyes landed on me.

—Dimple Maasi! she cried. —Wait! Relax. Breathe through the eyes!

I stared at her, confused. She stared at me, omniscient.

—Are you thinking of . . . eight? she finally uttered. Now I froze.

—Enough altoo faltoo! Kavita, Sangita, maybe you can get the key from Vipin Uncle and Vinanti Aunty's now? my aunt suggested briskly. She filled us in: —Our neighbors are traveling to Silicon Valley to visit their son and have kindly offered their flat to house Deepak's family.

Akasha was still staring at me.

—They are at present looking for the suitable girl for Akshay, my aunt added pointedly. Why? Had she gone missing?

—I'll come along? I offered, but didn't move, still stunned by Akasha's numerical telepathy.

My uncle shook his head. —We won't hear of it. The Americans rest now. Synchronize your clocks. The entire trip lies ahead of you. You don't want to sleep through it!

I certainly didn't.

Akasha leaned in to my ear.

—Those are *sideways* eights, she whispered.

CHAPTER 8

Gift Horse

Later that evening, I decided to unpack a bit. I threw open my suitcase and unlatched the heavily stickered bedroom wardrobe . . . to discover several sacks of basmati rice, enormous Tupperware containers of homemade chevda, and tins of Horlicks biscuits chockablocking the interior. I'd forgotten that closets also served as larders here, with the space constraints.

In my suitcase: the electric-blue box containing my wedding gift for Sangita. I took it out for a look. I'd wanted to give her something besides my photographic help, so I'd had my dear friend in New York, Zara Thrustra, create a pair of shoes for her.

This was no ordinary custom-made footwear. There was nothing ordinary about Zara, for starters — a Nietzsche-quoting drag queen who'd fled her native Pakistan when she and her family had received death threats due to her "outrageous" sexual (and fashion) leanings. In the box lay a pair of turquoise and amethyst platforms, gemmed and studded in broken bobs and bits that had been scored on the street, from Chinatown bottle caps to a Loisaida cinema ticket to a Harlem earring, and a Crown Heights diary key. Coins were always part of Zara's fashion currency, mostly lucky pennies, though this time she'd managed to get her hands on a few rupees as well, suturing a built-in anklet of the jangling coins around the platforms' upper borders. A fan of vivid feathers (probably pigeon, though spray-painted in arco iris peacock colors and removable by Velcro strap) jutted around the back upper heels of the shoes. The chunky heels were themselves transparent, filled with a clear liquid in which azure glitter created a snow-globe effect over an olio of marbles and jacks, along with the rope and knife and tiny Miss Scarlet piece from a game of Clue.

Miss Scarlet may have been Zara's nod to bridal red. But every other instance of red commingled with other colors (Sangita-style, funnily enough); as Zara had explained, her own life was an ode to artistic license, and nothing existed in a vacuum — even a hue.

Thus spake Zara Thrustra. A Nietzschean überquote adorned the box: *I say unto you: One must still have chaos in oneself to give birth to a dancing star.* Smiling at the thought of the look on her face once she got a gander of these flying feet, I transferred Sangita's gift into my duffel for better ensconcement, cramming it just behind a sack of basmati, and latched the door.

A pair of shoes always contained a magic slipper.

✳   ❋   ✳

Still later, Kavita and Sangita slunk into slumber beside me in our shared room. The apartment itself seemed netted in the dream-shift-gaze of REM, the sleeping in-ex-hales of my family dinghy-bobbing the space. But my body clock was all wound up. Eyes peeled, I disembarked into the living room, and did the thing I'd been longing to do since we'd arrived.

Dadasana: I sank into Dadaji's chair and peered at the painting on the wall across from it. I realized now why it looked so familiar: It was the precise daytime view from the window beside it, looking out over Andheri. I didn't know if it was the dreaming hour, but in the painting, the swashes of blues and browns seemed to conjure Dadaji's very face, organically part of his favorite outlook on Bombay: Gilbert Hill. I vaguely recalled a story of his first climb to the Durga-templed top, a vantage point from which the entire metropolis splayed gorgeously at his feet.

Through the grille, a slivered moon slit-lit the night, a star cradled just above the crescent. A memory rose of a wee me cradled in Dadaji's sheltering arms, him pointing a finger towards that peak.

—Rani, he'd whispered, and it must have been in Marathi, before my mother tongue was tied. —One day we will walk there, to the summit, you and I. And you will see, truly see, where you are.

I had no recollection of that upwards climb.

My thoughts turned to the other man in my life who called me rani, who treated me like the princess he'd awaited since birth. I tried Karsh now, to give him the local number Akasha had SIM-swapped me into earlier, but he didn't answer; he was probably smack at the start of his Adda show on the LES in New York.

I texted: *My night your day. Baited breath in Bombay.*

Funny how my love for New York swirled now into this metropolis, and my love for the great man of my past, in whose chair I rocked, into that of the man of my present and future, currently ensorcellingly rumpling still skins, spinning a distant room gold with a breed of music that had originated . . . here.

It was *here* that I could bring it all together. Sankalp the past present future into a seamless meld, erase those dividing lines I'd been straining against, like a blindered horse champing at a bit.

I lifted Chica Tikka, took in Gilbert Hill through my third eye. Moonlight etched its edges from the smog of night sky.

And I made a promise to Dadaji, to myself: This trip, I would remain as unblinking as my lens, let it all in, take it all in . . . and hopefully carry-on all of it with me.

CHAPTER 9

Blues & Country

Careful what you wish for: I remained unblinking well into morning. Each time I was on the verge of dropping off, that magical mystery door jangled as burtanwallah, kachrawallah, and possibly doodhwallah came and went. Not to mention the dhobi. Between these efficient barefoot visitations, the bedroom periodically creaked open as Maasi frequented the closet for the canister of sugar, of black tea, of cashews.

It was deep afternoon by the time I was freshly showered and heavily chai'd. The doorbell rang yet again and yet another man materialized within that magical mystery frame — but this one smiled shyly at me from the threshold, jingling a set of keys.

Eagerly, I grabbed my camera.

It was Arvind, ready to take me and my father to Juhu Beach.

*   *   *

Arvind dropped us off at the Samudri Ghoda Hotel, also known as the Seahorse — where many, many years ago my father had learned to swim in the neon-blue pool out back. I myself had effervescent memories of Gold Spot sipped under sky-size umbrellas, the cutie-patootie girl on the Amul butter packet furrowing as its contents jiffily melted. The rest of the gang would be meeting us here for the Deepak 101 dinner later; the poolside restaurant was renowned for its dum biriyani, according to my mother (who seemed to have developed a gargantuan appetite — and resolve — to eat her way back through time to her childhood).

This was also the first hotel where I'd be shacking up with Karsh.

We crossed through the buzzing lobby to the pool, which was inhabited by a treacherously fair-skinned chaise-lounged blonde in one-piece skin-tone bathing suit and a well-rotisseried half-dunked man, both staring off to the side at something in a late-day sun-stroked daze. I followed their gaze to the pavilion, and a small red-robed wooden stage area, its arched doorway strung with lights. Before it, clusters of white-clothed gold-ribboned chairs held their breath, backs to us.

—A mandap, my father explained. —There is surely a wedding reception taking place here. Those people in the lobby were probably awaiting the arrival of the groomsman on horseback.

A sweep of servers was busily setting up a buffet in the vicinity.

—Just imagine! So soon our own Sangita will be tying the knot.

—Or walking in circles, I said, referring to the seven steps around the fire of the Hindu wedding ceremony. —She didn't seem that excited about it back at the house, though, no?

—She is a very calm girl. Just like her father.

—True, that.

My father wrapped an arm around my shoulders.

—Maybe one day you will be here with Karsh.

—I will, I grinned. —In just a couple days!

—I meant . . .

—I know.

It was a tantalizing prospect: returning here someday and pronouncing our already implicit forevermore, in the country that had, in a way — by bringing our parents together in med school friendship — hitched us in the first place. I took my father's arm as we strolled towards the mandap. Closer up, I saw that the stage — which wasn't one unit but several knotted together — was in fact a metallic blue, so rusted it gave the impression of being wood from a distance.

—No issues, my father said now. He'd refreshed his Hinglish in no time. —You two have all the time in the world.

Camera out. A few feet away, a set of red-cloaked steps curved up towards nowhere; later, they'd be pushed against the stage where the couple would probably be making their own seven-step-circling vows, or at least posing for a photo op.

The stairs reminded me of our last visit to India, when the Sea Link bridge had been in progress, stretching its aching hand only about halfway across the waters separating these suburbs from South Bombay. I'd been inexplicably moved by this half bridge, at this valiant straining to make contact with the other side. Something about the stairs felt similar, though there was less desperation in their upwardly spiraling yearning. Perhaps because they didn't appear to be reaching for any*thing* — just a direction.

By the walled steps that dropped to the beach, the black-clad watchman nodded to us. My father nodded pleasantly back and tipped him for opening the gate. As we descended, I noted the guard's socks were implausibly white.

Onto the shore we stepped, then sank. A significantly different sight met our eyes today than the jam-packed Juhu Beach of my childhood. Dogs dug down, and a couple men also gullied in the sand, arms thrown across faces by the stone wall splitting hotels from seascape. A lone soul of indeterminate ethnic origin stood waterside, muscles rippling as he swung through a sun salute with verve and vigor and no expensive purple mat.

No swimsuits; no swimmers.

I missed the cacophony of the seaside of old. However, one advantage was a nearly unobstructed view of the Arabian Sea. The water wasn't blue exactly, but a brownish-blue haze, as if the bottom had been stirred up and never quite settled.

I couldn't be so close and not touch. My father, reading my fidgety feet, nodded for me to go on.

Here I stood on Juhu Beach, as far as I could see the only girl in clamdiggers and a Country, Blue Grass, Blues & Other Music For

Uplifting Gourmandizers tee, Birks in hand, eyes drunk on sea and sky — at last officially getting my feet wet.

I could feel something expanding.

As airplanes crisscrossed overhead, I considered then my true love across those waters, soon to be winging himself towards me. With my big toe, I did something a tad adolescent but immensely satisfying: scrawled an enormous *D+K* in a double-bubbled heart in the Juhu sand. Then I dragged a line from it to the lapping sea — my heart to his, to reel him safely in.

Another pair of bare calloused feet was soon beside me: my father's, his own orthopedic sneakers in hand now. I photographed him staring out to sea, a delighted smile dancing his eyes as the great ball of fire readied to take the plunge.

—Your mother and I would walk here, he said. —I'd ask her to sing song after song. *Zindagi bhar nahin bhoolegi woh barsaat ki raat*: My whole life I'll never forget this night of pouring rain.

He sang now, quietly but with great emotion. I loved this about my father: his off-key but sincere voice, resonant with pleasure and . . . was that a note of mourning? It was as if he were singing for a girl loved and lost.

—How many times I stood just here, he went on, —dreaming of what lay on the other side . . .

And how many times in recent years had I done the same, by the Atlantic Ocean, Hudson River, East River . . . any body of water that could eventually spill into this one, ferry me here?

—What's over there? I asked, pointing left to where the beach curved off, past the slew of hotels.

—Bandra. Once under Portuguese rule. An ancient fishing village.

To the right, where the walled backdrop gave way to tree and brush, a few high-rises elbowed up from a densely constructed area.

—Versova. And Andheri, of course.

We walked that way. Kids played cricket, a pair of simmering red chappals and single blue sole stumped in the sand.

—Down one of the next side streets is the Hare Krishna temple. We went there last time, remember, beta? Wonderful vegetarian food.

I had only a vague recollection of the temple itself but a clear memory of a moment during that outing, when my father had gently pushed me forward to receive the aarti blessing from the priest, guiding my palms over the proffered flame, then transferring the blessing to my forehead. When the little lit lamp had come his way, he'd passed his own hands over it — and then laid them upon my face, bestowing his own blessing upon me as well.

Now he spoke not only of the sands upon which we were strolling, but Breach Candy, where he and my mother had shared their first kiss. Shivaji Park, bordering the building society that had housed their wedding reception. Elphinstone College, where he'd first met Hush-Hush Aunty and Hear-No-Evil Uncle, two of the first Indian friends they'd have years later in the USA.

—All these memories, he mused. —Feels they happened only moments ago, yet in another life as well. Each time I come here, I wonder if it is the last time. I don't know if it's a remnant of how it felt to leave, really *leave* all those years ago . . . or also from having lost our parents, people, along the way.

I felt a sharp kick in my gut, and I didn't want to linger too long on this thought: that India for me, and my own Indianness, was so part and parcel of my parents . . . what would it mean to me if they were no longer? I felt a waylaying desperation to waystay, document this place to pieces, till it was broken down into morsels I could digest and convey with me everywhere. Always.

—So many years, he said now, eyes bright. —So many miles.

I took his arm, on the brim myself.

—So many *more* years, Bapuji, I said, squeezing his hand. —So many *more* miles.

The sun dove then, a santra aflame, sink-swimming exhilaratingly through the waves. A couple of the cricketeering boys skipped seaside, appeared as if they were leapfrogging over this star.

As the day dipped, activity keened, now back Bandra way: Bhel puri, kulfi stands, coconut-water-wallahs beacon-beckoned, mouthwatering nubs of land spotted at last from darkened sea. A lone jogger a pace off the breaking waves. The doubled camel-like shadows of couples here and there entwined against rock face.

By night, the beach evoked a half-deserted casino. Those samelevel stall roofs streaked mile-long neon light, like taxi headlighttaillight ripples in the rain. A hub of kerosene-lamped bustle: a long white fabric rolled out on sand, strewn with a gleeful geometry of objects. Parle biscuits; juice boxes, the balefire faces of the illustrated children spiriting up off the cloth. A bystander cast a ring, haloing one.

We'd walked for what felt like hours — it seemed we should have already been in that ancient fishing village, but it just kept bobbing out of bounds.

—We should head back now, my father finally suggested. —The others will be waiting. How anxious I am to meet Deepak!

We retraced our path. And as we passed the site of my romantic sankalp — where I'd carved those initials so joyfully in the sand — I saw: Only the D remained, the K water-washed, gullying into the line I'd drawn to link us.

Funnily, both hearts were intact.

*　❋　*

The wedding reception my father had forseen was off to a fragrant start now, guests gilded and glammed to the max, milling round the buffet tables. It was funny how close you could get to someone else's big day in India; in fact we walked right *through* it towards the alfresco restaurant area.

We were scanning the non-wedding tables poolside when we spotted a gangly man leaping up, waving as fervently as a NYC tourist hailing an off-duty taxi. At first I thought his impassioned greeting was for, say, the twin brother he'd been separated from at birth, but soon enough I spied the rest of our posse seated along with him, already cracking into papadums and lassis.

Had to be the dudewallah.

—Dimple, Rohitbhai, my aunt called out proudly, taking the arm of the mirthful man. —I'd like you to meet Deepak, my soon to be son-in-law!

Groomsman had already victory-lapped around the table towards us. And when, as a show of respect, he bent to touch my father's feet, Maasi shot my mother what I could only describe as a triumphant look. My father giggled shyly, as if he were ticklish.

—Uncle, I am overjoyed to meet you! And *you*, Deepak enthused, rising, eschewing my own toes, —must be Dimple!

—Congrats on everything, Deepak, I said as my father warmly hugged him. —I've heard . . . loads about you.

—As have we all, my father affirmed. —You feel like a nephew already!

Deepak pulled out chairs for us both, then raised his lassi sky-high.

—And so soon we will be irrevocably bound! To tying the knot . . . and joining our families!

We clinked glasses. There was something weirdly fresh off the boat about him. Although I guess he hadn't even gotten on the boat; *I* had. Kavita made a gesture of hanging herself with her dupatta, for my benefit. My mother had clearly done the ordering already, and now punctured the bread lid of the dum biriyani she'd been craving the entire plane ride over.

—We were just discussing the wedding, of course, my aunt briefed us.

—Your own as well! Deepak added, nodding to my parents. —That is, your anniversary trip. You most certainly must have taken one last look back at the Taj all those years ago! They say your return is guaranteed if you do so.

My aunt gazed at him as if he'd just broken down Fermat's Last Theorem.

—And it is the fate that this is true! she finally affirmed.

—Well, actually it's a *choice* Maasi and Kaka made, said Kavita, replying to her, referring to my parents, but staring at Sangita.

—It is a *confluence*, Deepak said diplomatically, or philosophically. —I can arrange a car for you from our Delhi office to Agra. What an example of Mughal architecture, this magnificent creation built by a king to express his love for his queen!

—Actually, built for a couple decades by a zillion lackeys for a pittance, said Kavita. —Not to mention elephants. Frankly, I'm not sure old Shah Jahan was getting any dirt under his nails.

—Twenty-two years, Deepak edified us. —If I am not incorrect.

—We will go to see it at dawn, my mother revealed now, as if uttering the fruits of a prophecy rather than an online tour agency booking, complete with confirmation number. —And during the moonlit night.

Kavita cleared her throat. —Actually, it's a *mausoleum*. A tomb to love. Shah Jahan's wife died, tragically, during the birth of their fourteenth child.

—And then on to Fatehpur Sikri! my father hurriedly chimed in.

Deepak nodded sagely then explained, apparently for my benefit, although I was already somewhat privy to these details: —Ah . . . a very powerful place. In the tomb of the Sufi saint who granted Akbar his prayer for an heir, you can tie a thread and wish on it, and it always comes true. When you are having success — when that wish is realized — you must return and untie a thread in thanks.

—What are you wishing for? Kavita asked my parents.

—Ah, we cannot say! my mother told her. —Not until we have made the pilgrimage.

My father winked at me. Uh-oh.

—We ourselves made the trip years ago to wish for Sangita and Kavita to find their mates, Dilip Kaka said genially. —And see?

—Well, then you have to go back to *untie* the thread, I pointed out.

—Only one, my aunt rued. —We are waiting so we can untie both in the same ceremony.

Kavita stiffened. Sangita was generously refilling her husband-to-be's plate, though it wasn't yet even half empty, and began conjecturing pleasantly about the biriyani recipe. It made me a little sad, and I turned away.

The sound system for the random reception we were nearly crashing had turned up a notch. I checked out the pavilion. I'd imagined it would be hard to spot the bride and groom since everyone was decked out in moth-burning materials, but they were a shoo-in: The bride — all in white (ivory, actually) — linked arms with the tuxed-out groom as they awaited with gobleted hands the pouring of the champagne, which a member of the serving staff seemed to be having a spot of difficulty opening.

—Isn't that unusual she's dressed in white? I commented, sneaking a shot of the server from our table. —I thought red was the bridal color.

—And white is the color of mourning! Deepak yelled cheerfully over the music.

—Which makes it the perfect color for a wedding, Kavita retorted. Her mother shot her a look, although my own stifled a laugh.

The server finally stuck the bottle on the ground between his feet and yanked with all his might, nearly toppling over as the cork whizzed out with a Serge Gainsbourg "Comic Strip" mega pop. Half the champers spilled to the pavilion ground, but he managed to rise to the occasion and swoosh the conjugal couple's goblets full before it all went to waste.

—Christian wedding, my mother deciphered now. —Unless that's Thums Up fizzing out the bottle.

Sangita squinted. —It's not exactly white, her dress. . . .

The bride was already presenting her glass for refills. The groom looked on with a mix of admiration and fear.

I took more photographs.

—It is so wonderful to have a pastime you are so skilled at, beta, my uncle remarked now.

Sangita looked like she wanted to say something, but then just stared decorously down into her plate.

—Dimple's pastimes win prizes and get published in magazines. In fact, she's here to *work* on her supposed hobby, Kavita interjected.

—Of course not *only* for that, I hastily added. —I'm so happy I'll be taking photos for the wedding . . . which is . . . *not* a hobby?

—Anything we can help you with while you are here, Dimple? Deepak asked now.

My aunt beamed. —Deepak is a weritable encyclopedia of information.

—I'm still trying to work it out, my photo project, I admitted. —I kind of want to just be open, see where my eyes lead me . . . maybe even follow a color. Like all the gradations of brown.

—Yes. In a city where so many long to be white, Kavita noted. —Did you know Fair & Lovely, that skin-whitening treatment, now has a product for your feminine intimate areas? I suppose so brown boys can pretend they're getting down with white girls.

She was channeling Sabz again. Deepak opened his mouth, then seemed to think better of it.

—Kavita! my aunt cried, horrified. —How can you speak of *intimacy* now?

—Oh, sorry. I thought we were talking about marriage. *Art.*

—Well, on that topic . . . I've been accepted to art school, Sangita suddenly blurted. —J.J. Full scholarship.

Now I opened my mouth to congratulate her, but caught my aunt looking utterly confused, so I shoveled some biriyani into it instead.

—How can you be accepted if you haven't applied? she asked finally.

—I guess . . . I forgot I applied? I didn't want to get my hopes too high.

Meera Maasi appeared less than thrilled with her daughter's show of academic initiative. Deepak sat slowly masticating, his factoid-full smile now frozen on his face.

—And no mention? my uncle asked gently. He looked almost proud, but one glance cast from Meera Maasi, and he changed tack. —So, beta, what are you going to do with art school?

Sangita stared at him a little helplessly. My father spoke mildly up:

—Hobbies do wonders for good health. Like sudoku and gardening. I find this really releases the tension.

—You don't need any of this altoo faltoo activity, Sangita, my aunt dissented. —*Marriage* will release the tension.

Her own, I had the feeling, more than anyone else's. I was beginning to feel a little myself — maybe it was contagious, or just a hunch that this conversation was going to end up lassoing me in.

My mother broke in. —It is not necessarily altoo faltoo, Meera. Especially if it is J.J. School of Art, one of the tip-top!

—Nor do I think Dimple's photography is altoo faltoo, Sangita said quietly now. Lassoed.

My uncle turned worriedly to me. —Of course not! That isn't what we were meaning, Dimple, beta.

—Uh, it's okay, Kaka, I assured him. —But I do think . . . if you find something you really love, it's always worth giving it a shot, you know?

—It works differently in America, my aunt went on, lobbing this back towards my mother. —Here, we think of others, of the family, the community. And besides —

I stiffened as I could feel an ace serve about to happen. . . .

—*Dimple* isn't getting married.

—Dimple, my mother said now, a bit sternly, —is in a very serious relationship with the finest of Indian boys. Karsh Kapoor.

—He's coming in just two days! I eagerly proclaimed, relieved to shift to a topic I was genuinely happy to discuss. My uncle smiled.

—Karsh Kapoor? Yes, we've been hearing about this Karsh. Kavita has been singing his praises.

—More than we've ever heard her sing *any* man's, my aunt added. —Does this Karsh have a brother?

—Me! Soon! Deepak alleged now. —I look forward to meeting my future bhai. But, Dimple, is he serious about his intentions? He will be careful with your heart?

—Totally, I assured him, wondering how this had become entirely about me. —He's particularly gentle with the atria and ventriculae.

—And never forget the auricle, my father, cardiologist extraordinaire, added proudly into the sound of no one laughing.

—What does this Karsh do? my aunt asked suspiciously. My father's voice was touched with pride:

—He's a student. At the NYU, like Dimple and Kavita beta.

—Software, my mother hastened to fill in. —The hardware.

—I thought Kavita mentioned he was jockeying? Maasi pressed.

—No issues. The *DJing* is just a hobby, Kavita snidely comforted her mother.

—But we do love hobbies! Sangita piped up brightly. —I forgot to mention Papaji, Mummy. Karsh is playing our wedding; we've canceled the other DJ.

My aunt visibly relaxed. —He is a *wedding* jockey?

—Really, he's a musician, I clarified protectively.

—A *classical* musician, my mother rapidly adjoined. —He plays the tablas. On the side.

—In front, actually, I corrected her.

—Well, regardless of from the front or side, we're looking forward to meeting him, said my uncle. —Where will he be lodging? We can always set up a room for him at Vipin and Vinanti's.

—Thanks, Kaka, but Karsh and I are going to be in hotels. Then you won't be so crowded at home, either.

He appeared stunned.

—Didn't my parents tell you? I asked, confused. My mother and father looked completely blank, though we'd gone over the details a million times.

—But you are staying with us, beta, no?

—For now. But the gig promoters are putting Karsh up, Kavita said, exasperated. —The rooms are paid for already.

—*Gig?* my uncle asked, baffled.

—*Promoters?* my aunt asked, horrified.

—In fact, we're at *this* hotel to start off, I explained, aiming for a mix of inspiriting and unswayable. —Then they're moving us to Bandra, I think. Lands End?

As soon as I'd named this suburb, no one seemed remotely interested in what the mysterious gig being promoted was.

—*Bandra?* my aunt faltered. What was so alarming about an ancient fishing village?

—Queen of the suburbs, Kavita roosed. —West, not East.

—You know what they say: If you throw a stone in Bandra, it will hit a pig, a priest, or a Perreira, Deepak grinned broadly. —Though these days, property developer might be more apt!

I had no idea what the hell a Perreira was (a sports car?), or why people were throwing stones at them. My mother leapt in again.

—No issues, Meera. By *coincidence* . . .

—Dimple will be staying in these hotels as well, my father, ever the honest man, concluded.

—With her girlfriends from NYU.

I raised my brows at my ab-fabulist mom; she lowered her own at me.

—Ah! I think Maasi thought you meant Dimple and Karsh were staying in the same quarters! my uncle laughed. My mother laughed, too, a touch too robustly.

—But even if they were, Deepak moderated. —Sounds like Dimple and Karshbhai will surely be the next wedding our family will be celebrating!

My uncle smiled. —Soon, soon. But perhaps Kavita will be next.

Deepak nodded reassuringly. —Don't worry, Mummy, Daddy. I will make sure to take care of Kavita, too. After all, she is going to be my Tai!

Kavita glared at him but Deepak had already turned to Sangita.

—And you, my darling, don't worry your pretty little head, he said, patting her on it now. —No need for you to fret about this art school. I was going to tell you later, but this may be the perfect moment: I have just accepted the job in Delhi — and put down a deposit on a wonderful farmhouse in Mehrauli!

Sangita looked up at him, startled. Meera Maasi literally paled a shade.

—Delhi? she whispered.

—I thought you could do the job from Bombay, Deepak? my uncle joined in, brow furrowed with worry now.

—My father believes it will be easier to have me in place, Deepak explained. —But no worries: There is more than enough room for you both, Mummy and Daddy! My parents will be happy to have you as well.

—But what about my *painting*? Sangita hazarded faintly.

—My jaan, we'll take it with us! Your Gilbert Hill will be the first painting we hang up in this new home!

I was pretty sure she'd meant her art in general. Evidently pleased with his own reply, Deepak lifted his lassi again to toast. Most of us had already drained our sweet-and-sour curd beverages and raised empty glasses.

Sangita's eyes were shiny with emotion.

—If you'll excuse me, Kavita said, rising suddenly. —I do believe I will pay a visit to the ladies'.

Her eyes were shiny, too. Not good shiny. I knew that look. She fled hastily for the foyer. I rose as well.

—Actually, be right back, too.

I clattered through the polished lobby, past the Kashmiri man flogging pashminas in the in-hotel store, and found the bathroom by the elevator bank — complete with smiling saried bathroom attendant, who uttered a *good evening, madame* as I entered. Inside, below one of the stall doors, I could make out Kavita's Vans.

—Kavita?

The door gave, and I joined my sister-cousin in the cubicle, where she was clearly not peeing but slumped head in hands on the lidded toilet. She glanced up at me with red-edged, furious eyes.

—Kavity, I whispered. —Are you okay?

—Am I okay? Dimple. I'm in a city founded on shaadi, matrimony, isn't it? Worse, a dowry! And now no end to the pressure on me to meet a suitable boy. Did you see the way Mummy was looking at me when they talked about Vinanti Aunty's son?

I thought they'd been looking at me.

—Yes, but wasn't part of the plan during this trip to tell the family about . . . your leanings?

—*Leanings?* I'm no Tower of Pisa, Dimple. When I love, I fall completely. And you see how frazzled Mummy is? I can't drop the bomb now. Once the bloody wedding is done and they can rest assured they've got one offspring who did the right thing . . .

—The wedding might not be . . . *bloody*, I suggested, leaning against the toilet paper dispenser. —Maybe she *wants* to get married. Maybe she's found the person she wants to spend the rest of her life with.

—But you have to *have* a life first.

I was leaning a little too hard; the toilet roll suddenly popped out and rolled away, out of the stall.

—Life might be all right for her, Kavs. For one thing, it's so unlonely here! Such a sense of community, of family.

—Believe me, you'll be craving loneliness at some point.

Very gently, the disembodied hand of the bathroom attendant passed a fresh roll under the door. I took it from her. Kavita gave me a *See?* look.

—But you're home, right, Kavita? That must feel nice, after so long?

—I'm not so sure this is home for me anymore, Dimple. It's not like I left it; *I'm* not like I left it. I can't truly talk to anyone here about how I feel, what I want. I mean, thank god you're here! But do you realize this is the first time we've been on our own for two seconds since you arrived?

The bathroom attendant coughed.

—I know, Kavita. But we'll find a way. Mallika Mulchandani's in town, too; she texted about meeting up tomorrow. You could join us, let off some steam?

I decoy-flushed and whispered:

—And maybe . . . you can try dating some other people? There must be a, you know . . . queer scene in Bombay?

Kavita rolled her eyes at me. —I'll show you the scene I've seen. In three minutes. Things have been a little on hold since those crackdowns on Bombay nightlife.

—So, what — the Shiv Sena's outlawed booty calls?

Kavita gave me a warning look. Fresh water bubbled back up into the bowl. She levered it down again.

—You know that little shop in Bandra, where I picked up those mugs? It's fantastic; the owners are like gurus of being yourself . . . but it's moving to Goa soon. I thought I'd bring Sangita along to begin to let her know what's going on with me. But she just seemed to find all the colors cute.

—Didn't the vibrators clue her in?

—Dimple! Sex toys are illegal in India.

I stared at her, making a mental note to wrap another pair of socks around the (very) personal massager currently holding its bunny breath in my suitcase.

—Section 292. Up to two years in prison . . . in the land that created the Kama Sutra, Kavita informed me, having clearly done her research. —Oh, and not to mention, homosexuality is now illegal *again*. That'd be 377. Which follows 375, 376 — the sections that kind of do not recognize *marital rape* as a crime.

She took in my surely freaked expression. —Just because they've built a few malls doesn't mean Bombay's all futureward, Dimple. Anyway, I'm not into any *scene*. You know that.

Just then, la dame peepee uttered a *good evening, madame*; I low-frequencied:

—Okay, okay. Just, Kavs . . . if you love Sangita, you have to be happy for her.

—Of course I love Sabina. With all my heart.

—Um. You said Sabina.

—No, I didn't. I said Sangita.

—Right. Anyway, Sabz sends her love. I ran into her on campus a few days ago.

—I know. She's been sending it to me directly, too. Even called to tell me it was the biggest mistake of her life: our breakup, her cheating. I mean, what am I supposed to do with that information, Dimple? How can I trust her again?

We stepped out then, and nodded to the toilet lady, who flicked on the cold water faucet and stood at the ready with her little towels. She gave us a sympathetic look.

A flush. Kavita turned her mirrored eyes to mine.

—It's still very hard to live without Sabz. And, frankly, it's pretty hard to live with your parents after you've been independent. You know, Dimple, sometimes it just feels like things couldn't get worse. . . .

Someone exited the stall just then. Behind our faces in the mirror: *Sangita*. Kavita and I slid looks at each other. How much had she overheard?

Sangita marched over now, bumped her hands into ours under the still running tap, and with uncharacteristic bluntness blurted out: —Worse? Than living with our parents? Imagine — I'm supposed to live with *Deepak's*!

We perused her sincere but twinkling eyes in the mirror.

Then all burst into giggles.

It felt like the three of us were we three again. But when we got back to the pavilion, Sangita suddenly looked miles away, staring out to sea. An instant later, I wondered if I'd imagined it, as her diffident smile slid back into place when she sidled up by her fiancé at the table. The bill had been paid — thanking very much Deepak's generosity, my aunt exulted. A long yawn escaped me.

—We should push off now, my uncle said. —Get some sleep. Especially you, Dimple! So you're in the pink of health for your real Bombay experience.

I nodded gratefully. I could tell Kavita and Sangita were spent as well.

Out front, the wedding party vehicle was instantly recognizable, so garlanded it appeared topiary. We split up into two cars: Deepak got a head start with the Pradhan posse (my uncle, aunt, and cousins). We Lalas went with Arvind.

—Um. Ma? I whispered as we pulled out the hotel drive. —Why did you totally lie out there about Karsh? And the hotel and all?

—I resent that. I did not totally lie, my mother replied, not whispering in the least. —I just spoke half the truth, Dimple. Full disclosure is overrated; we are not the Internet.

—They will not look upon it . . . well, my father surprisingly agreed. —When in India, do as India, no?

—Is that how they do in India?

—I don't want the family to feel we have become too Western Heston, lost all our values and morals, my mother disclosed.

My father nodded. —It is funny how we return to our roots here. As soon as I set foot to this soil, I do not want to eat meat, even fish, any longer. How I crave my simple childhood meals in Varad . . .

—And how I crave mutton! my mother exclaimed.

—And roasted chana! Singhdana! Remember that vendor at the top of Juhu Beach — the one with the silver beard? I wonder if he's still there. . . .

And they were off down memory lane — Memory Marg — spiraling back through the years, looking younger (and hungrier) as they collectively recollected delights lost and perhaps now possible again.

—The way you feel is your truth, I surmised. —Even if you tell a half-truth now and then. . . .

—Truth is beauty and beauty, truth, my father quotingly added with great feeling. —Gandhiji.

I was pretty sure it was Keats, but I reckoned Gandhiji would have agreed. I considered Sangita's feigned — or felt? — happiness at the table. And Kavita's commitment to following her hidden heart. My parents' half-truths were, I supposed, a way of protecting our freedom; maybe total bean-spillage *was* overhyped.

—I guess I'd rather lie and live the truth, I said thoughtfully, —than tell the truth and live a lie.

—Keats? my father wagered. I did a noncommittal side-to-side nod-shake, snuggling up between them.

—Remember that other song you used to sing when we would stroll on Juhu Beach? my father was saying to my mother now. —*Roop tera . . . mastana . . .*

My mother smiled and launched immediately into a pitch-perfect melancholically sweet rendition of the song.

—*. . . pyar mera diwana . . .*

They were gazing across me, into each other's eyes, like the young lovers they'd once been. My father accompanied her now, dropping into an off-kilter hum wherever he'd forgotten the lyrics.

And after a beat — on it, actually — with a delighted rearview glance at us, Arvind joined in as well.

—Lie and live the truth . . . I whispered to myself.

*   *   *

Back in Andheri, before we turned off to hit the hay, my eye was drawn to the stretch of wall behind Dadaji's chair, by the Gilbert Hill view window.

The wall gaped, blank, a square patch a shade brighter than the rest of the paint around it.

That presumptuous groom-to-be . . .

Sangita's painting was missing.

*   *   *

I washed up, got to our room. Kavita and Sangita were already tucked into the unrolled futon, courtyard lights filtering in through the grille. I was exhausted, but when I finally lay down on the not-quite-queen, sleep was the last thing on my mind.

My cousin-sisters were still up, too, toss-and-turning the dark. I decided now was the moment to give Sangita her gift; I was certain her eyes had hung on that space on the windowed wall, too, when Deepak had left, and I wanted to fill them with something beautiful. I cracked open the wardrobe, dug around, then handed the package to her.

—I was going to give it to you later. But maybe you can break them in before the big day?

Sangita looked up, startled, then tentatively lifted the lid. She unpacked the tissue, pulling out first one platform then the other, setting them atop the box, where they glittered as if strung with miniature fairy lights. We three stared. They were gobsmackingly grand, those shoes, and Sangita seemed too moved to speak, just gently ran her fingers over the collaged corners, the feathered heels.

—Cerulean, she whispered. And fell silent, smileless. Then, very carefully, she repacked the platforms in the glowing papers and placed them ever so gently back into Zara's electric-blue shoebox.

—You don't like them, Sangita? I said, astounded, disappointed. I looked towards Kavita for some kind of explanation, but she lay perfectly still under the thin sheet. —I thought you —

—They're wonderful, Dimple, Sangita replied quietly. —And all my favorite colors. But Mummy will never approve. And Deepak . . . ?

—You don't have to wear them for the wedding. Just . . . when you like.

—I'm not even talking wedding — I mean they won't want me to wear them . . . *ever*!

Suddenly, sifting up through the shadows, Kavita's voice:

—Then put them on, for god's sake. And *never take them off.*

I was stunned by her vehemence. But the box had already been pushed below the bed, and Sangita's head was now buried beneath the sheet. A muffled sound into her pillow grew quieter, then stilled. And a final whisper:

—But one of us has to live out Mummy's dreams, isn't it?

CHAPTER 10

NoSoBoho

The next night, Kavita and I were to meet Mallika (of *Ye aai Karshki bibi!* renown) in Bandra. To Kavita's chagrin, and maybe even mine, Meera Maasi insisted Sangita join us, to distract her from the fact she was fasting for Shivratri. I didn't see how our dinner would do that unless Sangita wasn't so sweet on ancient fishing village fare, but as Meera Maasi didn't hesitate to point out, in *this* country, one respected her elders' wishes.

We climbed downhill from Ramzarukha and scrammed into the narrow confines of a rickshaw at Shoppers Stop. A tight squeeze; maybe that's why the tuk-tuk hadn't taken off in triple-chinned America.

Please Do Not Touch Me read the sign on the meter, which, upon Kavita's command, the driver — one leg folded under him, bare foot of the hanging one sticking insouciantly out the non-door — levered to zero. I was reminded of the low-railed cramped seats of the amusement park rides of my childhood: flying chair swings, bumper cars — and a combo of the two seemed to be the ride we were on as we narrowly missed a paanwallah on the right, only to nearly veer into a massive *Horn OK Please*–adorned Tata truck to the left . . . which itself had barely spared the life of a grizzled man sitting serenely just off the scant sidewalk, on the road itself, mending shoes.

As we skewed what seemed to be directly into oncoming traffic, I spotted the roundabout rani, weaving between cars with an enviable, and inadvisable, nonchalance, sticking a procuring palm into the window of any slowing vehicle. As we passed, Sangita reached a hand out, calling out *Nandini!* It seemed she was going to yank her in with us, but my cousin-sister merely slipped a bar of chocolate —

one of those green-tea-infused artisanal ones I'd brought upon her request — into the hijra's hand and withdrew her own, smiling merrily as we rounded the bout.

—You know her? I asked, incredulous.

—Everyone knows Nandini. And she was so excited about your arrival — especially when I told her you'd be sating her sweet tooth!

So that's why Nandini had waved to me that day: She'd recognized the car.

Rickshaws weren't allowed to cross-Link into South Bombay. A no-go in SoBo — but onto highways? No problemo! Although I still wasn't certain where it was, I was pretty sure my perineum was getting a workout as I clenched all my muscles to keep from being jettisoned out of the rick. Sangita and Kavita casually chatted, as if we were lounging by a hotel pool.

Off the highway. Through Juhu, Khar, and finally —

—Bandra! Kavita announced.

Mallika had chosen the joint, apparently very hip and expat-friendly, which she referred to as NoSoBoho (the real name was something rhyming), landmark, as Sangita had informed the driver: *Kya ufzee.* Urdu? The tuk-tuk stuttered down a side street and pulled to a panting stop.

We stumbled out. At a first glance, it didn't look particularly more hip or expat here. Unless the cow in the middle of the road was American.

Sangita and Kavs displayed immense courage and cultural immersion by flitting through the (very slim to nearly nonexistent) shifting gaps between cars and ricks, occasionally patting one of the vehicles to remind it that humans were in the path of destruction.

I froze, obeying an internal survival-instinct stop signal — one the cow seemed tuned in to as well.

—Dimple! Kavita shouted in exasperation from The Other Side. —For crying out loud!

It was demure Sangita who, like something in a retro video game, dodge-darted back across to me, grabbed my hand, and zig-zagged me through the slipsliding stream of vehicles. Like a good expat, I closed my NR eyes and screamed the whole way, just like I did the first time I merged with traffic coming off I-95.

When I opened them, I was gazing up at the building behind Kavita. It was a big bone-bright KFC.

We spotted Mallika farther up the side street.

—Madame has arrived! Kavita announced, waving her down. —I almost didn't recognize you, seeing you on time.

Mallika, dressed to the nines, even tens, in a come-hither slither of a BCBG number, stood shivering outside a jewelry shop. A row of men all in white lined up beside her.

—Who're your pals? I asked.

Mallika shrugged. —Valets.

—All yours? Kavita grinned. —Why are you up here? I thought we were meeting at KFC. Landmark, na?

—This sidewalk is nicer, Mallika replied. —Come on, ya. My feet are killing me.

I glanced down at her ankle-strap stilettos.

—Nice shoes, Mallika. Pick them up on Linking Road? I asked, trying out my newfound knowledge.

—Hell, no. Kurt Geiger on Portobello Road in London last summer.

We pushed through an aaray of stalls selling T-shirts, dupattas, and flip-flops, and entered a building by a side door, then took an elevator to the top.

Inside, all was decked out in a weird mix of Goth and jungle hues. Images of half-humans grazed the walls, lion-haunched, bird-winged. Thatched umbrellas floated over a few tables, gauzy greenish fabric billlowing above us in place of a roof. No breeze had been evident outside, so I wondered now if it was exhaust from the neighboring KFC. In fact, come to sniff of it, the venue *was* a little redolent of chicken nuggetry.

We were ushered into a side room, A/C cranked to tempest power. Mallika now proceeded to remove her sweater, as did Sangita. Somehow, though teeth-clicking cold in the balmy twenty-one-degree outdoor weather (read: seventy degringos Fahrenheit), they seemed fine with indoor Frigidaire climes.

We perused the menu, a culturally confused (or enlightened) assortment of Indian snacks and Tex-Mex platters. Like so many places here, it also had an entire Chinese section. Those ubiquitous transatlantic sliders were available, too.

—First things first. A BandrAmbrosia, Mallika read off the menu. —Gin, triple sec, vodka, lychee liqueur, and 7 Up.

—Ew, I said. —I hate 7 Up.

The waiter arrived. He looked immediately Hispanic to my NR eyes (NYC branch).

—Can we get something more typical? I asked Mallika. Wasn't feni a trad Goan beverage? (And wasn't Bandra Goan-ish from its Portuguese roots?) —I want the full immersion experience.

—But of course, Dimple. When in Bandra . . .

Mallika nodded to the waiter with the ease of someone used to servants.

—. . . drink Manhattans! A round, please.

—Just water for me, Sangita demurred.

—Sangita, please. You've been fasting forever already, Kavita cajoled. —Deepak's good for more than one lifetime by now, isn't it?

—I . . .

But Mallika held up a hand that silenced my doth-protest cousin-sister.

—Ignore her, Mallika instructed the waiter, who nodded and shooed off.

—Um, thank you so much! I called after him.

—You must be starving, Sangita, Mallika said now. —You haven't eaten all day?

Sangita nodded weakly. —Just a few more hours . . .

—Fasting to fit in the wedding dress, my dear?

—It's a sari, Kavita snorted. —No one has to fit in a sari.

—True, that's the whole point: You can hide all your fat under the wrapping, Mallika said with a nod, though I wasn't sure how she'd know anything about fat, unless she'd read about it (or saris, given her penchant for French designer duds). —Then: Surprise, betrothed! Two wives for the price of one!

The waiter reappeared, set down our drinks, and stood by me tensely with a bucket and ice grips.

—How many cubes, madame? he asked. That had to be the first time anyone had ever asked me this question, and I certainly hoped it wouldn't be the last. I felt purringly indulged. However, childhood warnings to avoid water in India sprang to mind.

—Um, has it been boiled? I auto-asked. The waiter looked like he wanted to call his lawyer first.

—Why would you boil ice? Mallika inquired politely. —Oh, come *on*, Dimple. It's mineral water ice. We're in Bandra — expat central. If the H_2O was dodgy, this place would be out of business in a snap.

I chose three. "We Three," by Patti. A holy number: third eye. I wondered if Akasha knew. Half a Manhattan down and my goose bumps white-flagged it despite the frozen trio in my glass.

We passed the nachos, which I hadn't heard anyone ordering. Sangita chastely shook her head as the platter came her way, though her eyes bored ravenously through the disappearing dish. I crunched; she flinched. Mallika, who took a spoonful of guac, passing on the rest, stared at her.

—So? Then what? she asked now. —What the hell diet is this?

—Shivratri, ya, Sangita sighed.

Mallika raised her brows. —It's Shivratri? Oh yeah. I suppose it is.

—So on Shivratri, the goddess Parvati performed tapas, Sangita filled me in.

—Like dim sum? I wondered aloud.

—Ah, *dim sum* . . . Sangita moaned, stomach audibly rumbling. —No. As in prayers, meditation. To shield her spouse from the dangers of a moonless night. That's why on Shivratri, women pray for the protection of their husbands and sons.

—And daughters and wives? Kavita said through a tortilla-glutted mouth. —Screw 'em. *And today I will fast for the protection of the women in my life* said . . . no man ever!

—My theory is in return the husbands eat twice as much to become nice and fat so no other women will want them! Sangita chuckled.

—And if you don't have a husband? I asked, figuring a fridge with a lock must come in handy for these occasions.

—You fast in the hopes of having one, Sangita explained.

—And one like Shiva — the destroyer! Mallika added derisively. —Of your life!

—Shankerji, Shiva is the destroyer of *evil*, Sangita objected. She stared longingly at the feast on the table, twisting those beads around her neck. —He drank in a poison that could have destroyed all of creation. Halahala. But he did not swallow it, held it in his throat. Thus he is also called Neelkanth. The blue-throated one.

She touched her neck as she spoke, as if she felt that god's pain, then cleared her own throat.

—Anyways, they say it's good for your soul to stay up all night, dancing, playing music. The planets are aligned for maximum benefit.

—Well, we're in the right suburb, Kavita proclaimed. —For dancing and music.

—Let's go with the all-night vigil part, then, I suggested, having fast failed the fast.

—In Bombay? All night still means one thirty unless you're at an after-party at someone's home. Or a four- or five-star hotel — then you can soiree till three, said Kavita.

—Sadly, I'm not doing such a great job of protecting Karsh. . . .

—Karsh doesn't need protection. He's a strong man.

—Deepak is, too! Sangita jumped in, a little petulantly.

Mallika nodded towards Sangita's untouched drink. —Then what are you so worried about?

Sangita met her eyes, raised her glass, and took a sip. She glanced around the room as if an alarm might go off.

—Believe me, I fasted for a couple Shivratris, Mallika was saying now. —Upon my mother's command. But that didn't stop my marriage from falling apart; in fact, I'm in town *finally* finalizing the divorce. Starving yourself isn't any guarantee. Unless my ex was being protected from . . . me!

—*You* were married, Mallika? I gasped. Sangita took a bigger gulp of her Manhattan, reached tentatively for a nacho.

—Thanks a lot. Is it so surprising someone would want to bond me in helly — I mean holy — matrimony?

—No, it's just . . . you're so young, I said quickly. A grad student, she didn't look past her mid-twenties. —Was it arranged?

—Unofficially. I was dating a good boy from the same background. So it was inevitable.

—Like, Hindu from Bombay?

—Rich. From Malabar Hill.

That elicited a snigger from my cousins.

—We met in high school, Mallika continued. —Cathedral. Actually, in grade school, but we started dating in high school. His family was doing business with mine. And the assumption was always that Naveen and I would unite to bond the bloods — and businesses — even closer.

—Magnate-ic attraction, Kavita quipped. Mallika nodded.

—As soon as I finished undergrad, we got married. Three days at the Breach Candy Club, every family member got a little twenty-two-carat Ganesha when they left. Honeymoon in Bali, second one in the foothills of the Himalayas . . .

She sighed, perhaps nostalgic for that conjugal bed. —You absolutely *must* get a massage there. Ask for Ananda.

—Wow, I said, incredulous now in equal parts due to Mallika's tale of betrothal and the idea of turning up at the foot of the Himalayas . . . and asking for Ananda. —You didn't date anyone during undergrad?

Mallika smiled.

—I didn't say *that*. I just knew what was expected of me when I got back to Bombay. But New York had given me the seven-year itch . . . seven years ahead of schedule. We stuck it out awhile, even tried Manhattan together when I started grad school — which I did primarily to get back there. He did everything right, all by the book.

—Aw, too sweet only! Sangita cooed.

—In short, Mallika concluded, —nauseating. So . . . he caught me with Niket. I suppose I let him; couldn't see any other exit.

She turned to Sangita. —Highly recommended tactic if you're looking to get out of your engagement.

—Why would I be?

—I'm just saying. Cheaper than bribing the astrologer to misalign your stars.

—Astrologer? Sangita snortled. —Now there are computer programs to figure out if your stars are aligned, na?

—Is that so? I personally find the best way to confirm alignment with someone is to go sixty-nine. Shag 'em senseless and see if your eyes can line up after.

I turned to Sangita. —But I thought you used an astrologer?

—Both. A program and a star-chart reader. In reverse order.

—So what's better about the new date? I asked her.

—It's *later!* Sangita laughed. Mallika snickered. Sangita immediately grew serious.

—*Aacha.* So how's your alignment with this Niket been going, then? she asked her now.

—When in New York, Mallika replied. —And when in Bombay . . .

—Huh? So who are you dating in Bombay? Kavita interrogated.

—It's a quandary, Mallix lazily lamented. —In terms of experience, I'm too old for single boys my age and too young for the widowers, you see. I can't date anyone available: I'm the wild one who broke a good boy's heart, na? And, frankly, I'm not so keen on tying any kind of knot at this point. So I've found a way to . . . entertain myself in a way people can't talk about. At least to my face.

—What's that supposed to mean?

—I've targeted a new demographic: the unhappily married men of Bombay. Principally, but not limited to, South.

—There are so many married guys in their twenties? I asked, amazed. I didn't know of any in New York.

—No. They're not unhappy till their thirties or forties.

—Forties! So you're, like, into geriatric sex?

Mallika waved me off. —Take it from me, these guys want nothing more than a young supposed ingénue to marvel at all their minuscule victories — handed down from their dads of course — and ready to . . . worship the lingam, so to speak. Which, thanks to my liberal arts education, I've gotten damn good at.

—That's disgusting, said Kavita, unsurprisingly.

—Don't knock what you haven't tried, sister. Right, Dimple?

—I can barely remember . . . lingam worship, I laughed. —But I intend to refresh my memory the second Karsh lands.

Sangita's mouth was so stuffed with nachos at this point, she looked like a hamster preparing for a long, cold winter. In the foothills of the Himalayas. With Ananda.

—Sangita, don't listen to them, Kavita assured her. —You don't have to be a BJQ to prove your love.

Sangita looked perplexed.

—There are all kinds of love, ladies, Mallika disclosed.

—And . . . ?

She cackled. —And sex isn't one of them! Sex is about power. Always has been.

—Mallika! Sangita cried out now. —Think of those poor wives!

—The wives? They're anything but poor! And trust me, they all know what's up with their husbands. They're holding it together for the window dressing. It's a deal.

—But it can't be so easy for them, I said, considering it. —There must be a lot of broken hearts in all this.

—*I* am not the heartbreaker, Mallika said fiercely. —No one can break your heart but yourself. It's a choice.

Sangita shook her head, pained. —Mallika. This is worrying. You will never meet an eligible boy behaving like this.

—Exactly. I'm done with eligible!

—Why don't you go for some Bandra boys at least? Unmarried, preferably. They're the hip ones, na? The cool ones. And more your generation.

—Screw hip, Mallika replied.

—I think that's what she's saying, I clarified.

—No, I mean — too childish, too young. Too many goatees. Those patently ridiculous shorts to the knees — ugh! Such random T-shirts.

—Um. That sounds like Karsh, actually, I said. —Except the shorts.

—Karsh is different, Mallika assured us all, with a proprietary pride that unnerved me. —He's a bleeding heart in a warrior body. And he doesn't have that whiny end-your-sentence-in-a-question-mark way of talking that so many American desi boys have. Plus, all those Bandra expats are too trust-funded, pampered.

—And *your* crowd isn't? Kavita laughed. —Mallika, you get chauffeured to take a piss!

—We are old money, Mallika said grandly. —We know how to behave with the stuff. No vulgar SUVs that can barely squeeze down a suburban street. No tattoos at Al's and silly lopsided haircuts. I mean, do they do that on purpose? We are about understated elegance. Come to South Bombay — we'll show you where to put your lakhs.

She raised a glass. —Anyway. Here's to marriage, Sangita!

—Two weeks! I joined in, feeling foolish.

Sangita looked to her glass, but it was empty. She grabbed Kavita's.

Mallika grinned.

—Two weeks? Fabulous! So in case you change your mind . . . here's to being within the window to get your deposit back!

—You're a bloody fucking romantic, Mallix, said Kavita.

—Why, quite literally, darling. Sangita, you just let me know if you want me to get your man in trouble — and you out of it. I'm pretty good at that.

—Aaray, shat up, ya! Sangita slurred, but she didn't look too perturbed.

—No issues. I'm sure Deepak is a real catch. And probably a firecracker under the sheets. Make sure you test out the wick beforehand, ya? Dimple's doing that with Karsh, and I commend her for it.

Sangita nodded, embarrassed. I doubted she'd had much action even *alone* under the sheets. But, after a moment's hesitation, she clinked glasses with Mallika.

CHAPTER 11

Room 212

At last, the glorious day was here! Karsh's arrival . . . and our immi- nent reunion in our motherland. When his night and my day would once more tock together, beauty and the beat syncing the same shore.

And mergers of a bluer, more salubrious nature as well . . .

Actually, it was difficult distinguishing day from night as sleep had eluded me once again, up up and awaying with my butterflying anticipation. Karsh and I had texted back and forth up to the moment he boarded at JFK. And even once he was jet-winged, I remained wakeful and wired, obsessing over all the things I had to show him. Despite the challenges our coupledom had experienced of late, surely here we'd find an indelible reminder of all that had united us in the first place, a bridge back to our old two-headed, big-hearted self.

I'd been keen on picking him up at the airport (as had Kaka), but Karsh had informed me that Ravi (Mallika's contact, the pro- moter) had already organized a car to fetch him; he wanted to go over some details for his impending show ASAP.

—It's going to be a little hectic, rani, Karsh had explained from check-in. —But plenty of time to hang with your family once all this music business is settled . . .

No *problemo,* I'd told him. I couldn't wait. For all of it.

*　*　*

My own bags seemed not even to exist, so seamlessly did they flow from Arvind's grasp to Maruti trunk to, about forty-five minutes (and two miles) later, the Seahorse hotel porter's.

It had been my mother's suggestion that Kavita drop me off so we could get some girl time with my NYU roommates; Kavita had eagerly agreed (boldly adding how she so rarely got to *come out* in India). But to our alarm, at the last minute Sangita had shyly asked if she could join us.

As we emerged from the car, I was slightly stressing out about how to explain the lack of any other chicas involved in this fictitious girl time to her. But Sangita, stopping the porter from making off with another rickety rolling suitcase in the trunk, just waved to us.

—Okay, aacha! Have a lovely day! Sorry, I can't stay after all. We're working on Deepak's office today.

She ejected handle from suitcase. Where was his office? Simla? Before I could inquire further, she was off with a rick-hailing *Bhai!*, pulling the edge of her faded blue sari overhead.

I shot a querying glance at Kavita, but she was already passing through the metal detector, into the lobby.

I stepped up to the blankly cheerful man at the desk (name tag: Sunhil).

—I'm booked with Karsh Kapoor, arriving today?

He typed away, then looked up at me, this time with an expression of recognition now that I was confirmed in the computer system.

—Welcome to the Seahorse, Mrs. Kapoor!

Kavita gave me a look. I was probably giving myself one as well.

—Is there a problem, madame? Sunhil inquired. I burned my gaze into Kavita, beaming a no-issues telepathic signal her way.

—No issues, Kavita said. —I just always took her for a *Ms.* type.

—There is a message for you, Sunhil-ji went on. —Mr. Kapoor will be here momentarily but was detained at the airport. I hope this will not be too much of a problem for you, Mrs. Kapoor.

Kavita and I burst into a fit of giggles at hearing the name spoken aloud again.

—Madame is highly excitable, Kavita explained impishly, while

I fervently nodded. —She has not seen her husband in . . . almost a day? Newlyweds only.

—Ah, then you will feel right at home here, madame! It is the season, of course. We have weddings on nearly every evening at the moment! Please wait one moment. . . .

He glanced at his screen, rolling his mouse into a tizzy.

—I'm pleased to inform you, in celebration of your choosing the Samudri Ghoda as your honeymoon destination, we are happy to offer you a free upgrade to a seaview room!

He handed me two key cards.

Room 212? New York City's prime area code? It was a sign! Of . . . whatever!

Kavita saw me into this honey-glow seaview room: a warm (A/C not on), cozy (small), inviting (paid for by someone else, key worked), and utterly charming (warm, small, paid for by someone else) space.

A vase of radiant blooms! Such tiny bananas in the fruit basket!

Kavita drew the curtains, and the pane flooded with brown-blue Bowie-eye sea-sky. Below, that patch of electric pool blue was today perimetered by a bevy of brunettes. Bent over the end of the beach barrier wall, that pacing dark knight of a guard appeared to be pulling up a sock.

The message light flashed on the bedside telephone. While I dialed in for calls, the luggage arrived and Kavita dealt with the tipping. The first message was from a music journo named Flip, about kicking off the profile pronto upon Karsh's arrival. A second was from Ravi, detailing an address in South Bombay.

So Ravi wasn't with him?

The third message was for me, from none other than my parents . . . welcoming me to Bombay.

—Well, Dimps, Kavita said now, bidding me farewell. —Chalo. My love to Karsh . . .

She gave me a sneaky smile. —And yours to him, I'm sure.

And she was off. In a flash, most of my clothes were as well.

I dug around in my bag. Pulled out a strip from the Condomania pack and strung it around my neck like a lei (lay!), then stood there in my bra and boxers, glancing around the room for inspiration.

I was beheading the flowers, scattering petals upon carpet and bedspread, when I heard that much-longed-for knock on the door.

The baby bananas! I tore one off the bunch, stuck it between my lips like a randy monkey, flung open the door with a bushy-tailed:

—Karsh!

. . . then slammed it shut, mortified. A breath, and I eeked it open, peeked apologetically through the crack at the hotel attendant waiting there, shyly, holding a bottle of champagne.

—Um . . . yes? I managed, the freed fruit at once pealing from lips to floor with a defeated thud.

He appeared more embarrassed than me.

—Very sorry to be disturbing you, madame, he whispered. —But the hotel would like to offer you this in honor of your wedding.

He bent down, setting the bottle at the threshold.

—I'll just . . . leave it here . . .

He scurried away, probably not daring await a tip from a girl without pockets. When he'd vanished, I rescued the champers.

Had word spread so fast? For I'd barely thrown on one of the two fluffy white bathrobes when the door edged open (I'd never shut it) . . . and there before me stood another hotel attendant, bearing a wicker basket with a brand-new bunch.

—May I replenish your fruits, madame? he asked — courteous in tone but curious insolent eyes unyieldingly fixed on my bath-robed, condom-lei'd, hootch-handed self. Perhaps he was wondering what fate might befall the bananas.

I furiously shook my head, closing the door on his uninterrupted stare.

I threw off the lei, dramatically ripping up the condoms (along the perforation, of course, so as not to render them unusable), and threw them on the bedspread. Then I flopped down among the strewn petals, exhausted from my failed seductions.

When I heard the next set of knocks — these strangely rhythmic and overlapping (had the entire staff turned up?), I didn't budge.

But the ever-attentive fruit replenishers kept at it, finally ringing the buzzer.

—Ayurvedic full-body massage? a deep, thickly accented voice offered through the door.

—Um. I'll pass, I replied, then translated: —I mean, thanking you only.

A pause. Then a chortling.

—Rani! It's me!

I catapulted up. Flung open the door. And there, at last *here*, was he of the percussively skilled fingertips, a single tabla in hand. He returned it to the cylindrical case he was towing behind him, one wheel a little banged up from that airport carousel crash landing.

Karsh was five o'clock shadowed beyond the usual boundaries of his beard, fatigue lines below those crinkling eyes — my favorite shade of brown in the world — and a devilish grin I immediately attacked with my own, kiss-steering him into the room with one arm, slamming the door behind him and flicking on the Do Not Disturb light with the other.

I threw Karsh onto the bed and finally released my mouth from his (delicious, though slightly lagery) lips. Then I sat on top of him, victorious.

—Duggibug! I can't believe it's you!

He smiled. —It's always me. Me and you.

I threw off the bathrobe, revealing all my bra-and-boxer glory.

—You and me. Finally *here* . . .

—Imagine, he whispered, both hands in my hair now, pulling up from the nape as I so loved. I lay down, snuggling up beside him.

Now that he was here, it felt he'd never not been. I'd never not been.

He brushed a petal from my hair.

—Doing a little gardening? he laughed.

I nodded towards the condoms.

—Fertilizing, I sighed. —What took you so long?

—The usual. Gear check. They stopped me for the cables, cartridge, needle. And then they got stuck on the tablas — thought they saw some dubious drug dust in the duggi case. Must've been the talc.

The baby powder he sprinkled on his palms before finger-singing bayan and dayan (legendarily once one drum) to when-broke-it-still-spoke *toda, tab bhi bola* life.

—So how'd you get out of it? I asked.

He grinned. —I played 'em. Did a round of teentaal. They *applauded* me through after that!

—Hit the ground gigging? Off to an auspicious start, methinks! I effervesced. I smiled lecherously and slid a hand between his shirt buttons, onto his heart. —And we can be, too . . .

His excitement encouragingly palpable, with a bed-groan moan he exhaled.

—I know! L'Heure Bleu! I can't believe I'm playing such a hot venue in Bombay. Ravi says in a country of nearly one-point-three billion people — more than half youth, and a bursting middle class — all the elements are in place for me to take this city by storm!

Correction: His excitement about the *gig* was palpable. Well, I couldn't blame him. I was on the edge of our seat to see him break India, carry the light of his risen star in the South Asian (and now, beat by beat, subcultural-gone-mainstream) scene in the USA and shine it here, seduce this city into head-over-heeling with his particular breed of bhangra.

Nevertheless, I picked up a banana and seductively stroked it.

—May I replenish your fruits, sir?

He shook his head, still smiling, propped himself up on his elbows.

—I have to be careful, rani. I really have to watch what I eat and drink here so I don't get sick before the big gig . . . or the meeting today.

—From a five-star banana? I asked, incredulous. —What meeting?

He rose up now, all the way to sitting.

—I'm so sorry, rani, but Ravi wants to connect to go over the show details. I promise we'll hang on our own after.

—I thought you met with him in the car that *fetched* you?

—I didn't realize just the driver was fetching me. Ravi's going to call in the deets. Some place in South Bombay.

—Oh yeah, I said flatly. —Ravi left a message. Some place in South Bombay.

Karsh leapt up for the hotel phone like it might run away.

—Man, rani — why didn't you tell me?

He was scribbling down the instructions on the notepad while I pondered that. Um, maybe because I thought we'd be going wildly nonverbal for a few hours upon his arrival?

He hung up.

—Given the traffic in this town, we better leave a wide margin. I'll just jump in the shower, then we can push off. Don't want to be late for our first Bombay industry meeting.

—We? I said, surprised. —Our? Are you sure you want me to come along to an *industry* meeting?

—Of course! This is India; people always bring people to things. Besides, I want Ravi to get to know New York's clubbing photographer of choice.

He sat down beside me, planting a kiss on my forehead as he unbuttoned *his* shirt.

—*My* photographer of choice, he added.

I hesitated. But only a blink; the idea of roaming Bombay with my boy mercury, as the B-52s sang, sound and vision team back in force, was pretty all right by me.

—Yeeehaw! I grinned, then sang it. —*Around the world the trip begins with a kiss* . . .

I was about to begin ours, but at the last moment withdrew; his face was so serious.

—Thank you. It would mean a lot to me if you came along, he said quietly, and there was a hint of a plea in that tone. —To be honest, I feel a little out of sorts this time. It's strange to be here without family. . . .

I took his face in my hands.

—You're not without family.

—I'm sorry, he said quickly. —I didn't mean it that way.

—I know you didn't, I replied, even though I didn't know he didn't. But this was his big moment, not mine, and I wanted to support him — through the pain, and the pleasure as well. —I'd love to come, Karsh. And I can't wait to meet Ravi.

—Really? he said with audible relief. I nodded.

—Anyway, if you're getting to work, I might as well get to work, too. I can get some shots of you there, and I can always split and shoot the setting if it seems you two need some one-on-one.

I reached for my camera now.

—Speaking of which . . . no time like the present? Let me get my first shot of . . . Karsh in the motherland!

He froze for me. When I peered through the lens, I was disarmed to discover a mournful undertone to the manic smile. And when I clicked, I heard one, too, so low I nearly missed it. . . .

—The fatherland, he said softly.

• CHAPTER 12 •

White Noise

Driver 4303 was destined to be ours, and pulled up by the hotel entry to whisk us off to Marine Drive.

In the taxi, Karsh kept staring nervously at his phone, picking at a thread on the loose-flowing, casually elegant maharajah getup he'd ultimately settled on (hot out of Edison, Joysey; staple duds at his Adda gigs in New York). I sidled in closer to him, abetted by the fact there were no seat belts in the back of the car.

4303-ji glanced at us in the evil-eye-deflecting fresh-chili-peppered rearview, molten brown eyes split from the man.

—Missed call from Ravi, Karsh fretted as we passed a *you booze you loose* sign. —But I can't get a signal. . . .

—Sea Link, sir, 4303-ji announced, or explained. And next thing I knew, a river of ricks hearkening off left, we'd cruised straight onto the bridge.

The Rajiv Gandhi Sea Link. Through the toll, an unreeling in my belly not unlike at the moment of aviatory ascent. Aloft as if mounting the skeletal soul of a flying ship, eight lanes swung-hung, shimmering suspended over the sea.

The slant-spanning cables zipped past our open windows. And before us — skyline jarringly jaggingly modern, yet mirage-hazy from this distance — that other wavelengthening shore unfurling like a sleight-of-sight Manhattwin.

Unidentical. Sororal twins. Throat catch; scupped beat: the other side suffusing me with a sense of something both instinctively familiar and utterly alien.

Like love at first sight. The farther across the bridge we traveled, like a magic trick, that other skylined shore before us seemed to extend, unfold, undulate through an amniotic gauze deep into the southern distance, a matryoshka city birthing itself as we drove, infinitely expansive, intimately inviting — yet somehow always unraveling just out of reach.

—Wow, Karsh murmured.

—*Wah*, I concurred, as in *aaray*. I picked up Chica Tikka, turning to the back windshield to catch where we'd just been . . . and was swept with something akin to vertigo to discover directly behind me no bridge, no shortest-distance-between-two-points straight-lining back to that Bandra shore, but rather, this slithership giving us the slip: curving delinquently, deliriously, disorientingly off to the right.

How had I not felt that curving away?

Forward, peripheral vision, left: a thrust of near-prehistoric sepia, rust, russet and occasionally blue-tarp-tarned terrain, a ramshacklage of tiny boats, blinks of color along its craggy edge.

To the right: open sea.

All that in approximately seven minutes. The bridge let out in Worli, a sign to South Bombay (where I'd thought we were headed) indicating left, though 4303-ji soon after spun around and gassed off in the opposite direction, the congested arterial roads honking us out of that suspended dream state of a bridge.

And into another?

* * *

Despite the mind-numbing traffic, we arrived at the Inter-Continental with twelve minutes to spare — not too shabby, as IST (Indian Standard Time, meaning: late) was a given in this town. Karsh was always pretty particular about timing; he was a drummer, after all.

We got the elevator to the hotel roof and exited into a shimmering snowscape: ivory-iridescent sofas and seats, icy sunshades, milk-spill tiles. Fat white candles dripped in glass holders. White bowls burst a bloodbath of blooms, while ice buckets luxuriated, fulgent with bottled bubbles.

It was all so *clean*. White was a color you didn't see much of in pure form in Bombay, given all the grime and grit. A few white people even lounged around, sipping on long cocktails and dipping their toes in the upraised pool of glittering blue that put the ashen sea — just visible off the terrace edge — to Technicolor test. Palm fronds unfurled in the ocean breeze. It was like stepping onto a film set.

—It's so *Aryan*, I whispered.

—Indians are likely descendants of the Aryans, wiseass, Karsh laughed. —And we're in a hotel, remember, which may explain the gringo quotient. But, man, it *is* pretty amazing.

I nodded. No Ravi to be found, we walked to the glass half-wall running the rooftop perimeter, leaning over to imbibe the view. Eight floors down, the mulchy sea muddled a smudged sapphire sky. The air brimmed with white noise from all the rickless traffic below, curving off and away.

We sank into a sofa by the edge. To the side, a glass and aluminum bar, manned by deep-tawned, red-hatted, black-shirted men. I wondered where they hailed from, here in this city of dreams. And why I hadn't even noticed them initially, but only the pallor palette.

In fact, only about a third of the starletty folk lacksadazing on white cocktailed couches were white. The sipping Indians were several shades paler than the serving ones, and donned billowing shirts and skirts that kept them well sheathed from the searing sun.

The non-Indos went sleeveless.

—This is the life, Karsh murmured. It certainly was, though I wasn't sure it was that of the black-shirted related-to-me-looking man who came up now to take our order.

—Hi! I exclaimed, guilt-thusing. —And how are you today . . .

I searched for the name tag, found none.

—Ji? I concluded, using the term of respect.

The waiter appeared partly tickled, largely embarrassed.

Karsh jumped in. —Hi, boss. We're still expecting someone.

The server nevertheless proceeded to Houdini up small bowls of wasabi peas, cashews.

—Thank you so much . . . boss! I yapped. He nodded and scurried off without replying, thereby drawing to a close the shortest interaction I'd ever had with a waiter in my life.

—I think your enthusiasm terrified him, Karsh opined, amused. I whipped out my camera, clicked him, then snapped a few shots off the edge of the roof while he checked his phone every two seconds for a text from Ravi.

—I just hope he didn't forget, he said nervously. I was about to reassure him when:

—Karsh! someone called out. We turned to find a man, early for an Indian (only twenty minutes late), striding bullishly towards us.

He wore tight-fitting, big-belted blue jeans, major shades, and a beige shirt undone a couple buttons more than advisable, revealing a possibly braidable tuft of chest hair. Hero swaggered into the space, seeming oblivious to everything around him.

—Ravi, he announced, for my benefit since Karsh had already met him in New York.

—Dimple Lala. I'm Karsh's . . . girlfriend.

Swaggering in India seemed morally wrong somehow, and I was relieved when Ravi flumped down on the sofa.

—Ha! Lala. Good Gujju girl, I see. Always by her man's side?

—Half Marathi, I corrected. He didn't seem too interested in my rich and varied cultural background, and immediately popped a generous handful of cashews into his mouth. Like, *all at once.*

—Sorry, ya. Been waiting long? he asked Karsh.

—Na, Karsh replied, shaking his head. Since when did he say *na*?

—My driver was still drunk from Shivratri. So we ran a little late. He's parked streetside, napping it off.

Karsh looked concerned. Ravi scooped up another handful and shrugged at him. —They like to sleep.

—*They?* I said.

Karsh shot me a look. Ravi raised an arm sky-high and snapped, summoning the waiter back towards us. It was . . . boorish. But I tried to remain (or become) open-minded; it was all about context, right? Perhaps this gesture worked wonders as far as convincing venues to give Karsh gigs went.

The waiter appeared, complete with three-cube frozen smile.

—A round of these, Ravi instructed, pointing to the menu. —And wasabi dumplings.

I wanted to ask the waiter what his favorites were — they always knew best — but he was already off like a hound on the hunt for his master, and Karsh was saying grace:

—First, Ravi, I just want to tell you how grateful I am for all your help on this. I can't thank Mallika enough for the introduction.

—Mallika's great, I said. —And Niket. The glamourest love-birds on the circuit.

I didn't know why I felt the need to couple her up. Perhaps because I'd been tagged (by myself) as Karsh's woman, I wanted to align myself with other boyfriended-but-still-independent females who required profuse thanking.

—Niket? Ravi inquired, raising his brows.

—They're so inseparable people even refer to them as Malliket, I laughed. Ravi laughed as well, a little derisively. Why did he seem to have taken an instant disliking to me?

Was it my instant disliking of him?

Karsh, sensing the mildly festering undercurrent, dove in again. —I can't tell you how thrilled I am to work with someone of your caliber!

I wasn't sure what caliber Ravi was, since from what Mallika had said, it seemed this was as much an opportunity for him — to enter the music business and jump ship on his father's law firm — as it was for Karsh. But like the good Gujju girlfriend I wasn't, I sat silently (scowling) as Karsh sucked up to Ravi, who leaned back, casually allowing this verbal wankoff.

The wasabi dumplings arrived. I was craving Indian food, but the closest I could see to it on the menu was the use of cilantro in a Mumbai Mojito — three of which materialized before us now.

I downed my mojo, observed as they went over a checklist of equipment for the show. Ravi's right shoulder was slightly elevated; did he secretly sport a knapsack? His face was worn, but his shock of hair was uncompromisingly onyx. I wondered if he dyed it.

A thin-crust pizza with some weird shit on it (cue: endive, pungent cheese) wafted onto our table.

—You've got to try this — *divine*, Ravi said through a full mouth. He handed a slice to Karsh but didn't offer any to me.

—We live in New York, I sullenly pointed out. It wasn't that I needed a literal handout, but it was confusing. Was Ravi's lack of tending to me sexist? Or feminist? —Pizza was practically invented there.

—That's so American, he scoffed.

—Um. I *am* American.

He finished chewing and, after a beat, thunked a file on the table. No multitasker, this one.

—Enough small talk, ya. So let's run over some legal details for your sundowner show. Karsh, I'll need you to sign the contract for LHB ASAP.

He said ASAP "a-sap" instead of "A.S.A.P." It seemed odd considering the L.H.B. Not to mention I.S.T.

A.S.S.

—LHB? Karsh asked.

—L'Heure Bleu. I'm seeing Sam tonight so can hand it to him myself.

—Can I take some time to read this?

—It's the usual, Karsh. Very general.

—General in a contract usually means they option your offspring, doesn't it? I translated. They both ignored me.

—The LHB show is a make-or-break deal, Ravi said, fanning out the papers. —I had to pull more than a couple strings to get you this slot. It's a big night for them — a reopening — so keep these things in mind: The contract stipulates you may only play electronica at a sundowner. Ya? No R&B, mainstream pop. And absolutely no bhangra.

Karsh's mouth dropped open. I spoke up for him.

—Huh? But Karsh is *king* of bhangra. He *made* that scene in New York!

—Well, bhangra in *Bombay* is strictly wedding music, and maybe a couple tracks at that. Something you *definitely* do not want to be doing, Karsh. Weddings.

He made a cut-throat gesture.

—Actually, we're here for a wedding, I said. —My cousin Sangita's. And Karsh —

—But bhangra is so well *received*, Karsh interrupted. —From my experience.

—Not in the Bombay scene, Ravi enlightened us. —Here it's even considered a little . . . how shall I put it? Lower class.

I took that very personally on behalf of my ancestors and all the contemporary New York City club kids who danced with delirious abandon to these ancient-Punjabi-modern-hip-hop meshed beats. As well as on behalf of the lower class, though I wasn't sure I knew them.

I tried to give Karsh an insider look. But he was just staring at Ravi.

My mojito had vanished. In me, I was pretty sure.

—Well, Ravi, if no one in the *scene* plays it, I suggested, —then maybe it would be subversive of Karsh to do it. Like, Patti Smithish.

—Patti Smith?

—A forerunner of the punk movement, that whole seventies downtown New York scene, I informed him, enjoying a delightful matronizing tone in my voice. —And one of the first artists to meld spoken word and poetry into rock.

—Um. I know who Patti Smith *is*, Dimple. *Shooting at the walls of heartache, bang bang* . . .

—That's the other Patty Smyth, I corrected him. I suddenly felt depressed.

Karsh seemed to catch on.

—I think I know what Dimple means, he said, cautiously. —I do a kind of meld as well. . . .

Ravi held up his baas (stop) hand, then went on to inform Karsh that was a no-go: The big clubs were about Bollywood hits; the indie scene — electronica, trance, techno. That he couldn't be king of bhangra in the land where bhangra came from. That land had changed with the times.

Yadda yadda dahi wada. I figured Karsh would point out to him that bhangra *itself* had changed with the times: morphed in the UK to become what it was now — urban bhangra, what he played. That his meld, in fact, was that of India, the UK, and our New York — which was why it perfectly embodied him, even this generation. But what he said, finally, slowly, was:

—Well, it's not *all* I play anymore. I've been mixing it up more at my Adda shows.

—Karsh, Ravi sighed now, fire in his eyes. —If you break that deal, even with one track, you're out on your ass. Literally. Which would mean, I am out on mine.

—What, the crowd will protest? Karsh asked now, a little too timidly.

—The crowd may not even notice. Mumbai doesn't have the most discerning clubgoing audience in the world.

—But I thought Bombay would, I remarked. It was interesting that when it was negative qualities under discussion (or politically correct, usually American, expats talking) this city was invariably described as Mumbai: Mumbai terror attacks, Mumbai nightlife crackdowns. When emotion, longing, homecoming were implicated: Bombay. I wondered idly if a Bombay Mojito would taste different from the second Mumbai one we were now draining. Probably miles better . . . but leaving you suddenly missing your childhood pet and with an unquellable yearning for another round, which would be served after an excruciating wait — and maintained a tantalizing inch out of range.

—But the management would certainly notice a breach of contract, Ravi concluded, signaling the waiter's return and gesturing for another one of these less nostalgic rounds. —If you kill it at LHB, it will secure your rep. We could follow it with Heptanesia, this super-hot spot in Lower Parel. And if you get a following going, there's NH7 next year. Sunburn. Magnetic Fields. And after? Sync spots! Soundtracks! But you have to play by the rules.

I turned to Karsh . . . to find him lapping it up. And what was strange was, rather than this being an entirely new sensation, I felt a flicker of familiarity. Like I could have been naked on the table slathered in sashimi and it wouldn't affect the rattle and hum, the roll and the rock of this meeting. It reminded me of those rooftop city nights, when Karsh and his cohorts would get so into a jam (AKA communal jerk session), only they and their appendaged tablas, guitars, dhols existed.

—I've got some ideas for photographers for you, Ravi went on.

—There's this guy, Mahesh. Mesh. Part of a cutting edge design collective. A linchpin in the scene. Runs one of Bandra's only art galleries. They can be cross-promoting you at the same time.

This time, my man hopped up to bat.

—*Dimple* is a photographer, Karsh said, gently but firmly.

—She did all my website shots, for starters. In fact, that's why I brought her along today, so we could talk visuals, flyers.

Ravi shot me an *Are you still here?* look.

—That's sweet, Dimple. But I think we may want a more *local* perspective.

I nodded quickly, trying to look professional (it was all in the posture: straight but not rigid, slight tilt back, no eager lean-in; chin up).

—I'll be shooting Karsh around Bombay, and of course his shows. Behind-the-scenes stuff as well. I even got some shots in before you came. And look — a few from New York, if we want to play the transglobal card . . .

I pulled the digital out now, scrolling back to a recent Jackson Heights snap: Karsh in a mithai shop vitrine, angled trays of gulab jamun catching the light like doused disco balls — just the shade of his sun-drunk eyes.

—DJ GJ . . . get it?

Karsh's HotPot party night moniker. Ravi glanced at the photograph and shook his head, almost sadly.

—Karsh. Mahesh is a Bandra boy through and through. Does website design as well. Speaking of which — get your original tracks up. I didn't see any online.

—That's because . . . Karsh sheepishly admitted, —I haven't got any.

Ravi stared at him horrified, then spit out an olive pit. I swear it came out slow motion.

—Karsh. You've got to have a track. You'll probably never make any money from it. But it will show you're serious.

—I've never been more serious, Karsh averred, possibly never more seriously. —I'll . . . I was going to dig around Rhythm House for some inspiration.

—No self-respecting DJ will be seen anywhere near Rhythm House, Ravi warned. —Stick to Soul Seek, Beatport. And get yourself a hot girl to front your sets and you've got a whole other in. A spot of midriff goes a long way. Makes them feel sex is imminent.

—Well, I've got Dimple! Karsh smiled cheerfully.

—The kind of girl who appeals to both the Bollywood bling set and the Bandra hipster, Ravi bulldozered, unblinkingly, on. —Who makes a sex appeal bridge between South and the suburbs.

—Why don't you get the Sea Link, I said drily. —She's been itching for her big break, and you'll make a killing if you get a cut of the toll.

Ravi paused, as if working out the math, then concluded:

—Like that Shailly ladki. Shorten the hippie skirts, and she's got potential.

Shorten? India? Maybe it was me who'd hit pause on my notion of what went down (or up) in the motherland. But I had a faint glimmer of respect for Ravi now, if he could consider buzz-cut, blue-green-eyed, single-silver-browed Shailly a *bridge*. She was more like an island, though a hospitable one.

Ellis.

—Shailly? Karsh smiled. —Tamasha? We're hooking up with her later. Shy used to open for me.

Ravi seemed pleased. Too pleased.

This meeting was not shaping up exactly the way I'd envisioned. I'd pictured me and Karsh rolling in as we'd always done: D&K, K&D, KDNY, DKNY versus the world — our sound and vision *shaping* the world.

But I wasn't sure this was that world anymore.

Sour taste in my mouth. Cilantro? I looked away now, and the sky was a gift of phantasmagic fuschia as the sun, after many hours of diligent travail, began to rung downward.

Several cocktailistas were now ditching all cool and leaping to the call of their inner shutterbugs: crowding the barrier and snapping, ooh-aahing at the spectacularly quotidian event.

I felt a sense of relief to sight my tribe, at last unveiled. I shot up and joined them.

When I returned to the table, Ravi was saying, —Karsh. Sky's the limit. What is your *dream*?

—I guess . . . Karsh replied thoughtfully, —to play the music I want to play and have it be just what everyone wants to hear . . . in a festival that includes all genres, races, income brackets . . . and we all inhabit the same sonic dream . . . that moment when DJ and crowd become one, song and listener, dancer and dance . . . and that harmony, that unity, becomes our anthem. Our musical manifesto.

—Right, Ravi said a little impatiently. —I meant, what *sponsors* would be your dream? Coke? JD? Dewar's? Kingfisher?

Karsh glanced up, startled.

—How can you *dream* about Coke? I interjected. Now Karsh gave me a regard I knew well: Cut the sarcasm. I was chastened; this was his meeting, after all. —What I mean is . . . I guess you could. If it turns him into a global . . . icon . . . who can cross back over to the American market?

—Ha! Ravi laughed, a sharded sound that bounced off the white light of the bar. —That's so NRI.

—What's NRI about that?

—Who says you have to cross over to the American market for it to count as success? Need I remind you, *you* all left to pursue the American dream — and now you're returning in droves to trade it in here. But FYI: This is the *Indian* dream. And the Indians were dreaming long before there was an America. Hell, you all even thought you were *in* India when you docked upon your promised land.

He pushed the papers across the table now, towards Karsh.

—I didn't mean it that way, I said quietly, although I was surprised to realize, in fact, I had. My heart sank as Karsh took the tendered pen . . . and signed.

Ravi smiled and, with a good-dog pat on Karsh's shoulder, stacked the papers and slid them into his bag.

—Anyways. Maybe Karsh won't return to the States, if things go to plan here, he concluded.

Karsh nodded, eyes still on him — and filled, if the half-light did not deceive me, with what looked like gratitude.

—Listen, I think we're finished here, Ravi abruptly announced.
—I've got to get to my eight o'clock.

It was already eight o'clock.

—I'll get Sam the papers ASAP. Any questions before sound check, message me.

He rose swiftly to go.

—And, Karsh. For the show? I'd skip the Indian attire. You don't have to prove you're from here *here*. No one dresses like that. A little more cas, maybe?

Loads of desi hipsters kurta'd out in New York, I thought. What was Karsh supposed to wear here? Probably Nike, Levi's. Airtel, Samsung. Corporate-sponsor style. Ravi glanced at me, in my jeans and CBGB tee.

—Not *that* cas. But you know what I'm saying. It's all about image.

—What about sound? I ventured.

He didn't hear me. In a flash: gone. I imagined his driver being jostled up from a sun-drenched snooze . . . as I let out a massive sigh of relief. I hadn't realized I'd been holding my breath till then, and took Karsh's hand now and squeezed it.

—Frock — what a *relief*!

—I know! Karsh smiled. —I think I've found my man!

Was mine losing his mind?

—Huh? Sign a contract to *not* play any of the stuff you love? And did you notice he stiffed us with the bill?

—Dimple, relax, Karsh said. —He was in a rush.

If there was one thing that made me not relax, it was being told to relax.

I tried to remember to be happy for Karsh as we gazed out over the Arabian Sea. I imagined Mumbadevi, first goddess of this city: a supine sea creature with cresting skin, a hemisphere in her hair, body studded with jutting buildings, moaning with the poor, the groaning rich, the many mud-dumped years of reclamation. Obsidian breath darkly rippling across her imagined chest.

Whether she was drowning or floating, I wasn't sure.

Karsh turned to me, eyes both comforting and aiming to convince. He gripped my hand tighter.

—Dimple. He believes in me. He believes I can belong.

—He treated me like Yoko Ono, I pointed out.

—Well, see? He recognizes your talent, too! After all, she's also a groundbreaking artist.

—I think it was more along the broke-up-the-band tip.

Karsh reached over, gently tapped my nose with his index.

—Come here, you, he said, kissing the top of my head with great tenderness. —Dimple, it's not us and them. It's you and me. You're the eyes, I'm the ears. We're on the same side, okay?

He was looking at me with such love in his own eyes, something in me loosened. I nodded, though I couldn't swallow down the lump in my throat. Karsh grinned now.

—Let's go back to the burbs, he suggested, counting out rupage for the waiter, including a hefty tip. —I think I'm in the mood for a little . . . room service.

I nodded again, managing a smile.

Below us, the Queen's Necklace arched towards South Bombay, sea a stunning murk, nearly indistinguishable from sky. The Art Deco buildings flicked on their finery, Bombay glittering with promise and potential — and looking not so unlike New York at the moment.

Karsh's arm wound around my waist and pulled me closer. We peered over the balcony, possibly appearing postcard perfect to the innocent bystander: silently entwined, admiring one of the finest views in town.

—Karsh, I said quietly. —Just remember. You've got to have faith.

—In?

—You've always been so passionate about bhangra. And your passion makes listeners passionate. I'm not saying don't branch out — I mean, yes, there shouldn't be borders with music. That's kind of the point of music, to get rid of those. But all I'm saying's don't stop listening to your heart and what got you on this journey to begin with.

I thump-thumped my own with my hand. —The beat you gotta follow. It's this one.

Karsh raised his hand, and I awaited his answering thump-thump — our code that all was okay, our call to live from the heart, mine his and his mine — but a slight buzzing distracted him. The ominous hum grew louder, and a mosquito landed on his forearm. He swatted it now with surprising fervor.

—Shit, Dimple, he said anxiously. —I brought a ton of chloroquine, but I haven't started taking it yet!

—Karsh, I sighed. —You're not going to catch malaria here.

—The same mosquitoes frequent luxury hotel rooftops, he pointed out, sounding like my dad. And then his arm was off me, hand untwined from mine as he busied himself rubbing antibacterial gel into his skin.

As we walked towards the elevator bank, I cast a last back glance to Marine Drive, so many floors down. At first I'd seen a street, curving away. Then that majestic oft-spoke-of necklace, shimmering on bulb by bulb. But now, ferrying off into the chasmic quarters of this known and unknown city, that necklace, the queen's accoutrement, morphed in my view.

All I could see lain out below me, before me, was a massive scintillating question mark.

CHAPTER 13 *

Bandra State of Mind

I was hoping to turn that question mark into an exclamation point back in Room 212. But no sooner had we gone through security than a blue-jeaned slingshot of a boy rocketed up from a sofa where he'd been scribbling in a notebook with one hand, nursing a ginormous neon cocktail with the other. Within seconds, he'd accosted us, rousing Karsh out of his taxi-nap trance with a hugely enthu high five. I was impressed that not a drop spilleth from his goblet.

Notebook: Clairefontaine (my favorite). Pen: Seahorse logo'd. This was one swift worker.

—Karsh Kapoor? he cried, angular face nearly devoured by a cartoonish grin. —Flip Pinto! Shailly e-intro'd us? For that profile on you, from pre-gig to post? America Based Creative DJs?

—Flip . . . said Karsh, blinking rapidly with that intent look of recognition he reserved for those post-gig sidewalk fans he didn't know from Adam (Avi?). This time the rapid double-wink soon subsided, and with a smile of relief he high-fived back, a second time. They were up to ten. —Ah . . . *Flip!* Filip?

—Shailly told me you were arriving today, Flip nearly gushed. —I'm profiling her, too. I hope you don't mind, but I didn't want to waste a moment.

Pinto bro was a wiry fiery-eyed thing, with all the avid alert grace of a starving cat. Goateed and randomly graphic tee'd (damn! Mallix was onto something), he nearly passed for a skinnier bespectacled version of Karsh.

He glanced at me now, then down at my camera, with what seemed an admiring look.

I liked him already.

Karsh now introduced us. —Dimple, Flip. Flip, Dimple's my main photographer. Amongst other things.

Flip proceeded to high-five me then. Fifteen.

—A photographer with a real camera! Superb! Maybe we can collaborate on the final product, then?

I nodded overenthusiastically. What a relief to be rid of Ravi!

—So who's the article for again? Karsh asked now.

—Um, it's on spec. But so's life, the way I see it.

This was a positive approach to a total lack of income. —After all, one must not take oneself too lightly . . .

Quoting Nietzsche? In Bombay!

—. . . nor too seriously, I beamed back, joyously rounding out the überquote.

He raised sleek satis-gratified brows at me. —Let's just say I do it for the love. But that's why you guys do what you do, right? Vinyl for Karsh, and film for —

He took a glug of his swish psychedelic cocktail.

—Mrs. Kapoor, he said, big-winking at me. Huh? He turned to Karsh. —Sorry. I said your name at the desk, and I think they thought I *was* you, as I was welcomed in for guests' happy hour. They asked if Mrs. Kapoor would be joining — but I had no idea she'd be such a punkstrel wife!

He nodded to my CBGB OMFUG (at this moment, for *oh my frocking gods!)* tee, swiftly becoming my new BFF.

We had more drinks in the lobby, and Karsh filled Flip in on Ravi and the LHB plan.

—You know, the last DJs to play LHB before they got shut down are in town, Flip informed us now. —Braun and Blau. This is their last night in the Bay; they'll be in Bandra later, and we could start the interview on the way? I see this piece more as a conversation, with a little of my tagging along with you while you're in town, if you don't mind. I can show you around while we're at it — get your POV on this scene, introduce you to some peeps? Everyone's just starting to come back out of hiding after the patrols.

Sounded like a great opportunity to photograph Karsh in this milieu, prove my credentials to Ravi — and truly begin our adventure.

Karsh lit up like a Diwali firework. —Shy mentioned hooking up, too. . . .

—Yeah, she had a meeting Worli-side, checking out a venue for her next party, Flip said. —She'll end up at the same spot. Everyone does.

He raised his glass. —So what do you say? Want the quintessential Bandra experience?

Karsh and I looked at each other and smiled. Room 212 could wait.

—Chalo? Flip asked. *Rock 'n' roll.*

—Chalo! we replied.

*　*　*

As we rode through Juhu, Flip pointed out various venues where Bollywood stars I'd never heard of, but who all seemed to have the same last name, had gotten thrown out for drunken brawling. A family with some serious issues.

The sea sweltered outside; I could make it out in peripheral vision, though mostly I was staring straight ahead and desperately hanging on to the rick. We suddenly swerved down a long kaleidoscopic street . . . which it actually felt we'd been doing the entire time (even when we were going straight).

—Five Spice! Flip instructed the driver, who braked abruptly in what, naturally, appeared to be the middle of the road. Almost pronto, a perspiring boy with hungry eyes stuck his hand in the tuk-tuk. Guilt-reflexing, I forked over whatever bill bulged out of my bumpack first. Karsh culpa-tipped the driver.

We got out — which didn't feel that different, frankly, from being in, except there wasn't anything to hold on to anymore.

Before us, an expanse of darkened pane. Above: the sign FIVE SPICE. I wondered if asafetida was one of them, and was about to head in, when Flip said:

—Not here. Five Spice is the landmark for over *there*.

He was pointing across the street. I zoomed on it.

—Jan*a*ta?

—*Joon*tha, he corrected my pronunciation. —Or common people.

We landed up before a compact well-lit stall selling strips of those ubiquitous supari packets, a stack of paan leaves laid out like lily pads on the wedge of counter. Lighters, batteries, key chains, ketchup, and 110-minute STD calling cards bulged off the shelves — but it was Lucky Strike cigarettes that took up the main marketing space: three gargantuan boxes of them up on the back wall, centered and lit up like 3-D Rothkos.

A Ganesha calendar hung to the side, freshly garlanded, days and months so tiny as to render time irrelevant in the presence of the divine; a few inches upwards, another god of new beginnings beamed down at us from beside the smokes expo.

The purveyor of this motley assortment of goods looked at us as if he'd seen it all. He'd definitely seen Flip, from the familiar nod he gave him now.

—One Gudang Garam, Flip ordered, then lit up the single cigarette from a lighter dangling off a spiral cord swinging from the stall ceiling. He diligently posed for my shot . . . then led us down a slip of alleyway behind the building, to a shadow-scudding back lot. He gestured one floor up the building's back.

—*This* is the quintessential *Bombay* experience, he proclaimed, taking his time on the exhale. —A permit room.

We gave him a blank look.

—A permit room? I asked finally. —What, like where anything goes?

—Ha! Hold on to your knees, folks . . . for this, Maharashtra, is the only state in the country where you need a permit to drink or buy booze.

He went on to explain, incredibly, that Bombay was still in practice under Prohibition, and had been since Independence. Permit rooms, which sprang up around town during this period, were little irrigating pit stops for the licensed drinker.

—Anyway. So I suggest we booze up here before hitting the bars. You can even order by the measure. Same taste, no paisa waste.

And so around to the front and in and up, past the sultry ground floor to tippling top we went.

The room we entered, though pleasantly devoid of character, was crammed with plenty of 'em, but a waiter seemed to recognize Flip and sardined the three of us at a school caf-like table beside a pair who were either siblings or spouses (looked alike; were focused on their food rather than each other).

—Chicken lollipops here are amazing, Flip apprised us, nodding at the neighboring plates. He got up to talk to one of the uncles, I guess ordering.

No music playing here; or if it was, it was drowned out by the deafening drone of high-spirits chitchat. The lighting, though on, for some reason gave the impression of being off.

Soon, Flip was back, swiftly followed by Kingfishers served in bottles bigger than our heads, and a plate of those famed lollipops. He dove in with his fingers, which surprised me for some reason; I'd figured hipsters were knife-and-fork types, even in India.

—So, my ex-fiancée splurged and got me a lifetime permit; that way I get off faster in case of a raid, Flip now informed us. —But since you have to be twenty-five for hard alcohol, not to mention rolling in the rupees in most bars, I carry a bottle of Old Monk just in case.

He indicated his messenger bag. But I'd latched on to that other detail:

—Ex-fiancée?

—She was American and her visa ran out, he sighed. —And she ran with it.

That was one way to end a relationship.

—Anyway, he went on through full mouth, —no one really ever checked before, but during the recent crackdowns, the police started demanding to see these permits, which almost no one has, in order to find a legal reason to close down parties.

—What is it exactly?

Flip licked his fingers clean then produced a beautiful wallet — rich weathered red leather unfolding like origami — and from it, a rumpled paper scrolled with Devanagari script.

To my surprise, Karsh produced one, too, smoothing it out on the table.

—Ravi gave me a bunch today, he said. He had? —I thought they were drinks vouchers, not drinking permits! It just says I'm of age, right?

—Dude, snorted Flip. —It's basically posing as a fucked-up medical certificate. It pretty much says you're an alcoholic — that you need to drink to preserve your health! Better yet, at least in the Marathi one, you're referred to as a drunk when you apply — darudiya. And they ask for the name of the drunk's dad, too.

—No fucking way, Karsh said, amazed.

—I know. Bombay's becoming like . . .

I waited for Flip to insert the name of some Taliban-run nation, or a totalitarian Tea Party state.

—. . . Bangalore!

Huh? His phone went off.

—Damn, he said, checking a text. —Braun and Blau were spotted draining all the JD at the Jack Daniel's Rock Awards. I've got to pick them up; if they miss their flight, I'll be in big trouble with Birgit, the girl at the Goethe Institute. I'm trying to get into —

—Her knickers? I offered.

—Events management! he cried, mock-offended.

We had one more round of drinks before hitting the ground. . . . Flying.

* * *

One lovely perk about being drunk in Bombay was it relieved me of all terror of traffic.

My camera was glugging away, too — and though Flip had informed me that anything in Bandra was ten to fifteen minutes away from anything else in Bandra, this demented flow of a night could not be incremented so.

We took a tuk-tuk to Mehboob Studios, a whale of an architectural hunk somewhere by the sea. I thought Flip was flashing his alcohol(ic) permit and realized only after a beat that it was some kind of press pass. Philosopunk seemed to have a ticket for everything, and when he indicated my camera to the creds checker, announcing *Amrika photographer*, I got in on that ticket as well. Karsh was our plus two.

A throng of partygoers howdied Flip. As soon as we headed into the deep dunkeldark of the space, he instructed us, —Do not move. I'll make the rounds.

Inside Mehboob felt like being outside Mehboob, in an ample field beneath starless sky. With free Jack Daniel's. The next band on was fumbling around in this viscous black, fixing their gear on the stage up front.

—I'll let Shy know we're here, Karsh said. Then, after a brief textual exchange, —She's running forty-five minutes behind.

A beam hit the stage just as a shivery strum striated the space, revealing a quintet of rockers in jeans and tees. I was excited to note it was an all-Indian band, then remembered we were, in fact, in India. But then I realized I was still, in fact, excited. I gestured for Karsh to move up front with me so I could photograph them.

The musicians looked kind of old, and not very hipster, which made me relate to them more somehow. The lead singer's eyes screwed shut; when his lips parted, a lush whorl of a melody genied forth.

—*There's a firefly . . . in his hand . . . if he holds too tight . . . we lose again . . .*

A rapt bob-haired creature swayed beside me, a girl in a skin-tight yet somehow low-on-the-raunch crimson dress. Her childlike eyes zeroed in on the singer alone, her lips moving along to all the lyrics, an expression more proud than reverent. I conjectured she wasn't a longtime girlfriend, since she looked as though she were receiving the song like a cherished gift rather than a button-pushing irritating-as-all-hell thing she'd heard in its every incarnation from shower hum to final bounced-down form.

Or maybe she'd loved him still longer, deeper than that. A resplendent tattoo ran the length of her arm, bougainvillea blossoms dancing in the dark.

Her joy was so palpable I ended up photographing her instead of him. She reminded me of how I used to feel listening to Karsh.

—I can't wait till it's you leading the dance, I told him now. I slipped an arm around his waist; he interlaced his fingers through my hand. If I had a lighter, I'd be flicking it on, doing the side sway. . . .

Sankalp? For a lighter manifested that intention before me now. Flip, huffingly attached to it.

—Damn, I need a smoke. This just in: Braun and Blau last seen staggering into unknown vehicle. Direction: Pali Village.

And we were out. Through the dunkeldoor; swig of Old Monk. Rick-and-roll.

I was getting the hang of it.

*　　*　　*

Rumor had it we were back in Pali Naka — Lourdes Heaven, home of Toto's Garage, a heaving joint strung out with fairy lights, old-school Madonna blasting within hubcapped Nevada-license-plated walls. Suspensioned from the rafters, actual cars, garlands heavy petalling off their trunks. A bright red stapler dangled off a ceiling string; I photographed it.

Here, the dance moves involved lots of bum shaking, hip jerking, crazed smirking screaming singalong mouths. Moi's included.

According to an NRYB (nose-ringed yoga blonde) named India (what else) who'd just returned from hugging Amma (as thirty million had done so far and counting) and was now guzzling a round of welcome-to-the-Bay shots with us from Flip's old monkery, Braun and Blau had indeed been spotted here . . . and had blurdled off for yet another retro fix at 16th Road, the Hawaiian Shack, lei'd to the max (and also playing old-school Madonna for a euphorious crowd).

Somewhere between these venues, I was hit by a hallucinatory image of a small roadside temple, as illuminated as the surrounding bars. Within a pristine alcove, a brilliantly orange Sai Baba statue and a saried woman with erupting shopping bag just now kicking off chappals to pay him a visit. Gnarled rapunzelian locks of a magnificent banyan tree. A street sign reading LATE SHRI GULAM MOHD SHEIKH GULAM BHAI CHOWK above swirlycues of Devanagari script.

Next up: a dip into Sancho's and salt sting of a killer margarita (or maybe Old Monk in a margarita glass); slung-low sweet chair riots, a flamenco kind of feeling, tongue in flames from not-toned-down Tex-Mex taquito, that. A slip onto Escobar's eternal dance floor, too quick to register the tune, but plenty to forever remember a lanky long-locked solo-tango-ing scriptwriter with infectious grin from Shillong, a rock 'n' roll town up north . . .

Outside, a surreal lineup of overly straight-faced white-shirted men with the same haircut stared straight into my lens. Mallika's valets?

Then, somewhere around Linking Road, 15th Road (which somehow, very non-NYC-grid-style, fed into 33rd) . . . through a clatter of stalls (tees, bangles, belts) . . . and into a no-Elbo-Room elevator.

The poster on the elevator wall clarified things somewhat: *Wobble! Mumbai's premier bass-heavy night. DJ Slinky on the decks. Visuals by Mesh.* A calendar below listed nights hosted by Uri, Reji, Ruskin, Pravvy Prav, Bandish Projekt, Func International. Everything sounded vaguely familiar and totally foreign at the same time.

I hoped at least one of them was a girl.

—One of the only party nights in Bombay where people pay attention to the DJ, Flip informed us. —Braun and Blau'll end up here for sure.

Though on a roof, the space looked more like a sparsely decked-out basement: cement floor, caramel curtains, plants glowing faintly in the dim light, which bounced off the bar bottles onto Flip's glasses, washing out his eyes. It made him look, ironically, like a seer.

The wall behind him: sphinxed, seraphed.

A low rhythmic déjà vu drone like an amplified heart thump, a coltish stetho-skitterbeat across it.

And a whiff up the nostrilia of . . . another finger-lickin' genre.

Was this the same place? Adjoining Colonel Sanders's drum-sticked space? Tonight, tarpless, a ceiling of smogged starlight. And no SoBo hos in sight; more like so boho.

—Slinky's already on, Flip confirmed. —Ace DJ, from the UK.

He was scanning the roof, probably for Braun and Blau, when a dude with a shaved shining head and two gold-hooped ears rushed up and gave Karsh a walloping backslap.

—Karsh! Shailly told me you were in town!

—Pozy? Karsh smiled back. —Dimple, this is Pozy. He played the same festival I did in Cali.

Pozy instahugged me, nodding at my SLR. —The famous photog girlfriend! The film to his vinyl . . .

He turned back to Karsh and soon enough they were speaking DJ, talking like *they* were a party flyer. Eventually, Pozy gestured towards a side door past the bar, which was the source, I imagined, of the seismic tremor climbing my legs and thudding around my newly discovered tuk-tuk-activated perineum (which I was now squeezing for the sheer fun of it). Inside was indeed as Flip had described: The crowd was packed shoulder to shoulder, all facing the invisible-due-to-them decks, heads snapping back and forth, haunching up and down, surfing the sea-deep beats. The visuals were excellent — weren't even bound to the walls but projected around the space, video-tattooing this attentive audience in laser squirls of red, blue, neon green.

The crowd was clearly loving it, and if they'd been scared off by those crackdowns, no sign of fear here, just pure bliss merging with the bass. I got a few shots — most blind, camera held overhead — but was having trouble navigating the space, and the beats were doing my doused head in at this point. Plus, as usual, it all kind of sounded the same to me. Verse, anyone?

Bridge?

I figured I could get better pics on the roof, and exchanged the bassheads for the tobacchanaliast scenesters outside. The usual was going on — imbibing, inhaling, hand rolling, and a thick giggly ripple of flirtblurting. I wove through the crowd, shooting the human scenery, everyone trying so hard to be different, they ended up looking kind of the same, in that way hipsters do. But they were friendly hipsters, these. Brown ones usually were. At least to me. I even got several hellos and smiling nods from them.

And then Flip was back, Gudang Garam between lips and a chain of intros streaming from them. A mad o wot stylist/blogger with sculptural how-do-you 'do. A production designer/Everest climber. A NorBlack-NorWhite-donning half-Indian, half-Icelandic makeup artist (who appeared entirely Argentinian) soon shifting to Santa Cruz (the cheaper Bandra) from Khar (also the cheaper Bandra) — typical landlord pressure on single women to decamp their dubious moral vibe. A DJ/fine artist. A poet/WeThePpl-er/permaculture-eco-practitioner.

In New York, they'd all be slash-waiters.

Rumor had it a banker and private equity analyst swigged amongst us — but neither was admitting it. A scrap-plastic-bowtied boygirl was presenting one of those buttery leather billfolds at the bar now. She gave me a smile like running bathwater as she moved off with her brews.

—Wow, I said, feeling it rush over me. —There's so much love in this room!

—Ha! That's 'cause they're all shagging each other, Flip snorted. —I could tell you some tales. See, Lala: In South Bombay, they talk about you the second you leave the room. In Bandra, they talk about you the second you enter it.

It was a lot like . . . campus. In any case, it felt like we were at a private party, where everyone knew each other. And *knew* each other. I guess we kind of were, since those in this country who could afford the cover, for one, were few and far between (a hipster, after all, was often basically a hippie with a credit card. Who'd showered).

Karsh joined us now, tickling my lower back and radiating gig joy.

—Look! Flip said, excitedly motioning for us to pay attention. —Our coolest star of all . . . the new leader of our tribe!

The human wave parted, multi-heads spinning, to make way for what could only be described as a goddesslike girl who seemed ripped out of some tribal past and cut and pasted onto the scene. She donned a halter top patchworked in vivid mirrored fabric like our Rajasthani wall hanging. Her ebony hair, sparked henna in parts, swung freely to her waist.

She was immediately accosted by . . . everyone in the joint. But she turned towards us now, face lighting up. Her somnolently lidded eyes were Cleopatra kajal'd, and white decorative dots rained above her brows, bordering an intricately painted bindi. Thick silver bangles clanked down her enviably toned arms as she raised them in a dramatic salutation . . . revealing a hint of six-pack below her halter.

—Shailly? I cried. What had happened to the Lower East Side buzz-cut pink-haired punkstress of yore?

—Homies! she addressed us warmly, elegantly uncurling her middle fingers.

—Nice to see you, too! Flipping the bird is the new form of greeting?

—Dimple. It's a *mudra.*

She promptly dropped it and pulled me and Karsh into a hug, reaching over to rumple Flip's hair. I smiled.

—Frock, Shy — what, you play sitar and speak Hindi now, too?

—Um. No sitar. But I'm learning Hindi.

—Kya ufzee, I agreed, trying out my own brand of the national lingo. —Honed, woman. Been out harvesting the mustard fields?

—That's a little racist for an NYUer, na? she said good-naturedly.

Come to think of it, her sinewity was probably just from lugging gear. The hair, however, had to be extensions. How could it have grown so fast? The heat? In the mustard fields?

—But how can it be racist? I'm from the same race, I countered, though I wasn't so sure I was anymore.

—She's got to stay fit to keep up with her Crosstreet crowd! Flip smiled proudly. —How'd the meeting go, Shy? Venue confirmed?

—The Fifth Room seems game, she said excitedly. —Which is pretty gutsy, since the shutdown last time. We can't secure the mystery artists till they confirm . . . but it's looking good! You guys have to come if you're still in town. There's a big expat crowd; you'll fit right in.

We'd fit right in? I wondered what *her* landing card claimed.

—We're Bombay's number one antiparty, she concluded, though sounded like the Shiv Sena was a pretty close contender.

—And they're still drawing the best acts in town, Flip attested.

Shy smiled modestly. —It's probably the cheaper beer. . . . Anyway, we're doing a brainstorm set at Manhole next week, to figure out ways to ensure we respect the neighbors around The Fifth Room. You know, honor the fisherfolk — after all, they *are* the indigenous people of these once islands.

She was down with the Kolis, too?

—Looks like being Indian's working out for you here, I laughed. —How've you made traditional so hip? Dare I say . . . the E-word?

—Do. Not. Dare. This isn't exotic. It's a personal trajectory.

—Shy! It's me! Come on — what up with the Incredible India wibe?

She was about to jest with me like back in New York, when she noticed Flip had pulled out that notebook.

—Maybe modern-day India has a nostalgia for its culture preglobalization? she suggested. —Look at Raghu Dixit Project.

Gorgeous band of boys in lungis, all barefoot, singing in Kannada, Hindi . . . as well as English.

—They . . . *we* . . . eat that shit up, Flip affirmed.

—And Shaa'ir. She's shamanic.

I'd never seen a female shaman before. Nor a male shaman, come to think of it. I thought they were always pretty far above sea level, hanging with Castaneda and drinking mate from gourds.

—Blending cultures into a new cool, making up our own rules. That's what this tribe's about, Shy concluded in pull-quote friendly style. She handed me her card. In swirly script bound to a bar that Devanagarized it: *Shailly AKA Tamasha: DJ, producer, scribe, inquisitor, & cultural conduit.*

—Anyway, sorry I'm late, she went on. —Had to make an appearance at Mehboob, support some bands. And unfortunately, I've got to split: killer PT session in Joggers Park at the crack of dawn. Let me just go check in with Slinky.

She mudra'd off. Still buzzing, I pulled out my cam to shoot more of the scene. And double vision struck: I noted two identical gigantesque dudes in Tantra tees by the entry. From the way Flip's face lit up, I knew who they must be.

The pair were predictably tall — six foot plus — but unpredictably, unsunburnedly tan. And they sure were wobbling, which was a little nerve-racking, given their stature. They toppled through door onto roof, one belly-flopping across three seats at a terrace table.

—Dudes! What the fuck? Flip cried, sprinting over to pull an extra seat under twin two, who landed with a tremor that tipped the ashtray.

Karsh and I made our way over.

Flip sighed. —Dimple, Karsh. I'd like you to meet Braun and Blau.

I raised my lens and photographed the DJs, who were now snoring. In harmony.

CHAPTER 14

The Place That Started It All

Bandra — at least here, now — was a kind of desi Brooklyn. This surely portended well for Karsh's show.

—You know, Karsh, I whispered, —you've got nothing to worry about. Methinks an Indian DJ, from New York, playing UK-roots bhangra will really strike a chord here. This crowd is so Apple at heart — if New York loves you, wait'll these guys hear you!

We were outside the club now — after a frenzied exit that involved the staff's availing all remaining darudiyas of plastic cups to portablize their potions, and then a mad rush (club owners' last-call patrol paranoia?) out via the emergency stairwell, which seemed crazier than the party itself: dizzy with falling-over-drunk and sideways-high partiers tumbling down the trash-flecked steps, trying not to land on their faces. But Flip looked like he was just warming up, a visible six foot plus times two load off him now that the twins were taxied up and airport bound.

—A last stop? Or, a *first*, Flip offered cryptically as I noted that all that time we'd been in a strip mall. —Let me take you back to zero. Wanna see where it all began?

Need he even ask? I had a feeling I wasn't going to be saying no much in this Maximum City. For the infinitieth time that evening, we three were off, in our eternally recurring tuk-tuk.

* ✷ *

When we emerged from it onto Waterfield Road, Flip indicated a pubby place across the way.

—Lagerbay? Karsh asked, unconvinced.

—On the site of what used to be the magical mythical Zenzi, eulogized Flip. —Once upon a time, not so so long ago, this was the place that started it all. Zenzi was like . . . Bombay's CBGB. Not punk, new wave, but it became the platform for the Bombay indie scene. Shaa'ir + Func played their first show here. Sridhar/ Thayil. Even, rumor has it, the duo that makes up that mystery band, io, met here one night in the alfresco area where musicians played, artists gathered, chattered, coconspired. There were Open Mind nights, salsa classes, art expos, gay/lesbian events, stand-up, live graffiti. Kris Correya. Bhavishyavani Future Soundz. Indian Hipsters — this French duo — used to have a party there, too. Zenzi was the hub, the nexus, the catalyzer. The wheel. Built by expats, full of 'em, too.

He waxed on as if in a trance; the pub twisted and transmuted as my mind's eye filled with a glowing room, a tree growing right through it into open sky, and a group of like-minded creatives coalescing, subsumed by a space crackling with energy, synergy.

—People fell in and out of love there, Flip murmured. —Like anywhere . . . but here, it would end up in a song, a painting, a poem. An after-party where musicians would jam till the wee hours. When Zenzi closed, there was a ten-day farewell — and a kind of grief. No one wanted to say goodbye.

—Patti Smith played the last slot when CBGB shut down, I offered now, nostalgic for that Bowery venue I'd never known.

—So what happened? Karsh asked.

—Unhappy neighbors, broken regulations, Flip replied, shaking his head a little sadly. —The rules.

—Is there a new Zenzi? I piped in.

—Half the places we popped into tonight had a five-second new-Zenzi moment. But nothing's quite compared . . . until now. The closest we've got, a place with the potential to carry on that legacy is The Fifth Room — totally off the beaten path, just off the

Sea Link in Worli . . . and smack in the middle of a six-hundred-year-old Koli fishing village. Sounds like Shy made some headway today. But until then, no more Zenzi . . .

He paused now, then added:

—But at least *she's* still here. Tai.

He nodded towards a bordering shanty where a plump woman who looked like my grandmas squatted, face haggardly elegant, sari folds rippling, roiling on her lap. —And *here*. I got this from her.

He rooted around his pocket. I awaited the emergence of a New York City Metrocard for some reason, but what came out was a little ziplock bag with a suspiciously hand-rolled item in it.

—What do you say? In honor of the source.

—Shhh! I shouted, my eyes darting around paranoically. —Aren't you worried about getting caught?

Flip grinned. —Without some, you mean? Come on. Even the gods spliff up in this town.

He lit up, took a leisurely slurk off the joint, looking momentarily like a Bengali poet, and then magnanimously held it out. Karsh, to my slight surprise (given his mild case of hypochondria since landing), took a drag.

I looked at him. He shrugged.

—When in India, he said. I hoped for his sake it was organic.

—Pot and me, we've had our differences, I explained to Flip, passing on my go.

—Pot? Here, allay any doubts, Flip replied, digging into his alchemical pocket and presenting a carefully wrapped, mud-russet splodge. —Smell this shit in its raw state.

The scent reminded me of freshly laid tar on the streets across from Mirror Lake. And Silly Putty.

—Mmmm! I enthused, although I had no idea what shit was supposed to smell like. (Except my own. And even then.)

—Manali, dude. Best of the best. A pure Himalayan high.

He passed me the joint. I considered it skeptically.

—This stuff is really mellow, he insisted. —You won't feel any different.

—Then what's the point?

—I mean, you'll just be a mellower version of yourself. Frankly, it's a quintessential Bombay experience.

Lots of things seemed to be a quintessential Bombay experience according to Flip, and I guessed that's what I was here for. I supposed a mellower version of me couldn't be a bad thing. For starters, maybe I'd stop worrying about someone seeing us lighting up if I was lit.

—Up to you, Dimple, Karsh said gently. —How safe do you feel?

It struck me now that I felt stunningly safe. Here with Karsh, my rock-solid, and just as critically: in Bandra, where I was sure not to run into any relatives.

I took a hit. Maybe because I was so used to holding my breath in life, I ended up doing so quite naturally with the rock and roll-up.

Flip snorted, laughing.

—For fuck's sake, Dimple, you don't have to go totally scuba on its ass! Save a little for the rest of us!

It felt lovely, smooth. Himalayan. Were the Himalayas smooth? I tried to picture that snow-godded range, but all that kept popping into mind was sixty-five-million-year-old Gilbert Hill in an Andheri window.

—Who's Gilbert anyway? I inquired politely now.

My boys looked pensive. I appreciated the pensing.

—I don't feel anything, I added.

—I know. Isn't it awesome? Flip grinned.

After another inhale or three, that mellower version of me suddenly needed to sit. *Now.* Slowly, I lowered myself into an invisible chair.

—So. Still not feeling anything, Dimple? Flip asked as my Awkward Pose branched into Tree Pose.

—Nothing, I sighed. Moonlight slipped into my sigh and spun me slightly around the universe as I slid down into my inner self.

My outer self joined us. I found myself in a Tai-like squat on the sidewalk.

Karsh stuck a couple of gentle up-pulling hands in my armpits. I thought, *Isn't it the loveliest of ever to have someone stick their hands in your pits?* Such a safe serene sensation. I longed to give something back to the community. I rose, turned to Karsh, and jammed my palms into *his* pits. A perfect fit.

—Get a room, grinned Flip. He was perpetually grinning. Did that count as grinning, or was he simply a-grin?

—You gonna lift me? Karsh smiled.

I voce-forte'd: —You lift me. You *bring* me. A higher purpose. A higher love. Think about it. Let's go to Banganga!

—That a club?

I sotto-voce'd: —It's an ancient water tank somewhere on an ancient hill. . . .

—Malabar Hill, you mean? said Flip. —Yeah, that's ancient. As in old money. Dimple, you've had too much ganja.

—Ganga? The holy river?

—Um, that's the Ganges, Karsh filled in.

—Gandhi! I exclaimed. —We're in India!

—So, where next? Flip said. Karsh shrugged his smolders.

—We don't really have to go anywhere, I agreed. —I mean, we're already *here*.

—Where?

—*Here*. Isn't everyone always trying to get *here*?

The motherland. The fatherland, even. Ancient civilization. My father's mother, his sisters, in the garden of that joint house in Varad, swooshing around in their saris, frying spice, must, and pillowcase redolent in their braided and bunned hair — looking so unlike anyone we'd been hanging out with in Bandra this (was it this?) evening. Mosquito-netted swinging beds; my grandmother Ma staring into my eyes, not speaking, pupils mainlining with my soul as the Brahma Kumaris had taught her . . . and me bucking against the need to avert her gaze while maintaining mine, for some . reason ashamed to be beheld so piercingly. Yet unable to look away: Spying out from behind cameras had been in my blood even then. This memory frissoned me full force, felt more real than the night we'd just immersed in: Kingfishers at Janata, dubstep at NoSoBoho, a KFC landmark on Linking Road.

And yet . . .

What if the real India . . . wasn't even in *India*? But rather, amongst the diasporic denizens of other places? After all, those who'd git seemed to be hanging on with the tightest grips, trying to slow the tock of nervous tics in that throttlehold. The country itself moved on with the times, yet the ones who'd forsaken it struggled to freeze-frame it just as they'd left it — forming South Asian Student Associations, Indian community groups, stocking cupboards with mango pulp and agarbathi, as if to conjure and lock it into suburban kitchens.

What if it was about time, not place?

—Dimple. You are so stoned.

I shook my head, mulling it over. Mellowly.

—If I could just sankalp it . . .

—Sankalp it? Flip queried.

—Arjun it, explained Karsh, making a bow-and-arrow gesture.

—Expats, sighed Flip. —Always trying to name-drop your way into authenticity. You could always just try: Focus.

I squeezed my eyes shut, found myself doing pelvic floor exercises.

—Dimple, do you have to take a leak?

—No. Why?

—You've got this funny scrunched-up look on your face.

How to bring the India I had known — the one of my, my parents' memory — into harmony with the one I was experiencing right *now?*

—I don't even know what right now *is*, Karsh mused.

I didn't even know what out loud was right now. I opened my eyes . . .

Four older saried Indian women were waddling towards me on Linking Road, hands bouqueted with marigolds. A weritable vision from my past, down to the faint whiff of tarka that slipped up my nostrils as they approached.

My mouth dropped open. Himalayan smoke steamed out of it. I snapped it shut. My forebears, even in the land of bhang, would probably not be so pleased about this kind of non-strictly-yogic exhalation. But the clouds I'd emitted still seethed, bits of doobie sky hanging in the air for all to see.

Stealthily, I tried to inslurp, cumuli to cirri. To my dismay, more steam slid from my lips to join them. Like catching snowflakes, soap bubbles, it was a delicate duty; I opted to cloud-suck clandestinely via my nostrilia rather than continue my fish-on-sand gulps of the redolent air. So I sniffed around, attempting to hoover the smoke straggles back up into my system.

—Uh. Dimple . . . ? Flip asked. —What are you doing? Snorting pollution?

—Matching the outer universe to the in, Karsh speculazed.

I held finger to lips and jerked my head to the waddlers, just now passing us. Wide swathed hips, silver-veined braids swinging down backs, anklets jingling over bare feet. Bare feet on *Linking Road.* Which was famous for footwear! Yup, it was proof: Surely these were apparitions from my past, I deduced, as they daintily sidestepped potholes and rubbish and even cars in a manner reminiscent of phantoms wall-passing in haunted-house movies.

Ghosts didn't need shoes — I mean, they didn't exist, so most likely their feet didn't either. Maybe when you were in a civilization as ancient as this one, the past never truly left you?

And then it all made sense.

—Oh my *gods*. Get it? I hissed urgently. —*Linking Road!* Like, it links the past to the present!

—And also Juhu to Khar to Bandra to just about Mahim, Flip divulged.

—Seriously. Look at them! I *know* them!

Flip and Karsh tracked my gaze to the women, who walked dauntlessly on, weaving in and out of the traffic with all the chutzpah and blind faith of the devout.

—What, they from New York? Flip asked me.

—These brown people, Karsh said with a smile. —They all look alike.

They kind of did. But I had bigger blood ties to oh-my.

—You *guys*! Those were my grandmothers!

—You have a hell of a lot of grandmothers, Dimple, Flip said.

—They do this all the time. Every Monday night.

—They do? Karsh asked Flip.

—Some of them walk all the way from Borivali, Andheri, carrying their work clothes on their head, and change after.

—Into *what*? I whispered.

—What do you mean, into what? Into their work clothes.

—So they become, like, human in the day?

—*After* what? Karsh asked.

—Darshan, Flip replied enigmatically. —Tuesday's the big one at Siddhivinayak. There's even a hotline to check crowd status. Ganesha's day and all.

Flip was so intriguing! He said the weirdest things. And with such confidence!

I squeezed my pelvic floor again, and sure enough . . . another batch of saried women passed by! God of new beginnings!

Was I *birthing* them?

—More village elders! I yawped.

—They don't look that old, Karsh noted.

—Of course not. It's them when they were younger, I explained patiently. I was clinched with conviction. —We have to follow them! I barely got to know them in real life, and I am now being given this boon.

—Boon? Flip inquired.

—Like in the Ramayana! I cried, and began running after the waddlers.

—They're not going to outrun us. They're walking, for Chrissake.

Flip had a point. I needed to stay behind, well out of sight. After all, if the past was before me and I caught up to it, or if it turned around and spotted me, I might never be able to get back to the present. I slowed down and sped up a few feet, working out the math, then ducked behind a Styrofoam-cup-chokered bicycle parked roadside. The two-wheelin' chai vendor gave me a questioning look. I smiled sheepishly up at him.

—I don't want them to see us, I apologized, jerking my head towards my ancestors' backs.

—They don't see us, Karsh whispered dramatically, materializing out of nowhere. Flip stared at him, then me.

I crept out from my linear-time hiding place, sneaked a sidelong glance across Linking Road. Now: throngs of young boys in tees and jeans and *no shoes*, traipsing parallel to the saried women on my side. A few men. One girl in glittering top.

Karsh was just gazing fixedly at the traffic, human and otherwise, as if the secrets of the universe were contained therein.

—I'm into it, he disclosed, nodding à propos de nada. He looked more than into it; he looked hypnotized by it. —How *devoted* they are. How much *purpose* they have . . . Birds flying south for the winter.

Was that south? I wondered now where my progenitors would wind up this evening. Perhaps it would be an actual portal to time travel? A wrinkle in time?

The ancestral home?

—We should take off our shoes, I declared. —Then we'll mix right in. They won't be able to tell the difference. For the tesseract.

—I think they can tell the difference, said Flip, hiking up his Levi's, pulling down his Bauchklang tee, and taking a long drag on a smoke.

Finally, we got to a corner.

—I'm not going any farther, he announced.

—But *they* are, I pointed out.

—Dimple. I don't do Mahim. Long story.

He'd signaled over a rick. —Your grandmothers. Let them do their thing. Get in.

We got in. How could *Reclamation* be in a different direction to that of my forebears? But we veered away, following that sign. I felt a bellyache at abandoning them yet again — diasporically the first time, and now by turning right off Linking Road. Curving, swerving down a network of streets (or maybe it was just the loco motion of the rick), I felt we were leaving India far, far behind . . . as we entered the heart of . . .

—Bandra, Flip sighed with audible relief, disappearing from the rick.

—It's like déjà vu. It's like . . . we've been here before.

—That's because we actually *have* been here before, Lala, Flip sighed again, appearing in the rick with a Gudang Garam.

—In a past life.

—Um. No. Like, in the past two hours.

—It's like how I feel about India. Like . . . I've been there before, too.

—You *have* been here before, Karsh offered.

—In a past life? I tried again, desperate to have at least one of those.

—A few years ago, and a handful of visits before. Multiple entry.

Multiple exit: Flip had vanished from the rick again. Karsh and I were somehow back in Room 212.

And no one had even asked to see our permit.

*　✳　*

All that time traveling had left me both carnal and craving Bonne Maman apricot confiture. Which, it turned out, was not in the minibar. However, therein lay a can of pistachios, a Cadbury Flake, and other toothsomes that I devoured while simultaneously ordering room service. I hung up, leaving a titillating trail of Bombay mix snack crumbs to the bed, where Karsh was zoning out.

—You've got chocolate on your face, he commented impartially. I considered asking if he wanted to lick it off, but something about his comatose expression convinced me otherwise.

By the time the chili cheese toasts and faloodas and fries were magically wheeled before me, I was too tired to eat. Balancing the chili cheese toast and inserting straw in falooda seemed to require such painstaking effort, it exhausted me just thinking about it. So I tried to squeeze the vast feast onto a bread plate and stuff it into the minifridge.

Karsh shook his head, smiling.

I lay down beside him, clicking us into the dark.

—You saw them, right? I whispered. —It wasn't just me?

—I saw them, he whispered back.

Reincarnation. The cycle. Birth; life; death. Procreation.

Recreation. I snuggled up provocatively close to him.

—You know, Duggi? All this talk of the motherland, the father-land; it's weird, but it kinda makes me think about . . .

—I know. All I can think about is my dad. When you talked about linking the past and present, all those things you said about not forgetting our roots, the souls who brought us back here . . .

I said that? Out loud?

—I realized, Dimple, that on some level — even though I know he's gone, even though I didn't get to see him before he went — I'm here, in India, for him. To find my connection to him again. And, I suppose, to grieve.

He curled up on his side.

—How he loved bhangra, Karsh said. Then he drifted into sleep.

* CHAPTER 15 *
Tying the Knots

The next morning, I came to covered in straw wrappers. Karsh was out like a zombie *in* a coma *off* life support. I scooched in closer now, sliding my fingers down his boxers to aid in the rousing from the dead process. He mumbled something, half-asleep . . . but a downtown vertically uptowning response had commenced, a squidge of a smile just curling his mouth. He was opening his eyes sleepily, luxuriously at me — when the phone in 212 went off like a fire alarm. Karsh grabbed his forehead with both hands and groaned, hangover probably roused into action now more than anything else.

—Frock, I whispered. —Can we pretend we're not here?

But the ringing didn't desist, so I reached my free arm over his head and picked up.

—Hello? I sighed.

—Bacchoodi! a joyfully wakeful voice exclaimed. —Having a romantic morning?

I yanked my digits out of Karsh's boxers, as if we'd been caught brown-handed. Karsh startled fully awake at that.

—Daddy? Is that you?

—Aaray, who else? Just checking on you. Your mother wants to know if you made the free breakfast? The masala cheese omelette is a highlight.

—Um . . . no. But we're about to?

Karsh propped up on an elbow now, with some difficulty balancing his hungover head.

—How is the room?

—Everything's fine, Daddy . . . and with you? All okay?

—Of course! We are in *India*! And what a glorious day, isn't it? Throw open your window and greet it, dikree!

—I will. . . .

—*Now,* beta, he instructed mischievously. His laugh sounded like it was in stereo.

—Sorry, I mumbled to Karsh. I inserted myself into hotel bathrobe and drew the curtain a smidgen.

—Anyway . . . we just called to say hello. . . .

Sunlight: Ouch. The pavilion, backed by churning waves. A few pinkening people by the pool, and two browner men smack in the center of the space, waving excitedly . . . at me?

—Oh . . . my . . . *gods* . . .

Karsh rose then, came to stand beside me.

—I just want you to know we are always here for you, my dad was saying.

Down below, he and Dilip Kaka were cackling like schoolkids. Kaka even slapped his knees.

—We were just in the neighborhood for our morning stroll . . . like in the olden days! We figured we would make sure you got to the hotel all right.

—Of course we did, Daddy, I said. —Um, sorry you and Kaka took all that trouble. . . . You could've maybe just called from Andheri?

—This Internet generation! my father said jovially. —Nothing can compare to human contact, beta!

I sure as hell agreed with that; I'd just been hoping to have some with *Karsh*. Still, I couldn't help but smile, and when I looked over at Karsh, he was, too: They just looked so damn happy to see me.

Or us. My father seemed to crane his neck now.

—Karsh! Is that you? Have you been swimming? I learned in this very pool!

Karsh glanced at his boxers, and ducked down, lowering groin area from window view. I nodded for him.

—Lovely! Nothing like seizing the day! Well, why don't you both freshen up and meet us downstairs for the free breakfast? Your mother will be so pleased!

I surrendered.

—Okay . . . see you in a minute.

We clicked off. They waved until the curtain had been drawn completely.

I turned to Karsh apologetically.

—We've got forever, rani, he whispered. He ruffled my hair, and headed for the bathroom — popping three Advils before hitting the shower.

After, ablutioned and appareled, we examined ourselves in the mirror. I thought we pretty much resembled us. Except we were squinting, staring a little too long through reddened eyes, as if at a miniature painting instead of our own hungover reflections. Karsh dug into his pocket, handed me a vial of eyedrops. We each took a round.

*   *   *

Out by the poolside café-cum-breakfast buffet, Karsh pulled his shades off, then immediately stuck them back on when the full blaze of day hit his eyes.

—Very Bollywood look, dear Karsh, my father said, smiling warmly at him.

—His eyes are really . . . sensitive to the pollution, I explained. Then, just in case: —Mine, too.

Dilip Kaka abruptly pulled Karsh into a cuddly clasp.

—How delighted I am to meet you after hearing such wonderful things!

My father nodded. —And how . . . serendipitous you two are staying in the same hotel!

Karsh was clearly too fried to even look quizzical beneath those Bollyglasses.

My uncle now launched into a barrage of questions for him — mostly about how to fix this problem he was having with his Kindle, while my father and I took in the mandap being built again on the pavilion.

—What were your plans for today? my father asked. The men on the pavilion kept tying, tying the knots. No one wore a hat.

—I was thinking of shooting Karsh around Bombay. Maybe starting with this beach.

—Wonderful! Juhu Beach is our favorite, my uncle enthused.

—If you want to join, ji and . . . ji-ji's . . . you're both more than welcome, Karsh offered now.

—Oh, we wouldn't dream of it! my father demurred. —It is your first full day together in Bombay; we will leave the lovebirds alone!

My uncle winked at me. —We just needed to escape the house for a couple hours. Premarital sex, you know . . .

I stared at him, stunned. Kaka coughed, embarrassed. —Stress . . . *stress* . . .

My father smiled.

—We will drop you at the top of the beach. That's more like the Juhu you'll remember, Dimple.

*   *   *

And drop us off they — and Arvind — did. By the landmark juice bar, where the road curved seaward, Bandraward we got out, waving.

Beside the barriered path leading in, an ancient mariner of a snow-bearded man spread-eagled around a small fire on the ground,

cloth draped sari-like over his shoulder, roasting peanuts and load-
ing newspaper cones with the sea-salt-smelling mix. In the striped
earthenware pot, the nuts smoldered, half still pale, half gone
gold in the heat, wedged beneath a sort of iron. This was the snack
my parents so dearly loved, the closest (not close) they could get
to it back home the sticky sweet roasted chestnuts sold streetside
Manhattan winters.

I tapped my camera at the man; he gave a slight nod. I squatted
in mirror position, his smile gold-rushing his face as I snapped.
Then I stood directly behind him, shot the silvery moon of his crown
semi-eclipsing the cauldron of bronzing legumes.

It seemed there were so many more old people — at least in
view — in India. A bolstering sensation, and I felt a small satisfied
ache for Dadaji. But there were also so many more conspicuous very
young: A small child in man's striped shirt hanging well past his
knees stood by, solemnly watching on. I clicked Karsh buying a cone
of peanuts . . . and promptly handing it to this man-child who visibly
brightened, then continued on his way.

Onto the beach we marched, to find it was indeed more like the
Juhu of memory, those strolls with my dear grandfather — though
we no longer had to dodge snake charmers, loping camels, dancing
monkeys.

Dredged with debris: tiny scraps in rainbow hues *partout*, as if
in the aftermath of a great celebration. Karsh stumbled along beside
me, sipping a hotel Bisleri water and rubbing his head.

—Are you sure you can do this? I asked him, concerned.

—Might as well sweat it all out, he said, and nodded valiantly.
—I want your photos ready in time for the show.

Camera casing: a wigwag of palms. A long beach-length wall,
lolling with beat-up bikes, all meshed in a rusty hue, Sai Baba and
Ganesha images propped against it, as if holding it up. I turned
and nearly walked into a man with a towel-draped shoulder, flogging

a woven basket dizzy with pinwheels. Snap, clack: close-up of Karsh's face, haloed by the spinning pink, green, vermilion.

—Just keep wandering around, I instructed him. —I'll get you in some shots, and some of just the beach as well.

Wider angle: Arabian Sea to my left, more stands closer to the low-tide border. Stretches of stroller-, sitter-, vendor-mobbed beach interrupted by peeks of sand. Neon-shriek signs offered ragda patties, dahi puris, masala papadum. A pani puri stall, the one-crackling-gulp puffed breads exploding with chickpeas and mung. Translucent buckets of rainbow chutneys.

Swastikas — which originated in India, denoting auspiciousness (though given their later evil co-option, my mother didn't usually mention that one on her long list of credentials to the motherland) — decorated several of the stands. Images of the ubiquitous Sai Baba as well, like a spiritual Colonel Sanders, were splashed up beside *butter chana masala & sandwich, cheese chana masala cheese sandwich.*

Were these the snacks my parents had fed each other back in the day — much like the wedding cake that bride and groom had offered each other the other night? (And how could I possibly be hungry again?)

—Check that out, I mouthwatered to Karsh, nodding to the next vendor over. Roasted hobs of corn stuck into the crevices of a Coca-Cola carrier crate, the effulgence of the double hues — searing yellow, blazing red — dazzlingly setting off the unshucked cobs, the rusty pail beside them.

Even rust looked beautiful here.

No matter how wide my lens, I could feel Chica Tikka bursting at the binds, the blinks with all there was to take in.

Coffeetea guys, mustaches, no beards, wrists threaded with temple-blessed bracelets. One man marching with a bamboo stick, a bandanna tied around it for standout power, wooden lutes and flutes for sale.

Men leaning on Pepsi machines.

Saried women parked upon blankets in the sand.

Uneven-toothed kids with entrepreneurially bright and stunningly underfed faces, begging me to photograph them . . . then pitching me kajal, mehendi, the bindis stippling baskets balanced on their still nascent hips.

Children carrying children.

Another boy in Spider-Man tee manning a stall solo, table laden with pyramided paints, a big water bottle brimming with red liquid, wires: soap bubbles for sale, wands exhaling unhurried twists of iridescence to pop languorously over the Juhu sand.

Just beyond, the rides these tiny workers were too busy to partake in: a colorful Ferris wheel a fraction of the height and diameter of the Jersey ones I was used to — perhaps a dozen feet, tops — its Popsicle-hued seats perfectly still in the sun. Then, a roofless carousel, its menagerie raised about a foot off an oxidized wheeled mount. The creatures looked made of unmelting soap, a waxy unevenness to their tone. A turquoise-trickled sheep, unridden. Unbidden. White swans with lipsticked beaks, one donning a top hat (wise in this heat).

Shadows of gulls swept across the expanses of swan flesh. I figured I wouldn't shoot Karsh by the rides; they somehow made him appear smaller, despite being so diminutive themselves. We were passing a sand-stuck lemon-lime cart, when I laid eyes upon the most beautiful vision of all: a candy floss vendor and his scratched blue stand, sewing-table size, occupied primarily by a woklike silver bowl and decked out in bagged caught-cumulus cotton candy on wooden sticks, stuck along the length of a pole nailed directly to it. I moved in closer. Bundles of bared stalks that looked like they'd been snapped straight off a tree stood at the ready to be witched into cloudy glory. Upon the table: a silver rod, matchbook, those omnipresent rags like burp cloths (but here more likely sweat absorbers). A yellow screwdriver.

The man working the whole shebang was too cool for school: foot on pedal, cranking the contraption, one ear plugged with a headphone, wire disappearing into his pocket, other ear bare.

Quietly immersed, immaculately shirted, a burlap bag on the ground by his feet. Lost in his task but attentive to his audience, he looked . . .

Like a DJ!

I gazed into the cauldron where he was working his visual and olfactory mix. A hazy planet: dark fuschia rimming the bowl where the floss had stuck. In its center, a genie-gold orb, spinning solid to air, grit and dust skewed to dream brume, an ephemeral auroreole pink mist.

An ethereal turntable.

I moved in for the catch, filling my frame with the foggy beauty of the cauldron. Though he appeared not to notice me, I knew the vendor was aware of my movements by the way he held still for the click. A pro.

When I bent to pick up my camera bag, I caught my shadow pooling into his, and wondered at how different our lives were, here in a city we could both call home, in a sense. It was through photography that I could light our way, meld us together for a moment. I turned to share this with Karsh.

But Karsh looked like his own inner-world peace was eluding him big-time, as he frantically wiped sweat from his forehead.

—Thirsty? I asked him, worried. He was eyeing boxes of Bisleri mineral water at a nearby vendor, his own bottle empty.

Violently, he shook his head.

—They probably refill the bottles. We can't be sure it's safe.

—How about tea or coffee, then? I attempted. —Or barring that, a spot of coffeetea?

—How can people have so many hot drinks in this heat? Karsh moaned, pressing his head.

—I don't know. It didn't seem to concern you back at the hotel.

—It's probably because you have to boil water before drinking it here. See? Even the locals know it's not safe.

—Should we head back?

—No, I'm good. Just jet-lagged, I guess. Keep shooting, rani.

—Okay. Last one.

I squatted again, dropped Chica Tikka right between my knees, aimed at a nearby coffeetea stand and clicked.

When I rose, my eyes met another camera, a spanking digital. Before me, its carrier stood in striped shirt, pageanting for me, for us, a photo album of Indian couples frolicking in the shoals of the nearby Arabian Sea. Lovers, or would-be lovers, always in the same pose: arms wrapped around waists, knee-deep in breaking waves, whitewashed jeans on the boys, salwar kameezes on the girls.

—Picture, madame? the man queried, thumbing through the laminated pages. He halted on a photo where both boy and girl donned sunglasses, matching white belts, and jeans. This boy wore short sleeves, unlike most of the others pictured — an NRI?

It was getting harder to tell them apart. *Us* apart.

For a moment, I thought he was trying to sell us this shot — then caught his drift. I tapped my camera(s). He tapped his. I shook my head.

But then I realized, my head shake going side to side, that he had a point: We with the cameras were hardly ever in the pictures. In fact, we were his target demographic.

I glanced to the waters of Juhu Beach, in which no couples cuddled, though there seemed to be a few walking with wedded hands. I wondered if the album duos were Photoshopped into the waves.

Did Deepak and Sangita come here for evening promenades? My parents had; I tried to picture them now. Perhaps this could be part of their anniversary present? A saried city girl and the shy village boy courting her . . . incarnating a generation later into a Patti Smith–tee donning American desi and her via-UK DJ boyfriend.

I turned to Karsh, my cheesy grin already unironically in place.

—Come on, Duggibug! For the hell of it . . .

He tracked my seaview.

—I don't know, Dimple. I doubt the water's very clean — can't you get gangrene or something from that? Can we just finish my shoot? I may need to head back and lie down after.

I nodded, and shrugged apologetically to my co-shutterbug.

We headed hotelward, passing a row of stands selling squared strips of supari. Hypnotic in their foiled light, they draped the stall openings like glitzy prophylactic curtains.

—Condoms! I laughed, pointing them out to Karsh. But he just shook his head.

—Is that all you ever think about? he sighed.

* CHAPTER 16 *

Pink Noise

We worked our way up the beach.

—No seashells, I commented to Karsh, traipsing along behind me.

—My father gave me one when I was little, he said, suddenly reviving a touch. —A huge pink conch, a shankha shell. I think we found it together. It'd always been by the record player when I was growing up, and yet somehow I'd stopped noticing it. But then, years later — the first time my mom and I left him — he handed it to me, said to keep it by my side. He told me to put my ear to it, and the ocean inside would carry me back to him, and I'd be able to hear him as well in that sea sound. . . .

He caught up to me.

—Mom and I left him many times. His gambling, drinking . . . We were enabling him, she said. And each time we left, he gave me that shell . . . and each time we returned, I brought it back to him. But that last time I saw him — we were going to the US for good. I didn't take it, because I promised I'd be back, and he seemed glad. He said he'd hold it to his ear when he missed me so he could listen to what I was listening to . . . until that shared song would lead us to the same space again.

—Wow. Like a gramophone shell, I said, moved. —You know, one of those old Victrolas? Who knows? Maybe that's why you're a DJ.

—Who knows. It wasn't the ocean in that shell, I guess, because I never saw him again. It's just pink noise.

Pink noise. Karsh had explained that to me once: flicker noise, where every octave has the same noise power, turning up as pink light in the power spectrum.

—Well, that's not nothing. I'm sure he kept an ear on you.

I lowered my camera; he looked too lost in a private moment for me to invade with a click. I immediately forgave his hypochondria, those slights at the top of the beach. It couldn't be easy returning to India with no father for the first time.

—My Dadaji always told me to look to the moon when I missed him, and realize, truly realize, we were seeing the same one.

—I remember. I wish I'd gotten to meet him.

—It's funny, Karsh. You never told me about the shell.

—Incredibly, I forgot. Or blocked it. Until now, walking here. Or maybe it was the color of that cotton candy?

He squinted out to sea.

—It's strange being back here without them, isn't it? he said finally. I nodded, said nothing. Karsh looked a little woozy and I took his hand. Our footprints blundered into each other.

I wondered how long Manali stayed in the system as I was having a very high-altitude Himalayan experience of this Bombay beach. I could feel Dadaji's and even Karsh's father's phantom steps beside us. I could feel each grain of sand slipping between my toes, even the flecks that slunk undernail, the slather of sun sinking right to bone — the way the light was quavering, liquefancing the landscape. I felt I could go for miles, and was trying to beam some of that energy towards Karsh, when he said:

—Dimple, I'm not feeling so good. . . .

I glanced over just as he stumbled in the sand. Beads of sweat glistened at his hairline, and his eyes had a vague fuzzy look.

—Dugbug. What is it?

—I think it's the heat. And I'm starving. Do you mind if we get off the beach to walk back?

—Or the hangover. Sure.

A slew of pint-size gods painted on rock face. We turned right, onto a sidestreet. Palms fronded overhead, creating a shadowy path out to what was surely the blare and buzz of Juhu Tara Road. From the corner of my eye, a lion seemed to be levitating midair: a sculpted heavy-breath heave off a residential building.

The road nearly ended in a brick wall with a massive edifice behind it, a few kinetic, chaotic feet of street to adventure across to get there. It rang a bell. Literally.

—Ah! This must be the Hare Krishna place, I said to Karsh, that toll tale espousally high in volume as we neared. —I came here with my dad a few years ago. They have really yum cheap food. And fans, most likely. Sound good?

Karsh nodded with effort. We crossed with effort as well, but by now I was too weary to emit my usual scream.

On the brick wall, like spiritual graffiti, the words to the mantra: *Hare Krishna Hare Krishna, Krishna Krishna, Hare Hare, Hare Rama Hare Rama, Rama Rama, Hare Hare.*

As we passed through the entryway, the sound of clapping, percussions, grew louder as if announcing our arrival — then a gust of space, and the temple pavilion spilled out before us. Something in me relaxed.

To our left a metal detector guy nodded us over. Then we were gestured right, to a stall of footwear-filled cubbyholes. We left our shoes behind, passed the pavilion's footwash pool.

Up the curved steps of the multiply arched turrety-topped temple, the music swelled. Being barefoot on the marble felt fantastic — like dipping your feet in the shallows. We glanced at each other; Karsh appeared slightly enlivened. Despite the fact nothing so wild was happening, I giggled conspiratorially as we slipped inside.

Karsh nodded upwards. Where I'd expected roofing, a false ceiling: unhindered air above us, stunningly and oddly sienna with grey-blue undertones. A breezy petal-strewn courtyard.

Further inside, and up a few steps to the right: the inner sanctum, where a whole load of sonic and dancerly funk was going on.

—Holy shit, Karsh breathed. I nodded, my eyes filling to the lash tips with people: loosely in lines crossing the entire space, swaying arms raised, some clapping, facing forward, as if at a James Taylor gig during "You've Got a Friend," when everyone bonds for four minutes and twenty-nine seconds.

A small blue-curtained mandir-within-the-mandir here in the back. In it, hands folded on lap, a cross-legged, white-bindied, brown-skinned man, rooted in the most focused of meditations. He wasn't real, but the garlands of marigolds around his neck were. Karsh edged in to smell them, sighing contentedly.

Everyone had their backs to this mini mandir. I dragged Karsh farther in. Some of this everyone cast glances at us, but not looking like they minded so much. Above now, a chandeliered ceiling; a balcony ran the periphery of the next floor up, quotes scrolled along its top. Here below, arches bordered nooks to sculpted three-dimensional paintings of scenes from Krishna's life, like the glass-plated one we'd just passed, depicting throngs dancing beneath a leafy tree.

We could see now, latticed off at the room's front, threefold alcoves, like separate stage sets upon the diamond-pattern floor.

We could also see what everyone was staring at: To the side of each alcove was a saffron-robed smooth-headed monk, neck holy-threaded, arms dolloped with white paste, perhaps ash. These temple triplets were moving in no-sneak-peek sync. And like twins, just as my gaze fell upon the curving crescenting object in each priest's grip, Karsh and I whispered the words, eyes widening:

—Conch shells.

It was a sign! Of what, I had no idea, but it seemed a positive portent. The trio tilted big-band heads back and blew with brio through their shankhas, their over-one-shoulder robes bunching up like angels' wings. The honk of the shells was startlingly resonant, primordial, as if an utterance from the belly of a great, famished beast.

—Come on, Karsh! I said. —Let's hit the front row!

—I'm good here. You go on, Dimple, Karsh replied. He looked weirdly entranced. Or very hungover. I figured I'd nab him some great shankha shots and left him there, weaving my way to the front.

The priests were tipping water from tiny pitchers through the shells, shaking them clean. They then took hold of the deep-blue curtains over the alcoves, the crowd's anticipation palpable as they pealed them away to reveal a shock of tripled light . . . and the vision they'd all been waiting for:

Up the alcove steps, three gold-topped mandirs containing . . . *statues*.

No fire-eating gymnasts, snake charmers, stilt walkers. Not that I was expecting them. But the crowd's rapture at the sight of these immobile god and guru figures was astonishing. And contagious.

I couldn't wipe grin — or camera — off my face. The monks now faced the statues, swirling incense sticks around as if casting a spell.

Back glance: The crowd amped its arms-up sway. I zoomed into the mandirs. No Lotto tickets to be found here, but a plethora of other items: flute-fiddling Krishnas before turquoise backdrops, Krishna and Radha pairs, encircled by gopis — those milkmaid cowgirl devotees of the makhan-pilfering god. Double Krishnas raising arms in a frozen mirror image of the dancing crowds before them.

The statues smiled sweetly, childlike. But where was the famed blue skin of this flautist god? These Krishnas were porcelain white, almost Kabuki with their heavily outlined features and sanguine grins.

Before them, like treasure washed ashore: an aaray of seashells, golden vessels. On smaller pedestals, miniature versions of the same gods and, in the case of the human guru statues I now noted (one even *bespectacled*; the idea of perfection here generous enough to include astigmatism) garlanded photos, it appeared, of the same men. My father had explained this to me last trip: The larger statues were too big to bathe daily for darshan, so these miniature ones were used to represent them for this cleansing.

I wasn't sure how you could wash the photos, though.

Although the large god and guru statues bore the whitest of skin, the miniatures used for abishek were a deep brown — like the garlanded guru in that other mandir at the room's back.

And the white Krishna's upturned flute-playing palm as well as Radha's waving one: a rich pink hue. They looked mehendi'd, newly bridal: Radha and Krishna, the holy couple; gopis, the adoring (and perilously besotted) flower girls.

I perused the crowd, who appeared mostly of the brown persuasion, and spotted a possibly white girl — though with this city's solar wattage, even white went gold. Another NRYB: This one's dirty-blond hair was dreaded to the hips and she was nose-ring'd and earring'd like she'd had a lengthy tryst with a hole puncher. Her eyes were closed (and kajal'd), and she was grinning a very depilated-head, white-boy New York Hare Krishna type grin — maniacally, almost dictatorially, cheerful.

Rastagirl opened her eyes, caught my stare, and smiled broadly at me. I smiled back a little hesitantly. She swayed harder (which seemed to defeat the very essence of a sway), nodding as if to coax me into a round. I shook my head no, thanks, but lifted my lens in compensation, for which she magnanimously posed, offering an extra whip of her dreads.

I quickly turned my camera away.

The priests were now waving genie lamps in ever-widening circles towards the gods. Then they lowered them offstage onto a tray held by another priest, who turned and promptly bolted across the room . . . to offer them to the mini mandir brown dude. No one followed him, so I guessed the main activity was still taking place up front.

It was getting a little confusing. In church, where I'd midnight massed with Gwyn a couple times, you mostly just sat and stared straight ahead. But here, everything was everywhere.

A sudden heave and I was pushed forward with the crowd till I was nearly against the latticed gate. The priest before me was now taking finger-dips of conch water and flicking it over the devotees, who supped it up like desert pups. I'd just managed to steer my lens out of the way when — *splat!* — a grand wallop of this liquid blessing hit me in the eyes.

Earth, wind, fire, water; bhūmi, pavan, agni, jala — the elements on offer: When my vision cleared, they were twirling some kind of cloth . . . then, an instant later, as if by transmogrifying magic, waving some blooms about. I shot the singing, chanting crowd; when I spun back priestward, their sadhu spells had produced some yak-tail fans in place of the flowery stuff, rising and dropping in a swoony cascade as if of slow-motion-shot, long-haired headbangers — while the rest of the room sped up.

The mantra cranked. Some of the crowd were jumping up and down, as if on pogo sticks. The priests were now flapping peacock feathers, bells ringing in their non-fanning hands all the while.

Templegoers dosey-doed a couple steps forward, a couple back, arms raised as if they were part of a hoedown stickup. Everything seemed faster, louder. It was making me a little anxious, like gym class. Were people *yelling* the mantra? I turned to discern a couple guys planted towards the back with mics, bvox-ing the space to ear-splitting volume.

Hare Hare!

Surround sound. A man fell to the ground, narrowly missing my feet. I was about to help him up when I noted a few more men doing this and realized it was on purpose. Rarely did Hindus lie down on purpose. These particular ones prostrated themselves in a state of curiously inert elation. Dreaded Deadhead stalker girl was back, inching in, nodding into my face and overdoing it with the dance moves. Cornered, I reluctantly hands-upped. She smiled triumphantly. It made me feel lonely. I cast my eyes around the room so Karsh and I could exchange looks. We were always so in tune, so . . .

Where was he?

I peered into my camera, using it to survey the space. A shock awaited me. Karsh, who'd stayed a slight distance behind, was tilting back and forth to the beat, eyes intent on the stage action. He didn't look like he felt left out at all.

His expression made me nervous. It was completely devoid of irony. It wasn't looking at me, or even *for* me.

And then he did the most outrageous thing of all: He raised his arms overhead . . . and began to sway.

As if we were a seesaw, my own arms abruptly dropped like lead.

The holy-men trio synced up again on their individual stages, blew their mollusking trumpets with gusto.

A strewing of roses. A last ding-a-ling of the golden bells.

And it was over. As the crowd sundered, I wiped my eyes and sought out Karsh . . . my camera landing, after so many snaps, upon a NO PHOTOGRAPHY sign. I hesitated.

—It's okay, a voice spoke low in my ear. —You can take a picture.

One of the bvox boys stood beside me, holding a small pouch like many of the devotees had. He smiled, I supposed an enlightened smile.

—A hundred and eight tulsi beads, he explained, following my eyes to the pouch. —You're new here.

It wasn't a question.

—*We're* new here, I said, indicating Karsh, just now approaching as if stepping out of a dream state. He was still a little wobbly, so

I guessed with some relief that his swaying moves had more to do with a dearth of electrolytes than that mantra. —Karsh. And Dimple.

—Where are you from?

—New York.

—Ah. New York — a very significant place for Hare Krishnas. For ISKCON, the International Society of Krishna Consciousness. I'm Gopal. Come. Have lunch with us and we can answer any of your questions.

I wasn't sure we had any, other than what was for lunch. Karsh was nodding frantically, famishedly, like it was the invite of a lifetime.

—And you must meet Gokulanandini, who lived in New York once upon a time as well, Gopal continued, guiding us towards the back of the room. —My name means "protector of cows." Another name for Krishna, who was a cowherd.

An image of Krishna atop one of Patti Smith's horses whinnied into mind. A cowboy god!

—We'll dine with the devotees, Gopal said, walking us through a set of doors into a kitchen/café where numerous 108-tulsi-bead-pouched individuals were lining up, ladling their banana leaves carefully with vegetarian cantina nosh: aloo bhaji, chapati, basmati rice.

We joined. Karsh exhibited none of his usual hesitation with the food on offer here; he must have been ravenous. Leaves loaded, Gopal led us to a table and dug into his own banana boat with expert fingers, dunking rice in dahl.

—Such an auspicious day, he said now, side-to-siding.

—What's the occasion? Karsh asked.

—*You* are the occasion. You have discovered us — and Godhead! Karsh cracked not a mischievous look my way. Dehydration?

—Thirsty? Gopal inquired now, clearly making the same diagnosis.

—Very, I said, worried.

—Ah — well, here comes Gokulanandini with paani for all!

The bearer of the four stainless steel cups, it turned out, was neither male nor Indian . . . but the dreadlocked white-gone-golden girl with the multiple-entry piercings. She distributed the cups and sat, beaming round at all of us as Gopal made the intros.

—Wow. You don't look like a Gokulanandini, I finally said, unsure of what one of those would look like in any case.

—Gokulanandini is my Hare Krishna name. Like Gopal used to be Sanjeev.

—Sounds like taking a DJ name, I said, stuffing my face.

—Frock, I feel so much better already — that water-fight part really woke me up, too. Great for a hangover!

Karsh shot me a look. What? I mean, weren't the Beatles — those reefer-ridden musical geniuses — into this religion? And even the gods must experience hangovers in Hinduism, right? Bhang. Chillum. All those spiritual quick-fix elixirs?

—For hanging *around*. It's great to hang around, Karsh said now, swiftly scoring the gold for lamest cover-up ever.

—I'm glad you are enjoying the lunch, Gopal nodded. —Are you a vegetarian, Dimple?

—Part-time vegetarian, I replied. He gave me a quizzical look.

—Whenever I'm not eating meat, I explained.

—Dimple, he gasped, stricken. —I know I don't really know you, but if I may say something? I urge you to stop eating meat as soon as possible. The path you are on can lead to no good.

He was exuding that bossy brochure vibe. He and Gokulanandini were clearly in cahoots.

—You're right, I said. —You don't really know me.

This dude had pushed a button I didn't even know I had. Karsh intervened:

—What Dimple means is —

—I think Dimple knows what Dimple means, I assured them, amazed Karsh could jam the same button so quickly. —*Sanjeev*.

—Gopal, my three co-diners corrected me.

—Dimple, you should really at least cut onions from your diet, the many-named man recommended now.

How could he presume I included them?

—Huh? Isn't that Jain, the no-onion thing?

—These underground roots — onion, garlic: They excite the system too much, Gopal disclosed, like that was a bad thing. —They are linked to an argumentative nature.

—Argue the point, Karsh added gently, likely for my benefit. —Not the person. Who said that?

—You. Just now, I replied, suddenly feeling highly shallotted. —Bad ears for a DJ, no?

—I don't eat meat in India, Karsh reported now, not mentioning that this was due more to hygienic angst than anything else. —Or at least a lot less.

—A *DJ*? Gokulanandini exclaimed, probably fearing for Karsh's spiritual purity. Then, hopefully, —Weddings?

—Karsh is DJing a big show at L'Heure Bleu tomorrow, I off-handedly announced, to support her in her fearing. —It's just down the road from here.

—Isn't that the venue that was shut down when they found intoxicated people there? Gopal asked, worried.

—Isn't that every venue? I laughed cruelly. —I mean, how else would you even know it's a *venue*?

—I studied computers, Karsh interjected. —Tech work.

I couldn't even look at him in case he'd turned into my parents.

—Yeah. As in algo-*rhythm*. Well, you've got something in common, anyway, those places and this one, I went on, directing my comment at Gopal and the cowgirl. —All those dancing masses. The singing, the music, the ecstatic look — that happens at all of

Karsh's shows. Even people falling on the floor. Except it's him onstage, not Krishna.

—They weren't *falling on the floor.* They were supplicating themselves before a higher power, Gokulanandini sighed now. —Surrendering. You should try this, Dimple.

—You first, I suggested.

—And, Karsh. As a music lover, you will so appreciate the 7:15 darshan here — and George Harrison's Brahma Samhita. He was a Hare Krishna, of course.

Gopal nodded. —You should come to that one, by all means. But of course the most powerful darshan of all is the first of the day: four thirty A.M., when your spiritual powers are at their peak.

—We never see four thirty from *that* side, I told them. They ignored me.

—The mantra has inspired many musicians. The Fugs, and Nina Hagen, too, Gokulanandini informed us. She'd probably dated a musician when she was still Amy from Minneapolis.

—And of course Hare Belafonte, I snickered. No one got it. Did the abstinence from stress relievers so many devotees practiced (sex, drugs, rock 'n' roll) include eschewing a sense of humor as well?

—Wow, you two get here so early for these darshans, Karsh broke in, sounding impressed. —I mean, Bombay traffic's killer. Do you live nearby?

—I live right here, Gokulanandini said, smiling and patting her heart.

—Which chamber? I asked. —Ventricle or atrium? Or the unforgettable auricle?

—*Here.* At the ashram.

—I am only here visiting. My father has had surgery, Gopal said. —I moved recently to Vrindavan.

—Oh. I'm sorry about your father, Karsh said with great emotion. —I . . . I lost mine not so long ago.

Gopal and Gokulanandini immediately laid their hands upon Karsh's. Gokulanandini got a bit of dahl on Karsh's wrist, but he didn't seem to notice.

—Oh, Karsh. I am so sorry, Gopal said quietly. —Perhaps a visit to Vrindavan would be just the cure to help heal your heart. Have you ever been?

—Krishna spent his childhood there, the most beautiful place in the world! Gokulanandini added. —And *so* much *grass*!

I perked up.

—And so many cows! Gopal added. I perked down. —You really need to be surrounded by grass and cows to maximize your spiritual sensibility.

—Do beaches count? I asked. —I mean, what about everyone here? They seem pretty maximized.

—That's not what Gopal means. Gokulanandini smiled patiently. —But this urban environment can dilute the innersphere, corrupt the channels. Introduce impurities.

I longed to recommend a loofah.

—I hope one day to move north as well, she added dreamily. —So I can truly become one with Godhead.

This sounded strangely sexy coming from Gokulanandini's . . . pierced . . . tongue. That also seemed a pretty good way to introduce impurities.

And as far as urban environments went, I thought, my father and my uncle seemed pretty adept at finding their Zen here — even in dogged Bombay traffic, in most populous suburb Andheri.

—I don't know, I countered. —Seems it'd be a no-brainer to zone out around cows and grass. The real trick would be to be enlightened in the crazy day-to-day. On the streets of this city, for example. In a crowd. In a club.

—You can't trust anyone! Gokulanandini decried now, passionately and, as far as I could see, à propos de nada. She'd clearly been cheated on. Probably by that Fugs-loving bassist. —Only God. We here are all married to Krishna.

—Even him? I nodded towards Gopal, who seemed a little flummoxed about how to reply.

—We are Lord Krishna's devotees, she went on, eyeing Karsh. —Like the gopis. We don't need anyone else.

—You know, I mused, —I wonder if the word *groupie* is etymologically linked to *gopi*. . . .

A silence.

—I mean, all those girls all over Krishna.

—They are not *girls all over Krishna*. They are cowherds, Gokulanandini nearly squawked. —They feel *divine* love.

—Radha, his wife, doesn't mind?

—His wife is . . . Rukmini, Gopal replied. He cleared his throat. —One of his 16,108 wives . . . but principally he had just eight.

I let that sink in. For him.

—But there are only *four* regulative principles to lead a pure spiritual life! he spin-doctored now. —It's quite simple, actually. I urge you to desist this DJ lifestyle, Karsh: the illicit drugs, the sexual licentiousness . . .

I laughed. *I wish!*

—Oh, Dimple, Gokulanandini said sadly, shaking her head. —You poor, poor thing.

—Trust in God, Gopal stage-whispered, and now he blazed his eyes into Karsh's. —The way you would trust in your *father*.

Karsh's dad hadn't really been one to trust — hence Karsh and Radha's so long — but I figured it wouldn't be good form to point that out simply to argue with Gopal. The point, not the person.

—You know what's so strange, Karsh said now. —The shankha shell. Dimple and I were just talking about it on our way over. My father — we had a connection through the conch. We'd listen to it to hear each other when we were separated. . . .

Why was he telling these strangers something he'd only just revealed to me?

—Karsh. That is *beautiful*, Gokulanandini swooned.

—They say you can hear the music of the spheres inside that shell. Om, the sound of creation, Gopal divulged. He went on to explain that Vishnu's conch symbolized life; shells that spiraled clockwise indicated this infinite expansion. The ones that went the other way were linked with Shiva, the destroyer.

Karsh was leaning so far forward listening that Flip's lighter now fell out of his upper pocket, onto a banana leaf. Gopal looked betrayed.

—It's for . . . incense. Agarbathi, Karsh quickly explained, to my total nonsurprise.

—I am relieved to hear that, Karsh. You know it requires great lung power to blow a conch.

—In ancient times that was how warriors announced battles. Like Arjuna in the Mahabharata, Gokulanandini supplemented. —They blow it at weddings, too.

—We'll have to blow one in less than a couple weeks, then, I smiled to Karsh, thinking of how startled Deepak's face would be if we did.

—I didn't realize! Gopal exclaimed. —Heartiest congratulations to you both!

We didn't bother to correct him; after all, at the hotel, I was currently clean-livin' Mrs. Kapoor. I was relieved to see Karsh flick me a grin.

We rose to go. Gopal and Gokulanandini rose with us.

—Your father loved you very much, Gopal said, his arm around Karsh's shoulders now. —And you were meant to find us . . . through the music of that shell.

Emotional manipulation! Dude looked sincere — but his sincerity was pissing me off. They accompanied us out through the mandir space, to the false-ceiling courtyard.

—Go on, then, Karsh, Dimple. But please do consider all we've discussed.

—And remember, Gokulanandini said, —there is always a home for you here.

—And in Vrindavan, Gopal added. Gokulanandini hugged Karsh a little longer than necessary, compared to the paltry embrace I received (and bestowed).

—Everyone's trying to go to Mars, to the moon, she said urgently. —But the world inside is much bigger than the one on the outside.

Karsh nodded urgently back at her.

I took his hand, interlaced it in solidarity. But he was still nodding as we left.

＊　＊　＊

Out on the street, the urban environment smacked us gloriously in the senses.

—This city's so dirty, Karsh said now. —You know, they may have a point. I don't think it could hurt, a little detox, purification of the soul. I, for one, felt like hell till we went in there.

—Well, you know what they say: Bright lights, big shitty. You were hungover, Karsh. And hungry. So I don't know how much purity has to do with it. Believe me, I don't think it'd take much to throw some of these guys off the straight and narrow. Did you see how Gopal's face lit up when she said *Godhead*?

—Dimple. That's extreme, even for you. In fact, you were kind of rude back there.

—I'm just saying. Those two clearly need to engage in some illicit onion action. It's usually people who get dumped or don't get laid enough that become spiritual seekers, after all. Otherwise they start wars.

—Is that all you ever think about?

—Is that all you ever ask me?

—And even if you're right, he went on, —there are worse things you can do with a broken heart than become a Hare Krishna.

—Like . . . lie? I mean, come on, Karsh — computers? Agarbathi?

—I *do* work with computers. And I am a nonsmoker.

—Since when?

He pulled out Flip's lighter and chucked it into an otherwise empty bin surrounded by heaps of trashfetti.

—Since now.

I stared at him; he stared at me. Then he reached back in and pulled it out, wiping it off on his shirt.

—Well, maybe after this gig. Ravi gave me a little hash stash that might be nice after the show — or during, depending on my nerves.

Now, that was more like my Karsh!

—They'll need to cater the console, considering how long your munchies last, I teased him. He was smiling, too — but it was a distant smile.

—Gokulanandini was beautiful, wasn't she? Like she had some inner light.

—Gopi girl had some outer light, too, I snorted. —She's white. I mean, gimme a break: Gokulanandini?

—She just seemed . . . to make sense.

We cut back through the beach, in silence now. Suddenly, Karsh's eyes fell on something half buried in the sand, a glimmer of dusky pink, and he darted forward, knelt to lift it.

I caught up to him.

—What, Karsh? What is it?

A curved slab of pinkish-white rock. He lay the stone back down, but his eyes were looking elsewhere now, to the horizon. He shook his head.

—Sometimes I wonder if I was only dreaming. Or maybe he lost it, gave it away — you never know if things have the same meaning for other people.

—He'd never give it away, Karsh, I said.

—Never say never, Dimple, he replied quietly, but there was an edge to his voice I'd never heard before.

I looked down. Chica Tikka on my hip, silhouetted in the sand like a swaddle-slung baby.

My own feet. In Bombay. Karsh's: now out of frame.

They'd said the blowing of the conch symbolized the start of battle. And I'm not sure why I even thought this, but I sure hoped it wasn't the start of ours.

CHAPTER 17

Console

Finally, it was the day of Karsh's gig. I couldn't make sound check. As it was a sundowner show, the check was pretty early — and it was also the afternoon my parents were flying to Delhi for honeymoon two.

Karsh didn't insist.

—Forget sound check. You've seen it all before.

—And you've got the visuals anyway, right? I fretted, unsure about leaving him alone on his big day. He'd been more nervous than I'd ever seen him — except, oddly, *post* his California shows. —You've run them, and it's cool?

I'd laid the final touches on the images of Karsh in Bombay and New York last night, during my then-helpful bout of insomnia.

—Sure. Listen, Dimple. You should see your parents off. Just turn up a little before the set, shoot the venue then?

Maybe he was being extra understanding, making up for how tetchy things had been between us as his nerves worked overtime. He'd snapped at me twice already, though he was immediately remorseful after, and he'd been vanishing into his noise-cancellation headphones for increasing spells. I'd even spied him in front of the mirror practicing DJ *facial* expressions and intonations on his usual call to dance:

—Desi dance cohorts! Let me take you on a *journey* . . . ! Nooo . . . let me take *you* on a journey. . . .

Some of those facial expressions were astonishingly Ravi-like. Even Amitabh Bachchan-like.

I began to grow anxious, too.

But no one needed to know that.

*　*　*

I accompanied my parents to the domestic airport in Santa Cruz, driven by Deepak (bigger car, though still a squeeze) and joined by Sangita and Kavita. (The former was doing wedding errands with Deepak after, and Kavita was sneaking off with me, ostensibly to shoot the sunset, but in fact for the sundowner set.)

My cousins and Deepak waited in the car, neither quite parked nor in motion, as I accompanied my parents in, wheeling their one suitcase. As if I were the one leaving, and for a post-nuclear-war bunker, my mother tearfully pressed a box of granola bars and two packs of Huggies aloe vera wipes into my hands, my father slipping me a ziplock of refill meds: Advil, Tums, Imodium, Zantac, and, for some reason, folic acid — the same items he'd supplied me with when I began NYU.

A barrage of parental advice:

—Now, promise you will not be up to any altoo faltoo business. . . .

—Do not hang around Colaba at night. . . .

—Or the mills . . .

—Or the beaches . . .

—Or the slums . . .

—Take taxis, or have Arvind drive you. Or Deepak.

In other words: Stay in?

—Or just stay at home, beta, *relax*, my father suggested, confirming my suspicions. —Enjoy the hotel.

—Um. I kind of wanted to see the city.

—Does the hotel have Internet? You can do a lot of sightseeing without even leaving your room these days, he informed me. —Always wear insect repellent.

—Try to stick to home-cooked food, my mother added, though I wasn't sure there was a lot of that going on at the hotel. —But do *not* miss the free breakfast. Especially when you shift to Lands End and that four-star — well, five-star, as they call four-stars here. If I recall correctly, the akuri is divine. Basically bhurji — almost like mine. Just take a Zantac first.

—But they put garlic in it, na? my father queried her now.

—Check in with family regularly, my mother went on. —Should we call you every night?

—I think you'll be more prone to worry if you call me and I don't pick up right away, which might be the case if I'm . . . in the middle of applying insect repellent? I advised them. —Daddy, Ma, this is your city! I'll be fine.

—We know it is our city . . . my mother said slowly.

—. . . and that is why we are worried, my father concluded.

Though we'd only be apart a little over a week, monsoonal parental tears were a-rolling when we split ways at security. As I watched them pass through the detectors — back-glancing the entire way, and waving fervently as if *I* were about to set sail, never again to return — I realized the tears were in my eyes, too. It felt strange, epic, even, them leaving this city, me staying behind. As if, in some funny way, despite the fact they'd still be in India, I, without them, no longer would be. I hadn't realized before this trip just how much my geographical historical coordinates were tied in to those of my parents, a twisting twirling umbilically bound compass you could spend a lifetime trying to detach. Or hang on to.

I really would have to find my own Bombay.

It was a thrilling concept, but I felt a pang of loneliness when they finally moved out of my line of vision.

As I exited, I startled a moment, thought I peripherally caught a six-foot-and-then-some blue suede brown-banded cowboy hat. My heart, illogically, lifted. I turned eagerly to say hello — and found myself checking out the robin's-egg-blue-hued turban on a wonderfully elegant Sikh gentleman.

I was strangely disappointed. As I headed back to the car, I wondered what that international airport cowboy was doing right now, which frontier he was framing with that twin SLR.

Rejoining the posse, I was swept with a nervy anticipation for Karsh's impending major moment as we found ourselves heading towards L'Heure Bleu.

The club was relaunching tonight after a spate of seedy events. Well, two: One evening, a couple Bollywood stars came to blows there, butting egos in the dining area and, oddly, given they weren't so tall offscreen, destroying a chandelier in the process. The next, rumors of a rave had spread — although joining the concepts of Bollywood and raves was a little like a Zen koan, along the lines of clapping with one hand. A police commissioner had busted into the place, flailing a cricket bat, pulled out a videocam and begun taping whoever was there. It *was* cricket season, but this seemed a bit much.

The whoever-was-there were mostly fine diners and deal makers who were clearly not raving, merely ravenous, and in the end, all the buzzkill fuzz could charge the place with was a faulty gas cylinder. However, everyone in the joint had fled upon the emergence of the cam — probably more likely due to the company they were keeping (not their spouses, according to Mallix) and the deals they were making (often under the table) than the drugs on hand (coke, a little MGMT — or was it MDMA? — and the ubiquitous reefer).

Juhu Tara Road seemed to lengthen as we drove along it. To my surprise, Deepak dropped the *three* of us off across the street from the club landmark, a Juhu branch of Café Coffee Day, announcing he could do with a quick caffeine hit, then stick-shifted off to find parking. Kavita seemed to take it — and then me — in stride: My salwar-kameezed cousins stepped up to either side of me, hooked an arm each, and launched us into that pinball-on-speed traffic tap dance, pausing briefly on the midpoint island, a paltry purgatory, before diving into the multilaned chaos once again.

—Dimple. Drop the heavy breathing. We're across now, Kavita informed me.

My heart was still pounding; I was growing more and more stressed for Karsh as we drew closer to the venue. In the way twins can sense each other's chills and thrills, I could feel his own nerves shuddering through my system, too. I took a breath, decided I had to be calm for the both of us — infuse him with the kind of cool he had in New York, strolling into those venues as if by chance . . . before dropping the most dance-frenzy-evoking set of his life, or anyone's. Every time. Every life.

We climbed up — past the squatting scrubbing soap bubble boys, one beating sidewalk with a long-haired bamboo-handled brush that looked like it had been plucked directly from a tree (or ISKCON priest), his partner in existential events tipping the bucket of suds out before him, a tandem almost telepathic act of such Sisyphean proportions in this exhaust-choked atmosphere, I was nearly moved to tears — and into Café Coffee Day. Sangita insisted on buying our drinks; when I figured she was out of earshot, at the counter, I shot Kavita a look.

—We have to tell her, Kavity.

Before Kavita could reply, Sangita had returned with her obviously bionic ears and inquired:

—Tell me what?

A highly uncaffeinated, sleepy-lidded man served our off-the-cricket-season menu concoctions — a Fanatic for Kavita, Nirvana for Sangita, and Blue Maniac for me. We busied ourselves passing around the drinks, which all tasted the same: sugar mixed with syrup.

—Okay, here's the deal, I confessed, taking a swallow of these worryingly palatable sweetened sweeteners. —We *are* going to shoot the sunset, Sangita . . . but at L'Heure Bleu.

—LHB? You mean where PJK and ABK had their bout of violence?

Was this Morse code for the actors who'd bashed hanging lamps? Correct: Sangita looked alarmed, as if contentious Bollywood stars lurked in our near vicinity, readying to jump us.

—Uh. Yeah, I guess . . . but it's also where Karsh has his *first-ever Bombay gig*! I squealed.

She sat back, flabbergasted.

—What? I can't go like this! I look like an oily aunty, with this coconut oil treatment!

She ran a hand through her particularly lustrous locks, caught a glimpse of herself in the reflection of the Bisleri-filled fridge. —And I'm not dressed right!

—You're in India, Sangita. And a friend of the DJ's. No problem. I mean, no issues.

—In any case, we'd never have escaped Mummy's suspicions if we'd dressed any differently, Kavita pointed out. —I wear salwar kameezes all the time at Karsh's HotPot parties in New York. Our friend Zara comes in saris. Sabz and I even used to . . .

Her voice trailed off. The two had always color-coordinated their kameezes, swapped scarves in an amorous dupatta dance during their favorite numbers. —Anyway. Don't worry about it. You're getting married — what do you need to look fabulous for?

—Not that you don't, I jumped in, guiltily. —Will Deepak freak? You can blame it all on your wayward ABCD cousin.

Sangita sighed. —No; he's had one or two business dinners at LHB. But it's just imperative we run this wedding errand today. Maybe we can come in for a quick hello and be off? Let me just check on him. . . .

Her phone dinged his reply within seconds.

—He still hasn't found parking, so he'll just meet us there, she informed us.

—Chalo, then, I said, rising. —This is a sundowner and, even in India, the sun sets on time.

*　*　*

There was nothing blue about the entrance to L'Heure Bleu.

But a giveaway: Like a rabbit hat trick behind the pithy paan-wallah stand, throngs of impeccably coiffed, manicured, waxed (threaded?) girls postured on the sidewalk, by the hefty dude closest to that unblue unmarked door.

These girls were around the same height (a little higher than me), throwing a type of smile at the door dude that confirmed he was the bouncer: the doe-eyed giggly picture-me-naked smile.

It was odd seeing them work the bouncer look during such unabashedly sun-soaked hours. But the better to see these shining lovely ladkis, all, in white jeans, cool capris, sequined halters, hot-to-trotting in shockingly flat and sparklingly threadbare footwear I couldn't imagine donning for New York City clubbing. And there was a tension amongst club queuers in New York that didn't exist here; even the ones who knew they'd get in, like Gwyn, emitted a kind of conquering energy. But these creatures exuded a balmy ease. They'd been in since birth.

Not-so-goateed boys flocked around these balmy girls as well, but unlike at HotPot — or even in Bandra — they were strangely unremarkable. Nothing stood out about them, though they emitted a general *ambiance* of well-groomed good looks (shout-out to the dhobis).

Me, I'd donned my HotPot double-dhol tee, a tasseled turquoise vest I'd scored around Ludlow Street, faded look-poor-on-purpose jeans, and Birks. In fact, I wondered if I was so cool for school I was actually expellable here amongst the semi-glitterati.

Sangita and Kavita sore-thumbed in their salwar kameezes and dupattas. Kavita, however, had mitigated the aunty effect with her leopard-skin leggings and checkered Vans. But Sangita was in total old school ankle-cinched baggies and chappals.

You know you're doing something wrong when the bouncer isn't even bothering to bounce you.

—I thought we might be walking in the sand, Sangita whispered now, and I felt bad she'd caught me scrutinizing her feet. Was I so worked up about this show I was going Wintour on her peds? I had to get a grip.

—Who knows? I smiled. —At this rate, we might be.

As the bouncer succumbed to the no-split-ends feminine wiles of one compact chica extending an unlit cigarette, I carped the diem and got us through the unmarked portal. Before us, a long alleyway stretched, walled to the right, partially open to the left, allowing in a surge of sea breeze mixed with traffic exhaust. An exhausted breeze? A few more freshly pressed folk were in this line, and looked upon us with a mix of disgruntletude and admiration as we, led by me, onwarded directly up to what appeared to be a maître'd's stand. I figured we were home free . . . but as the maître held up a hand in the universal gesture of cease and desist, I guessed he was in fact the second bouncer — who looked so much like the first, I wondered if it was just one guy running up and down from post to post.

I grinned, too exuberantly perhaps.

—We're on the list.

The bouncer blinketh not.

—With the DJ? I elaborated in self-doubting American-desi style. The clipboard remained unconsulted. —Karsh Kapoor? DJ Gulab Jammin'?

—We're DJ GJ's entourage, Kavita said slyly. —In all the way from New York.

—*City*, I added, in case Poughkeepsie had been insinuated. And GJ it was; there we were, on the list.

Kavita and I now passed through with an ombre'd random who'd stepped up and, in a classic velvet-rope-cutting move, was acting like she was with us. I could see Sangita getting left behind.

—Memsaab, bouncerman addressed her now, making a respectful term sound cheeky. —Strictly no desi attire here.

—Everyone at Karsh's . . . GJ's . . . New York gigs dresses like
that! I cried.

Deepak now arrived, looking rather like he was in fact here for
the paanwallah and had made a wrong turn; he'd likely bribed his
way through door one.

—It's her wedding in less than two weeks, he proceeded to
unhelpfully offer. —*Our* wedding! We're here to hear some of the
DJ's tracks for it.

—Where did you park? Sangita asked him anxiously, as if
this — and not the possible non-entry to Karsh's big show — was
the main concern here.

Deepak mumbled something to her.

—We do not hire wedding DJs, Bouncer Two retorted. —Next
mandap to the left.

—Dude. Give us a break, Kavita sighed. —They're just being
ironic.

The bouncer looked confused by the big word. I thought
Sangita and Deepak would be offended, but Deepak's smile faltered
not . . . and Sangita actually looked like she was about to laugh.

And then we were in. *In* in. We slipped through the second door.

Arriving. Frock — it took so bloody long in this city!

I was no longer bowled over by venues. I'd seen them enough
in the buff, during the day, sound checks, and knew it was the
magical moment when you became one with the music that transformed the place, blurred the lines between outer and inner
space. I'd been shooting a lot of Karsh's events this way: the Before,
where a room was just a room, and the After, when the alchemical occurred — like the dip of photographic paper under rushing
river water, currents cameralessly caught by a flash of lightning, a
full moon.

But this place was a whole other category: a snazzy stately ship deck of a room. My eyes shot immediately to the flung-open doors at its far end, filtering in sun-drenched sea-sky-scape. Out on the terrace, poised between whitecaps and contrails, I could just glimpse Karsh behind his console, Flip trailing close with that Clairefontaine.

Me and Karsh. We were funny that way: so synchronized it was silly. I could practically enter a room earplugged and blindfolded and know he was there, and where. As if on clairvoyant cue, Karsh lifted his eyes just then, caught my gaze and held it with such warmth I got chills. A brief tick in time, but the you-and-me-ness of it: eternal.

He was either going through the motions for Flip or sound check had run late. Sometimes checks ran right into sets, and I wondered if this was going to be the case tonight, given the room tone of low woofered drone. Zoom: Karsh was, I could tell, superexcited. As he breeze-shot with Flip, his features flowed in unison — brows, mouth, cheeks up — and he leaned his nodding-to-the-beat head in to listen to le punkosophe's obviously uproarious running commentary, judging from his bursts of delighted laugher. And that laughter was looser, richer since he'd spotted me. Catching Flip's eye, I grinned at him, a wave of affection washing over me. Upon his tee, an überquote: *And those who were dancing were believed mad by those who could not hear the music.*

I reloaded Chica Tikka; since Karsh was at work, I might as well get to it myself.

—What say we case the space?

—We'll case the *bar*, Kavita suggested.

—Yes. We do not want to be disturbing your work, Sangita agreed, as if this was why Kavs wanted to throw it back. —Nor Karshbhai's.

They nodded me on. I began clicking my way towards Karsh.

We had that dance down: me shooting, him spinning, our double-eared-and-eyed beauty-and-beat beast covering every sonic and visual angle. Even the night we first truly met at HotPot, when I'd been shadowing Zara with my camera: He'd seen, from the balconied DJ booth, that I'd been shooting to the beat. His beat.

Stepping onto the deck was zero cool: out the dim passageway into the expansive brilliance of the Juhu evening, sand-stretched wave-breakered miles to every point on earth. No stars above — though the flickering jets from Shivaji Airport unzipped the welkin with wishes.

—Holy cow, I breathed. Flip nodded at me, face lighting up.

—It's going to be great, right? Karsh whispered.

—It's already great, I said. —Go on; don't mind me.

He seemed afloat in that knockout backdrop: the Arabian Sea—melt swelter of end-of-day Indian sky. Instead of the stout sweet-sweat ferment scent of Karsh's usual venues, a salt-flecked breeze perfumed the air.

Everything I laid eyes upon moved to the rhythm of Karsh's song. Or maybe it was me, syncopating.

Back inside, most were whisking tippleward. At the end of the bar, I saw Sangita sitting quietly in her salwar kameez, Deepak standing by her, he sipping a Kingfisher, she a Thums Up. Kavita was surely downing something lethal.

Sangita. She was a trouper, coconut-oiled hair and all, which she'd at some point swiftly braided.

Kavita gestured for me to join, heading my way. She waved our guest-list vouchers at me, then glanced at her watch.

—Look like it's time to get wasted!

I got the feeling she was already well on her way. We rocked up to the saffron sandstone counter, she coxswaying as if down a lopslid gangway. The bartenders were silently focused, none of that sallying chattiness you got so often in New York, where they were all surreptitiously, desperately trying to figure whether you had leads for financing their indie film while they nonchalantly poured.

She blinged (all) our vouchers, awaiting their attention. The mix of impeccable South Asian girls and boys was now combo-ing up with other ethnic groups: a tall lean black man (unless he was South Indian), a possibly Euro couple (unless they were Fair-n-Lovely desis). As I ordered a Kingfisher, I spotted Ravi amongst them, as usual too many shirt buttons undone for my liking.

He was earnestly imbibing with a corporate type, just two bar stools away. I figured I should greet the frocker. Tonight we were on the same side, after all. I caught his eye, which fell upon me, then Sangita, Deepak, Kavita. And, with the merest nod my way, he turned back to RoboCorp, continuing his conversation. I exchanged looks with Kavita, feigning a sneeze for her ears:

—Ah . . . ah . . . *arsehole!*

Unfortunately, or fortunately, this was precisely the moment the managerial man strode off, leaving nada between me and the object of my disparaging nasal expulsion.

—Caught a viral, Dimple? Ravi asked coolly. —Bombay too cold for you?

—Certain aspects of it, Ravi, I said. I turned to the bartender. —Actually, make that a *Manhattan.* Please.

I raised three fingers before he cube-queried me, thanking him obsequiously. Neither he nor Ravi were impressed.

Kavita leaned in coquettishly.

—Ah, *Ravi.* Your reputation exceeds you. . . .

Before he could reply, she seemed to catch someone's eye and swept grandly down the bar, murmuring, —I think we're going to need another round. . . .

—Um. Ravi. That . . . *was* Kavita. And this is Sangita and Deepak.

Sangita and Deepak smiled broadly, openly — almost idiotically — at him.

—Ah! The wedding people? Ravi asked, sounding, I thought, derisive.

Deepak nodded happily, however.

—Are you a married man? Deepak asked. It seemed he was implying something, although he may have simply been asking Ravi if he'd himself had a wedding. Ravi offered up a minimalist side-to-side nod.

Sangita peeked up eagerly from her Thums Up, and either in a move to smooth things over, or exhibiting complete cluelessness about the not-so-nuanced insult inherent in Ravi's tone, said, —It is such a pleasure, Ravi. I am truly looking forward to this evening. I can't tell you the last time I went out dancing!

Without batting an eye, Ravi replied:

—Garba?

My mouth dropped open at his reference to the traditional Gujarati dance performed at Navaratri. I mean, I'd been embarrassed by my sister-cousin's outdatedness — but no way in bloody hell was I letting him insult her! I was about to suggest to Ravi that he run outside and see if he was there, when Deepak, staring at him with a surprisingly cool blaze in his eyes, very calmly replied:

—Dandiya raas, in fact. Where sticks — or swords — are used. He nodded towards Sangita. —She's a demon slayer, this one. I'd watch out.

RoboCorp returned, schmboozing his way onto the stool, this time with a sheaf of papers. With Ravi obscured from view, my ears abruptly tuned in to the low throttle of the bass.

Casting a pointed look Sangita's way, Deepak muttered something about heading out.

—Sorry, Dimple, Sangita said, rising after her fiancé.

—Oh, don't go, Sangita! I cried, surprised to find I actually wanted her to stay now. —I told Karsh my reservations about that idiot, but he seemed immune to my opinion. He's just been so worked up about this show. . . .

—No issues. Please do not lose focus: This night is about Karsh's career, na? But I, *we* have to run a quick errand.

—Where are you going? Kavita asked, reappearing with another half-drained whiskey. —Don't let that chutia scare you off.

—It has nothing to do with that chut or this chut, Sangita assured her. It was unnerving hearing this graphic cussword fall from her innocent lips. —We have to visit the caterer; it is the last day we can make changes. In any case, this does not sound like the kind of music Karsh will do at our wedding.

—It's still the sound check? I offered.

—I am not sure electrical songs are my favorite, Deepak said mildly.

—But you'll be back for his set, at least some of it?

—We will try but cannot be making any guarantees. Traffic.

She and Deepak headed for the exit. I took her arm.

—Sangita, I said quietly. —I'm so sorry.

She smiled, and it was with such kindness, I was certain she'd truly heard me.

—No sorries between sisters, she said.

And she was gone. So fleet, exiting.

—Let's hit the ladies', Kavita proposed now. —I think I may throw up.

—I know. He's nauseating, that Ravi.

—No, it's not that, she whispered. —Not *just* that . . .

She opened her mouth, looked about to burst into tears . . .

. . . then let out a significant belch.

—How many've you had? I asked, nodding at her sloshy glass. She held up her thumb . . . then slowly added index, middle, ring, and pinky.

I secured her arm. —Okay. Come on, Kavity.

Beyond the bar, the bathroom gender-split, though the sinks in the ladies' were shared with the men's, separated by an opaque screen so you could see the silhouettes of man-hands washing, drying, gesturing . . . or, in the case of the girls' side, reapplying makeup. Frock, these ladkis knew how to work the kajal. They seemed more than happy to pose for my cam, when I nodded to it and then to them.

The pee-tendant beside the NO PHOTOGRAPHY sign didn't seem to mind my shutterbuggery either. I stepped into a stall and took a technical break; when I came out, I caught Kavita glancing around nervously, paranoically oversoaping at the sink.

—Kavz? What is it? You look all loo-gitive, like when you used to hide from Sabz and Upma at HotPot.

—Dimple, Kavita whispered. —Precisely. I keep thinking I *see* Sabz.

—Stress not. She's safely — or unsafely, for New York — at NYU.

—Well, if she's in New York, she's emo-texting me at some very strange hours. Four A.M.? Five?

The blue hour.

—That's when people send those kinds of messages. Anyway, she'd hardly come to Bombay and not say. Or at least, not get a local SIM card.

—I suppose you're right, Kavita relented. —Maybe my eyes just see what's on my mind.

—Abetted by what was not so long ago in your glass. Trust me, no Sabz doppelganging going on here. For one, no one looks even remotely pissed off, except Ravi.

She belched again, and spit something into the sink.

—Bloody hell, I said, digging into my bag. —Here.

—What's that?

—A Zantac and a Tums, Ms. Premed. Thanks to Mom and Dad. Although they likely thought we'd be using them against food — not alcohol — poisoning. Let's get you some water.

As we exited, I noted the giant jowly guard by the men's room door, beside a sign claiming The Use of Drugs Will Not Be

Tolerated. Although mine were strictly over-the-counter, I hastily shoved the ziplock back into my pack. Kavita lurched off to nab some agua, but I lingered a moment as I observed, just beside the bathroom bouncer, first one, then another male exiting with downcast shifty eyes. All were fervently rubbing their noses — and not in a single-nostril-breathing type way.

This was surely no drink-on-the-permit-room-cheap crowd, if they could afford nostrilian combustives. I raised my cam, hunkering after this fantastic organically split screen: runny-nosed club kid, immobile bouncer, No Tolerance sign . . . when the bouncer mobilized and shook a warning finger at me.

I lowered both head and camera, hoping to sneak a shot while feigning a packaway, when there was a tap on my shoulder. Was the drug lord going to monitor my antacid stash?

It was Flip. Had he just exited the toilet? No visible nasal dandruff. He pointed to Chica Tikka.

—Lala. Not here. You're giving off that moral police operative vibe.

When we emerged, I figured Karsh was still taking part in history's lengthiest sound check as my zoom revealed a mere handful of people on the terrace. The tuneage was Buddha Bar pseudo.

—Let me know when he's on, I told Flip. —I'll shoot the action at the bar; everyone's there. . . .

—Dimple. He *is* on!

—Already?

This was peculiar. At Karsh's HotPot nights, it never took any time to get people moving — plus, this wasn't even his music. And what up with those psychedelic visuals on the back wall?

This crowd seemed to be on IST in terms of dance spirit. Maybe my visuals were, too. I headed terraceward, figuring I'd give Karsh a little paparazzi ambiance to help push things along.

I passed Shailly at the end of the bar. Alone.

—Hey, Shy. Where's your crew? I asked, worried now.

—I've been trying to round them up. But most can't afford the cover, or are going to drink first and show later. If you ask me, a lot of them are still scared to land up after what went down here. But at least some of the usual LHB crowd is here. They'll get it heaving; they just need to warm up.

—It's twenty frocking degrees! I groused. —Celsius!

—That's cold here, she smiled apologetically.

The music, a loungey electronica, wasn't an overtaking kind, the breed that bewitched you, made you drop dishes to dance. It felt more like background hum, perhaps because that's how the LHB crowd was treating it.

No one, save Flip, who hovered to the side hanging on to his Kingfisher, had eyes on the DJ. And no one seemed to be listening, either.

Even me.

The only other folk anywhere near the console were three black-shirted, way-biceped dudes, arms crossed before them, all eyeing Karsh — but not with any notable pleasure. I was pretty sure I'd seen one of them serving sliders on our way in.

I mostly hung back when Karsh gigged. I didn't want to be the front-row groupie girlfriend; plus, I was usually too busy shooting the space — or dancing my shoulders off in it. I stuck to the sidelines now as well but could sense Karsh's mounting terror at the unresponsive crowd. His eyes met mine across the room, and they were wide and worried. I wasn't sure he'd ever been faced with a dance demographic that didn't throw it down, and my return gaze was possibly concerned, too.

He cut such a lonely figure, suddenly. And it struck me we were, for the first time in forever, in a roomful of mostly strangers. Disturbingly static ones. We'd gotten so used to our fam gang:

Karsh's parties Stateside were gatherings of friends as much as anything else — like the vibe in Bandra the other night.

These sleeksters just kept chatting away. If people vocalized at an Apple show, they were either singing along or praising the sound. Here, it was as if Karsh — with that mega console, laptop, and all that painstaken gear — was invisible. Inaudible, even. A few people even drifted back indoors, *away* from the speakers.

Flip spotted me now, and backed up till we were side by side.

—What the frock? I whispered.

He shrugged. —Look, don't sweat it. This crowd . . . they can rarely tell apart genres, just sway with the current trend.

Then why weren't they swaying? And if they couldn't tell the difference, why was LHB so stringent about defining the styles you could stylus?

I thought: Screw Ravi and his arse-backwards advice! If Karsh had been playing from his heart, surely they'd all be going mad with motion. What did Ravi even know about the way to a crowd's heart? Or anyone's?

And where was he anyway?

This was Karsh we were talking about. *Karsh* knew the way to the heart; after all, his own pulsed to the beat, blood coursed to the bassline. This was the man who went one with two tablas, rolled with the dhol, and Stateside could, without fail, unpin even the staunchest of wallflowers, unfurl them onto the dance floor in whirlwinding bloom. I'd seen it; he'd done it to me. His call to the floor — to let him take you on a journey: The crowd crewed up for that trip every time. Without ever leaving the room, we rounded the world, the clock, DJ GJ our guide — bringing us hot off the Punjabi harvest those ancestral bhangra beats so many of us had near-Fallopian memories of, hip-hopping them all together in an irresistible soulful skitter of a path to our present-day New York City selves.

Before I knew it, I was sending him, the musical captain of this swilty ship, a salute, a signal. I netted Karsh's wide eyes in mine, lifted shoulders and brows in a bhangric shrug. But this time it was an instruction, a summons for him to play from the heart. He didn't shrug back but knit his own brows, unsure. I pointedly scanned the gabbing ebbing crowd and shrugged back at him with more vehemence. He scanned them as well . . . and this time when he looked to me, I pointed to the dhol graphic on my chest and pounded my palm *thump thump* on it, nodding: Go on!

And he heard me, got the message. I saw it and it was magnificent to behold, like he was remembering something from so very long ago, before even our time, our story became our own; this force now poured through him, fortifying his backbone, leveeing him a couple inches higher . . .

Off the gangplank. Our eyes locked, our limbs loosened. It was him and me. Me and he: we — dual-eyed and -eared. We were the world, and we'd gather everyone into it like we always did. Take a blank page, fold it into a fortune. Double a zero, tip it to infinity.

He thump-thumped back.

With renewed vigor, Karsh now studied his tracklist, fading out the trancey number, notching up another dial. I knew the song before he dropped it — the one he always saved for me at HotPot, the ringtone that signaled his calling on my cell. And then, that base of grace rising in the mix, those exalted opening strains I'd once confused for *itchy itchy eye:*

Gur nalon isqh mitha hi hi . . . !

Love, sweeter than gur. It was cosmic. Dholphoric. We the tabla tribe, creating a unified beat with our two stretched skins. And that husk-rustic voice rang primordial, magnetic — Malkit Singhing it — then Karsh's own overflowing it . . . count backwards from one, ready to rock, here it comes . . . his mic'd up call to his desi dance cohorts: *Let me take you on a journey* . . . And I let him, would always let him. I lowered my camera and went out there, into the place we made, were *making* together.

I danced my heart out and in, to within inches of the console. Dancing for him, for us — paving a pathway into this city with rollicking shoulders and firecracker feet, a line from his Juhu sand heart to mine . . . from the land of we diasporic offspring to this terrain of our mothers, our fathers, our grands . . . screwing the lightbulb into pulsing celestial light, my palm poised as if to catch the great glowing solar orb that was now dipping, dunking into the Arabian Sea behind him . . .

In New York, this bhangric shrugfest on the HotPot floor was usually so no-elbow-roomed, the dancers became one not only with the music but with one another: fleshtacular contact — hips bumping, hands skimming, eyes joylocked as vox wand-wove that chorus of *hi hi's* and *ho ho's.*

But here, it was like spinning in deep space.

Off to the side, Flip nodded his head to the beat, true, but was busy scribbling away in his Clairefontaine. And the only other dance manifesters were this one slithery wick of a white — beige? — guy doing some kind of trippy Woodstock moves to the bang-on beats. There was always one like this in the New York crowd. In fact, maybe even the same one.

And the other groover: a dreamy girl in flowing skirt who was now just before Karsh, engaged in a very odd, yet oddly familiar dance — swaying side to side, singing along though her lips aligned not with the lyrics, as if she were badly dubbed. She held both hands up, palms out in a kind of surrender . . . then released her ripply ponytail, windmilling topknots-per-hour dirty-blond dreads, eyes fixed on Karsh like a groupie.

Gopi! That devotee from ISKCON — moving just the way the masses did there . . . only now she was before a console, not a mandir.

In fact, it was probably the Hare Krishna mantra she was chanting.

Just as I realized this, two more figures flung themselves onto the dance floor with almost wanton abandon, and launched into *another* familiar dance:

Full-on high-octane bhangra moves. Performed by a goofily grinning man leaping around like an aerobics instructor, and a salwar-kameezed woman artfully dodging her own dupatta, thick black coco-loco braid giving the air a good lashing as she whirled up and down.

Sangita and Deepak.

A bench-pressed bulk of an Indian man now broke loose from one of the sleekster pockets and moved swiftly towards Karsh, something playing on his upturned lips — a compliment? A request for more? My heart lifted.

I was close enough to hear — and the space, now loud enough he had to shout — as he leaned in towards Karsh and bellowed:

—Hey, Mr. DJ. Want to play my wedding?

Karsh looked up at him with a gaze so hopeful it hurt, and was nodding, smiling, when the Indo-hulk spat, —Bhanchod! Play some real music!

Sister-frocker. Not the most poetic of appellations. At the top of my lungs, I yawped, —*Brother-frocker!*, but no one heard me. Or got it. Even me.

A mind-frock, more like: a hot club, a white blond Rasta Krishnite, and a couple of trads throwing it down — it would have looked sure-shot subversive . . . in New York.

But here, in India, the concept of Indianness probably wasn't something Indians were trying to subvert. Or prove.

I did a 180, then 360; spun around again in confirmation: a 720? Most of the irredeemably loose-lipped crew had prattled back into the dining area. A few continued their terrace twaddling, foot-tapping but otherwise tune-immune.

The space now appeared a tilting, careening ship-deck-near-wreck.

Behind Karsh, the aphotic urge of the Arabian Sea blending with shadowed sand seemed poised to swallow him up, just as it was draining the psychedelic hues of the sun-done sky.

L'heure bleu it was at LHB. The very same place appeared a whole other venue now. Back to zero: It was like watching a HotPot party night in reverse, a slow rewind of people flooding off the dance floor and towards the bar. . . .

Even the music sounded suddenly distorted, pitching frantically in volume and zigzagging cross-fades.

Back at the decks, a battle of console control was in fact now taking place. One of the hulking black-shirted servers was literally wrestling Karsh off the Serato box. But Karsh wasn't giving in so easily — how could a DJ just cut off a song midflow?

By the next *itchy itchy eye*, another man had appeared: the RoboCorp who'd been deep in discussion with Ravi at the bar earlier . . . and who now assaulted Karsh with a deluge of Hindi, or maybe it was Marathi. His gestures were universal: He was clearly instructing him to quit the console.

—But I'm . . . I'm taking you on a *journey!* Karsh attempted shakily — and, unfortunately, right into the mic during a momentary gap in the song.

Ooh. This was bad. A second delivery of the line . . . and with that negative conjunction: *But.* I cringed.

It was too late. The plug was pulled from somewhere, only Karsh's plea resounding humiliatingly through the room . . . followed by an abrupt, bone-chilling hush.

And then, the worst: The door-two bouncer appeared, gripped Karsh by the arm . . . and jousted him out from behind the console!

Black-shirted server dude actually stepped in, shut down Karsh's laptop — and took over the decks. This seemed to disobey the very vocational laws of the universe. How could you bounce the *DJ*?

—Hey! You can't treat the artist like that! I yelped as Karsh was led past me, hanging on to his control record. —Or he's never playing here again!

—That would be correct, sister, the DJ police retorted.

—Dimple, Karsh hissed now, to my shock. —Drop it. Just go.

I froze, stunned. What was going on? How had our double-featured creature been sacrificed so fast? And in the moment of silence before our new supposed DJ launched into the venue laptop (and a fuzz of something generically electronic), a ticktock clickclack like metronomic metropolitan rain: the only sound whittling empty air.

Mallika burst onto the terrace in her teeter-heels, Ravi inches behind. She glanced from Karsh and the bouncer to me and back to Karsh again.

—Sorry, traffic, she exhaled. —Did I miss it?

—You didn't miss a thing, the bouncer replied.

—What? It's over?

—Oh, yes, Ravi spoke now, arctic eyes on Karsh, then me. —I do believe it is.

Mallika turned then to lay a comforting hand . . . on Ravi's shoulder.

And, as if under arrest, Karsh was led out to the dining area.

I followed a beat later, nervously observing as he, clutching stomach, bolted for the bathroom. Shailly hung back at the bar, nodded a warm hello to Ravi *and* RoboCorp, then caught me staring.

—Shailly! I seethed once they'd passed. —You know these people — say something! They can't do this to him!

She glanced around the space, then leaned in to me.

—We can't piss off the management. A gig here's good money; I don't want to get blacklisted.

—What about friendship?

—Dimple. This isn't about friendship. Nothing can kill it between me and Karsh — even though he's too proud to play my party, which I'd suggested he do in the first place. Guess he's used to being the main act when it comes to me, but whatever. It's business. I put a word in here for him before Ravi even got on the case, even sent him a bunch of track suggestions since it's not his usual deal. To be honest, he fucked up, plain and simple. I can't put my own livelihood in jeopardy — not just yet, anyway. Not till Crosstreet's truly up and running.

I just stared at her. I guess it made sense Karsh might find it odd to second-bill for the act who'd always opened for him in New York. But it hadn't occurred to me there might be a touch of sour grapes in that resistance. I wasn't sure what to say, so opted for:

—Well . . . since when are you such good pals with Ravi?

—Since I'm such good pals with Mallika, she said with a shrug. I glanced back at Mallika, at the other end of the bar by a livid Ravi. They stood slightly apart, but there was something funnily intimate about this distance.

It fell into place.

I lowered my voice. —But he's married, no?

Shailly shrugged again. —What's a piece of paper?

Mallika stepped up then. Ravi was now, it would appear, groveling with the manager dude.

—What the fuck was that all about? Karsh was playing bhangra? Didn't he sign the contract?

I didn't think the what's-a-piece-of-paper argument would work here.

—You said yourself, Mallika, back in New York, remember? That his sets would go down a storm here.

—Dimple! Why would you or he listen to me? Ravi's managing him. It's *Ravi's* reputation at stake. The last thing he wants is to go crawling back to Daddy and South Bombay like all his spoiled brat friends to ask for money — near forty-year-olds needing written permission to buy a car! He's trying to make his own way, and I respect that. He just clearly chose the wrong team to make it with.

Whose side was everyone on? I could barely speak, and beelined for the bathroom. Just outside it, Sangita and Deepak were now helping a keeling-over Kavita collect her things.

—Dimple. I think it's time we push off. Will you be all right? Sangita asked me. —Do you want to come with us?

I gave Kavita's shoulder a squeeze, torn but clear.

—I have to stand by Karsh, I said. —Seems no one else is.

They left; I waited by the bathroom door. But when Karsh came out, it wasn't his stomach he was rubbing. Flip followed, swiping his own nostrils and sniffling a little much.

—Flip, I whispered. —*Seriously?*

He shrugged. Why was everyone shrugging? It was a mockery of the very music that had just been banned from the premises.

—Just taking care of the artist, he said. Karsh was already downing something at the bar.

—Go easy on him, Shailly muttered to me now, appearing by my side. —He gets a little manic on Charlie. You should've seen him in San Fran.

Charlie? Karsh? He'd neglected to mention that wee *deet* to me. So had that been relief in his eyes when we reunited after Shaky City, I wondered now — or repentance? It sure as hell explained his return jitters.

Why hadn't he just told me? It was amazing how clear our corner of the bar was, like all this negative energy was pushing people away.

—Yeah, I said, halfheartedly fronting. —Manic . . .

—You should've seen it — he was up all night there, by turns feeling like a genius and the world's greatest fuckup. I told him to skip the blow, especially here. New city, new scene.

—Uh-huh.

—Dude even dropped his sacred tabla case and ended up bashing up the wheels. Like, on purpose. I mean, stick to hash, you know? Mellow shit. Cheaper, too.

Ravi was up by Karsh now. Karsh glanced at him with, affirmative, undeniably manic eyes.

—Still here? Ravi inquired icily. Three cubes plus.

—Ravi . . . I'm so sorry. But I really was just trying to take everyone on a journey, honest. . . .

—What fucking journey? And *desi cohorts*? The journey you take them on with bhangra is to the Punjab. To India. And an outdated India. We don't need a ticket to the motherland, fool — we're already here!

Though Mallika had painted Ravi as the black sheep of the brown family, he was nearly baboon-red in the face now.

—You signed, for god's sake, Ravi fumed on. —So you're not a man of your word, isn't it?

—I was . . . trying to be, Karsh stammered, —true to myself.

—Well, you're a self-indulgent sham, Kapoor. I was so wrong about you.

—Ravi, I'm sorry. I fucked up. I — it won't happen again. I promise: next show, by the rules.

—Next show? You think this place is going to roll out the red carpet for you anytime soon?

—But surely there are other venues? Karsh whispered, wild-eyed.
—I, it's an innocent mistake. This music — it works where I'm from.

—Then go back to where you're from. Take *yourself* on a journey, Karsh.

Ravi stormed out. Karsh froze, then turned towards the bathroom again, and its clearly tolerating hurly-burl of an attendant. I leapt up, caught his hand.

—It's going to be okay, Karsh. But . . . maybe you should go easy on the substances?

I worried suddenly about the hereditary nature of becoming an addict. Not that this had been his dad's drug of choice: booze, more like, and betting. But still. That glazed blaze in Karsh's eyes was new to me.

—You know, why don't we take down that sign? he replied, disentangling himself from me. —And *you* just stand there instead, exuding no-tolerance?

It felt like a kick in the gut, but I tried to stay cool, comfort him.

—You don't need him, Karsh, I attempted weakly. —You're not thinking clearly. . . .

—You know what I don't need, Dimple? I don't need any more of your great advice.

—Huh?

—Ravi was right.

—Ravi's an idiot!

—No, Dimple. *You* were wrong — and you were probably just doing it, goading me on to play like at HotPot, to prove your hold on me to him. *I'm* the idiot for listening.

I tried to steady my breath. What was it — breathe through the eyes? But my vision was blurry, and it didn't sound like my Karsh speaking.

—He's not the boss of you, Karsh!

—Who is? You?

He just stood there, staring me down. I felt my eyes watering . . . and then glimpsed a softer, older substratum to this raging new skin. I latched on to it for dear life.

—I feel, Karsh whispered, —like I've lost my father twice. This was my big chance. Ravi's chance. And I blew it.

—You don't only get one chance, I whispered back. —Not everything is make-or-break.

—You do, Dimple, he said, and for a moment, it felt we were having a completely different discussion, one that, if I thought about it, cut too deep.

Shailly stepped in now, taking his arm.

—Karsh, baas, ya. You can make it up to him.

—Why? I cried. —We don't have to suck up to him, them. This isn't the only club, the only crowd!

—Um, it kind of *is* one of the only clubs and crowds in this scene, Shy pointed out.

Gokulanandini joined us now, blithely smiling as if she'd just had a totally different experience of the evening.

—What are you doing here? I asked, more edgily than I'd meant to.

—Lovely view of the sunset. They don't lock us in the ashram, you know.

She proceeded to take Karsh's other arm. None left for me; what, should I grab his lingam?

Gokulanandini went on. —Karsh, listen. Everything you need is inside you, if you practice the correct life. A life of devotion. For God loves you . . . whether you are a DJ or not.

I tried to catch Karsh's eye, but both of his were trained on her. I recalled with a pang how he'd described Gokulanandini as, what was it? Luminous?

—It probably wasn't the best night to play, honey, Shy added.
—A reopening. My last Crosstreet party? The Shiv Sena shut it down before it even started!

—Because of the immoral women in tiny skirts standing outside doing unmentionable things on the Koli fishermen's path? Gokulanandini asked sweetly. No, ISKCON clearly did *not* deadlock those doors. —I heard.

I got the feeling, as far as the party police were concerned, the unmentionable things were . . . women standing outside in tiny skirts. Or just women standing outside. (Or just . . . women.)

—Probably more likely the drugs, Shy said. I noticed just then that she was in a tiny skirt, although still inside. Ravi would be delighted.

—The crowd didn't seem so scared in Bandra the other night, I noted.

—Well, Ravi messed up a little on timing, Shy admitted. —That French dubstep act's on in Lower Parel tonight, start of their residency. Lazy Gonuts Gondolier. That would've drawn a lot of the Bandra crowd; free entry first few hours, too.

—Well, why don't you tell him that? I nearly yelled. I glanced around but didn't see Ravi anywhere. —He's blaming it all on Karsh.

—I doubt he's in a receptive mood at the moment. Anyway, if anyone, Mallika should tell him.

—Those songs, that set always works so well in New York, Karsh said, shaking his head.

—You're in India now, Shy replied. —And must partake in the Indian dream . . . even if America is at the heart of some of it.

The Reeboks, the Levi's I'd seen all over Bandra the other night. The Domino's Pizza delivery motorcyles; the Subway sandwich shop with free valet parking. A flashback of focaccia-flooded bread baskets somewhere.

And not a roti in sight to save your life. Shy had a point. I wondered if Ravi picked up this sentiment from her, or if it was common knowledge around these parts.

—India. America. It doesn't matter where we are from, Gokulanandini remarked sagely. —We drew the borders ourselves;

we can erase them with love. Love. The great eraser. After all, earth viewed from space is just a beautiful blue ball. . . .

—I wish I were in space, then, Karsh lamented. —I mean, New York burnt me out, so I came here for a spark. The UK hasn't been home since forever. And now, I've just blown Bombay.

—You are a citizen of the world, Gokulanandini concluded serenely.

—What's the point? If no one in the world will have me . . .

I'd never seen him quite like this, even in those months after he'd gotten word about his father. Such downcast eyes — as if he were teetering on the edge of the earth when the earth was flat.

You have me, I thought. But for the first time, it felt a small succor, given the circumstances and how tuned in to everyone *else* he was. The dead air thickened; I could almost see him sealing off from me.

And then Shailly stepped through that wall, both arms around Karsh, forehead tipped to his forehead, eyes locking his into hers with a near gravitational pull.

—I'd have you, she said quietly. She must have meant at Crosstreet, perhaps. But he gazed at her with such gratitude, it was painful. For it was a regard I recognized — one he'd cast my way many a time when I'd handed him precisely the right words, the perfect silence during a low moment. Hadn't the dolorous murk of months after his father's passing been all about that?

But now it was aimed at her, and my heart tightened around this view.

When had I lost the ability to console him?

—Chalo, ya, Shy suggested. We moved towards the exit, which such a short while ago had been an entry.

—And Karsh, Gokulanandini said gently. —Always remember. The world *inside* is the greater universe.

I got the feeling she didn't mean the dining area, but I took a last look anyways. The room appeared just as it had upon our arrival;

that musical alchemy hadn't occurred here, transformed it. In fact, despite the drinking crew, the increase in diners now, it felt somehow empty, bereft.

I glanced back through the flung-open doorways seaside, caught a glimpse of the terrace. To add insult to abrasion, out there under the tropical jet-plane-sparkling sky, the crowd was now actually dancing . . . to the waiter's set.

Before I could block the view, Karsh caught it.

—Look at them now, he said.

*　　*　　*

I followed the trio out, a demoted roadie loaded down with gear, somehow including Karsh's laptop.

As we stepped out into that young night, Gokulanandini floored me by beginning to sing the sweetest song — a lullabye? — in *Hindi*. Or Urdu? It was familiar, trilled a plangent thread through the honks and hollers, the rickety racket of the still-buzzing street.

Was it . . . *"Jana Gana Mana"*? The national anthem? Talk about inappropriate! No — talk about appropriating! Shy joined in, too, with a weirdly colonialist undertone as well. From my shaadi-chafed perspective, it seemed she and Gopi girl were walking down the aisle with Karsh. I tried to quell the feeling that tonight I was the giveaway.

Flip hopped up out of nowhere, wheeling Karsh's LP trolley, and relieved me of the laptop. I smiled wearily at him, grateful I still, apparently, existed. He raised his eyebrows at me, then shrugged: *What can you do?*

We stood around by the paanwallah. Flip even bought a piece, and a small silence ensued while the wallah rolled up and slake-limed the areca nut.

—It didn't go down all bad, Flip attempted now. —Sweet visuals; everyone was commenting.

Huh? Karsh didn't start at this revelation; was that why he hadn't wanted me at sound check? I turned to him.

—I brought yours, Dimple. It's just . . .

—Yeah, yeah, I said. —Ravi.

Shailly smiled now. —Same dude who designed my last Crosstreet stuff. Mesh. He was here earlier, shooting.

Flip spat his paan. I suddenly just felt lost.

I sneaked a glance Karsh's way. To my surprise, and relief, he appeared lost as well. I was pissed about the visuals — but for better or worse, right? Maybe he just needed a reminder of where he was from, who he was — and who he was *with*. This coked-up frantic-eyed Karsh wasn't the one I knew, and I worried the distance between us would only lengthen by evening's end if we didn't call it a night, quit while we were only a little behind.

Karsh seemed to feel the same, eyeing the ricks now. I looked at him; he began nodding at me.

But Flip begged to differ. —Come on, guys. Don't bail! Let's go have the quintessential Bandra experience. I've got an Old Monk in my bag to kick things off.

—I don't know. . . . Karsh trailed off.

I held my, *our* ground.

—I haven't caught any *zzz*s since we got here. Let's get your gear back safe and sound, Karsh.

Karsh hesitated, then handed me the control vinyl.

—Thanks, Dimple, I appreciate it. The laptop's pretty much it, and the LP case. The rest is on loan.

He nodded to the others now. —You're right. I don't want to end the night feeling like this.

—Karsh? I tried again, a little feebly.

—Go on, Dimple, he said dully. —I'm going to chill a while. Maybe powwow with everyone about Plan B.

How the frock was a Hare Krishna devotee going to advise him on salvaging his rep in Bombay's DJtronic world? I took in the motley crew . . . which now included the rickshawallah pulling up to Shy's beckoning hand. He appeared the friendliest of the lot, and I drifted towards him for asylum.

—Seahorse, Gokulanandini instructed him, like I couldn't say it.

—Meter! Shailly added. The driver grudgingly flicked down the lever. As I bent to get in the rick, Shy leaned in to me:

—I just don't think he should go home yet. Might be better to get the shit out of his system. Sweat it out.

—That's what *I* was thinking. *Sweat* it out.

She didn't catch on. Why were DJs so bad at hearing?

—Cool, then. We'll get him on his feet, Dimps. And he'll be back with you and better than ever before you know it. After all, everything here closes at one thirty.

—Uh-huh. Hotels, three.

I was surprised to find myself fighting back tears. I supposed it couldn't hurt to try to sleep. Was I overreacting?

As my rick made a surely illegal spurl-a-round to head us off in the right direction, I caught a glimpse of that Café Coffee Day — now more accurately appellatable Café Coffee Night, though I could have sworn I could still discern the silhouette of the squatting Sisyphusians. The sight of it comforted me; it appeared a small visual oasis, a resting place soap-bubble déjà vu amidst the grime and garrulosity of the nonstop street, the battering battle in my head.

Unchanging. As if nothing had even happened back there — to Karsh. To us.

And perhaps nothing had?

CHAPTER 18

Insecurity Check

I crawled into bed, knocking the fresh jasmine flowers scattered on the pillows to the carpet. I kept my phone in one hand and flicked on the TV with the other. But there were just too many Indians on air, dancing and singing and newscasting and looking generally like the LHB crowd. It made me feel like a failure. Like *I* should be dancing and singing and looking generally like the LHB crowd.

I switched channels. But the flatline laughter of US sitcoms on satellite now made *America* feel like a failure to me.

Maybe something was wrong with my phone? Or Karsh's? (Please?) Someone had mentioned signals vanished around the Sea Link. Were we near enough to disappear?

I called my cell from the hotel phone to find it, unfortunately, working. But maybe texts weren't?

Then suddenly: *Gur nalon isqh mitha hi hi* — Karsh's ringtone! I fumbled to answer his call . . . but my phone wasn't ringing. I stared at it, confounded.

The song continued: *Gur nalon isqh mitha ho ho!*

It was coming from outside my window. I threw open the curtains. It took a quick seaview glance — at the spotlit mandap, buffet tables, ribboned palms, and dance floor ebullient with shoulder-shimmying divinely dressed folk — to see: A wedding was going on.

Gur nalon isqh mitha, gur nalon isqh mitha . . . !

With unabashed enthusiasm, the wedding DJ was playing that song.

And everyone was dancing.

*   *   *

One thirty came and went. All over Bombay, the bars were closed. My eyes: not.

*　　*　　*

Nearly three thirty.

Had he run out of battery? Fallen asleep? If anything had gone wrong, Shy or Flip would surely have called me. Unless *they* were what had gone wrong?

Where the frock were they? I could resist no longer and tried Karsh . . . but his phone was switched off as the vastly vexing, almost smug-sounding woman on the recording informed me — first in Marathi, I assumed, and then, clearly showing off, English.

I hit the sack, sacked the lights, and tried simulating sleep, figuring I'd worn myself out enough with worry and fury to fool myself into actually believing it.

A click of the door opening . . .

I continued my slumber act, slit-eyedly observing Karsh's silhouette entering.

It felt like spook spotting. He quietly set down his bag, slipped out of his shoes, then paused, possibly looking at me; a sigh, a sip of bottled water, and into the bathroom. Just ajar, and I could see his shadow sifting about inside, the soft scuff of clothes falling to floor. Door closed: a toppling gush of bathwater, split-second silence, then the smooth ominous rush of the shower.

Water stopped; hush-tone towel to skin. He was taking great care not to wake me — fool that he was — door barely slivering as he glided out, flicking off bathroom fan and light. He dug around his suitcase; from his bend and rise, it seemed he was easing on a pair of pajamas.

I bemoaned the PJ-less days of old. But at least he was coming to bed. I deepened the sound of my breathing and closed my eyes, awaiting the sinking of his side.

But there was a mere mattressqual dip as he perched on bed edge.

What stopped me from reaching an arm out to touch him, pull him near — confront him? Seek reassurance?

Maybe I knew you shouldn't ask a question unless you're prepared to hear the answer.

Plus, I was sulking.

And then the near-unthinkable happened: Karsh pulled his shoes back *on* and rose. I caught a whiff of the noxious fish-story fumes of his treachery — Johnson's Baby Shampoo — and opened my eyes all the way as he stealthed to the door, clicked it open, and stepped out. The glare of the corridor lights spotlit his freshly kurta'd figure.

Kurta?

The 212 glinted above his head.

And he was gone.

I froze momentarily, then skedaddled to the bathroom. Aquafresh: uncapped. His toothbrush: wet. My toiletry bag had tipped, spilling a couple of goods by the sink and revealing the corner of a transferred Condomania six-pack strip. I yanked it all the way out. One. Two. Three. Four.

Four?

I dumped the contents of my bag onto the counter: Burt's Bees lip balm, various skin care sample sizes, dental floss, Zantac, a stash of toothpicks from Lucien in the East Village. Yet no preemptive pair to bring that four up to a grand mollifying total of six.

I hated Shailly. I loathed Gokulanandini.

Where the frock does a freshly showered sure-footed double-condomed kurta'd DJ go at 3:42 in the morning in Mumbai — or even Bombay, for that matter?

Perks of being an insomniac: No matter the hour, you could turn secret agent spy girl at the drop of a hat. I got up, pulled on my jeans. Birks. Phone in pocket, room key in other, so no risk of data wipeout. Skip the camera; I wasn't sure I'd want to remember what I was about to witness.

No. Take the camera. Witness.

* * *

I stuck my nose, followed by an eye, into the hallway. Way down it, I saw Karsh still pacing by the elevator bank. It dinged open. In he went as I hit the well, took the stairs.

Two floors down, I was about to burst into the lobby, when I glimpsed the elevator touching down, two, one . . . and Karsh stepping out. I ducked back into the stairwell, peeked out after him.

He strode out the back doors, turning 2-D lineation towards the pool area. I followed a safe distance behind, though the jaunty concierge nearly blew my cover:

—Good . . . morning, Mrs. Kapoor!

I tried a smile back but kept moving. And it occurred to me as I exited into the temperate night, trailing that silhouette slinking its seaward wall path:

Perhaps it was she who was the real ghost.

* * *

The light from the twenty-four-hour hotel coffeeshop paved the way to the drop wall. I lurked poolside, cloaked in the shadows of one or two still sprawlingly oblivious umbrellas, and watched Karsh move along that barrier, to behind the Fire Evacuation Point palm tree.

I could just see him lining up his figure with one of the still-clad areas of the bones of the mandap, a perfect near–four A.M. hiding place.

And then: He stepped up onto the dividing wall — and jumped!

I nearly shot out of my hideout in anticipation of Karsh's last hurtling scream — when I recalled the wall wasn't so high, and banks of sand lay below. Considering the snoozing canines that other day, the greatest danger, I figured, would be landing in dog shit. Me, I was already in some kind for sure.

I slipped stealthily from umbrella'd table to table and found myself mounting that same divider.

I took a breath. Invoked my inner Nancy Drew (minus that doofus Ned Nickerson), and slung myself over and off . . .

Ouch! No springy dune cushion awaited me; a knee-scraper. But there was no time to waste licking minor wounds. I rose. Dusted myself off. And, Birks in hand, continued the chase.

I gulped in the salty breeze, wildly, wickedly awake. Finally, something productive to do during my insomniac hours — stalk my boyfriend!

Wall gave way to bramble, rust, and brush. Lamplight threw halos to the moonscape sand, where I could now discern Karsh's prints. I followed, then glimpsed their owner well down a side street. As I turned right onto it, Hanuman the monkey god cheered (or jeered) me on from whitewashed tile, followed by a crucifixed Christ accompanied by another, less afflicted, Jesus and Mary, pressed against raw rock face.

Juhu by night was another place altogether. An arboreal sky over cobbled road. As I walked on, I noted banks of sleeping rickshaws parked to either side, backseats blanketed with dreaming drivers. Seeing so many tuk-tuks clustering like that, I felt I'd stumbled upon an entire carapaced species unto itself, a dozing herd of wild urbanlife. I never suspected a rick could be so quiet . . . though a faint peal of crackling music, rife with strings and swoons, filtered from one, staticking down the street towards me.

Karsh had vanished into the forward distance. I passed now the tune-playing tuk-tuk, an aloft lion just atop it.

A leonine serenade: I knew that king of beasts. And well before the street nearly ended in that edifice — before I crossed over and laid palm to it, tracing the strains of that mantra printed direct upon glowing brick, I knew where I was headed. Perhaps had known from the moment my soles hit sand.

A jingling singing winging into the not-quite-dawning day. I turned through the gates, into the pavilion. I ran my bag through with the somnambulist metal detectician, deposited my shoes with a more wakeful man in the illuminated P.O.-box-type stalls.

That percussive sleigh bell song grew louder. . . .

A pair of well-worn red sneakers was in one of these cubbyholes. I half expected to find a couple seductress stilettos leering against them, but the shoe storage space was largely empty, chappaled if at all. I turned, faced that open-arched marble edifice, dream-luminous at this hour. Followed the water-cupped-sweet crooning into the courtyard now.

Above: My eyes dilated with stars. By my feet, umpteen leaves patterned the floor, danced in a slight breeze around the pillar bases.

4:32 A.M. After-party: the pre-sunrise brahma-muhurta first and most effective darshan of the day. Up the steps, in the temple's heart: those swaying praying devotees, chanting their love to the here unblue-skinned god.

I slipped inside, to where they gazed towards the triple stage I'd seen . . . just a day ago? Many donned similar robed apparel; perhaps the ones who lived here? Aureoling the perimeter, those 3-D sculpted paintings were illuminated, as if Krishna were dancing through his days in the very air around us, like the throngs of followers-to-be beneath the leafy tree in that one to my right, I read now, depicting the 1966 day the USA branch of the movement was birthed . . .

. . . in Tompkins Square Park?

In utero sensation. I stepped across the rose-petaled floor, lining up on the women's side.

Dirty-blond dreads at the forefront, Gokulanandini leading the sway.

This time when the three monks bluesed their conches like busy Dizzy trumpeteers, tilting up to throw it down . . . as bells brouhaha'd and grown men fell prostrate to the floor . . . as the crowd raised unblushing unselfconscious arms in the air, singing that mantra with such love, such faith, a no-verse all-chorusing conviction — *Hare Krishna Hare Krishna, Krishna Krishna, Hare Hare, Hare Rama Hare Rama, Rama Rama, Hare Hare* — syncing to the sound vibration, the joy of the japa: I understood what had drawn Karsh here.

Music, motion, dance, devotion. Song and surrender. A knowing wonder.

I pushed forward on the wave of waltzing women; following the followers, I tried to feel it, catch their bliss. These were jubilant gods, inviting gods. But something in me still resisted that joy, that invitation. No blue these Krishnas' skin, but a deep sad swathe of the hue in my belly. Up front, I ran my hands over the priest-proffered flame, coving that aarti, fire favor cupped close to me. I remembered my father, blessing me doubly, huge-heartedly.

When I turned back, instead of returning to the women's section, I entered the men's. I knew exactly where he'd be — exactly where he'd been that first time, when his swaying had so startled me.

Second row to the back, now cross-legged on the floor. I stared at him sitting there, my Karsh, and saw how like a small boy he looked, hunched over in the midst of the praying masses. But a small strong thing at that. On his face such a tranquil expression, as if he were dreamlessly sleeping . . . but from the steady stir of his lips, whirring fingertips on the string of beads in his hand, it was clear it was a wakeful dream.

And then, for an instant, a flicker: He wasn't really my Karsh. He was a person going through his own shit, his own journey — clearing a path through a certain kind of pain that this evening had clarified I could do little about. Yet, with this realization, for a moment, something in me eased off. His peace became . . . my relief. I tried to hold on to this generous and surprisingly mature sentiment, but it slipped my grip like an eyelash wish, promptly replaced by that tenacious old current of fear.

He wasn't my Karsh? Then whose was he?

His eyes, closed, a strangerness beneath that veneer of familiarity. Palms still cupped, I was moving towards him to pass him my blessing . . . when I spotted Gopal beside him, chanting with closed eyes as well, the two boys' wrists gently bumping as they worked their way around the beads.

I froze, hands inches from Karsh's head, loath to break this reverie. And to be honest, I wasn't sure how pure my blessing for him was. I just stood there staring, nervously waiting for him to sense my presence. But then — how would I explain? That I'd followed him all this way — for what?

It was Gopal who opened his eyes and stared back at me, pupils wide and knowing. A slow burn crawled up my neck. He gave me a gentle side-to-side nod. What the frock did that mean? Hello? Goodbye? Pass the aarti already? Don't?

Or simply: Go.

My head began to pound. The incense, the ghee, the cloying scent of fallen flowers. And just before releasing that invisible benediction upon Karsh's head, I had second thoughts, lay my now cold palms upon my own brow and slowly retraced my steps, out the way I'd come.

Perhaps selfishly, I had the feeling I was more in need of a blessing tonight.

Karsh didn't see, didn't follow. And I was no longer following either.

* CHAPTER 19 *
Blueshift

I packed up; we had a few hours before checkout and shifting hotels. Karsh still wasn't back, was probably shaving his head and changing his name, for all I knew. I hit the free breakfast, drowning sorrows in copious quantities of masala tea. My mind funneled that first-visit image of him swaying at the temple, arms raised in a musical surrender, so jarring to me for some reason. And today, I was ashamed to discover, I was even more perturbed by that expression of peace and well-being he'd had on his face — a peace and well-being I couldn't take any credit for.

But once eggs settled in my belly, I began to calm down. Hunger could account for my hopelessness, couldn't it? And lack of sleep could make you neurotic, too . . . na? It was a form of torture, after all — just see how crap new parents always looked — so maybe I was making a big deal out of nothing. Karsh *had* to come back at some point (could be he was stuck in traffic even now). There'd be an explanation, and we'd have a laugh about the entire epic night.

I returned to the room. Sankalp. For there he lay, on his side of the bed. I moved in closer to where he rose and fell in a sea-deep slumber, the sun now up and away, a blinding hot-air balloon in the window beyond.

Something in me gave then: He wore his baby face when he slept; I'd seen it in Radha's photo albums, from which his father had been neatly snipped out. Actual photographs, in soft cushy books, protected by sticky yellowing sheets curling off the edges.

Lying here now, he looked like my Karsh again. So familiar it was almost difficult to see him.

I must have been staring hard, because his eyes suddenly fluttered open.

—Already ready? he asked sleepily.

—I made the free breakfast, I said softly. —You know Mom's going to ask.

I sat tentatively on the edge of the bed.

—You were out like a log when I got back last night, he said.

So Gopal had kept mum?

—Over the lag at last, I lied. —So . . . I didn't hear from you last night?

Karsh yawned a little too long. —Oh. Yeah. I knew you needed your sleep. Didn't want to wake you in case you'd finally found it.

—Yeah. It's just your phone was switched off, so I was a little worried.

He didn't say anything. Maybe this was too much brainwork for him so early in his day?

—So what did you guys end up doing? I asked, yawning a little too nonchalantly as well, as if I was already bored with his reply.

—Oh, not much. Just hung out a while with the crew — a couple more DJs joined . . . got some Bombay duck at Soul Fry . . .

—Gopi girl eats duck?

—It's a fish, Dimple.

—Still. Isn't that illicit or something?

—Gokulanandini wasn't there. She hurried off home soon after you left.

—*Hare'd* off, you mean?

I was trying to bait him to tell the truth, but unfortunately keeping it taunt-free wasn't my forte. Karsh, who'd looked about to say something, decided against it.

—And then? I attempted.

—And then . . . nothing. And then I came back.

—Wow. I didn't even hear you. Or feel you . . .

—Yeah, well. I was pretty wired, so I just listened to some tunes, worked on my set. Hung out at the pool café for a while. I guess I just needed a little quiet time.

He clearly hadn't been in the environs of that banging bhangra wedding. But why was he lying?

And why wasn't I calling him on it? I supposed as crazy as his ISKCON excursion seemed to me, dishing that I'd jumped the barrier onto curfewed Juhu sand and stalked him would perhaps come off a tad more bats. And something about the way he'd looked there had seemed so private, even in that devotee-jammed arena. I didn't feel like I could enter that space just yet. I wasn't sure there'd be room for me.

—The sound of the sea . . .

His voice drifted. And here, in a room with just us two, I felt suddenly claustrophobic. I jetted into the bathroom for fear my face revealed too much, took a breath — and my eyes fell on a spa voucher on the counter.

I could do with a little Ayurvedic cleansing, I decided. When I went back into the bedroom, I pulled the cover up to his chin; his lids were slipping.

—Have some more quiet time, then, I whispered.

He was already out like a light.

*　*　*

Luckily, the spa had a slot for me. I vanished into a cavelike room by the pool where over the next couple hours I was kneaded and rubbed and oiled and scrubbed into a submissive bliss, tinged with sentiments of a scurrilous nature. Overactive brain sinking rapidly to a restful pulsatory nest between my legs, I found myself deciding Karsh's deception back in the room had been minimal; after all, I'd hidden something from him, too — and there were far seedier facts we could be covering up from each other than ashram-frequenting ones.

Asha, the masseuse, expertly twisted my . . . earlobes. If Karsh and I were having so much trouble hearing each other, I thought now, perhaps we should steer clear of speaking altogether, blissfully submit as well. . . .

I'd let his secret go — couples were allowed lives outside of each other, weren't they? As long as they spent enough time *inside* each other, I concluded.

Ahhhsha! Bum massage!

Enlightenment struck: We should have sex! Lots of it!

Asha pulled at my toes as if agreeing. The most beneficial of unions: And me and Karsh, we had to wholeheartedly meet halfway — all the way — in other realms as well. We needed an adventure! Flashbulb: I suddenly had an idea, thanks to a wise wee wing-fixing wizardress, of an outing that would feed us both visually and sonically — a return to our roots, in a sense. I couldn't wait to share it with him.

*   *   *

Post-Ayurvedic massage and wash-and-blow-dry and speedy, stunning — and strikingly inexpensive — eyebrow threading, I arrived back to Room 212 in the most sprightly of humors. Despite my spa shower, I still reeked of jasmine, oil lending a crimson sheen to my now superstraight hair, Sparklehorse tank top gorily stained, eyebrows curved in what I hoped was a knowing and wise and sexy arch, and body so knee-weak unknotted from all that head to toe tending-to . . . I was ready for a little knowing-wink arching action with my man.

Karsh was up — against his laptop screen. His noise-cancellation headphones were inserted firmly in his ears.

Undeterred, I sauntered Ayurvedically up, seductively plucking one plug out and reenacting the nether-region-butterflies-inducing lobe probe and inner-canal caress magoddesseuse Asha had just to me ministered.

Karsh glanced up, startled. —What the $f-$?

Okay, maybe not so seductively, then. I removed my auricle-exploring index and flopped down on the armchair beside him.

—Oh. Sorry.

He was already back to staring at his seventeen-inch monitor; I would've taken half that in a heartbeat. At a glance, I could see a Word doc, social media page, two websites, and several downloads in progress, all open and active on-screen. He left the one head-phone dangling and, without peeling eyes away, asked, more gently this time:

—Can I borrow your ears for a moment?

—Sure that's all you want? I attempted again. No sordid response forthcoming, I backtracked. —I mean, you sure you don't want the eyes? They're a little more in tune.

He did that vague smile-smirk-snort — the *I'm not really listen-ing, but you must have said something funny (at least to you)*-a-roo.

—Which do you like better? he asked earnestly now. —DJ Cosmological Redshift or Blueshift?

—I don't know either. What kind of music?

—No! I'm testing out new DJ names . . . and ensuring no one's nabbed the domains while I'm at it. But I'm torn — redshift's an increase in wavelength, seen in an expanding universe, which is cool . . . but Doppler blueshift's experienced when a source nears its observer, like a siren. Which is pretty sweet, too.

—But you've got a DJ name, I said, confused.

—I've been thinking about what Ravi said. Gulab Jammin' . . . well, it's kind of cheesy, isn't it? Using a food for a DJ name?

—Not as cheesy as using a food adjective to denigrate a food-inspired moniker.

—Dimple, seriously. How often do you see people trying to be cute with food puns when they write about India? Like *currying favor*, or *a spicy masala of comedy and drama* movie reviews. It's overdone, and kind of reductive, given our rich tapestry of heritage and culture to draw from.

—I don't see how Redshift's drawing from our rich cultural heritage, I pointed out. —Why don't you try DJ Indus Valley Civilization or DJ Satyagraha AKA Passive Resistance?

He still wasn't laughing. I touched his arm.

—Look, you don't have to do everything Ravi says, I said gently. —Or some random corporate sponsor. You're your own person. Aren't you?

—Of course I am! But Ravi may be up for giving me another chance if I show him I'm committed . . . and changing DJ GJ is something I've been toying with for a while now anyway. So any suggestions, or just the usual sarcasm?

I decided to go satyagraha myself and passive(aggressive)ly resisted a comeback. I was doomed if I had one, done-for if I didn't. But I did have a serious answer.

—How about Karsh?

—Huh?

—What about *Karsh*?

—That doesn't mean anything!

—Of course it does! I cried. —And when people get to know you, your name will be identified with a certain sound.

I was nearly bouncing in my seat with sincerity. —Speaking of which. I think you're stressing too much about replacing your bhangra beats. It was the wrong venue, that's all — I mean, that's what made you who you are in New York!

—There's no scene for that kind of music, he said. —No one hip drops bhangra here.

—For frock's sake, Karsh! You want to know what the problem with the Indian hipster is?

He raised a brow.

—They don't know what's really cool.

He gave me a *huh?* look. I was probably giving myself one as well; where'd that come from? Then I remembered: cowboy hat, crinkly smile. A vague sense of secrecy wisped through my system.

—I know this music's not for people like you, Karsh began slowly. —The music of now, of the future.

—Karsh, it's not like I've got Gregorian chants on my playlist.

—We're in a different place now. The same rules don't apply.

I wondered for a moment if he meant the music, or us.

—But I thought the whole goal was — pardon the platitude — to be true to yourself? I said, unsure now of what was going on. *People?*

—But how to be true changes with the times, with technology. And maybe that's what makes it so hard for you to accept this part of my journey, Dimple.

—What? What does?

—You just don't really . . . change with the times. Keep up.

—What's that supposed to mean? Is this a race?

—I mean, let's see. How long did it take you to change from film?

—I didn't *change* from film. I supplemented.

—Of course you didn't *change*. And why did you supplement?

—For convenience, portability, postability . . .

It was also nearly required as part of the NYU program, but I kept that bit mum.

—And if you use modern technology for convenience, he went on, —are these photos quote *true* anymore? Or has Canon become your corporate sponsor, compromising your vision in the process?

I guess he meant my Digital Rebel, not my single-lens heirloom.

—Um, it's not like Canon's wiring me any funds for my work. And how did this become a conversation about my authenticity as a photographer?

—The second it became one about mine as a musician.

—But I'm not doing it to . . . to sell cars or eighty proof, Karsh! Or to kowtow to someone I barely know —

—Ravi just wants me to make a living here, and some of that might come from sponsors. This is a country with millions living below poverty level, Dimple. Money isn't necessarily evil; it's just necessary.

—I don't think the people singing to sell deodorant are down there. I think they're sticking their heads pretty far out above poverty level, actually, I remarked. —It's an expensive hobby, music, after all — all that gear, rehearsal spaces, transport.

Karsh suddenly looked up at me.

—*Hobby?*

—Look, I said, fumbling, —I don't mean it's evil; I just mean . . . art. Love. Not everything's about money.

He stared at me coldly, unflinching. Siberia.

—That's easy to say, he finally replied, —when your parents are footing your tuition bills.

I couldn't speak. I mean, they were.

—Dimple. We've got to switch hotels by noon, he said, too calmly now. —To Lands End. The Centauride, at Bandstand. I don't want to run up a late checkout fee here; Ravi's contacts have already been generous enough. He's organized a car . . . so I can bring along your stuff if you have something else you'd like to do with your day? I'm going to be working and, hopefully, meeting up with him and some music folk till late to come up with a new game plan.

The categorical *get lost* inherent in that superficially helpful non-question rang loud and clear. I rose from the chair, not daring look back lest I'd left an Ayurvedic bloodstain behind.

—Okay, sure. I was just going to ask if you wanted to come to Chor Bazaar with me, I said dully. —They've got some great vinyl stalls there apparently. . . .

I trailed off. It wasn't just about the vinyl, I wanted to say. It was about him and me having a gallivant, hanging out, finishing each other's sentences — he filling my ears and me his eyes with what some would call an unmissable Bombay experience. But instead, what came out of my bungling beak, dictated by my pathologically caustic soul, was:

—But of course, no self-respecting DJ shops at Chor Bazaar. What would Ravi say?

—Rhythm House, he corrected me vaguely. There wasn't even an undercurrent of contempt to hold on to. —Now, if you'll excuse me, I have to get to work on my track. Ravi needs me to prove I'm serious. And, believe me, I am.

—We must not take ourselves too lightly, nor too seriously, I advised, relying on the überwords of another as my own seemed to be birthing all breach.

But Karsh wasn't listening anymore. Or looking.

There was still red oil all over my head from my Ayurvedic experience. Had he not noted he now had a titian-haired girlfriend?

And then it hit me that Karsh didn't really see me anymore.

And I was tired of hearing him.

If you didn't share a sense of humor with a person — your boyfriend, no less — or a soundtrack . . . or a seascape . . . or a bed . . .

Well, I wasn't going to share Chor Bazaar with him.

* CHAPTER 20 *
L'Arrivée d'un Train en Gare

Leaping onto an about-to-depart Bombay train was a bloody good way to get over myself. Elevated heart rate beating out the broods, realizing my story was but one of a gazillion . . .

After a superfilmi swaggering cowgirl entry, breathless and giddy — and feeling as though I'd been granted a second lease on life — I looked smugly around at my traveling compatriots for some kind of recognition of my triumph. I, Dimple Rohitbhai Lala the First, at last was upright on a Bombay *train* — alive!

However, no one blinked twice upon my intact, if slightly wobbly, materialization in the compartment. I guess they were also on a Bombay train. Alive. Possibly for the hundredth time that week.

By good fortune, it seemed I'd entered the women's section of the Western Line. This brown line route (as it appeared on my chai-smudged, Akasha-printed, *Paris Spleen*–screened map) was filled with variations on that hue, down to the rows of chappaled and brown-ankled sneakered feet that skidded, then settled on the reverberating floor of the train as it lurched forward in a rocketlike hurtle-gurdy.

I desisted worrying about the welfare of my derrière and swapped to stressing about that of my own brown-suede-shade extremities, so vulnerable in Birks. But Bombay feet (and rickshaws) seemed to have bat radar, veering a hair away from but never upon my terrorized American toes, which were still, I saw now, sporting remnants of blue crackle polish from when Amanda and I had done them up one rainy riveted dorm night.

Grant Road, Grant Road, Grant Road: I beseeched my ears to tune in for this call, closest stop to Chor Bazaar.

As we chugged into the sunnily committed day, I clutched camera bag to pelvis, folding my map into "Loss of a Halo" so as not to scream lost cause to my fellow passengers.

I was in the standing section, separated from the seated zone (in which several people were standing nonetheless) by a silver-barred window over a blue half wall. In that sedentarea, saried, blue-jeaned, salwar-kameezed, and mostly ponyplaited SPF-8-max women and girls packed the sky-hue seats, clutching handbags, shopping bags, cell phones, the scintillating aquas and santras of their attire glimmering against the slippery shades of the compartment.

The train halted at Mahim Junction. A bevy of vendors approached it, offering *coffeeteacoffeetea* and a cornucopia of vegetables, which seemed to go down a storm with a cluster of ladies at the back.

After the next set of passengers stepped on and off (and I could pride myself on not having been pushed on and off along with them), I let the surprisingly soothing *Grant Road* mantra go backseat hum in my brain, and took in my surroundings again.

In that matter of moments, those same saried ladies had gotten down to work: chattering animatedly, chopping, peeling, grating chunks of okra, aubergine, ginger — an economical way to get dinner, or I guess lunch, started whilst in transit.

A silvery cadence caught my upturning eye: the intermittently fanned ceiling of the train compartment was adorned with myriad handrails, dancing in sun-spindrifting harmony, a few of the steadier semicircles clasped by tawny hands. I lifted camera to eye, to create a ceiling sea whirlpooling about the steadfast fingers of an Indian woman in an ultramarine sari, her gaze towards the grilled window.

I zoomed. The woman was in fact not in a sari, but blue jeans and yellow tee, torso to hips mostly covered by a decussating scarf. She leaned back as if pulling a rein, her dreaming face lifted to a bolt of sun in the glinting compartment. Suddenly, she opened her eyes, met mine. I expected irritation to rent her face, but she just smiled slowly, luxuriously at me, held still for the camera.

I clicked. She nodded, opening and closing her eyes in sync: a catlike benediction. Something about her soporific movements (and the fact she hadn't yelled at me) slowed my senses; I sank into my relief, closing my eyes as well, breath rhythming up with the rattle and roose of wheels to tracks. . . .

Before I knew what was happening, the train had pulled to a stop and I was inelegantly ejected onto the platform on a wave of human commuters.

I was also (and a little absurdly, in terms of timing) doing the Train Dance: shuffle scuffle — *shebam! pow! blop! whiz?* I desisted, stood eye-of-the-storming in the swirl of rushing Bombayites. When it all settled, train doors sealing, I saw the blue-and-white-etched sketch indicating I had indeed been in the Ladies' Coach.

And now, I realized two beats too late, having surely tumbled out my camera-cradling grasp: so was my *Spleen*-screened map.

I felt the first pulse of panic, glanced around to get my bearings.

Neon-lettered signs called out KURLA, GHATKOPAR. Others declared: THANE, DOMBIVLI, KALYAN, AMBARNATH, BADLAPUR, KAR-JAT, KHOPOLI, ASANGAON. Another: SLOWFROM THANE. What the frock was *slowfrom*?

Other panels bilingually filled in the details: 9-car, 12-car, some fast some slow — which took me a minute to realize meant local and express, wasn't a weigh-in on which one to bet on.

Was I going to be late?

For what? I went slowfrom as well, my somewhat pointlessly resumed mantra consoling me about what had seemed a traumatic loss of locus as I realized: Not only did I have nowhere to be at any particular time, but I had no idea how to get nowhere, anyway.

Which meant . . .

I could go anywhere! I could *be* anywhere — nobody knew where I was! (Me included!)

I decided to explore.

Wandering this way — maundering among the multitude, holding my own pace and simply reading the signs — itself felt like traveling. I loved that sensation at Grand Central as well, with its dome of indoor stars. I wondered now if I could find a visual angle, a link between the two stations. Track Bombay and New York together.

I passed through an area where a zillion commuters were all camped out on makeshift mats, crunching papadums and chevda, slurping cola and chai. They seemed to be slowfrom as well. The outdoorsy picknicky vibe reminded me of staying up all night with Gwyn for Arcade Fire tickets that summer before college, singing "Deep Blue" to keep awake.

My Grant-ra was immediately replaced by another loved number from that epic band:

Strange how the half-light . . . can make a place new . . .

The station was inhabiting this half-light on a grand scale.

Exhale: a witting sinking to swimming pool bottom. A cathedraling sense of the candlelit, the sacred.

It was difficult picturing the brilliance of the day outside. Though it wasn't exactly cool here (despite the whirring of a few precariously placed fans), it *appeared* cool, and my perspiration eased off.

Were these the train lines my parents had taken to med school back in the day? Where my mother's rain-lengthened sari had once been trapped by the door, and my father — who'd been working up the nerve to declare his love wonderfully too soon that monsoon afternoon — watched from the platform, dismayed as it disappeared into the distance, an emerald flag to a seemingly unattainable land?

My practical mind kicked in. Unsure whether I could leap back on a train — and unclear as to which unattainable land I longed to attain — I figured I'd see if I needed to buy a new pass.

In the north wing, I got in line. I was up next, when I realized: I didn't want to go anywhere.

This was my destined destination, the station itself.

And I also realized: Today I loved being on my own.

So I turned away from the booth, took in the ticketing area. And suddenly recognized the space.

I was in VT, Bombay's Victoria Terminus. Well, now CST: Chhatrapati Shivaji Terminus, as the overhead sign proclaimed. In Mumbai.

To have ended up here, I must have been on the Harbour Line, the blue line, rather than the Western. And I felt tangled up in that hue now, realizing the deeper reason I'd recognized the terminus. I didn't want to think about death when all around me was Life. But who hadn't seen that image of the young rucksacked gunman in cargo pants and Versace T-shirt striding in that '08 day and gunning down all those passengers, those would-be passengers — who could never have foreseen the journey they'd be forced on, fated to. Blood on these marble floors.

But once red, the room was now, I noticed, cast in a bluish haze — a spirit fog.

A blue room. I was in a blue room. Was it my gaze tinting the space, worldviewed through a deep blueshift? But just the hue the doctor ordered, and this one steeped in such beauty it spun my sadness round to something softer, more wistfully alive.

I sunk myself in that shade and found myself experiencing a surprisingly serene moment in the midst of the symphonically human hustle-bustle. Stone swerved, embellished with flora and fauna. Pillars plumed up to the domed sky, flowering into arches in a symmetrical arboreal flow. A Roman-numeraled clock echoed the spidery script of the ceiling architecture, time uttered in an outlier's tongue.

I craned my neck farther — to be met by an astronomical ceiling beaming heavenly-body bigness back down at me.

I kept craning . . . nearly back-bending now, to meet that sky with my eyes. Though a sense of blue pervaded the space, upon a closer look, it felt as if other hues had *swallowed* blue. Neelkanth.

The stars were faded — chartreuse nearly, awash in sea green.

Oh, so quiet. I unlidded Chica Tikka. This was the shot I wanted of Victoria Terminus. Something huge had happened here — the wished-upons and the wasted, the blink of the dead emitted in this celestial haze, time-traveling back to us through the light-years.

And this was my link to Grand Central. What I'd wished for — sankalp: the starry night of the terminus ceiling bridging two great cities. Prone seemed the only way to catch these stars. But I wasn't sure what would happen if you lay down in a train station. Especially this station. Would they call in the medics? Or would you get trampled alive when a particularly popular train began boarding?

Or arrested?

Only one way to find out.

I dropped to a squat . . . then lay flat on my back.

Lifted Chica Tikka to eye . . .

Something about the roof softened from this angle, evoked bedding, plush-studded mattressing to sky-sink into. The greenish haze went bluer. Free-falling — but upwards into upended hull, the cupped hand of that constellation.

Shifting the frame opened a portal. Hillbacked hours cloudspotting with Gwyn rushed back to me, stargazing backyard sleepovers. Childhood afternoons on the shag rug, tipping the room upside down in our collective imagination: tiptoeing cross-ceiling, a chandelier's cavalier flip, a somersault of bonsais balancing clay pots on tentacled bottoms.

I was swept by a piercing longing for that feeling again: the company of a kindred spirit. My commonsensical mind told me I had Karsh, family, friends galore. And hadn't I just been singing the praises of solitude? But there'd been such a familial freedom, an ease and meld, thrill as well — a discovering, and instinctive scripting of the world we were living — in a childhood friendship that simply wasn't comparable to anything since.

I ached for Gwyn. Someone who'd shared that childhood sky. With whom, beneath it, enveloped by it, she'd, we'd grown — flown the unknown. She who could see what I saw, and show me a thing or two, too.

And this sky, here. Now. Wow.

Frock, it's beautiful. . . .

—Very, Indie Girl.

The voice, near familiar, entered me like steam on a blustery day, instantly launching a kindled tingle up my spine.

I turned. I only needed lower my gaze a touch, as the bearer of that warming, wondering accordance was quite tall, tawnily brawned.

Even at a nanoglance, I knew that wide-brimmed silhouette. He tipped the hat at me now. Then, eyes uncovered — those blue-brown grey-green eyes the shade of stirred-up sea — he stepped towards me.

CHAPTER 21

Superdensecrushload

Cowboy donned not boots but Birks. My mouth foolishly agogged, and I was struggling to rise when he fell-swooped beside me, his own SLR in hand, and lay down.

—All alight in the Star Chamber, he said now, and smiled. —So you've found one of my favorite places in this city.

A languidly commanding near-British Indian boarding school accent, like some of Mallika's crowd had — except his was sonorously shot through with twang. I hadn't noticed at the airport.

Our heads aligned, lying down.

—It's already one of mine, too, I said. —Cowboy.

—At your service. Almost didn't recognize you with the new 'do.

I touched my head: still slick. Asha and that Ayurvedic experience seemed miles of moments away. . . .

Camera balanced on belly now, he crossed his arms behind his head — as if he were recumbent in a lazy-day field instead of on the floor of one of the busiest train stations in Asia.

He pointed up with a mischievous grin. —On a clear night, they say you can see Orion. . . . I'd lie like this in Ooty. Years ago. The stars were so many there . . .

—. . . was barely room for sky, I said, nodding as I recalled a hill station visit many years ago with my family.

His grin expanded, gaze still up. I tried to keep mine there, too, but kept sneaking a side peek at the way the little parentheticals wrinkled gleefully around his mouth when he smiled.

—Far preferable to queuing for tickets, no? A whole other kind of superdensecrushload.

—Superdensewhat?

—The term invented to describe the sheer numbers of people here during rush hour.

—Superdensecrushload — I love that! I cried. —So cosmic. Romantic. Maybe people who fall madly in love in train stations should get their star charts checked against *this* sky.

—Absolutely. Love's like transit, isn't it? So much of it's anticipation, and the traveling's the point — sometimes it's even best when you never get there, or don't even know where you're going. Just the direction . . .

It seemed perfectly natural we were already discussing the locomotion of love. Conversations got intimate fast when you were lying down.

I tapped my camera bag. —I was just making flying saucers a minute ago. Letting my flash hit those glinty bits. It's so amazing up there. . . .

—You know what's just as amazing? What's *below* our feet. Well, backs. Somewhere just about here, on the site of Bori Bunder, lie the remains of the temple of Mumbadevi, the city's patron saint, goddess of the Koli fisherfolk, Bombay's first inhabitants — for whom the metropolis is named. Mumbai.

—Frock, I whispered. —So the beginnings of Bombay itself lie just beneath us?

—Yes, ma'am. Legend has it the temple was built by Mumbaraka, a giant who ransacked the city at the time. The Kolis prayed to Brahma; he birthed from his own body an eight-armed goddess who knocked the giant for the punch. Mumbaraka built the temple for her, begged her to take his name. Mumbadevi symbolizes Mother Earth; some say she has no mouth.

—Mother Earth. Well, I suppose so, if she's down there.

—No longer. Except her energy. They've got the goddess in a new temple in Bhuleshwar, by Zaveri Bazaar — the diamond market. *New* being a relative term in this town, of course.

He lay there with an athletic ease, a sinewy lion at rest, hat half-tipped across his forehead. Space seemed to give, make room for him. I usually felt I was bumping up against it. Both inner and outer.

But not at the moment. At the moment, everything fit.

Cowboy was tall for an Indian. White, pink, noise — a colonialist interference in his geneaology? But his burnished skin belied that . . . and then his hazy eyes belied that skin. In fact, every layer I arrived at seemed undone by the next.

A spectacular perfectly circular birthmark bobbed above his left nostril. My right. I suddenly felt like touching it.

I guess I liked examining things so closely . . . because I was a photographer? My sidelong was getting a little full-on, though, so I swung my eyes back up. But not before he'd met my gaze for one rimple in time.

—They say the goddess will grant your heart's desire if you ask her sincerely, Cowboy whispered now.

—Even if you lie on your back?

—As long as you tell the truth on your stomach.

That open-prairie sand dune Doon School type accent rendered his comment even more . . . cheeky.

He was staring at me. I wondered if he was mind reading.

He nodded, sideways. —Go on. I won't watch.

—Wha—?!

—Make your wish.

Ah.

—You're covered, he added. —If the goddess is out, you've got all those stars as backup.

Your heart's desire.

Stargazing upon a goddess in a station built for a queen . . .

I wanted to roll onto my side and face him, my unexpected accomplice.

And then, something very strange happened. Though the adjacent trains tracked along my vertebrae and commuter footfalls thudded quietly in my belly, from above and below: a lush engulfing silence. And within that silence, an inner shift — a psychic wall sliding open to reveal a vault, a passage, another room. A shortcut to a long road.

An opening.

It struck me then I wasn't wishing for anything, had been so lost in the moment, I wasn't lost at all.

And then I realized my wish had already been granted. In recalling Gwyn, hadn't I also called upon someone to kin with?

I turned now to stare at Cowboy. And caught him staring at me. The same way I'd once-upon fallen into that book of Ansel Adams photos, catalyzing, sparking the idea that this was what I wanted to do with my time, my life — an immersion so complete, I lost sight of page, image, printed word — a fall more like flight, a flight more like crash-landing in the very heart of the matter . . .

In that way, I fell now into those eyes.

In those eyes, a catch of tiny Dimples bobbed, unshored.

I fell . . . towards myself?

—Hey! Ye kya ker raha hain? Utho, utho!

We both turned, startled, up to find we'd finally inspired a reaction. A somewhat official-looking man (upper pocket pens; pants and shirts same color) was wagging an admonishing finger windshield wiper–like over both our faces. It wasn't clear whether the problem was the cameras, our position, or my train of thought — but it was clearly imperative we move.

I got up first, glanced back at Cowboy. The stars etched on tile below him splintered out with a confident velocity, turning him into a kind of urban angel for a moment. I reached my hand back down to him, my coconspirator in supine single-reflex crime. He took it gently, but rose completely of his own accord.

We exchanged complicit smiles — even with our chastiser's

glare upon us — then brushed off our jeans, kicked into our Birks, packed up our SLRs. Strangely dissimilar twins, we exited in a comfortable silence, wending our way through the crowd towards the entrance/exit. I could feel the heat from Cowboy's palm hovering an inch off my back as he guided me.

Out to the sidewalk, and a heavier, smoggier chaleur. Throngs, saried and suited, gathered by the red-lit sign hawking more destinations: *Panvel, Titwala.*

Bandra!

The day's brightness struck us like a flashbulbed mirror; it was difficult to see in so much light, pupils shrunk to pinpoints. I turned to Cowboy now, a silhouette against the sun.

—That was so beautiful. . . . It's hard to imagine what happened here just a few years ago.

He nodded. —'08. It was crazy. First they crept in through that little fishing village . . .

—Cuffe Parade.

—Exactly. Then they hit VT — this station — Café Leopold, two taxi explosions, at Vile Parle . . .

—And . . . how do you say it? Wadi Bunder.

—Yes. Why do you know so much about it?

—I dunno, I said. —Why do you?

—I was here.

—You were in Bombay at the time?

—I was *here* here. About to board a train, in fact. It was a very, very close call.

I swallowed hard, digesting this.

—And you've come back, I said finally. —Aren't you terrified? I mean, you nearly died!

—Yes, I nearly died, he quietly replied. —But, on the other hand, I completely lived.

That was a way of looking at it.

—You're very brave, I said now. He shrugged.

—I guess I'm revisiting some places that were very painful for me back then. I . . . things changed a lot after that. In a way, it's my first time here with no agenda, no timetable. Unaccountable — nowhere to be, and perhaps no one to be with.

Perhaps?

—Have you been away long? I asked.

—Feels it. I suppose I'm just trying to find my way back. Back to Bombay. And part of that's . . . running into those rooms. I tend to step right into the fear, the pain — it becomes something different then.

He glanced back at the terminus then again to me. —You can reenvision, rewrite it. Shift borders and move on. Look at you — you lay down for your art. You don't have the usual bounds.

My art. I liked how that sounded; that's how it had felt.

—I've been thinking a lot about borders, I told him. —Dichotomies. Especially now that I'm in India.

—International borders? Cultural?

—I thought that's what it'd be about. But turns out it's more . . . innerspatial. Intergalactic. Borders between people, art, life, past, present. It just seems so narrow to limit it to your ethnic background. Sure, it's a part of it. But the number of times someone's asked me where I'm from . . . as if that's the answer to *everything*. Do you get that, too?

He laughed, nodding.

—And sometimes, once you name it, I went on, —you're *stuck*. It can be tricky feeling free when you're pegged down by all these coordinates.

I didn't know where all this was coming from, but here it was . . . and it felt like a revelation to be uttering it. Especially to such rapt, wide-brimmed attention.

—You're a daughter, a sister, a friend, a student, a slacker, I said. —You're your job, your project, your major. Immature for your age, too old for your years . . . You know, it's so wonderful being anonymous today.

—I've been having that kind of day, that kind of stay, as well, Cowboy replied. —It's not a desire that's easy to explain to —

—. . . those who know your name, address, e-mail. Three-digit security code. Your parents, your family, your friends.

For some reason, I didn't say *boyfriend*.

—Does anyone know you're here right now? he asked me now.

—Like, existentially speaking, or meaning at the train station?

—Same thing, we both said. We both laughed then. It felt good to laugh.

When was the last time Karsh and I had *laughed*?

—No, I replied. —I guess not. I mean, even *I* didn't know I'd be here.

I didn't mention my parents would be very nervous indeed about my proximity to the sites of any kind of attacks, however long ago; it didn't seem very Indie Girl. And *nobody* could know I'd braved a Bombay train. Especially Karsh.

—And it feels?

—Kind of cool, I admitted. He nodded, kicked a pebble from a Birk, tilted his hat.

—I got an idea, he said. —How long are you here?

—Not long.

—Okay. For not long. If you're looking for a new way to see yourself, to redefine your place . . . maybe you have to —

—Change the address?

—Exactly. Let's make a deal, Indie Girl.

I could feel where he was headed, and it was thrilling.

—Yeah. Let's.

Freeing . . .

—You're Indie Girl.

—You're Cowboy.

—We don't worry about who we are, what our names are, what they call us —

—Where we're from, where we're going —

—What we're doing next —

—What we did before —

—Unaccountable —

—I'm not counting —

—Accountable to no one —

—Even ourselves.

He offered his hand. —For the next however many not-long days, you and me, we live in the now —

I stuck my own out and shook his. —The out of frame.

A warm grip, a stronghold. He hesitated.

—Listen. I guess I don't know where I'm off to in the big picture anymore . . . and I'm kind of in between places at the moment . . . but I *was* going to jump in a cab to Cuffe Parade now. Part of my running into those rooms project.

He stepped off the curb to hail one now, but his eyes were on me.

—Not to break the rule already, but a technical question, he said then. —Were you on your way somewhere?

And I don't know why, but I only wanted to be on my way to where he was going. And what could happen in a licensed taxicab anyway?

I pulled my ticket out of my pocket, tore it in half — in *two*. I handed him one.

Fast train, slow; 9-car, 12. We'd gone further without them.

I told him, —You know. I dropped the map.

He opened the door of the taxi, gesturing me in. Once seated, he looked me steady in the eyes.

—I'm so glad you did, he said.

*   *   *

While Cowboy instructed the driver, I turned back window-ward . . . and was bowled over. I'd been so busy exploring the inside of the terminus, I'd forgotten it had an outside at all.

In one lingering glance, this:

The entire incredible edifice was bathed in a rosy, nearly brick-and-cobble Tribeca light, a Pink City glow from the settling day. It appeared an arched and angled, friezed and reliefed, boisterously balustraded birthday cake bursting forth from all its sandstoned, limestoned, marble-wood-brass-iron facades with elegant last-minute restraint. Wishing-candle-lit from within, the station called to mind Jaipur palaces, the Gothic and even Gotham, a meld of influences, human and even animal. Stone emboldened the walls, gargoyled, monkeyed, rammed, elephantined, owled, chameleoned — an inquisitive jungle marveling down at the manic migratory human zoo below.

Out of frame. I could barely take the whole thing in.

The entrance gate we'd exited from was crowned by a lion. Tiger. Peacock . . . *windows*: Oh my.

Had I died and dropped to heaven?

Humans were amazing. They could make things! I wanted to make things. Beautiful things.

I *wanted.*

It was only with this side, then backwards, glance, well after we'd stepped into this taxi now slooping south along Dadabhai Naoroji Road, that I realized: By my internal women's compartment arrival here, I'd bypassed the outside entirely, gone straight to the heart — maybe for the first time in my life.

Like Cowboy and I'd just done.

I turned back to him, to the here.

—I can't believe we met again, I said.

He smiled. —After eight hundred years. Believe it.

* CHAPTER 22 *

Wave

We got out at Cuffe Parade. The day was on a downglow, and something in us had gone quiet as well.

I wondered how it would feel to see the very unsuspecting shore where those young men had rowed up, oars gouging a near-silent rift through waves that would stretch, staggering and shuddering through the city for that eternal hellish night.

I tried to remember where I was when it happened. Had I seen it first on the news, online? A roaring image of the Taj in flames, half dragon, half stone. The thought: not possible, not again, not there. But, tragically: possible, here, again. That deep hole that had sundered me as a smaller girl — when the double towers of my own city had crashed volcanically down . . .

I braced myself to feel it all over again as we exited the taxi.

And here we were, stepping off into that very space.

The world was surprisingly muted here, just off the main road. Dusky hulks of beached fishing boats rose up before us, cuttering the view of the sea behind into slight moon-tipped swerves.

—This way, Cowboy gestured, or said, I wasn't sure. I followed him around the prow of a sand-dug dinghy, and we began to wind through the little fishing village.

All was hazy with grain and rust, warping wood, and the shadowy skin of the Koli fisherfolk who wove in near silence through this shipped maze. It felt, as it often did from my plastic, price-tagged American perspective, that we'd stumbled upon a ghost town of sorts — though dredged up still evoking a sense of being under, currenting us gently in. Cowboy took out a lighter, thought better of it, then gestured for me to hand him my cell phone; I did, and he lit the way with it. We wound down a silty passage, prowed and sterned with the sides of sea vessels, a city built of boated walls and twists of tarp sky. Underwater sensation again, till suddenly round a curve, this amidships artery tillered out onto a scant stretch of beach.

From the way Cowboy stopped and stared at the water, I knew it was here. Exactly here.

Submerged scatterings of Koli conversation filtered through the air. A smattering of rocks pitched seaward. Upon these humps, here and there, fishermen sat. We sloped farther down the beach. Scrolls of nets tumbled on the sand to our side, straining with what looked like heavily luminous stones. Off to the right, the coast curved away, the lights of Nariman Point flicking like star shards in the distance.

And before us: the sea. That sea.

Rock the boats. All those little lights and buoys . . .

I wondered what the fisherman just behind us — a ghostly Dadaji gazing towards that ever-elusive horizon — was thinking. Or maybe less thinking, more feeling. The sea must never leave his limbs, I imagined, like a surfer could likely discern the roaring tug of reckless water, even on dry land.

Earthed mermen and mermaids. I wondered if they dreamed seascapes, lungs still salt-blown, sleeping eyes flooded with water, flecked with silver scales, a dream that rocked slowly as it unreeled.

Then again, maybe there were more practical concerns that animated their night visions than that. Money owed and borrowed, sick kids, dowries. Arguments, to-do lists.

But still. To have found your sea self — in one of the most congested, peopled, urban centers of the world. Even I felt a kind of liquidizing in my own limbs; floaters — we all started that way, but it was pretty boggling to be only a couple minutes off an auto-buzzing Bombay street and to feel so cradled by water.

Completely contrary to my expectations, standing here at Cuffe Parade, I felt no fear, no black hole in my gut, no doom-mongering sense of the sunk state of humanity.

From the corner of my eye, I caught Cowboy's slouchy but rapt ocean gaze, hands hanging loose at his sides.

It hadn't occurred to either of us to take a photograph here; it didn't feel right, to the point I hadn't thought of it at all. It felt funny to see us both cameraless — almost as if we were naked. Good naked.

My own gaze lost its askancity entirely and I just took him in. He was mostly shadow, but I detected a reverence in even his relaxed stance. My usual hunger to run and throw my arms around this world (begging forgiveness on some level) was replaced with a softer desire for a more subtle embrace: to sit beside a sleeping child — but not hearken too close lest you wake her.

A gentle nod streetward: *Chalo?*

I nodded back. *Let us go then, you and I.*

As we turned, I reached towards one of the great glowing nets, wondering why someone had gone to such lengths to hook-line-sinker a bushel of stones. But when I touched it, the net gave easily, the rocks fell about like air.

—Thermocol, said Cowboy quietly.

—Huh? I said, and translated Hindi English with apparent fluency. —*Styrofoam?*

I had to laugh. Nothing was as it seemed, was what you expected it to be here.

✳   ✳   ✳

—Thank you, Indie Girl, Cowboy said when we were back in a cab again, heading my way and his way, which for part of the path, he claimed, would be the same.

—No. Thank *you*, I replied. —For sharing that with me. It couldn't have been easy.

—Are you kidding? It couldn't have been easier.

The experience, this day, was written all over my body: My thighs stuck together with sea air. A window gust flung a torrent of hair into my eyes. I could feel my curls had sprung back, knotting like netting themselves; this was going to take more than a hotel-size-bottle of conditioner to undo.

Cowboy gently pushed the springy strands from my eyes. From the scalp, fingers pulling briefly along my roots. I shivered.

—It's pretty crazy, I said, meaning the hair.

—Now, that's the Indie Girl I remember, he replied, meaning the hair.

Our eyes locked. Neither of us meant the hair.

I turned abruptly, focused gaze through pane. We approached the Sea Link, its inverted-Y bones luminously uprearing a ghostly white mast skyward, multilaned traffic deck curving towards Bandra. My pane tautened with those cables, angling us into an open-air dream.

Cowboy left me my space. But this time, the silence was awkward.

Seahorse to Centauride: The taxi pulled up to Bandstand, to Lands End; a towering edifice. I was a little sad when it did. I thanked him and the driver.

I was about to exit when Cowboy suddenly lay his hand on my arm, nodding his head in the direction whence we'd come.

—Remember, he said. —I'm just on the other side.

I wondered why he hadn't pointed out his hood when we were in it.

—I'll wave to you, then, I said, trying on a clumsily cheery grin. —Look for me.

—I have been, he said, so quietly I almost thought I'd misheard him. He lifted his hand from my arm; it stuck a moment to my skin.

—Salt, we said, a unified whisper.

Salt print. I felt strangely halved without his touch . . . though more whole having had it.

—Well, thanks again for the ride, I said, door shut, speaking through the cracked window. —So . . . so long, I guess.

He shook his head, still smiling.

—We'll meet again, he said.

Before I could ask where, when, he was gone, I was gone.

*　＊　*

I lay down to sleep. Or, tried to. Hours later, eyes still peeled, alone in the more-than-queen, less-than-king new hotel bed, I realized I'd been unconsciously running the salt test, touching my skin off and on, a delicious but agonizing ache suffusing me after this intensely long, wide, deep day out.

A trembling in my pocket.

Nine missed calls from Karsh.

And I hadn't missed them.

CHAPTER 23

Old Beginnings

With a mite of misgiving, I showered off my day — all signs of salt, of sea. Then lay back down on the bed . . . and succumbed to insomnia.

She was my most ardent follower, my loyalest companion, and now led me to a state that felt weirdly akin to euphoria — like when gut's hollow but the hunger moves to your heart, decapitatingly levitating your head in the process.

But I was me, of course, so a moment later, this feeling seamlessly dipped into an unmeandering melancholy, capsized me in the deepest blue. It wasn't an entirely unpleasant sensation unless I named it, boxed it up, and judged it. So I named it, boxed it. Judged it.

Time ticked on. I tried breathing *Om*, which made me miss my family, then *Now I wanna be your dog*, which made me miss New York. Thus I found myself chanting *Grant Road*. But the latter resulted in my inner focal point being a pair of sea-haze eyes, which I then struggled to oust from mind's gaze, to replace with another pair of honeyed ones.

This unmeditative tug-of-war was highly unrelaxing.

I tried focusing on my breath. Unfortunately, instead of having a soothing effect, this freaked me out — sounded like the creepy in-ex-halations of another person lying in wait inside my own body.

Click of a key swipe. I dropped decoy lids over my wide eyes, registered Karsh's quiet return to the room. He showered . . . and this time crawled into bed beside me. Had he been back to the ashram? Out with the DJs? Both? Tonight, I found, with my own secret excursion securely spiraling its way into my mystifying DNA, I wasn't really so interested in the answer.

I used to love to watch him sleeping. Dusky mornings at NYU, roommates out of town (or in someone else's bed), as the light fell stripingly from the venetians and he lay there lambent, we lay there entangled, our limbs and scents and breaths indiscernible. Me gazing at him; he'd open his eyes, fill mine with his smile. The opposite, too; me waking to his face, cheek propped in hand propped on elbow, just watching me, enveloping me in the love that great pop songs were made of. Major chords: heart-swelling chorus. *True* rhyming with *blue* and *you* in the most poetic of manners.

And now?

Lying here alone moments before hadn't felt that different from when he was here beside me.

So when the hour came, he still in the depths of rapid eye movement, I slipped out from under the sheets, got changed, and headed down to breakfast.

✳ ✳ ✳

When I returned to the room, Karsh was up and at 'em, head still wet from the multiple-jet-spray showerheads. He glanced up when I walked in.

—Where were you, Dimple? he asked. It wasn't an accusation, which made me feel guilty.

—At breakfast?

—No. I mean yesterday, and last night. I tried you six times.

Nine. Probably best not correct him.

—Oh, sorry, I didn't see. . . . Signals go down around the Sea Link?

He turned to the window, taking in a bit of that bridge now, as if it might nod in confirmation.

—I figured it was high time to get on with my photography, I

✳ 238 ✳

added truthfully. Then, partially (unpluraled person) truthfully,
—So I took a ride around South Bombay . . .

He drew the room-length curtain wider. Kingfishers, kites
swooped in tilting halos, just missing the glazing as inch by inch the
paned wall turned all Link, and that distorted echo of seaface across
the bay. I looked away.

—Great. Show me? Your pics?

When was the last time he'd asked me that?

—Um, they're all on film. Not digital. Anyway, sorry I missed
your calls, I repeated. —What was up?

—I just called . . . he began, and then suddenly turned back
towards the bridge. I busied myself with picking at my cuticles,
which I was pretty sure had evolved precisely for moments like these.
His Linkward gaze made me feel he knew . . . something. But then
he sat on the wide inner sill and faced me. —I wanted to apologize.
I've been really . . . touchy. Out of sorts. Not myself lately. It's like
I've been on drugs or something.

—You kind of have been, I pointed out. I sat down beside him
but a slight distance away. It happened too naturally.

I dared peek through that window now: a stunned silver sky,
slowly steeping in lightning sun. Stories below, the Sea Link eased
widely awake, swarming with traffic, hoisting its cabled sail into the
winging day, and Karsh spoke as it did.

—I've just had a lot on my mind. I guess I didn't realize how
much baggage I've been carrying around about India, about my dad.
I just need another chance. . . .

Was he asking me for one? I softened at this plea.

—And Ravi's going to meet with me later today — maybe give
me that chance. Seems those French dubsteppers dropped out.
Some kind of visa issue, so there may be an opening coming up at
this really happening place in those renovated mills.

—Oh.

—*And,* he added, —I convinced him to give *you* another chance as well. So if you want to come down with me to have a look, shoot the venue, you're more than welcome.

A little out of fear, truth be told, I wanted to see if a chance was all it took. But I couldn't forget my vow: to my work, this city. Myself.

—Thanks, Karsh. Maybe I will, I said gently. —I was going to check out some old-school Bombay today . . . and you could join, too, if you have time before the mill thingy? I mean, if you're available. I was thinking of hitting up Shivaji Park — where my parents got married — and this famous Ganesha temple on the way over. For that anniversary present?

—I'd love to see these places. They're like my parents, too, after all.

Perhaps that's why we were acting so sibling-like lately. In fact, a part of me — and a worryingly big part — could see Karsh as a brother, and without warning, abruptly did. Without the physical element to our relationship, he fell almost too tidily into that category.

And then I understood my new, perhaps deeper motive as far as a joint outing with Karsh was concerned: It wasn't just about my desire to create a new memory with him. A niggling feeling in me was praying a day out with Karsh could come as close to joyfully discombobulating me as it had with my cowboy near-friend near-stranger. Maybe if we had a shared experience, we'd find a bridge back towards each other? And it couldn't hurt to invoke the elephant-headed god of new beginnings to lend a hand (or trunk), could it?

His woeful eyes tipped me off that perhaps he felt the same.

*   *   *

And so it was that we set off for our destination: the Shree Siddhivinayak Ganapati Temple, Prabhadevi, near Shivaji Park.

Sangita, it turned out, was going from Andheri right through Bandra and, ambitiously, eventually, distant (in traffic minutes, not so much miles) Kala Ghoda for some errand I assumed was wedding related. She offered us a ride.

It wasn't driver Arvind but Sangita herself who pulled up before the hotel at the designated hour. It took me a minute to recognize her behind the wheel of the sky-blue Maruti.

—Sangita! I exclaimed through the rolled-down window. —You *drive*? In Bom*bay*?

She shrugged. She looked totally different in the driver's seat. Taller, somehow, even though she was sitting down. No makeup, but skin aglow (or a-sweat), she'd donned faded jeans and a loose button-down shirt, stained red and blue here and there. Her hair was piled in a bobby-pinned tousle on her head, and a pair of magenta heart-framed shades rested on it, like love was on her mind.

About a half hour later, she dropped us off on a mayhemic marg, indicating for us to cross over. Before she drove off, I saw her reaching into her handbag for something — and then lighting it up.

—Was she *smoking*? I asked, incredulous.

—Everyone here's smoking, Karsh laughed bitterly. —Simply by breathing. This has to be one of the most polluted cities in the world!

He relaxed a little, wrapping an arm around me. Somehow, it felt like ages since he'd done that.

—Let her have her fun. It's all over in a week.

—Or maybe, I said, entwining back, —it all begins then?

We continued on foot, crossing multilanes of cars and buses before hitting a riddle of jigsaw sidewalk on the other side, set off by a rusting barrier gate. An army of intrepid phoolwallahs, however, was seated on the street itself, stringing marigolds within finger-sting knee-scrape distance of the whizzing traffic. To our left, sidewalk stalls sold street food and Harry Potter mobile phone cases. To our right, a woolly banyan was tacked up with ads for karate training and Ayurvedic hair oil. A man at tree base sat rolling what looked like laddoos, a few rupee bills secured below his staunch cross-legged knee.

And people, people: a crush of devotees, bouqueted and bin-died and in beads like Sangita's. The street *was* the sacred. No need for pew-kneeling silence: Here, in Bombay, the sacred bleated, bar-gained, honked, haggled, gossiped, and giggled. It loitered, lolled, rushed, strode, shoved, drove, cycled, bullock-carted, and even, as I'd heard in Bandra, break-danced and longboarded (no mean feat on potholed streets).

It even mooed.

A big-eyed bovine face peered out at me now from around the banyan. A saried woman paid the cross-legged man, scooped up one of these ediballs, and fed it to this sacred cow, who'd perhaps sojourned here, Linking Road devotee style, from the middle of that Bandra street.

Was this where all my grandmas had been headed?

—Imagine seeing this in Springfield, Karsh! Animals, humans, gods, all come together like this . . .

—Do I have to? he said, busily squirting antibacterial gel on his palms. —*Springfield's* starting to look like a spiritual retreat now.

—But it's kind of cool, too, no? I insisted. We were going to have a great experience if it killed us! —Just transplant this crowd to the States — what's the equivalent for pilgrimages there? Black Friday sales?

—I dunno. I suppose, in the US, everyone has their own per-sonal journey to take.

—In their own personal car. It's kind of lonely when you com-pare it to the personal journeys everyone takes *together* here.

A sure hand clasped my shoulder. I turned to discover a chubby but vigorous middle-aged saried woman at the other end of it, carrying perhaps what would best be described as fervent flowers. She squeezed past me, shifting Karsh a few inches to the side to do so.

—I'm sorry, do I know you? Karsh said drily, erupting into a coughing fit, I figured on purpose. But she was off.

Sarcasm was definitely catching — but I seemed to be losing mine the more he caught it. Maybe there was a limited supply; I hoped to gods I'd still have some left when I needed it.

Ahead, the pavement widened, spires brightened. Serpentine lines now purposefully joined, human tributaries flowing in one direction, weaving around the chaiwallahs, the coconut splitters, the scattered flower vendors with their single-crate offices. Our joint destination: the arched temple, its gold-tipped orange-flagged skyline peekabooing over the treetops, a billboard, the next building . . .

I aimed my camera. A tsking index appeared in the viewfinder. A guard: horizontal head shake. No photos allowed.

Sidewalk gone pavilion. Scores of devotees temple-entering along the roped-in lanes farther ahead, others exiting, turning back to contemplate it, hands reverentially clasped. We, however, were both staring as a business-suited man now prostrated himself right there on the ground as if before Ganesha himself.

—I guess maybe I just kind of wish I had that, sighed Karsh, eyes fixed on the man.

—Had what?

—That kind of devotion. It must be so nice. To surrender to something.

—Well, I'm sure you do. To music. To . . . love.

—It doesn't feel like a surrender with love. . . .

A glim of hope.

—The other person's just a human, after all, he went on. —With their own baggage and shit to take care of.

—Oh. Thanks.

—I just mean, it's not like surrendering to God, the universe, the cosmos. Something bigger than our tiny twisted lives.

I just stared at him.

—Excuse me, could you hold my camera a second? I think I'm about to swoon.

—Dimple. Don't take everything so personally. It's not all about you.

Well, why the hell not? I mean, Cowboy would never say something like that! He'd probably say . . . the cosmos was embedded in each and every one of the twists of these lives, and it was in human relationships that we could discover the universal, and thus the universe.

Wouldn't he?

I took a couple steps away to hide the tears blindsiding my eyes. I turned my back to Karsh, fiddled with the lens.

I found myself yearning for a sign again, that things were going to be okay.

In my viewfinder a splendid child stood, upturning her face with an all-seeing regard, cheeks glowing in the sea-swollen light. Auburn-veined, the otherwise night thicket of her hair. Her arms brimmed with cellophaned roses.

This child must have seen my tears; her eyes widened, and she offered her tiny hand to me.

I was reaching out to take it, grateful for that angelic extension of friendship — *see? the sacred: everywhere!* — when she abruptly withdrew it, then, in an almost paper-scissors-stone move, palms-upped it, other hand plunking into her hip.

—Didi! Bakshish — khana!

Sister! Money — food!

Oh.

I guilt-o-matically scrounged around my pocket, procuring a

hundred-rupee note for her. She gestured upwards with that paper-scissors-stone palm: clearly paper.

I sighed and dug out another fifty. This was possibly a mistake as an entire slew of rose-vending three-foot-something homo sapiens materialized out of nowhere and began marching ominously towards us.

Well, two.

—Dimple! What are you doing? Karsh whispered. The air rippled thickly, perfumed. I pulled my pockets inside out to reveal there was no more dinero to be had, but the tiny army continued its pungent advance, undeterred.

A couple of people near us (probably natives) shooed them away. And here's where the brazenly bumpshove crowd worked in our favor: We were, within moments, swallowed up by it, rescued from the child vendors . . . and ejected into one of the roped-in lines for the temple. I could glimpse cubbyholes for our shoes, indicating we were close to stepping into the inner sanctum.

Karsh was busily texting away — probably to Ravi. Every now and then, he sneezed. I blessed him.

The pavilion was bedecked with phoolwallahs of every order now. It was like a convention — garlands choochooing chameli; lotus splaying out almost rakishly on offer. Bloomburst effacing the cement environs with sheer rowdy vivacity.

At the entrance, we kicked off our shoes, readying to enter. Karsh gave me a genuine smile now, grouped our footwear tidily together to hand to one of the foot locker men.

New beginnings, new beginnings . . .

I took a breath, took his hand.

Barely across the threshold, I could sense the temple interior aladdining in incense and oils, so flower-powered it seemed constructed of petals in parts. All around us, men, women, and children pressed forth, arms heaped with blossoms. As Karsh valiantly accompanied me towards this den of olfactory overload, it dawned on me: There was one man in my life who'd never let the flowers die in my dorm room. Before those blues could brown, he'd always brought me the next drippingly giddy bouquet.

And here he was, standing beside me.

Actually, here he was nearly keeling over, coughing and sneezing and gasping for *air* beside me. . . .

Choking sounds; even though I was pretty sure his trachea was in the clear, I panicked and Heimliched him . . . but this only made him cough harder. And thus, before even entering the temple of our new beginning, we slid our shoes hastily back on and scrammed.

His attack subsided a little.

—Frock, Karsh! I gasped anxiously. —Are you okay?

It was a little late, but overcome with a deep quick wave of affection, and regret, and guilt (mostly the latter two), I dug into my bumpack, bestowed upon him a Kleenex. He looked gratefully at me, eyes watering.

—Sorry, Dimple. I don't know what happened. But my sinuses really hate it here. I'm really sorry, but I don't think I can go back in.

I tried to pat his back, offer him more tissues.

—It's cool. No . . . issues.

The way out was much quicker than the way in. In moments, we'd ducked out of the line to find ourselves on the pavement by the whizzing traffic. When some vendors came too close with an aloha of garlands, Karsh gestured them urgently away and plunged back into his Kleenex. His eyes dripped thin rivers.

—You're allergic to *flowers?* I asked him, stunned.

—That would appear to be the case.

—But you never seem allergic in New York.

—I think New York flowers are part concrete, he sighed, gazing at me bleary-eyed.

—It's funny, but your whole system seems to find Bombay hard to digest, no? I said, not unkindly. —I mean, you seem to have no resistance here to . . . to outside influence.

We both stood awkwardly around as this morphed into a different exchange.

—I just really feel I should go with what Ravi says, Karsh said quietly. —He knows this turf. And he's taken me under his wing. I want to make him proud. I *should* have made him proud; he had a lot at stake with his faith in me.

—You want to make your father proud, I said, quietly as well. Karsh stared at his phone, but no texts were open. I took his arm. —But just doing whatever Ravi says isn't what would do that. You've got to follow *your* path. I mean, your dad's not even here to see it now, Karsh.

—Thank you, Karsh said. —For pointing that out.

—I don't mean it in a bad way!

—How can you possibly mean it in a good way?

I fumbled.

—I just mean, what would make your father proudest would be you being true to yourself. Even if you end up on the road not taken. Even if no one else would approve of how you got there.

I was starting to get a felonious monk of a twinge that I was now having a slightly different chat . . . with my own conscience. Karsh looked weepy again, but no allergens were in proximity.

—Karsh. You — you have to keep the smile, because you know it's all just an illusion.

—No, Dimple. I think, actually, that my father really *did* die.

I fumbled again. —What I mean is . . . freedom. You need that . . . as an artist. No obstacles.

—There's too *much* freedom! Karsh cried. —In fact, I think the opposite's true: I think you need some kinds of limits as an artist, some constraints to work against. They're not obstacles; it's a framework. Too many choices and it's easy to not make any. You could just go crazy in the void.

—But maybe it's not a void. Maybe it's a . . . well. A wishing well.

—Then you can wish for your freedom. And I can wish for structure.

—Rilke says to live the questions.

Karsh just shook his head.

—Dimple, he said. —We've returned to the place that in a way brought us together . . . but sometimes I look at you and I don't recognize you anymore.

I stood very still, in case that would help him.

—You mean you don't see me anymore, I said softly.

—No, he said. —I mean *recognize*. You've gotten . . . I don't know. Colder. Harder.

—Maybe you mean stronger?

The tearful ambush readied in my eyes again. I thought about Cuffe Parade — how instead of the expected horror, I'd found a kind of peace. You never knew what you were going to feel, sometimes, till you felt it. Maybe you *had* to run into those rooms — in order to find the exits. Or a new entrance.

I longed to explain that to him.

—Karsh, we've both lost someone who meant a lot to us, here in India. And you know what? Maybe we *should* take the train. I mean, I don't know if there's one around here, but it would be like getting back on the horse after an accident. . . . You know, when I arrived at the house in Andheri, I thought it'd be devastating, seeing all the places Dadaji used to be but isn't anymore. But it was actually comforting — even being in his favorite chair.

—My father didn't fall off a chair, Karsh said flatly.

I floundered. —I just mean . . . maybe it's a way for you to get over some kind of fear? To rewrite, or reenvision, what's happened, so you can move on?

He was staring at me like he couldn't believe his eyes.

—I'm just saying, life is —

—A test, he said coldly. —I know that.

—Not even that. It's . . . an opportunity.

—Yes. Maybe for you, right now. So go ahead. *You* take that train; *you* rewrite what's happened. But don't make a mess of someone else's life while you're busy taking advantage of those opportunities.

What was that supposed to mean?

A taxi was pulling up. Karsh's hand was raised.

I hadn't meant to downplay what had happened to his father, was just hoping to bring it all together. To make something from nothing, from something precious unmade. Otherwise, what was the point of even doing art? Or anything?

—I'm just trying to try to help you, I said, with utmost sincerity.

—Trying to try. Wow. Impressive. And, really — are you? Or are you just trying to justify your own way of doing things . . . to help yourself?

Did he know?

Know *what*?

Apprehensively, I looked to his face, expecting an incinerating disapproval in his gaze. But I was met with a very different sight.

Karsh had tears in his eyes. But these tears were a far cry from flower-fueled.

No sneeze, no bless you.

—I'm just saying, I whispered.

—I'm just asking, he said dully.

But he didn't say more, and I didn't answer. I just stood there frozen with my camera in my hands, wondering what to pray for, how to pull it all into frame and make it better.

The guard approached us again, and indicated exasperatedly for me to stow it.

I put the camera away.

Karsh got the taxi; I took the street.

*   *   *

For a half hour or so, I traipsed on, vowing to myself again to focus on my work; it was the only thing even remotely in my control.

Or maybe not. Finally, at Shivaji Park, amongst the walkers, the wooers, the cricketeers, footballers, and hanging-arounders, I looped the grassy expanse where freedom fighters had once gathered, seeking a match to the building society that had housed my parents' union so many years ago.

I couldn't find it.

But I did stumble across a heartstopping horsebacked statue of Shivaji, this one sculpted without sword drawn — a mere outstretched arm leading the way into battle.

It occurred to me then that the only way to truly end a war would be to reach out, clasp that other side.

But I couldn't reach that far. That high. And besides, he was looking somewhere else.

new endings

After Prabhadevi and Shivaji Park, I caved. It was our fresh start, dammit. Another chance: He was giving one to Ravi; I'd give one to him.

And maybe he'd give me one, too.

So I headed down to meet Karsh at Heptanesia, the mill-gone-club where perhaps Ravi was booking him a gig even now.

Lower Parel. I exited my cab, half hoping to debark into an urban wasteland, strewn with extinct-mill-haunt half-hewn textiles, trash bin fires, broken underfoot bottles, and wasted Warholian Chelsea Hotelish (but brown) artist-psychos running around, engaging in mind-bending blood-tingling rituals involving paint, absinthe, and crazy sex . . . any sex . . . (please?).

I found myself in front of a massive mall.

I burst out laughing. If my father, who'd been so worried about my sojourning to this part of town, could see me now! Seemed the main peril around these parts would be maxing out your credit card.

My path eventually cross-streeted, veered by a sign with a gargantuan question mark on it, then dead-ended at the Heptanesia compound. I must have appeared authentic with my camera gear, or the bouncer was inauthentic, because after the initial metal detector test, I passed into Hepto, no problemo.

The room was ampitheater-like, space-age seats slanting down towards a stage upheaving this very cool space alien shaved-head pair — a skinny guy with specs and a slouchy, slivery shard of a girl. The guy was spaghetti-westerning a guitar, and the girl was leaning indolently into the mic mumbling *fuck fuck fuck.*

Sweet sound check.

It took a minute for my eyes to adjust to the blue-tinged dim, and when they did, they landed on Karsh.

He was seated with Ravi and a superhot, evidently Euro woman (undue diligence paid to belt; cardigan tied round shoulders via cuffing sleeve bottoms together; thin lips; bobbed hair). I acknowledged my inner sexist as my first wager was she was just a damn fine girl at the bar — then realized she was perhaps the booking agent.

Why were all these music industry people so good-looking?

Body lingo (no lean-ins) signaled some tension at that good-looking table, though. Karsh spotted me and nodded; the other two were intensively tête-à-têting. I figured I'd best leave them to it. I tapped my camera at Karsh; he gave a subtle *go on* signal back. As I passed, I got a couple side shots of his dim-lit broody face, cutting out everyone else.

I circled, shot, and exited. Karsh texted me to meet him at Rock & A Hard Place. It was around the corner from LoZo's — a vogueing new spot in the same compound. I followed the building around onto yet another dirt path, past an ogle of Indian men who didn't look like they were headed to any of these venues (and who my NR eyes deemed dead ringers for those exodused millworkers), and beyond the bend, past a brilliant wall painting of a multihanded creature spinning vinyl, till I fell upon the entry to LoZo's.

I peeked in. From Bombay mill to Brooklyn swills: airy cool brasserie interior, exposed pipework, brick walls, bulbs strung off wires. I was just about to shoot a wide angle when I caught a familiar face on one of the shabby chic sofas, sitting a little stiffly and clutching a drink that looked pretty stiff as well.

—Mallika? I said, tentatively approaching. She started, glanced up, and looked around a little nervously.

—Dimple . . .

No one was with her, though a couple half-drained, foam-fled cappuccino cups dotted the table, as if she'd just had company.

—What brings you here? I asked. Her face looked different. Bared.

—Oh . . . I'm meeting someone later, she said dully.

—So . . . wow — this space is really cool. Very Billyburg.

She shrugged. —It's all the same bartenders from the Bombay Gym. You just can't fucking get away from South Bombay.

Weren't we in South Bombay? Was this Lower Parel where all worlds (well, all upper middle class to wealthy ones) met? One of these purported Bombay Gymkhana bartenders was looking my way. I nodded hello. He signaled he'd be right over.

—Did you want something, Dimple? Mallika asked now, unenthused.

—No . . . I have to meet someone, too, I said, not sure why I was being secretive about Karsh and Ravi. Mallika was shaking her head at the bartender to keep doing his thing.

—I'll let you go, then, she said, the clear call to clear out. And then I realized why her face looked different. No kajal around the shadow-ringed eyes; lipstick bitten off, but perhaps not by a kiss . . .

Had she been *crying*?

She was watching me almost pleadingly. And then she said it again, quietly.

—I'll let you go. . . .

And so, heart a little heavy for whatever her plight might be, I went — off in search of my own.

I circled the compound and finally found Rock & A Hard Place, an international chain that was considered cheesy at best out West but here in India was propped as an epitome of cool.

He wasn't here yet. Ravenous, I went ahead and ordered our usual slightly bloody burgers and fries from the not-quite-upscale diner menu — which, excepting the presence of a few more veg versions than usual and an optional addition of paneer, was pretty much identical to the tourist-trapping NYC branch. Save for the bands plastering the walls — Indus Creed, Men Who Pause, Pentagram, Dualist Inquiry, Sky Rabbit, Wild Mercury — the decor was, too. I hoped there was a female drummer in at least one of them.

Or just a female.

Karsh entered.

—Hey! I waved overenthusiastically, a cheerleader on speed. —I ordered for you.

He didn't seem to hear me. As usual.

I rah-rah'd on. —Um . . . Heptanesia! Wow! Excellent spot for a comeback.

—It's over, Dimple, he announced flatly. For a second, I thought he meant us.

He sat with a sigh and laid out his tale. His meeting had been a total downer. The club wasn't so keen on replacing the French dub-steppers with a brown guy spinning the kind of tuneage they'd seen in spyphone clips from that botched evening at L'Heure Bleu. Ravi's take was they were a little wary about that breach-of-contract busi-ness; how could they trust him? And in the end, the Francofunkists' visa extensions were looking likely to come through in time anyway.

Our milk shakes arrived. High-SPF vanillas.

—Do you think they boil the milk first? Karsh whispered.

—Karsh, I think it comes *out* boiled in this heat, I hush-hushed back. He appeared skeptical but took a tiny sip and went on while I slurped away.

Since that night at LHB, Ravi had been ruminating on a lot of things in his own life. The mess they'd made of it felt like a meta-phor, a signal. They both needed a break to reassess, see in a new light: Ravi maybe had to consider reviving his legal practice, or a return to Daddy, and Karsh had to conjure another way to come to terms with the loss of his own father . . . which Ravi had diagnosed as being at the root of his erratic Bombay behavior.

In short, they both required a kind of closure if they were going to move forward at all — an impressively perspicacious conclusion to a meeting to book a gig. Karsh looked low, and I tried to as well, though I felt a geysering hope: Perhaps he'd embark on a new Bombay adventure that might pave the path to return him to himself? Us to us? I couldn't believe my powers of sankalp when what emerged from his mouth was:

—It's a sign. On the day of our new beginning, for me to lose my second chance at a first chance? I think someone's telling me to try another path.

I nodded passionately.

—You were so right, Dimple. I've been fucking up.

It wasn't the most lyrical of apologies, but he was no lit major and I'd take it.

—I need a . . . musical detox. I'm full of noise. Inside and out. I need . . . *silence.*

I kept mum; did he mean right now? Our waiter slid up with our Mexicana burgers guac'd to the top.

Karsh pushed his plate away. I gave him a questioning look.

—Sorry, I just lost my appetite, he said. He was definitely bumming. I took a bite of my own.

—Should you be eating that? he asked now.

—Um . . . should you be asking me that? I said through a full mouth. —What else am I supposed to do with it? Wear it?

—It just seems . . . I don't know. The *cow.* In *India.*

—I think everything's a lot cleaner and safer here now, I soothed him.

—But the cow is *sacred* in India.

For some reason, I'd pictured my burger as hailing from a Western vaca.

—Is *that* why you're not eating? You want to switch to chicken? Is the chicken sacred in India, too?

—All living creatures are sacred.

—I'm pretty sure these ones are dead, I assured him.

—I've given up meat.

—Since when?

—I've been gravitating in that direction since my father passed on. You haven't noticed?

That didn't really make sense, since his dad had been a mega carnivore. I shook my head; had I stopped seeing him, much as he'd stopped hearing me? He did often opt for fish when we went out . . . but that didn't make someone vegetarian, did it?

My burger was looking and tasting increasingly unappealing, but I forced it down my throat. Karsh had that look in his eyes — windows to that so-open-minded-it's-narrow-minded mindset so many hippies, for one, seemed to have once you got to know them.

I pushed the menu towards him so he could choose something else.

He shook his head, pushed it back. —You know, my father became vegetarian in his last days. He lived like a monk, apparently, in some rental in Mazagaon. I was going to go see the house. But I can't bring myself to do it.

I nodded, masticating.

—I've been thinking a lot about dharma, those four principles they talked about at ISKCON. No eating of meat, fish, eggs. No gambling. No intoxication.

As if on cue, our (ordered by me) Kingfishers landed before us now.

They were to receive the same fate as the sacred cow: The waiter was about to crack open the second one when Karsh held up a hand.

—Could I have a fresh carrot juice instead?

We both — me and the waiter — looked at him like he was crazy. I mean, not even a guava, mosambi juice? The waiter shrugged and was about to take back both beers (sexist!) when I iron-gripped them and nodded.

—It's okay. I'll sin for the both of us.

Now the waiter looked at me like I was loca, but a little less off my rocker than Karsh. A small victory.

He popped off the caps and headed off.

—Karsh. *Carrot* juice? What's wrong?

—Actually, he replied, —it's what's *right*, Dimple. I need to purge my system. Ravi was almost more upset about the drugs than the show fiasco! And I have to admit: The party lifestyle takes its toll. . . .

I took a swig from each bottle.

He opened his wallet and Exhibit A'd the drinking permit . . .

—I was carrying *this* around, declaring, as it docs, that I'm an addict, even implicating my *father* in this.

. . . then swept it up and ripped it to shreds.

—Seems there was some truth to that, he concluded. —So I'm cleaning up. New beginnings. And actually, maybe I better begin by leaving this space.

—Rock and A Hard Place is hardly a *space*, I sighed.

—Gokulanandini says it's very important I live and breathe in a pure environment.

Bitch.

—Oh. So that's why she was hanging out at L'Heure Bleu?

—She wasn't *hanging out*. She came to save me — can you imagine? Devotees sometimes make that sacrifice when they see people losing their way. They come back down the mountain to help us up.

Mountain? He was tidying up his mess now; I wondered if he was going to tape the whole jumble together later.

—We went to the ashram that same night, actually, he went on. —To be honest, I've gone back since. She talked to me, really talked to me. Told me I need to harness my energy, that I shouldn't be so influenced from the outside.

I took another swig. My swallow was all I could hear; I found it ironic they weren't playing any music in this . . . *space.* Now that Karsh wasn't so interested in sound anymore, I found myself craving a jukebox to thunk on.

—Sounds like Gopi girl was influencing *you* from the outside, I said finally.

—She influenced me from the *inside.* She *reminded* me of the inside. That I am not only a DJ. I am a whole person. And a person is also a soul.

Excuse me, but hadn't I said pretty much the same thing to him (had I)?

—And it's *Gokulanandini,* he added. —Gokulanandini's her Hare Krishna name. You should respect that.

—Amy's probably her actual name, Karsh. You should respect her parents.

—I do, he said passionately. —It's amazing: She speaks perfect Hindi, reads Sanskrit, studied Bharat Natyam. She really must have been Indian in a past life.

—Or you must have been white.

—Look, I don't want to pick a fight about this, Karsh said with a sigh. —And I'm sorry, but I can't stay with you for now, Dimple. I think I need a change of scenery.

I was scenery?

—I'll be there tonight, he went on. —But I'll head out tomorrow. I need to keep some distance till I sort myself out, purify my environment. You can have the room to yourself — it's paid for, in any case.

All this had happened in a music industry meeting?

—How is our environment not pure? I asked him now.

—All the *alcohol* . . .

—That's called a minibar, Karsh. You don't have to sleep in it.

—The *condoms* . . . those S&M devices . . .

—Excuse me, are you referring to Le Lapin? It's only S&M if you whack yourself over the head with it.

—It's illegal, you know. Having those kinds of . . . tools . . . in India.

—Think of it as a personal massager. And need I remind you? It was a gift from *you.*

—From a previous me.

—And *you* were the one snorting your way through the suburbs, I added. —Not me.

—Again, a previous me. Maybe I needed to veer far and fall hard in order to open my eyes.

I was beginning to painfully regret ordering those burgers. Maybe we wouldn't be veering so hard with a side of paneer? I tried to steady my voice.

—So . . . where will you stay . . . that's so pure? I finally asked. *With whom* was the real question.

—All I know is I've got to get out of this city. Deep-clean my soul.

—For how long?

—However long it takes. These things can't be marked off on an agenda, Dimple.

—Well . . . I stalled, grasping for a thread, even though I wasn't even sure what I was fighting for. —What about Sangita's wedding?

It's kind of short notice if we have to find her a new DJ. Or are you doing this because of what Ravi said about wedding music?

—I'm making up my own mind, Karsh said defensively. —It's not about what Ravi said.

—*Riiight* . . . did Ravi say that, too?

—Anyway, I already texted Sangita I was having second thoughts. On the way over. I'll get a sub sorted for her — although she didn't seem too disappointed. Maybe she was turned off by L'Heure Bleu, too.

It certainly hadn't looked it, the way she and Deepak had been throwing it down that evening. But perhaps the off-the-floor ridicule she'd been subjected to had stung too deep?

I tried again to imagine how that entire experience must have stung Karsh. Sitting there, eating, drinking nothing at a laden table, he looked so small and irretrievable, like at the four thirty darshan, though a kind of truce had infused his lostness there. My little boy blue. I felt a pang.

He was the hole in the record, I thought. I was the hole in the camera.

—It's funny, said Karsh. —I came here, to India, to find myself, my roots. Our roots. But I guess I feel kind of lost, like I just can't quite find what I'm looking for.

—What do you think that is, Karsh? Because maybe that's part of the problem.

—I don't know. I guess . . . I want to belong. I want a musical family, a community that makes me feel like I did in the beginning.

—But you had that in New York. You still have that in New York.

—Yet in New York, I'm always trying to get to India through the music, he observed. —And it's not the same anymore. That moment — the start. Watching a party grow up from a basement, a few kids dancing to my parents' UK albums, Bally Sagoo, from when it all began over *there* — to become one of New York's most happening club nights, through the love, word of mouth, sound of roots being thrown down . . . being at the *beginning*. That's over. Today's kids, they probably think, I don't know . . . *Slumdog Millionaire* invented it all.

I used to get hung up about that kind of thing, like how back in the day, Madonna and Gwen Stefani were the reason white girls wanted to wear bindis. Hell — they were the reason *brown* girls wanted to wear bindis! But then I realized: If a door opens, walk through it. Plus, *Slumdog* was a case of brown folk opening a brown door. Well, and Danny Boyle.

—Karsh. So what if some people discover a sound through a movie soundtrack? They still love the music; it sparked something for them. Doesn't that count?

—Then maybe it's me. Maybe it's something I need to do as an artist, to find that spark again. I just don't feel it anymore. Any spark.

He looked so earnestly at me. Did he mean us, too? I tried to remember to be his friend, not just his spurned lover. Not easy. So I let him talk, just kept chewing my sacred cow.

—You know, I can feel the beginning of something here, in Bombay, he said thoughtfully. —Something I might be able to connect to, call home. I just don't quite know how to get in. . . .

I nodded, I hoped sagely. That was how I'd felt when I'd discovered the New York desi scene a few years back.

—And I don't think I can get *in* . . . till I get *out*, he concluded. —It's tough connecting with your inner space in a city like this. Even Ravi goes to Alibaug just to get away from it all.

—I think Alibaug's like the Hamptons, Karsh. I'm not sure you get away from Bombay there. And spirituality shouldn't be determined by your surroundings, no? I insisted. —You can't just keep running. . . .

I was beginning to feel a sick little feeling. Karsh, however, looked rejuvenated.

—It's a sixteen-hour train to Mathura, he said now, and this moment felt it had always been written in our fate. —Or a flight to Delhi and then a three-hour drive. That's where Krishna was born. And Vrindavan's close by as well. Gokulanandini and Gopal have organized everything; I'm welcome to stay there however long I need to find my center again.

—I can't change my ticket, I mentioned, though I wasn't sure it made a difference.

—Mine's open-ended, Dimple. I'm just going to have to play it by ear. But I'm ready to leave this city, that's for sure. I need to be in nature. Around grass and trees . . .

—There's grass and trees in Shivaji Park. There's grass and trees in Jersey, I pointed out, in case he'd forgotten. There was grass and our two trees in Tompkins Square, though now I wasn't so sure this reminder would be to my advantage.

I was dumbfounded. He was leaving? I'd only been here a week. And *we'd* only been here — not even. What about our great Indian adventure?

Or were we meant to have two different ones?

—I did try, Dimple, he said. —I played with all my heart.

—I know you did, I said. I had, too, I thought, and I was confused and terrified to realize now that maybe giving your whole heart wasn't enough to keep you with someone . . . nor enough to keep someone else out of it.

He asked for the bill. I hastily tried to pay for all my misdeeds, but he insisted on more than splitting it. We rose to go. He and I — were we even still we?

—I was so naïve. Arrogant, even, Karsh said as we stepped out from the dim café.

When all the mill real estate was used up, my father had conjectured that time with Hear-No-Evil Uncle, there would be nowhere else to go, to develop land, make homes, in this town.

Karsh's shot at the mill was used up, gone — and so, it appeared, he would be, too.

—In a country of one-point-three-billion people, he was saying now, —more than half youth culture, and a middle class as big as all of America, I thought: Someone has to love me. . . .

—Someone does, I said quietly, although I wasn't sure how much I still liked him.

—Yes, he smiled. —*God*. God does.

CHAPTER 25

Brown Girl Sings the Blues

I let him go then. He wanted an early night; me, a late. I needed desperately to breathe through my eye: a spell with Chica Tikka to quell this feeling of an ending in the ether.

I found myself back at Heptanesia. A proper queue had formed, and ads for beers and mobile service providers were being projected on the brick wall facing the compound. Sound-check-stamped, I stepped on in.

The space (yes, *this* was a space) had already transformed in that wizardly way I so loved. A spaceship vibe: drinkers and diners drip-dreaming downslope, backdrop bar alchemically aglow, like the liquid control panel to the experience. It was possibly the coolest music realm I'd been in. Except for CBGB (which I'd never been in, as it shut down before I was of even fake ID age, but still had to reserve top of my list as a matter of principle).

I'd expected an entire band on now, but still that space alien pair lurked onstage — audienced this time, a flashbulb occasionally striking out from somewhere in the wings. The boy was spaghetti-easterning, the girl now slouching into the mic, belting out a torrent of punk-inflected country-bluegrass-blues balladics.

—*I went back to Bombay . . . but I was the only one . . . who remembered your name . . .*

The music, magically apt, seemed to speak to my experience in such a spare singed way. As if possessed, I worked my way through the bob-nodders, the slow-lo groovers, right up to the stage, and began shooting.

—*All the people had changed . . . but the man at the bus stop . . . been there forever . . .*

They nodded me . . . right onto the stage. Entranced, everyone dissipating but the two, I joined them, made three, shot the set.

Just before they jumped ship, the boything leaned down to me with alert, eddying eyes.

—Did you realize you were moving like us — to the music — the entire time you were shooting?

—So I've been told, I admitted.

—You could be a drummer, he went on. —The bass. You had the beat, every beat, in your body.

—Ears in your eyes, the girl added, handing me a card: two lowercase letters afloat in that otherwise empty space. So this was io — Jupiter's lunatic lover.

A dude with a glorious tie-dyed Technicolor turban now emerged from the wings.

—Great set, he enthused, slapping the aliens on the back. Then, turning to me, he extended a hand to shake. —Mesh, by the way.

The annoyingly talented through-and-through Bandra boy himself? I tensed for the showdown.

—Dimple, I said warily.

—I know, he replied with a wildly uninhibited wisdom-toothed grin. —I've been hearing about you. Always nice to connect with one of our tribe.

I was bowled over. Hearing about me? So this wonderkid was no enemy, rather, was photographic family. Isn't it? I could feel myself nodding up and down, then side to side.

He held up his digital case. Like mine. A tribal twin, no less.

—Send me those shots, ya. I've got an idea brewing.

—Send? Take 'em.

It was as good as a sanguineous pinprick, spit-swapping sibling-hood: from my flash drive onto his digicam.

Then me and Mahesh, we aimed at each other, clicked good-bye. Or maybe it was hello.

* ※ *

I was in a magnetic blue mood by the time I exited. Clearly, it had been a good plan to keep my eye to my work. I hoofed it into the descending day, reflecting on how, whenever I took photographs, I oft forgot all sorrows. And before I could catapult into that downwards spiral of renumerating them now, I saw I'd been so lost in my thoughts, I'd in fact gone astray, mislaid in the mazelike netting of mill passages.

My phone vibrated.

A text from an unknown number: *Still lost?*

A spinal jolt. It had to be him . . . but how did he know?

I messaged back: *Map dropped.*

A reply: *Shall I help you find your way?*

Yes. It was him. I recalled then how he'd lit our way through the sand-dune ship-sided labyrinth at Cuffe Parade with my phone. Had he called himself, gotten my number then?

I was Indie Girl again. No questions, no coordinates — that was the deal.

I texted back:

Help me lose it.

* ※ *

I returned to the hotel with yet another secret, guiltbrain figuring I'd better give Karsh one more shot. When I entered the room, I nearly tripped over him about to hit the hay . . . on the floor.

—Uh, doing a thread count? I asked. And then, flashbulb: This regulative rule had been building between us for ages, I realized, although it had been numerically christened only recently. —The fourth principle?

* **266** *

—Yes, Dimple. No illicit sex.

—Too bad. I hear it's great for clearing the mind. And nasal passages, I commented. —And excuse me? Are you calling me illicit?

—Of course not. But sex outside of a committed —

—Are we not committed?

—Well, a committed bond . . . to marry, to procreate . . .

—We can do all that later, I said. —But shouldn't we get in some practice first?

—Dimple. We must practice mercy, self-control, truthfulness, and cleanliness of mind and body. I mean, it seems all you think about is sex.

—Maybe I wouldn't think about it so much, I said slowly, —if we would actually have it sometimes.

To be honest, though, I wasn't even sure I wanted to do it right now.

—Remind me to tie a rakhi on you this summer, I added a little snidely, referring to the holiday where brothers and sisters honored each other.

—I need a break, he said now, quietly. —We need a break.

So this was how it would end?

I tried to think of the next thing to say.

I was met with a resounding snore from the floor.

It was official. I'd been sexiled. I watched him sleep a while, my irritation mounting, magnetic blues repelled. Then, out of nowhere, I found myself trying out the mantra (very quietly, in case his ears were still on loan):

—*Hare Krishna Hare Krishna, Krishna Krishna, Hare Hare . . .*

But after a few rounds, instead of feeling uplifted, I was overcome with a wave of depression. *Hare Potter. Dirty Hare.* I mean, how long did I have to wait for inner peace to hit me? *Hurry Krishna* seemed more apt.

I replaced it with *Grant Road*. And in an act of CBGB-esque defiance, I marched into the bathroom and dug Le Lapin out from its giggly pink tissue paper.

I jammed in the cord. Switched it on. And got ready to have my first-ever round of robot sex.

Not. 110 voltage accessory. 220 socket. You do the math.

*   *   *

Four A.M. The blue hour — the infinite jiff of epiphanies, of aartis, just before the light of day would blind us into habit, our roles, routine. And lying awake in bed, it struck me: I'd gotten my wish — for Karsh to take a break from his musical path, connect again. For me to hit the photographic trail, connect again. Only thing was, I'd forgotten to mention I wanted us to remain linked in the process. *Guess we didn't specify same flight. . . .*

Vrindavan. Where Krishna spent his childhood. A god saturated with sky, the blackest shade of blue skin. It was funny I hadn't fought for us, I thought, implored him to stay. I'd never have predicted this a week ago, perhaps even days ago. Never have foreseen this hue:

Black and blue.

Krishna: the god who held the universe in his mouth.

Mumbadevi: the goddess some claimed had no mouth.

And me with nothing left to say. Karsh had said it all.

* 268 *

* CHAPTER 26 *

Unsupported Transit

I had a window before Karsh returned from ISKCON to pack up and set off on that spiritual journey north. I didn't want to be here to see it.

Hideout: first person at the free breakfast, last to leave. But now: Where to go? What to do?

I glanced at Chica Tikka. I was back to zero. And a return to zero seemed logically to include a visit to this city's first goddess. Besides, I could use a little granting of my heart's desire about now.

Whatever that was.

So I loaded my camera. Walked down to Bandstand. Got tuk-tuk to train. Took train past Grant Road, right to Marine Lines. Hit the road, quick rick.

Landed up at Zaveri Bazaar.

*   *   *

The morning was in full bojangle by the time I craned my neck to take in Mumbadevi's temple. Pinnacling to the highest point in the surrounding lanes of dust and diamond, the structure was creamsicled in colors to induce a severe sugar rush: butter yellow, frosting pink, pista-kulfi green, ripening to gelato bravado tip-top. Flags wanded off a balconied bit of scaffolding. I pictured an Indian princess letting down, letting down her (ebony henna-highlighted) locks — and dupatta while she was at it.

Frock, just climb down your own hair already. Or get a buzz cut. No one's coming.

I ducked under a sky-high banner and, unsure of darshan times, hightailed it into the ghee-streaked courtyard. The temple doors were just flustering open, casting their day-moon light into our eyes. Our — meaning me and apparently every other resident of this metropolis, who all seemed to have had the same idea today. I hastily kicked off my Birks to add to the outdoor pile. Swept up in the press of would-be worshippers, I was thrust inside, a doorman clanking the gates shut behind us.

We were promptly blocked at a second gate. Relative silence, save the shuffle and shove of anxious humans readjusting themselves in the several-shades-dimmer interior.

In terms of lighting, that is. As far as color went, it was high noon here: inner walls swarming as much as outer with beast, botany, dancing deities. I grabbed my camera excitedly to click, and was met with a no-ifs-ands-or-buts head shake by a temple guard, then jounced with the momentum of the devotee crew down the L of the lane.

A counter, manned by hot-pink-appareled sadhus, ran the length of it, before the main attractions: the temples within the temple. I strained to peek into the first alcove, but was immediately tided along by the human wave to teeter before the second.

It was all moving along so damn fast. Forget queuing for spirituality; were we now racing for it?

I tried to point and shoot, but this time the hot-pink holy man raised a hand. I braked frustratedly before him as he rummaged under the countertop (handcuffs for crimes of a photorious nature?) before conferring upon me a half coconut, whole marigold, and toothache of little pink candies with a thermocol-esque quality to them.

And in the moment my treat-not-tricks sadhu bent, I glimpsed her: the divine celebrity herself, shrined behind him. From a low draped stand, sharing her digs with a host of other deities and vahanas (vehicles, the deity's mount), the Koli goddess glowered magisterially at me, her face a flabbergasting tangerine. I was astounded by her almost brutal beauty. And bling factor: Flowered, crowned, nose-studded, gold-necklaced, and richly robed, it was as if she'd been shopping in the bazaar herself.

Before her, a tiger.

Behind her, a kind of throne.

But most shocking of all, upon her: her full bright *mouth*.

Mine opened. A hiss of speakers crackled to life, then — *bang!* Music! The sound was a spine-jolt bolt of tribal drone punctuated by blustering vibrato as I was joggled from my reverie and corralled with the crew via the behind-shrines zone back out through the moon-day doors. All before I'd even clicked.

Outside, the next avid bouquet-bearing bevy fidgitched for entry, this screening apparently accompanied by those live temple bellringers and resident DJ. Frustrated I'd had no capture of the divine (and had been so busy trying to frame the goddess I'd entirely forgotten to wish for anything) I scoured the piles of shoes.

No Birks. Double-check. A double negative.

So I wound my way through the temple courtyard, trying to keep an eye out for my sole mates, paan stains, sand, dust, trash, and seething pebbles amassing between my toes. Unsoled as a pilgrim. A two-time cindergirl.

Past the temple shops, with their mosaic lidded roofs and saffron, god stickers, nail polish; the cross-legged men, haloed by coconuts, packaging prasad, a few stringing blooms with the care and grace of violinists. The little cave of staring sadhus, foreheads smeared with ash paste and vermilion. The wall-camouflaged cow who'd discovered the sole blade of grass in the vicinity . . .

I stepped onto Zaveri Bazaar, out from under the banner I'd assumed declared this was the home of Bombay's patron saint, only to look up to find it in fact announced: NAKODA BULLIONS TRUSTED FOR

PURITY AND PRECISION. GOLD COINS/BARS: .5, 1, 2, 5, 8, 10, 20, 50, 100 GRAMS. SILVER COINS/BARS. SILVER NOTES. Followed by a website address.

A few feet from temple turret I noticed now a Tata Sky satellite dish tipped upwards, as if blaring all the sacred energy contained within those walls out to the secular metabolism of the surrounding marketplace. A loudspeaker to the gods.

Or perhaps it was cupping all the human energy out here and funneling it into the temple itself, it occurred to me now as I took in the babel of the bazaar.

The temple was already nearly obscured by scaffolding, street-lamps, a grimy blue police van. And here on the market street, signs: MEHTA JEWELERS. SUNRISE GOLD. ETHNIC LOOK (huh?). Oxidized A/C units. Posters of gurus and gods and politicians. Strings of peppers across shopfront doorways to ward off the evil eye. Poles wound with cables to where, windows bulging with gullioned busts displaying chokers like thick, crusted, yellow-gold foliage.

995 AND 999 PURITY. Camera to eye: Passersby reflected in the glass as if donning all this precious mineral — on all the wrong body parts.

Sugarcane presser; Mahajan Gulley. Clicking along, I soon forgot my scratchy sunbaked soles; funny how after you feel something for a while . . . you stop feeling it. Or rather, I realized: It becomes something different. Though a hot tectonic mess was plating my heels, it felt good, actually, to *feel* this city. In some small way, it made it near possible for me to feel the people around me, inhabiting it as well.

What was *their* heart's desire? Or, who? Sankalp: careful.

Women in sky-spooling saris carrying antacid-pink purses. Men casually balancing gigantic beehives of baskets atop heads. A sadhu winding threads round the wrist of an unwitting about-to-be-bakshish'd tourist. Chhuriwallah mad-pedaling a rusty unmoving bicycle, sharpening knives off his own-haunch-horsepowered

mid-handlebars grindstone. Small girl with overbite beating a pro-
testing drum as still smaller warpainted man (with second set of
crimson brows round stop-light bindi) thrashed a thick whip to the
mote-float ground — and then smite his own back, shrieking, awhirl
in bells-belted skirt . . . his skin somehow still unwelted.

Herein the holy: All these people making a living. Making *lives*.
Me too?

Below me, the street in that jigsaw interlock — which I could
feel for the first time puzzling together upon my own searching
soles — like all of us, with our own jaggedly tender tales to tell, pars-
ing our paths.

I follow, follow, followed it, sure it would lead me home.

*   *   *

The Huggies aloe vera wipe deepened from sienna and cinnamon to taupe and tan, then greyed over. My underfeet glowed,
surprisingly pink, soot still circling the below-toe calluses, riverbed-
ding the dry cracked heels. Riding onto Mohammed Ali Road with
its landmark Mandvi Telephone Exchange on the way back, I pulled
out my phone. Changed that unknown number to Cowboy. And
then texted him:

It isn't true, what they say. The goddess has a mouth.

Passing by the Mahalaxmi Racecourse with its stakes-raising
wonder fillies, well before the Link could wipe us out, already, amazingly, a reply — and one that both thrilled and terrified me:

I'd like to see it.

• CHAPTER 27 •

a Single negative

I got out at Bandstand, climbed the slope to the hotel entry. Security checked all but my bare feet — which carried the most information about my alibi this day than any other item on me.

Shoeless, the entire space changed. The gleaming lobby felt pool cool, like wading more than walking. An acute sense of exposure in the elevator — and then near-invisibility via inaudibility, padding softly down the carpeted corridor. It was akin to sleepwalking, a kind of dream espionage.

In the room, soles sunk into a deeper plush, a denser silence.

Karsh's carry-on: gone. That wheel-stuck tabla trolley, too. Table laptop-clear, no back-pocket-rumpled flyer pile — only today's *Times of India* pristinely rolled upon it, somehow immune to all my personal headline news.

And just beside me, below, other signs of shoelessness: no pair of red sneakers by the entry, laces always intact, backs scuffed down where the nimble-toed wearer had pried them off.

I'd swiveled them around once, those shoes, when he'd forgotten them on my summer doorstep, to point into my house in New Jersey.

Suddenly, I missed my Birks so acutely I wept. If I could somehow conjure them back onto my feet . . . would his sneakers reappear as well, followed by his feet, legs, the whole of him? Of us?

In the trash bin, one remnant of his stay here: a crumpled pale pink envelope. It looked familiar, and I extracted it, smoothing it out. The landlord in Mazagaon, that letter: *He left these.*

It felt difficult, too precious to trash again, and I folded it up, slid it into my camera bag pocket.

My phone dinged.

Cowboy: *Juhu-Bandra-Worli . . . You?*

Cowboy.

Indie Girl: *Bandra. You.*

And so we made a date. Or they did.

*   *   *

The place he'd suggested was on a little landslide of slope, a slight challenge to navigate in the purple peep-toes I'd brought along for the wedding. In the entryway, I ransacked my brain for a reason not to head on in, but not a single negative came to mind. And for every inch of me that bucked to run away, a mile of me went galloping into that room.

Behind the streetside wall, an alfresco section paved in white gravel. I wandered through; no one here save a couple bartenders, viewable through a porthole overlooking this front part of the restaurant. I followed around that bend, telling myself I was doing nothing wrong, would keep one foot on the ground.

And in a country of one-point-three billion people: no one at the bar but him. Even before I laid eyes on him, everything in me pivoted in his direction, like I had some kind of internal compass that knew, remembered the way. And he turned towards me as well, a smile lighting his face in a manner I felt on my own.

I wanted to hotfoot it towards him so much that I slowed down completely. A confession on my tongue, but the one that emerged surprised even me.

—I don't have a permit, I whispered.

—Indie girls don't need permits, he whispered back, eyes twinkling. This was true; no one could catch us. We weren't us. He patted the barstool beside him and I joined him. Our eyes were level.

I no longer had one foot on the ground.

—I . . . have to go after, I blurted, setting my camera bag on the bar. He had no camera. —I have a . . . meeting.

—Worry about after after, he said easily. —It's good to see you, Indie Girl. What's your poison?

—Halahala, I replied, still whispering. He said something to the barman, who'd appeared out of nowhere and disappeared back into it.

—Did you sleep after all? Cowboy asked now, picking up like we'd never left off.

—Yes, I lied. —No. You?

—So deeply, he said. —It felt like an extension of that whole day. Night.

All those little lights and buoys . . .

Chiarascuro: The bartender from nowhere was lighting rows of wicks. Another server swam near-silently throughout the tabled space, setting these candles down for no one. For us.

—To disorientation, I said now, raising a glass that had material-ized. A clink; a swig; a swilling thrill. I was stirred but less shaken. And now his voice again.

—Speaking of which, oh, found girl who longs to be lost . . . how are you doing with that out of frame? Boundary, border control?

I mulled it over: Karsh had chosen the spiritual; me, the physi-cal . . . with a vehemence in part to spite him. But truth was, in being physical — a part of the touchable, tangible world — I stum-bled upon the spiritual at all turns, like my dirt-toed experience of the sacred street today. And although I was no longer quite Karsh's girlfriend, I didn't feel like an ex, either.

—Recent events have led me to believe I don't think I can choose a side, I concluded now.

—Ah. But contradiction is in the eye of the beholder, isn't it?

—Truc. And I no longer feel like beholding it. Seems I'm developing a penchant for spilling over.

He nodded. —I hear you. Me, I no longer feel a need to feel complete. On either side, even both together. Ain't gonna happen. Why do we think we need so much to belong?

—I guess to feel less alone, I ventured. —Though I'm beginning to think hermits may be onto something.

—But you *are* alone, Cowboy said, not unkindly. Lonestar belt buckle and faded jeans. I didn't think he meant just me, or was getting psychic on my situation with Karsh. —And incomplete.

Strangely, that comment only made our us-ness more apparent.

—But at least we're all alone together! I declared cheerfully. —Maybe there are no sides. Maybe we're always just riding the bridge. You know. Try to lasso this.

He smiled. —Worli-Bandra, Bandra-Worli. Does your horse scare on them?

—Hell no. I think my horse has more of a fear of getting *off* them. But luckily, me gots a flying horse. . . .

I wasn't even sure what I meant, but it somehow still felt true.

Horses. L'Inde. Darkroom. Light passing through a pinhole, forming an inverse image.

—Muybridge, Cowboy said quietly. —With a single negative, proving the theory of unsupported transit.

I nearly dropped my glass.

—Muybridge? He's one of the reasons I turned to photography! I said, astonished . . . and not . . . at the coincidence.

—*Horse in Motion*'s how I turned to film . . . though I've returned to photography for the time. Trying to stop motion a little, I guess. Better to see where I've been.

—Muybridge made movies before movies even existed. Even invented the precursor to the movie projector . . .

In unison, and what a weird and wonderful unison it was:

—The zoopraxiscope.

Stop bath: The two of us stared at each other, glasses in hand. But it felt we'd been staring forever. Had we blinked even once?

—Funny that when you stop motion, I said, —horses fly.

—At the right shutter speed, he agreed, —anything's possible.

—Unicorns . . . I whispered, testing.

—Of course. In fact, the first unearthings — stone seals depicting them, from twenty-five hundred BC — were from some of the main Indus Valley civilization sites.

Mom'd be feeling pretty righteous: these legendary creatures . . . invented in India.

—It is said whoever drinks from the horn of the alicorn is cured of the incurable, he added. He raised his glass. I was already guzzling. —And Harappa and Mohenjo-Daro seals or not, the Indian ass exists for sure. I've met him. Many times.

I couldn't even laugh, my throat tangled up. My poison was a queasy elixir, one I had a feeling that was more likely to *make* you incurable.

My heart was pounding so hard my horn, the glass, the bottle went seismic. I suddenly sensed flight, a breath away.

—I have to go, I murmured. A pushmi-pullyu, this resulted in my freezing completely. But then, I thought:

Which kind of flight was a breath away?

—You don't have to do anything, he said gently.

Away or towards?

—Just do what you want, he said.

Part of the fear of running *towards* something, I suspected now, was that it likely involved an *away* from something else.

—I'm *going* to go, I announced, woozily rising. The world tipple-turvied, came crashing back at me when I did so, fraught, outlined, cornered, its unrelentingly inflexible stretches.

He didn't rise, just gently waved away my crude and flurried presentation of rupees. He nodded towards my camera.

—I thought you usually wrapped her up in there, he said, eyes lingering a little upon my *Horses* tee. My heart.

Goddess with no mouth: a loss for words. So I picked up Chica Tikka and aimed her at Cowboy.

—Smile! I said. It sounded absurd.

—Don't hide behind your camera.

—I try to connect through my camera.

—Put down your camera, he said. —And connect.

So I put down my camera. My mane tumbled into my eyes, and he pushed it away, unearthing an iris into which he continued to gaze.

—You can be yourself with me, you know.

—I can be whoever I want with you, I said. —Hell, how would you even know?

—Whoever you want to be is who you are, just waiting to happen.

I got the feeling it was already happening, and a surge of panic filled me.

—I think whoever I want to be, I whispered with an urgency that had nothing to do with my urinary tract, —is in the bathroom.

—See? he said gently. —Flight.

So I fled.

CHAPTER 28

Unbombay

I didn't really have to go to the bathroom, but now that I'd said it, of course had to seek it out.

Once there, I stared in the mirror.

You are here now, I told myself.

I needed, as usual, a sign. That this whole *feeling* I was getting around Cowboy was kosher. Or halal. Halahala. Or, ideally, vegan.

A true doctors' daughter, I washed my hands at the sink. Interlace, tips in palms. As I did, I noticed a microscopic black scrawl of graffiti to the mirror's right. I leaned in, zoomed:

If you're reading this right now, you're my fucking soul mate!

*   *   *

When I returned to the bar, I was giggling a little stupidly to myself — *that* was my sign? How . . . vernacular! I half expected him to be gone, dreamed up and done. But there he was.

The first thing that came out my mouth was an absurd chortle accompanied by this decidedly non-chortle-inducing comment:

—It's just . . . I want to find *Bombay* . . . the *real* Bombay . . . *my* Bombay. . . .

It felt like a nursery rhyme. If rhyming *Bombay* with *Bombay* and *Bombay* counted as a rhyme.

He grinned. —Superb! Was it in the loo?

—Hell, no! I'm not even sure it's in Bombay!

—Aha! Then you've found it! he said, not missing a beat.

—That's right. It's in *Unbombay.*

—Unbombay. I like that. Where I'm currently having a drink and damn good conversation with you . . .

He dipped finger in glass, sang the rim. A theramin hum. —You know, it was an ugly time — personally, the whole place over — when I was here some years ago. Now I've had a chance to rest my eyes, I thought the city . . . people . . . deserved a new look. A redefine.

—And? Now that you're here?

—Now that I'm here . . . I'm still never quite here! It's hard to explain.

—I know what you mean. That big *Are we there yet?* in the sky. It's like . . . the Heisenberg uncertainty principle . . .

—You can't measure something because the measuring mechanism changes it.

—Exactly. That's why you can never get there — because soon as *you* get there, *it's* not there! And frock, it's tricky pinning down a place in a photograph, isn't it? Places pose for you, too, I think — just like people.

He nodded at me to go on.

—What I mean's, even with places, you have to earn their trust to get them to open up. To make something really beautiful. And I guess I'm trying to earn Bombay's.

He was *really* looking at me now. So I spoke to the white stucco wall.

—Um. Like . . . Atget with Paris, I said.

—Or Cartier-Bresson's Paris, I added, upon getting no reaction.

—Yeah. Robert Frank's America! I mightily declared. Then I took a break and offered, —Nan Goldin's?

Just as I'd suspected, university-lingo-type name-dropping was primarily invented and utilized to keep you a safe distance from the subject at hand: usually yourself.

He raised an eyebrow, still twinkling, still staring.

—Things, places, people also open up, he said, —when you trust yourself.

His eyes. That birthmark. An accordion of tiny lines across his lower lip.

I felt slightly sick. Good sick. I wasn't sure what to say.

I didn't trust myself.

Then, and I don't know where it came from, I let slip, —I lost someone.

I was thinking of Dadaji, but then, seamlessly, of Karsh.

—I'm losing someone, I said.

And then I thought of everyone in the world who was alive right now and would one day be gone. The earth, in relatively mere decades, inhabited by no one here at this particular moment in the time-space continuum.

I pictured myself, out of scale, improbably the world's last survivor, alone upon the 33-1/3 rpm spinning planet — upside-down now, though truly there was no such thing, maintaining a desperate simian terra toehold as the rest of me stretched, even ached to wing into empty space.

Dark matter. Suddenly, desperately, wingingly, achingly, I missed Cowboy. And he was just an inch, a moment away.

—I'm losing someone, too, he said quietly. —It's okay, Indie Girl. Nothing lasts forever, but nothing ever goes away.

The way he was looking at me it felt like he never had.

We were molting, skin-shedding our way out of time. Bombay, New York; Unbombay, Anewyork. It could have been anywhere. Everywhere. It was here. When I would look back on this moment — which I was already doing — it would seem we were aloft, beyond even the rigging, barstools dissipating, everyone if anyone around us collapsed into white noise, brown noise.

Blue-beamed hum. Eternal split second.

All I registered was this light, dimming now. Candlecadabra: flame-flicker faces, an illusion of motion. Indigo wax in ruby holders pooling us into an unplumbed ocean.

—We met in another life, Cowboy said. —Maybe it was another life within this life.

—They all are, I replied.

—Yes, they are. And yes, we did.

Did we? Did *what*? Guilt kicked in, probably clogging some chakra.

—I already have someone I did that with, I blurted. I felt mildly oafish, like I'd been gifted a cosmic moment and was getting all plebby with it.

—Yeah? You can only have that once? he asked. —So where is he or she?

He didn't sound sarcastic — maybe curious, maybe slightly bemused.

—Um. He's in a Hare Krishna ashram. I think.

A beat. Cowboy's face broke out into a big smile.

—Seriously.

—It's almost worse than if he were with another person, I admitted. —I mean, how am I supposed to compete with frocking *Godhead*?

—If he's blocking you out, then something else is going on. It's not you. It's not Godhead.

—There's definitely been a block, I said. I gazed into my abruptly poured (by me, now) beer; it spumed to the top, me and it in a froth. —I don't get how this could have happened to us. He's supposed to be my jeevansaathi.

—I see. Your life companion?

—Yeah, ha-ha. Please spare telling me I'm too young to know who my life companion is. I'm either getting that or when's the wedding from some of the joint family contingent.

—It's not an age thing, Cowboy replied. —I was going to say once more: And you can only have one?

—I'm supposed to have only one.

—*Supposed.*

—I mean, it would be a scheduling nightmare, wouldn't it? If you had a lot of life companions?

He didn't look convinced.

—Listen, Indie Girl, he said. —What if The One is just a social construct? The stuff of romcoms and conditioned minds.

—To prevent total anarchy?

—It's just different people can be right for you at different times. Or even more than one person, Cowboy explained with a gentle shrug. —He'll still be in your life for the rest of your life, even if it's as a memory, an experience you've ingested and input into all you do, whether you know it or not.

Even more than one person? Was he one of those political-status-Very-Liberal open-relationship types who shagged your maid of honor in the name of carpe-the-diem bohemia? I wondered now if Cowboy had a girlfriend.

And I reminded myself: I had a boyfriend. (Did I?)

—Or maybe it will be in more obvious ways, Cowboy went on, seemingly oblivious to my socially constructed romcom-conditioned chain of thoughts. —But life is complex. In motion. Doesn't it seem you might need more than one companion to walk its twisting shifting road?

—Sure, I said. —You *might.* I mean, isn't that what Hinduism's about in a way? All those gods to describe one journey. But there *is* something really freeing about being with one person. The right person. Even *a* right person.

—Which is?

—For one, all that angst about meeting someone, or being with the wrong person, or even people, I said. —Adios. And that energy gets freed up, can go into creating a kind of . . . A sanctuary. A jumping-off point. To *make* things.

—But to make things, you have to be open. And sometimes being open . . . well, people get left behind if they can't evolve in that direction with you. Or if they try to keep you on the straight and narrow when you really want the —

—Crescent. But maybe he's on one right now, just knows a different way to the same place, I reflected. I couldn't bring myself to say Karsh's name. —Maybe you just have to take the aerial view. I mean, it could be he *needs* to make this journey.

—But do *you* need to make it, darling?

The tail-wagging wet-nosed puppy in me leapt at the term of endearment. I tried to calm down, remind myself some people said things like that to everyone.

—Have you heard that saying, he went on. —How we aren't bodies with spirits inside, but rather, spirits stuck in bodies?

—Frankly, if he had it his way, I think we'd get rid of the body altogether.

—Ah. Purity?

I nodded.

—995 and 999, I said. —And so many talk about freeing yourself of your body to achieve it. But as my mother always says, my body's my temple and my home . . . and I don't *want* to free myself of it, dangit! I've just started *enjoying* it. And how can it — *that* — not be pure if you love someone? If you're focused on each other and finding beauty in all of it?

Cowboy's gaze unwavered upon me.

—You're right, he said. —How can it not?

Something jiggered then, in peripheral vision: To all outsiders, we were seated securely within the frame, talking about me and Karsh. But somehow, for just a flutter, we were speaking of the two of us, can't-touch-the-bottoming in this bar, this uncity, unbeknownst yet known, and a moment, perhaps once experienced . . . or still to be experienced.

—It's all in the way you look at it, he added.

I nodded. —We should know. We're photographers. All we bloody do is find all the ways to look at it.

Our hands were inches from each other. His on his knees, bunched up on the barstool, mine gesturing vaguely just above them.

Before I knew what I was doing, I'd dropped them and taken both of Cowboy's in my own.

Oh.

They sure had a lot going for them, those hands. They were warm, they were strong. They knew how to use a camera.

In the eternal split second I began to wonder at my rashness, he'd intertwined his fingers through mine and given me a little squeeze.

And I don't know where it came from — perhaps I sensed an ending of sorts in this beginning — but what emerged from my mouth was a question viscerally painful to utter:

—Why does death — someone's actual death, or just thinking about your own — make some people want to renounce the world . . . but it makes me want to just run up to it, into it? Throw my arms around it?

—Throw your arms around it, then, Cowboy said quietly. —What's the worst that can happen?

I suddenly felt shy.

—I don't know. It won't hug back?

He smiled at me and shook his head.

And then he hugged me.

And — pressing every inch, iota back into him, almost as if swapping skins — I hugged back.

*   *   *

We rose up, a unit now. Walked through the bar, across the silvering terrace, which seemed much easier to navigate this time, and out the door onto the tilt-a-swirling street. The night was inky blue, writing us.

—Do you want to take a walk? he asked.

—I'd love to, I said.

But, much to the simultaneous irritation and voyeuristic thrill of the passing ricks, it took us almost an hour to leave that Union Park side street.

Landmark: strangers kissing. Not walking. Not strangers. Still kissing.

Did it count if it was in another country? An uncountry?

I had a feeling it did.

CHAPTER 29

Tangled Up

His car was round the bend, a sea-green Jeep. "If You See Her, Say Hello" was playing now, and he and me, we were like that other album cover, *The Freewheelin'*, Suze Rotolo and Bob Dylan, shot on the corner of West 4th and Jones in '63. A photograph, they'd said (Janet Maslin, actually) that had inspired countless young men to hunch their shoulders, look distant, and let the girl do the clinging.

But here in this stick shift, it was Cowboy who reached over with his left hand and caught my own, wove it with his. A no-cling connection.

—I can drive with one hand, he said, smiling. And he did, pulling out from curbside. I could hold one hand with two of my own, and I did.

—Lands End? he asked now, another question underlying it.

—You're just on the other side? I asked slowly, answering it.

He nodded.

—Just when you cross, don't turn around. But I've got a place by Union Park. . . .

Was that what he meant by "between places"? And then, he spoke the unspoken: —I can always circle back.

Unmapping our way. We'd barely left the curb when I turned to him. I lay a palm to his cheek; he looked at me as if no one had ever done this, as if he couldn't speak. So I did.

—Always, I said. —Circle back.

✳ ✳ ✳

We backed up into the same spot. I could just about sidelong see the silhouettes of we, intertwined, zoopraxiscopic on that sidewalk. Ghosts from just moments before.

Unmoored. If we'd been buoyant at the bar, now the farther we walked, the deeper we went. Sound drowned; a natural silence.

No one on this little lane but us. He stopped now before a low-sloping bungalow, a topple of angles against eventide sky. Reached for his keys.

Just before entering: winged fin fleck. A tiny blue girl brush-stroked upon doorframe, floating — floundering? — trying to hang on to something. Someone.

—And one morning, she appeared out of nowhere, he said now, ease-opening the door. —In the sea. A fisherman dreamed her. And she somehow came to be.

Whoever you want to be is who you are just waiting to happen. The me I just was: a mere frame away in a stop-motion series behind us. The she I would be: towing me over the threshold.

Sandals kicked off. Tailwind, into that umbrous space.

—All we have is now, he was saying.

No presents, just your presence.

—Let me see you, he was saying. —No labels, no borders. Really see you.

Less full feathered, the first words to emerge from my mouth in millennia:

—Naked, you mean?

—Of course.

I was shy . . . but Indie Girl took over.

We stood before him, there on the edge of the bed. We thought about naked. Good naked: young and free, sure-gaited and foolhardy, ungainly yet graceful. Foal finding footing, headlong and headstrong.

Trusting.

Horses. I pulled Patti overhead, she, Robert, cascading to the floor. Girl overboard. And just like that, the me I was to be caught up with the rest of me.

—That map, I said now, wonderfully nervous, terribly calm. —It's kind of confusing, this city — Thirty-fifth Road almost slides into Thirty-fourth . . . yet nowhere near Thirty-sixth . . . then from Thirty-third you get Sixth, Seventh . . . follwed by Thirteenth. I mean, Manhattan's easy. Mostly straight lines with a few bends and twists. But *here* . . .

—A little at sea?

He unbuttoned his deep tan shirt.

—Very, I breathed. —It's a diaspora thing. . . .

Our jeans cast to deck like midday shadows around our feet. We stepped out of them.

—And then, I whispered. —Janata: Landmark: Five Spice. Five Spice: Landmark: Janata. Like, you can only get close, never quite there.

He was running a finger along the upper hem of my boxers.

—You *can* only get close, he whispered back.

And then our second, and last, skins fell, all that had stood between us and . . . Us. His appreciative gaze — he was a photographer, after all — set me swiftly, mostly at ease. I stood still, basked in it.

He was taking my hand, leading me down beside him onto, into the rippled bed. In-breath. And before the waters sealed over my head, a capsizing into that fathomless yonder, I knew what it would feel like: a moment's panic, the fear of going under — and then, a baptism of desire, a willful whelming, lips up-hailing a goodbye message to the land I'd left behind.

Was that shore really only inches, moments away?

Skin to skin: a quickening. For the second time this evening, no feet on the ground. I lay on my back, unadorned. Unashamed. From the beginning, we'd gone straight to the inside after all.

He was propped on his side, against me, head of sunbronzed-moonburned waves in one hand. He'd always been beside me. With his other hand, he drew my own through his fingers. He'd always drawn me through his fingers.

—How does anyone ever know where they are here? I finally managed.

—You have to feel your way. Once upon a time, this city was seven islands. . . .

He lay a palm on one of my shoulders, lightly squeezing it, then the other. —Bombay Island. Parel.

Those fingers across my throat. Then just above my breasts.

—Mazagaon.

Just below them . . .

—Colaba.

One palm fell upon my stomach, kneading it, the other, breathtakingly upon my face, fingers tracing my mouth, which unhinged, no resistance.

—Old Woman's Island.

That hand gliding (uninstructed!) up my nape, gently pulling up from the roots, then his other joining it.

—Worli.

I slid my own hands back to clasp his, and dukefuls of my hair with them. I recalled that neck of the woods was just on the other side. Then I recalled nothing as his lips followed the path of his palms in reverse: from the nape, up over my chin, to my own.

Deep-sea kissing. His mouth had always been inside my mouth, mine in his. Direct communion: how to learn a language without speaking.

He pulled up a moment, stared me long, wide in the face.

—Exquisite, he whispered. I didn't know what to say.

—Where the bridge ends, I finally whispered back. I waved my arm to the right, where I believed The Other Side to be.

He ran his hand along its length, intertwining our fingers at the end, pointing left along with me.

—Correction: Seaface over there.

Shifting our outstretched linked arms, he pointed us window-ward. —Westward ho. And the sea's thisaway.

—Jai ho. Okay. But I'm not even quite sure where we are *now*. . . .

—Chuim Village. Landmark: You. Me. But the world's our oyster. I'll show you. . . .

He drew his hand back down and off my arm.

—A macro view: Borivali, Goregaon, Andheri, he said, fingers pianoforte across my clavicles. I tried to blank out Andheri and what that connoted. It was surprisingly easy.

—Airport.

That hand not above, not below, but *upon* my heart now. I took a sharp breath, lay my own upon his.

—*Bandra.*

Then sliding it down my side, he wrapped my waist in his fingers — his whole palm halfway around it, nearly.

—Matunga, Dadar.

A firmer grip, pulling my hip into his navel.

—Worli . . .

Again? Where the bridge begins? Were we going in circles?

Then fingertips were kissed . . .

—Wadala Road, Chowpatty . . .

. . . all the way to toe tips . . .

—Colaba, he confided in my feet now (he could trust them not to tell). —Microview . . .

And then he was not only mapping but imprinting this city onto, into my skin — indelibly, I had a feeling. I forgot about borders, boundaries. First base, second, a barrier at the waist — it didn't seem sensical to draw these kinds of lines on flowering terrain.

Fingers charting the lines, lips dotting them, tongues joining dots. Lexical scale; an elliptical geography.

He licking a link from Vile Parle . . . to Santa Cruz . . . Khar Road . . .

Then me, a retrace; minor detours.

Hand back on my heart, but this time his mouth as well, and it was I who shuddered:

—*Bandra* . . .

We remained, allegretto, in Bandra a long moment, during which time it felt my nipples were going to firecracker from my breasts. But just before they did, he rolled over onto his back, unraveling me up onto his belly.

—Mahim, he announced.

Stretching out against him, it was I who added, —Junction!

Horizontally, we aligned quite well, skylines sideways syncing, despite the discrepancy in our vertical heights.

From the Gateway to Le Marais. What the hell. This was Unbombay.

Very SLOWFROM THANE. His palm-up fingers pushing exploratorily in . . .

Change: BADLAPUR. My palm pull-pushing those fingers . . .

Even ASANGAON . . . I bent down to kiss him, deep as —

He bit my upper lip.

I buried my face in his neck. Endless inhale. Pheronomenal.

—Exhale, he whispered. He lifted my face with both hands; I gazed into his own. Then, dramatically, his half-smile wholly vanished as he hip-holdingly heaved me *onto* it. . . .

Lower Parel. Now fingers lips were tongue: no distinction, talk about borderless —

A little more Upper Worli, por favor; my own well-versed fingers joining in the fun . . .

Something. Very. Strange. Is happening . . .

Slip road leading into me: a condensening upsurge. But deep, deeper in: a taut widening, funny little inner suction-snap, quick strong wing flap —

Combined, allargando: a weird whirlpooling up . . .

. . . surfing the operatic apogee of a high-tiding wave . . .

. . . a half-heartbeat's sustained-note stillness, silence — and —

Audible hiss. Malad Creek. The lakes: Powai! Vihar! Tulsi!

And she was found floating in the sea . . .

I was that kind of girl?

Me: shudders, shivers; stunned. He: very still. For a moment, I worried I'd drowned him. I began to lift off, slide southside, when —

—Wait, he managed to utter, coughing a little. —Where there's one . . .

Dream of a fisherman's wife; I couldn't believe how much I wanted to engulf every inch, moment of him. Of this. But who was I to deny him his evidently identical desire? It was —

Oh . . . my . . . *gods!*

A tickle, a flicker, an ache, a pulse, a sparkler, saltpetering —

He, we: *again.* Suffusion from that slip road; inundated, levitatingly excavated shore. And it wasn't the same river twice — this visit so flesh-bone-blood melding I half expected my entire lower half to have deliquesced by now.

Only I had ever come even remotely close to doing this to me.

I fell onto my back. A breather, his baited with mine: eyes into eyes — and this just as intense, more so, than any of it.

A face I barely knew that I would never forget. And I could see he was memorizing me as well.

I hoped he had a bad memory so he could memorize me again and again.

Another long, deep kiss . . .

Laying his full length upon me . . .

Wrapping my legs around his back . . .

Both of us tumbling back over.

He on his back now. An arm's-length detour into his own condomanic stash. But first my own lengthy detour (de force) onto his lengthy de tour. Then rising, pulling me up, then securely down onto his lap. A sumptuous conviction. Saddle swells; swaddling everything around him like my entire body had been built to snap around his in a heartbeat, pendulating together, instinctively close.

All we could get was close. The outside in now; like remembering something — an old aching truth. Back to zero, no longer half. Can't touch bottom: a melting math.

We rocked there, very gently, like those buoys and boats that night at Cuffe Parade. He was hugging me so consummately his arms nearly doubled around me. And then, much as I wanted to stay steeped, buried deep in his skin . . .

I needed to see him again. He, me.

I dragged my face from his neck, gazed up at him. His every atom, or maybe even mine, seemed to have a gravitational pull; I was amazed the furniture wasn't flying. We couldn't stop staring into each other's eyes. I couldn't stop touching his face. He couldn't stop touching me touching his face. Our combined breath sinking every other sound.

The world now inside us, seaswellingly expanding . . .

— . . . — . . . — — . . . — — . . . — — — . . . — — — — — :::::

He sighed, all his muscles at last giving, then lay us both back down, turning to face me.

—Together, he smiled, kissing me tenderly on the mouth. —Again.

The tips of our noses touched. And still, that bluish-brownish haze of his eyes remained somehow indefinable, not to be captured.

But looking into them — into the unknown — that's where, once again, I found: myself.

Me in his eyes, him likely in mine. Him in my body, my being; me — him.

Incarnate. And I wanted to reincarnate. Encore again again. Freewheeling; no stops.

—Goddess beneath our back, I murmured.

CHAPTER 30

Border Control

Gur nalon isqh mitha hi hi!

It sounded off, cell phone buried at the bottom of my bag but still audible.

Gur nalon isqh mitha ho ho!

I froze up. Cowboy immediately wrapped an arm around me. It was a tender act — which a moment later appeared near farcical as we both just lay like that, perfectly still in the dim, as a third inappropriately festive round dholed and drummed into the room.

Gur nalon isqh mitha . . . !

Frock, how many times had I set it to? Was it going to ring forever? I began to laugh a little hysterically. It just sounded so damn upbeat.

Or maybe that was a sob, from the very gentle kiss on the forehead Cowboy gave me now. I sucked in all sound, looked away as:

Gur nalon isqh mit —

And finally silence, interrupted a beat later by a tiny ding to indicate a message had been left. The deeper silence of our hushed slowed breathing bobbing up.

—Do you need to check that? Cowboy asked softly.

I shook my head, tried to drain my mind. Above, a trio of blooms fogging corner post. Then I burrowed my face in his chest — hiding from myself in his heart's hollow. But my ears still strained from that painfully joyful refrain of a song first heard what seemed many, many summers ago — one that hymned of a higher love I'd never imagined could bring me to such a crushing low.

Despite his warm discernment, I felt utterly marooned.

Random Bombay sounds rose up: a chidiya, a chaklee, a pipe groan; wheel.

Below that, the hum of the room.

And in my ear: Cowboy's heart, thudding like falling fruit, belying his calm and calming exterior.

* * *

With that ringtone, another more worn and weathered map superimposed itself on the one we'd been charting, uncharting.

Karsh and I had made New York our own; *I* had made New York my own — through Chica Tikka, through life. All these experiences — there and here — collided now with such luminous intensity I squeezed my eyes shut, felt so searingly alive I worried I might be about to die.

Petite mort. The French term for orgasm. That little death pierced the heart of my ecstasy, so poignant my stomach clutched. My life with Karsh passed before my eyes now, with all the hurtling focus of an express train. . . .

A subway ride to Dyckman and Broadway, Zara Thrustra's on Seaman Avenue to pick up those blisteringly blue shoes. Heading back downtown, swinging around the sticky metal flu-catching poles — landing with a whomp on his lap with 125th's sudden stop, he bruised but grinning: *You pack a punch for a little thing.* Morningside Heights; Harlem. 116th — Columbia University and that Hungarian coffeeshop, a porcelain plate of broken biscuits. Animal Blessings at St. John the Divine; bridled horse led to altar (or were these vahanas blessing us?). Cathedral Parkway; 86th — the jerky jostly math of a vampirically lit subterranean labyrinth. Museum of Natural History and never making it inside: a kiss that running-leapt us from missing-link dino-bird time to the present, our own planetarium of sparks flying off the Columbus Avenue sidewalk just before the elegant edifice. Four seasons of Central Park: mist fall-thick on Dipway, Driprock. Cross-country skiers up CPW; glacial trees fearless in their fragility, spraying icicled light miles like an arctic sprinkler. Daffodil delirium, a riot of rollerbladers heralding spring, clocks flinging themselves forward with wanton abandon. Lying on our backs, Strawberry Fields sun in our eyes, Shakespeare in the Park *wherefore art thou*, time stretching, literally longing, with summer.

Port Authority — splitting a massive salt-studded pretzel. Penn Station — falling asleep on his shoulder, Boston bound. Christopher. Jane. A loft on Mulberry: impromptu party — rooftop slow dance — into my ear, he, telling me something that had gilled my heart so, I thought I'd never forget it.

I couldn't remember it now.

An alphabet of bridges so beautiful, a bit of you died to behold them.

Tunnels we'd cruised through, radio cutting out chunks of song, the delirious joy of music lunging back to us at the other end.

NYU spilling into the city itself. Skateboarders, hackeysackers, Union Square unicyclist in wire halo. Houston. HotPot. Tompkins Square. Our bench.

Sex with Karsh had been a beautiful, safe place: sinking into the known, so porously close it became unknown at the same time. Affection the bridge between intimation and infiltration. Friendship blanketing the edges of these encounters with something warm and worry-free. Even rushing off to class, we carried each other inside each other, ever nurturing that third being we made together.

What I'd just engaged in here had been the opposite, sinking so deep into the unknown, it became nearly known. Creating a third space rather than a third entity.

Feeling now so rawly, nakedly alone. Yet it was a familiar feeling, at the root of things, all things. Enlightening, nearly, if it weren't so goddamn scary.

Or because it was.

At most, we pressed our solitudes together. But Karsh's had encircled mine so roundly, protectively, it had turned second skin.

City Hall. South Ferry. Lady Liberty thrusting up her triumphant hand, a perpetual hello. And yet I couldn't pick up that phone, couldn't say that hello.

—I've got to go, I whispered now. —I'm sorry.

—No sorries, he said.

I had no idea what to tell him now, sought a tidy box for the mess I was surely making.

—So . . . ? I finally uttered. —How does it end?

—It only begins, he said.

I rose to go, this time self-conscious, charting my way back to my clothes via bed shadow, corner darkness, a penumbric trail.

—We will meet again, Cowboy said quietly. I couldn't look at him. Because when I did, I forgot every other place and person I'd been and only wanted to meet, to meet, to remain in a state of greet again.

L'arrivée d'un train en gare. This city was made up of crumbling amphitheaters, ancient water tanks, I thought as I pulled my overboard clothes back on overhead. It was an odyssey of Pisas and Penelopes.

And I realized, despite it all, I was still leaning towards a *Yes Yes Yes.*

＊　＊　＊

I went back to the hotel. Seventeenth floor.

As expected, no one was home. Through the window: Arabian Sea. Bluish through panes. Brownish, I knew, when you stood just before it.

I took off all my clothes. Again.

I stood in front of the mirror, and, as if out of body, examined my wayward self. I could as if for the first time see the true beauty of my physical being, and felt grateful and ashamed I'd complained so often about it before. Perhaps it was simply when I tried to squeeze into sizes and shapes that didn't match, mummifying fits, that the self-doubt and downwards spiral began.

I stood there for a very long time. On the surface, I was still. On the inside, tidal.

I suddenly felt the full impact of what I had done. The repercussions around the bend. The pain this could cause were it to be discovered — the pain it was causing me even now.

I looked myself hard, chasteningly, in the eye.

But the girl in the mirror was smiling.

*　*　*

And it struck me that, after losing the map, losing my boundaries, losing my way: It was the first time I'd thought of this place as home.

CHAPTER 31

Sister Cities

After about five eternal minutes of lying there alone, philosophizing, I put myself in a cab with my set of keys to Ramzarukha, speeding up the Western Express before you could say *kabbadi, kabbadi, kabbadi.*

Back in Andheri, I went pranayama, took a deep breath, and stepped in through the magic door.

To find: my uncle and aunt, Kavita, Sangita, Akasha, and even Deepak sitting around the table, drinking tea.

—Dimple! they all cried delightedly.

—Beta, we have missed you! my uncle exclaimed. —How wonderful you came by!

I cringed; I hadn't been expecting a full house — had just been longing for a semi-populated sense of normality.

Something about their expectant expressions, combined with my highly strung state, caused me to laugh a touch spasmodically. It began as a hiccup, evolved at lightning speed into a gaspy, nearly gastric guffaw, and quickly Vesuvius'd into a full-body convulsion.

—Dimple! Are you all right? Kavita fretted, jumping up and readying her back blow. Then she diagnosed: —Asthma.

Sangita suddenly flung her head back, shaking with giggles, too. She seemed possessed, but from under her face-flung disheveled hair I could see she was staring at me. I stared back. Something passed between us then — I didn't know what it was, a kind of bond? *I won't show yours if you won't show mine?*

Luckily, no one else seemed to catch this telepathic exchange. Meera Maasi was already off to the kitchen to boil something, tea being the salve to any malady in this town.

And Akasha brought out her guitar.

—Shot through the heart! she burst out. She strummed her way over to me, shook her bangs wildly in my face, then fell to her knees, still whipping her head around. The bandanna flew into my lap, a nation surrendering.

I began to panic as she proceeded to lay all the blame on me, was on the verge of genuflection, of some kind of confession myself . . . when I realized she was singing that Bon Jovi song. Kavita was quicker on the uptake than me, as she joined in almost stridently on the chorus.

And then, weirdly, Sangita did, too — in fact, leaping up! — just as Kavita and Akasha dropped out.

—*You give love a bad name!*

Deepak tittered nervously now, rising. Sangita looked him right in the eye with a swoony crooner expression, but repeated that refrain with badass conviction.

—Sangita! Sit down at once! Maasi cried, coming back from the kitchen. —What will poor Deepak think?

But Deepak — shockingly — was *smiling*. At *Sangita*.

And she was smiling back.

—No issues, Mummy, Deepak soothed her. —But before I go, it is time to reveal this new and improved work from our resident artist — and our gift to you!

He undid a package that had been tucked behind the sofa, then rose to hang its contents on that blank patch of wall.

Sangita's painting was back in place.

Dilip Kaka gazed from it to the grilled view of Gilbert Hill my grandfather had so loved, clucking his tongue happily.

—Deepak got it framed for me, Sangita shyly revealed. —I'm calling it *Sister Cities*.

—Sangita, beta, this is outstanding! Kaka proclaimed. —Such a weritable likeness! Yet . . . something looks different?

Meera Maasi peered in more closely, stern face softening.

—It is lovely, Sangita. And this hill is filled with so many tiny, tiny paintings. What are these little images?

—I redid it. A collage of New York and Bombay, since the people Dadaji loved most and who loved him most are part of these two cities, Sangita said quietly, blooming with pleasure. —Actually, Dimple's photos of New York and New Jersey, and even some of her Bombay ones, were a basis. I sketched off them. So it's a collaboration.

—You did? It is? I said, amazed. She nodded, smiling.

Deepak bade us farewell as we admired the tableau. It was impressive. Sangita had applied her gift for portraiture, both human and landscape, and miniature painting to great effect: This first-glance acrylic replica of precisely that mount out the window was in fact composed of teeny New York City taxicabs, delicatessen awnings, runway avenues, subway stops — all, I could see now, pulled and painstakingly rendered from photos I'd sent the family over the years. And, of course, the dreaming dust, sweltered clench and clang of the city in which we now stood. Perhaps Zara's magic slippers, with their urban collage, had been an inspiration? Often the muse was right under our nose. Why not upon our toes, too?

She'd even managed to swirl the upwards winging stairs of Gilbert Hill with bits of fin-flecked bridges from these two smittening metropoli.

Most remarkable of all, Dadaji's face was evoked, part and parcel of the parched pealing sky, the slum-blue beached terrain, that upthrust hunk of pre-pendulumed land. I hadn't been imagining it (or had I sankalped it?): Head: temple top. Hair: cumulus. Eyes: headlight-taillight. Smile: George Washington Bridge–Rajiv Gandhi Sea Link.

As her parents grew emotional over the canvas, Sangita looked like she was experiencing a different but just as intense feeling herself.

—This painting, the original even, was one of the reasons I was accepted to art school, she suddenly blurted. —I've registered. I begin next term.

Meera Maasi glanced up, stunned.

—You *what*? How will you do that from Delhi?

—It's a full scholarship, Sangita replied, skirting the location issue. I could see she was trying to hold herself very still. —And I'm an adult. Besides, don't you like my work?

—Of course we like it. In fact, it is proof you need no schooling for this pursuit! Kaka smiled.

—Is that why you're giving it to us? Maasi cried indignantly. —What is this — chai paani?

—*Chai paani?* How can you call this gift *bribery?* Sangita echoed, incredulous.

—Be practical, Sangita, my aunt said, a shrill edge creeping up into her voice.

—Yes. *Practical.* That's gotten me really far in your opinion of my career, Kavita interjected now with a bitter smile. —And *I'm* premed!

—What's *that* supposed to mean, Kavita? Sangita burst out. —I want a career in art, too.

Meera Maasi just shook her head. Western style.

—You're getting married, Sangita. You don't need an outside job — you can apply all of these skills to your home. Believe me, it is enough work running a household.

Sangita looked her dead-on, and a little coldly, even for my comfort.

—Is it?

—Yes, Mummy, Kavita joined in. —Is it really?

My aunt was speechless. My instinctive response was to pass the singhdana, but she didn't notice. When she finally regained her voice, the words spluttered forth on a stilted, sad breath:

—What are you saying, then? About . . . my entire *life*?

—I'm just saying there are lots of two-income households these days, Sangita insisted, though her eyes had loosened.

—But Deepak alone will be a two-income man! Maasi vociferated. Kaka moved gently towards her. Strengthened perhaps by his proximity, she added, —And who will look after the babies?

—What babies?

—Don't worry, Mummy, said Kavita slowly. —If Sangita doesn't want kids, I may still adopt, or find another way to make you a grandmother one day.

Meera Maasi's silence seemed to steel itself.

—Yes. You will have to adopt if you keep running around the way you have been, she said finally.

—Running *around*? Kavita laughed bitterly. —Premed is running around? In any case, it's a good *backup plan.*

I was pretty sure we all knew that wasn't what was actually being discussed. I decided to hang on to that bowl of peanuts.

—Yes, it is, Maasi said. —Look at Karsh Kapoor's mother. Luckily, that woman had obstetrics to fall back on when things didn't work out with his father.

I was about to protest . . . except it was kind of true.

Sangita jumped in now. —And me? If I give up my career, what am I supposed to fall back on if it doesn't work out with Deepak?

—*Doesn't work out?* That is not an option! And for starters, you must live in the same city — the same house!

—You don't *fall back* on ob-gyn, Kavita hissed; it seemed mostly aimed at her mother, though she was shooting Sangita a hard look as well. —You train for a million years, deliver two million babies, pay three million in US malpractice insurance. . . .

—Kavita. No man is going to want to —

—Maybe I don't *want* any *man* to, Kavita cut her off. —If I were a boy, you'd be happy I was going to med school!

—I don't know if you've realized this, my aunt said slowly, —but you are *not* a boy.

Kavita glanced up and down her own body then up with an *Oh my god! You're right!* look on her face. Then she snapped out of it, strode to the entry area, that slumped heap of chappals.

—Well, this trip's decided it for me, she announced now, pulling on her little pleather jacket. —I want to stay in New York. Practice there. Oh, sorry — I mean, *run around* there. And live on my own!

She kicked off chappals, slipped on Vans, picked up her knapsack, which had been by the door.

—And, by the way, given the circumstances, she said, casting me a look, —I think it's best I stay with Dimple and our NYU friends. In *Bandra*. I want to do what *I* want. Not fulfill some fantasy of yours.

—You've always just done what you wanted! Maasi cried.

—Well, said Kavita, a serration to her voice that startled me. Hand on the door handle, she looked significantly around the room, at her parents, her sister. —At least *someone* in this family has.

She threw open the door. When Maasi finally spoke, what she said threw me even more.

—You're just like your aunt. I'm surprised you're not *her* daughter.

Kavita stopped dead in her tracks. I was stunned, but I wasn't going to let this one slip through the cracks.

—That's a big compliment, Kavita, I announced loudly. —To both my mom and you. And me, too.

—Of course it is, my uncle agreed just as voluminously, giving Maasi a warning look.

—Yes! It is! Kavita exclaimed, turning back into the room. —Dimple has it all! She's following her heart in her art, and she's followed it in love, too. She's all heart!

Sangita joined in. —And she hasn't had to choose between them. Her work is going great — and she has a wonderful boyfriend, a serious relationship.

I decided now might not be the time to mention I was in a serious pickle more than anything else in the realm of love — and perhaps art as well, if they were as connected as they seemed to be.

—He's a *DJ*! my aunt scoffed. And then, incredibly: —And a *wedding* one! How serious can that be?

—He is also in the software, my uncle pointed out, looking at me with sorrowful and sorry eyes.

—Dimple, what are your plans with Karsh? You must be careful. It is important to . . . to be from the same place, Maasi said, then nodded a little sternly at Dilip Kaka. I wasn't sure why since their own marriage had been arranged, CKP to CKP.

—We're both from India. From America, I informed her.

—But he is *Punjabi*! my aunt exclaimed, as if we didn't all know that. I mean, *Kapoor*, for gods' sakes.

—Yes, I said. —Indian. American.

—I don't know if you are aware, but Punjabis are known for being . . . party types. Alcoholics. Just look at his father!

And Gujaratis were stereotyped as tight-fisted, when my father's hands were constantly giving, granting — even his own aarti blessings to his daughter, I thought. And Marathas were known for being very brave and very clean (according to my aunt), when I was possibly neither, though my mother was both. And how many Sardarjis did it take to do whatever? None, because I wasn't telling that joke! I felt wildly defensive of Karsh. He wasn't mine anymore; maybe we'd never been each other's for the taking. Maybe no one was; you just decided who to lend yourself to, give yourself to along the way. But it was still my duty, my desire, to protect him. Trying to sound respectful, mostly by lowering my voice, I finally said:

—Actually, Karsh doesn't drink, Maasi. Or smoke. Or do drugs.

Or do me, I thought to myself. I opted not to add the *anymore* to any of these attributes.

Kavita nodded emphatically.

—In America, in New York, we are all the same! she declared. —You should see at Karsh's events, when he *DJs*: Punjabis, Marathis, Gujaratis . . . Irish people! Latinos! African Americans! Muslims — *yes*! Boys with boys, girls with girls, girls with boys! Bankers and bohemians! Everyone is dancing together!

—Everyone I know in Bandra dances together, too, Sangita concurred. —I can see why Kavita wants to shift there.

—Everyone dancing in Bandra is from New York! my aunt cried, perhaps not incorrectly. Though maybe with a little Toronto mixed in.

—I'm done with drawing all these lines. Just like Dimple. She and Karsh will never be apart, Kavita asserted. —Because they are *free*. They may have met through their parents, but they came together of their own accord. They support each other as artists. They're best friends.

A pregnant pause.

—Like me and Sabina were.

—Sabina Patel, my aunt whispered.

I looked out the window to Dadaji's hill.

—We should climb it one day, I whispered back, training on that turreted peak. But I wasn't sure anyone heard me.

—It's not about arranged or not arranged. It's not about girl meets boy, Sangita added, stepping closer to Kavita. —It's about trust. Loyalty. Respect. Humor.

Other people have ached like this, I told myself. *Somewhere, in lots of places, right now, people are in much greater pain than you. This isn't a war. This isn't starvation, assault, robbery, even global warming. It's just your heart, and it's still beating. You are not alone.*

Kavita nodded urgently to her sister.

—And when you find that kind of kinship, two souls truly meeting? she said, near desperately, near testing.

—You have to clasp it with both hands, and hold it to your heart, Sangita nodded back, very calmly. —And never let it go.

Kavita was still standing by the open door. But it was I who used it first. I burst into tears, ran out of the room before anyone could ask me why, or where I was going.

*　*　*

I didn't get very far, of course. To the courtyard slaphappy with cricket-playing kids, mothers, fathers, dadajis, ma-jis observing them with end-of-day fatigued pride and abdication. In a matter of moments, I felt a hand on my shoulder.

—Dimple, you okay? Kavita asked me, eyes moist with concern. I just shook my head. —I'm sure she didn't mean that stuff about Shilpa Maasi. And sorry about all that NYU friends business back there. It's just . . .

—Do you need the hotel?

She nodded, a little sheepishly. —I just need space for a bit. I have a meeting. It might go late.

Her hushed tone worried me.

—Kavita. Are you okay? Who are you meeting?

—Someone special, she whispered. —And you can meet her later, too, if all goes well.

Another set of footsteps and a rickety sound rolled up behind us. Sangita, dragging her battered valise, now in another plain blue sari. She looked at Kavita.

—I'd like to meet someone special, too, she sighed. A silence. What did that mean? —Anyways, it's cool, we can go. Daddy said to take some girl time; he's deep-breathing with Mummy, trying to calm her down. I've got some things to take care of a little south as well. Share a ride?

Kavita and I nodded. We all headed down the slope of Ramzarukha, linking arms like when we were the kids playing kabbadi in the courtyard.

At the bottom of the drive, by Shoppers Stop, Sangita turned to us as a rick drew up.

—Where to? she said. But we all knew. And we all said it.

CHAPTER 32

Kamra Obscura

Sangita asked to be dropped off near St. Andrew Church.

—You want me to take your bag to the hotel? I asked her. —So you don't have to lug it?

—No, that's okay, she said quickly. —I'm meeting Deepak.

—Again?

—I've got to drop some things off for him. And I don't want to overwhelm Karsh.

—I doubt you will, I assured her. —He's out.

I wasn't sure I felt like discussing just how far out he was at this point — and drifting further from my life — so I gave her the catch-all: —In a meeting.

The rick stalled so Sangita could dismount.

—Are we going to see you later? Kavita asked. —There's someone I might want you to meet.

—Message me where you'll be. I'll meet up with you in a couple hours.

As Sangita disappeared down the lane, she pulled her sari overhead, sheathing her locks from view.

—What was that all about? I whispered. —The double life of Sangita Pradhan.

—The double life, Kavita sighed, —of all of us.

I shut up. I'd almost forgotten about my own, because it didn't feel double when there was only one of you leading it.

Kavita was staring at me with wide worried eyes: Was she onto me?

—What do you mean? I finally said.

—Dimple. Sabz is here.

We landed up at the hotel where Mrs. Kapoor still technically had a room. I got a second key for Kavita. As we rode up, she filled me in.

—You know she was invited for the wedding. Ages ago. After all, she's the roommate who made my first year at NYU bearable, as Daddy and Mummy know her, and Sangita, too. But I never expected her to show!

—Have you seen her, Kavity?

—Not yet. But today's the big day. Leave it to Mallix, of all people, to pave the way. She claims we belong together — that our love is still true, even if Sabz wasn't true to me.

Turned out Sabz had been staying with Mallika for the past couple of days, preparing for contact.

—I don't know why I'm so nervous, Kavita said, glancing around the room. —Nice nest you lovebirds got . . .

But for me, these digs were depressing as all hell. I tensed, expecting her to ask me where Karsh's stuff was, but she was too wrapped up in her own tale to notice.

She flopped down on the bed. —You're so lucky things are so easy between you and Karsh. No sneaking around, no double-timing history . . .

I started to feel nauseous, and excused myself to freshen up.

In the bathroom, the two-bathrobe blues infused me immediately upon entering.

But I showered. I changed. All I knew was I had to get out of this five-star mindfrock. Kavita was meeting Sabz. Sangita was meeting . . . Deepak? What the hell. I had to be in a meeting, too.

—I'm going to get to work on my photos, I told Kavita. —Feel free to use the shower, whatever.

She was already at the minibar, slugging Jack.

—We'll meet up later, she said. —If Sabz and I are still talking, that is.

I handed her the second key.

—In case you're not talking, I told her. —In the bad way, or the good way, too.

✳   ✳   ✳

Sundowner. I walked waterside, never once lifting my camera, vision blurred, doubled, troubled, tantalized by sensation: skin sun touch stung, heart revving hum, an incessant below-naval hammering. A bellowingly bit-lipped retuned body, mine, thrumming with the summons of that camera obscura, a darkened kamra — the karma of that room.

A sign, tide-side: DO NOT THROW POOJA FLOWERS IN THE SEA. EVEN THE GODS WOULD NOT APPROVE.

I felt I'd walked miles. I wondered if I was getting nowhere.

A text on my phone, just then:

Are we close?

Depends where we are, I replied.

Heading to Carter Road . . .

No. Me. Bandstand.

Same road . . .

I'd walked till one became the other. He asked me what I saw. A café. Coffee Day. He told me, *That's a landmark.*

He told her, *Let's meet there.*

She told him, *I'm crossing.*

He told her, *Go nowhere . . .*

I stood perfectly still outside that space. The juncture of Carter Road and Off Carter Road, as it was known. The border between frame and out of frame. Fear and anticipation.

That sea-green Jeep sidled up. Half door half open. I slipped in, didn't see where we were going or how we got there, just that pair of hazy eyes, front then side view, charting out the route.

And then, again: sundrowner. A light-tight room. Here in that kamra obscura. Developing.

Contact sheets: *Bed, Bandra.*

He was staring at me as if seeing me for the first time. Finally, he spoke.

—I feel so connected to you. Can I ask you something?

I nodded hazily.

—Are you the bridge?

I suddenly thought: Maybe I was. The missing link. Not even in terms of what I meant or would mean to him, what would transpire over time. But in the sense that where I'd thought there could be nothing, there was something. Where I'd seen dichotomies, disparates, impasses, an impossibility — it was up to me to bring them together. A bridge between two unknowns — whether that be a stranger turning friend or the you you thought you were meeting the you you were somehow destined, destining yourself to be, if only for a moment, both sides equally valid, impartially necessary to support that transit. It wasn't the waters that were the worry — but rather the two sides, where there was no conjoining.

And we were conjoining, all right.

—Sea Link? I replied, lying there like a beachcomber mermaid on our Chuim Village skiff. Solarized despite the day dip: half shored, half swimming.

—A forty-five-minute journey taken in seven minutes. We're making up for lost time.

—Do we have seven more? I rolled over and whispered. —With some major delays?

He nodded.

—Then, I said, —throw me back in the sea.

Were we still here?

We were. Suspension of silver. Salt. Skin.

In deep: no ripple, no wave.

Was I falling in —?

—I — I said.

—I do, too, he said.

We *did. We* did. We *were.*

Showering . . .

Dressing . . .

Outside, about twenty Celsius. Inside had felt like one hundred
Fahrenheit. The perfect temperature for making a color picture.
Nothing was black and white.

My pupils stone-skipped: wide, wider. Walking, dazed, down
the darkling lane. His cell phone buzzed then, and he glanced
down: a sepia image of a young boy, a mini cowboy on-screen. It
resembled him; a picture from his childhood?

He looked like he was contemplating not answering but, upon a
fourth vibration, did.

I pretended not to listen, kept my eyes averted. But he was all I
heard.

—*Yes,* he said. Then, —*No.*

Then: —*I'm just finishing a meeting.*

Then, pause, so gently: —*I do, too, baba.*

I came ungilled, breath held.

We walked in silence a few paces. Passing a lone streetlamp. I'd
stepped out of its halo, was washed out in the sinewy shadow of a
banyan tree, when he turned to me and smiled.

—You look beautiful in this light. . . .

I was in the dark when he said it. We got to his Jeep. He asked if
I needed a ride or a rick, but he was hailing a rick as he did.

Yet his eyes: They were still full of a kind of love. Or was it my own gaze, reflecting in that haze?

I said I didn't need either. Wasn't going anywhere.

And then he was gone. And I was still there.

I decided to burn the last few frames of our exchange, if that's what it had been. Stop processing.

Remain in the safelight.

CHAPTER 33

Blue in the Face

I'd prepared for, and even looked forward to, a mind-numbingly long trek, but Out of the Blue, where the girls were meeting for a nightcap, was about one horse-in-motion frame from where I was standing.

Despite the hour, the space radiated an ambiance of deep dappled sky. I couldn't see my cousins, or Sabz, or Mallika, who'd been invited along. The front area spun round with low tables and seats piled with tasseled cushions — the kind that look invitingly plush but, when you actually sit on them, are too far down, your graceless descent marked by spilling limbs and immense difficulty in straightening up.

Finally, I spotted Mallix. From her perfectly chignoned coiff and lined lips, it seemed she had a little of her mojo back, at least compared to that sighting at LoZo's.

—Dimple! Where the hell have you been? she demanded without delay. I wondered if I was walking different. I mean, Cowboy was obviously not my first time, but it was my first time at double-time.

—Um. Traffic?

I sat awkwardly in the low seat, took a mammoth gulp from someone's cup.

—This coffee's frocking amazing! I exclaimed. Mallika stared at me.

—Dimple, she whispered. —Are you on drugs?

I wondered whether to run with this. She shook her head.

—It's fresh mint tea!

My phone buzzed. I slammed my hand over it.

Mallika narrowed her eyes. —Aren't you going to see who that is?

—It's not important. What's important is seeing *you*! I grinned clownishly, raising my free hand for an unreciprocated high five. Slowly, I set it down on top of the other one . . . then, ever so carefully, moved it to the side of my pinned-down phone. —Where is everyone?

The phone dinged now: voice mail left. I fumbled to switch it off.

—Sabz and Kavita are on their way. They were getting reacquainted.

I could sense we only had about a minute's worth of small talk left, and luckily, Sabz and Kavita showed up within that allotment, acting like arriving together was totally normal.

Actually, it felt kind of normal. For one, their vibe was a tad tense — just like their good old last days together. Kavita's mouth was set in a line, and she chose a seat across from Sabz for good measure.

—Hey, Dimple, Sabz said, nonchalantly and yet irritatedly, as if I'd just been hanging with her back on campus five seconds ago and the proximity of her to Kavs was not breaking news. Her spiky 'do had naped down a bit. Though she still sported those thin-rimmed specs, she was squinting, slightly suspiciously, which I supposed meant defensively. On her finger, a split-sky geode ring.

—Uh. Hi, Sabz. So you changed your mind about the patriarchal objectifying nature of conjugal unions? I said, remembering one of her choice lines about why she didn't want to come to the wedding anyway from a few weeks ago.

Kavita shot me a look to shut it, and lo and behold, soon-to-be-patriarchally-conjugated valise-trawling electrolyte-drink-swigging Sangita arrived, in blemished jeans and tee, sari nowhere to be seen. Where had she changed?

—Did I miss anything? she asked, scanning our faces and tightening her ponytail. —You all look kind of funny.

—Just waiting for the face readers and palmists to show up so we don't have to talk, Mallika said, nodding towards a nearby vacant table with signs for both.

—And where are they? I ventured, playing along. —Hanging with the Todas, singing ghazals?

—The Todas don't sing ghazals, Dimple. You're mixing your tribes, Sabz corrected, raising her rock-ringed finger.

—Face readers are everywhere, Sangita piped in, pouring herself a cup. —They're just people who are open to connection, communication. Who pick up on signals. Artists.

—Well, there's a lot of shit to pick up these days. Wi-Fi, cell phones, satellite, Sabz commented. —It's got to be clogging the clairvoyant channels.

—I think everyone has that power, I jumped in. —And all the stuff that drives people to make art — basically, fear of death, of being alone — we all have that angst. Maybe some people numb it with talk shows, or bake it away, or kickbox it into oblivion . . .

—Or screw it out of their system, Kavita added sweetly.

—Whatever, I said quickly, wondering if I could blame my own tryst on a primordially morbid fear; it was an angle, and I filed it away just in case. —But everyone's got those feelers; we just don't always extend them into the universe.

—Everyone in a privileged economic *stratum* in a relatively safe *country* who is not, like, *fighting a war or dying of famine*, Sabz agreed in her discordant manner.

—But it may be true that artists, artistic people, feel it more: the vibration, the connection. That's why so many signs come to us, Sangita remarked. —For example, today I was reflecting on a different kind of blue. And a woman getting into the rick in front of me had this Cass Art bag — that London art supplies shop — and on it was the word *cerulean*. And that was exactly the shade I was mixing!

—I *love* when that happens! I chimed in, although I wasn't sure it ever had to me. Still, I felt relieved for some reason. She smiled at me, then glanced at the menu.

—Maybe, Sangita, you saw the bag out of the corner of your eye first and that's why you thought the color, countered Mallika.

—Or maybe Sangita *thought* it . . . and that bag appeared just then, supplanting what had been a Prada clutch only moments before, Kavita suggested.

—I'd be fucking pissed if some art supplies sack replaced my Prada clutch, Mallika snorted.

—It's probably a consumerist conspiracy, Sabz hypothesized. —Maybe ads have been subliminally whispering *cerulean* to us for the last year.

—I think these signs come to us because we're desperately screaming to the universe for *help*! I blurted, getting worked up. —We're begging for it! For someone to tell us it's going to be okay — there's some sense in the chaos, a little piece of fate and destiny so we can relax our grip on the wheel for just one bloody minute and not have to feel so . . . *lost* . . . so *confused* . . . so *guilty* all the time!

I was met with a dead silence. Maybe I'd gotten carried away. Sabz — Sabz! — turned to me with a look of such compassion I nearly wept.

—Yes, she agreed. —So we're a little clumsy sometimes, trying to make sense of the world, of ourselves. Maybe if someone could just cut us some *slack* . . .

She dared glance at Kavita.

—Or perhaps the problem's when you cut *yourself* too much slack, Kavita replied frostily.

—We must first forgive *ourselves*, Sangita proposed now. —So we are free to be who we want to be, to love who we want to love.

—Or shag who we want to shag, isn't it? Kavita added testily.

A slightly uncomfortable silence ensued during which I tried to figure out who knew what about whose sexuality at this table. Then I realized everyone kind of knew everything about everyone at this table. Except about me.

—We are free to shag who we want to shag, Mallika pointed out. —Always. A certificate hardly keeps people in line — guarantees monogamy or love forever. Trust me.

—That's terrible, Mallika! I cried. —To say . . . to Sangita.

Sangita didn't look particularly perturbed, though. Nor Mallika.

—No matter what the wedding, Sangita said with a nod, —it's a gamble what you're bedding into.

—I have no problem with the idea of marriage, of making a commitment, Kavita spelled out, glaring a little too significantly at Sabz. —If you choose the right person.

Mallika shrugged. —Whatever that means. You know, monogamy doesn't necessarily mean love, friendship, commitment, either.

—And likewise, just because you've been physically involved with someone else doesn't make you any less committed to the one you love! Sabz declared. —Sex is just sex. Short-term encounters, short-term. They in no way invalidate the longer-term ones. You can be loyal without being faithful.

—So if you cheat on someone you love . . . ? I hazarded, figuring I could get the girl consensus on my own behavior, incognito.

—Everyone makes mistakes! Sabz cried vehemently.

—But what if it's not a mistake? I cried, almost as vehemently, then lowered my voice. —And it's a different kind of true?

—You get over it. You can move on, Sabz insisted, clearly under the misimpression I was having a conversation about her, or anyone here but myself.

—But what if you don't want to move on?

Mallika's eyes were conflagrating my Knock-Knocks tee. I tried to burn my own into my tea, then worried I might frock up my fortune.

—Then there's always a risk your short-term becomes long, said Kavita, looking at Sabz now. —Like a *year* long.

—It wasn't a year! Sabz argued. —Okay. An academic year. But that's much, much shorter.

—Whatever, said Kavita.

—There's always that risk anyway, isn't there? Mallika put in now. —The second you step out the door, all the city's offerings spread out before you. Society is obsessed with sex. Horny OK Please.

—You think it's obsessed because we're having too much — or not enough? I ventured.

—We need to have much, much more sex! Sangita laughed bawdily. I thought of the Wife of Bath, that gap between her teeth. —Then we can stop thinking about it all the time and just get on with our lives.

I guess she'd say that, storing herself up for Deepak and all.

—There is plenty of mating, Kavita dissented. —But not enough *soul* mating.

I dared look up from my saucer.

—You know, I was in this bar earlier, I told them, —and I saw this piece of graffiti that said: *If you're reading this right now, you're my fucking soul mate.*

—Priceless! Mallika squealed. —That just highlights the random nature of the whole enterprise. Or the fact you have to be piss drunk to believe in soul mates.

—Maybe it *was* your soul mate? Sangita mused.

—It was in the women's room, I said, shaking my head.

—So? Sabz snapped. —Why can't two women be fucking soul mates?

—Well, maybe if they *fucked* and *mated* only each other, they *could*, Kavita pointed out.

—Well, maybe they're ready to do that, Sabz replied. —Maybe if they didn't have to pay the price for eternity for a few months' error . . .

Kavita's mouth was a closed book, but her eyes a jungli one, and she rose now.

—Excuse me, she announced shakily, staring pointedly elsewhere.

Sabz reached for her hand and missed.

—Kavita, she whispered, near desperately. —I . . . I can. I *do* . . .

We followed Kavita's gaze . . . to the face reader, who had finally arrived, bringing along her own impervious expression. Kavita bolted towards her. Sabz dropped her head into her hands.

Mallika tilted her own, eyes on me.

—What bar? she asked, too calmly.

—Huh?

—What bar did you see that graffiti in? The soul mate thing?

—Um . . . I don't know.

—Since when do you go out drinking without us? Who were you with?

—I wasn't with anyone. . . .

—So? Now you drink alone?

—I just went in to use the toilet.

—When? Went in from where?

—I was shooting some stuff in . . . around here. There. And . . . that bar just seemed like a more sanitary option for a technical break.

But Mallika wasn't going to drop it so easily.

—What were you shooting?

Sangita glanced at me, then gloriously intervened. —Graffiti, obviously. With me. Chappal. Waroda. All that street art?

Sangita, it turned out, was the real face reader.

Just then my phone, on the table, buzzed again. Mallika reached over and picked it up.

—Nooooo! I screamed, like a kid whose crush list's been nabbed in the playground. I wrestled it back from her so hard the table shook, non-coffee splashing the surface.

—Um, I was just handing it to you, Mallika said, stunned. —Dimple — what? Are *you* having an affair or something?

I stowed the phone into the outer pocket of my camera bag, spastically shook my head, and continued extending my *No!* in reply to this query.

She flumped back in her seat and stared at me.

—Oh . . . my . . . *god*.

She looked like she was about to whomp the table, but she just tightened her grip on its edge. —I was just kidding, but . . . you *are*!

—I'm having . . . an artistic experience? I said. Who was she to talk to me about affairs? Then again, who'd know better?

—I knew it! So. Who is he?

—You don't know him.

She narrowed her eyes. The rest of my audience was captive, speechless.

—Honest, I said. —I mean, *I* barely know him.

—Oh, like that's better?

—I mean . . . but I *do* know him. In, like, a spiritual way.

—Don't tell me he's been feeding you that Old Soul shit. Like *We met in a past life* and all that crap? Did he ask you if you'd read *Shantaram?*

—I've never had this kind of connection with someone before, I whispered.

—That sounds familiar. Didn't you say that verbatim about someone else not so long ago? Sabz asked. It was interesting no one was mentioning Karsh's name now that we'd moved on to the mortification segment of our impromptu adda. I was grateful, but didn't want to thank them in case they reconsidered.

—Um. Yes. Probably. And it was true at the time . . . but maybe different people are right for you at different times in your life?

—Don't you think the *same* person could be right for you at different times? Sabz appealed urgently. Kavita was hunched over at the face reader's table, nodding fervently, her back to us.

—That a quote from your mystery man, Dimple? Mallika correctly conjectured. —Like, you're right for the eight o'clock show, and then someone else is on for the ten P.M. performance. And wifey covers the daylight hours. Some people think *many* people are right for you at *all* times!

I was beginning to long for the relaxing analgesic company of nonintuitive people.

—Who is he? Bombay's a small town, she probed.

—Amongst the middle class and the wealthy, Sabz corrected. —It's hardly a *small town* otherwise.

—So, Mallika persisted. —Name?

—I couldn't tell you, I admitted, unusually (and probably not credibly) truthfully for me these days. Cowboy? Like she'd buy that? Anyway, that appellation was between us, however made-up it was.

—Sworn to secrecy? So he's married, Sabz hypothesized.

Mallika nodded. —Probably from South Bombay, then. Bombay Gym type. Kids in boarding school. Wife listening to self-help DVDs, *setting her intention to manifest her desired reality* bullshit. Summer flat in South Ken.

—I don't really know, I confessed.

—Then he's from Bandra, Special Agent Mallix concluded. —In SoBo, people only screw people with memberships at the same clubs. In Bandra, however, people only screw people they just met.

—Who said anything about screwing? I fumbled. —And I know a *little*. Like, I think he lives . . . just on the other side.

—Worli. Same thing. Frankly, I think the Link was built to facilitate Bandra-Worli hookups.

—Even the *Link*, I said, losing myself momentarily in the memory of that night, returning from Cuffe Parade, that bridge a sail to an uncity within this city. —It's like a symbol of our connection. . . .

Sabz snorted. —Ten years to build, double the budget, and in the end, doubtful it saves any time at all, with all the traffic now clogging the arterial roads on either side! Symbol of connection? Have you ever checked out under the Link, Bandra-side? You know how much farther out the Kolis have to go now to fish?

I had to concede I didn't.

—It's not really the *end*, Sangita piped in. —The Link is only half-finished. Five minutes into it, and it drops off into the sea, so bring your buoy — that's a slip road that gets you to dry land.

Sabz was still highly agitated. —Most of this city can't even afford to cross it! I heard the government was supposed to build a walkway, but seems they've scrapped plans for this, too.

—Really? I just kind of thought it was beautiful, I admitted sheepishly, considering how, although now it could get you all the way across, this fabled bridge could still only be half-finished, halfway crosswater . . . when it was stranding-you-halfway-across-the-water half-finished the last time I came here, too. Somehow it made sense.

—That's so NRI.

—You're an NRI, too, Sabz! Anyway, forget it. I don't want to frock over the fisherfolk. Or the non-toll-affording class.

—Dimple doesn't want to fuck the *fisherfolk*, Mallika sighed significantly. —Or the poor. Only the mysteriously unnamed wealthy of Worli! He'll never leave his wife, you know.

—I don't want him to.

—So he has a wife!

—I don't know. But I just want to know he's out there.

—Or he's in *there*, more like.

—Mallika, I said tetchily. —Since when are *you* so against —

But she cut me off, a quietly raging fire in her eyes now.

—Dimple. Don't turn into a home wrecker. Not yet. Not ever.

I was tempted to ask Mallika what the exact status of Ravi's home had been upon her entry, but didn't think I was in a position to be chairing the Q&A.

—Not fun when it all hits the fan, she continued. —Getting ambushed by the wife's sister and friend and told what a mess you're making. And actually receiving a call from said wife, a plea to cease and resist, saying the two of them can heal if they're just given a chance without you in the way.

Two foamless cappuccino cups at LoZo's painting a thousand words . . .

—And worst of all, she murmured now, —he thinks so, too. Even though he cares about you, even though you're not looking for him to leave her, he's not looking to leave. But where does it end, if you don't know what you're looking *for*? It's not so great having a secret love, if it keeps the love secret even from yourselves. So I say, when love enters the room, hit the fire exit.

She seemed a little sorry. A strange look to see on Mallika's face.

—Well, I whispered, —that's not exactly my situation. . . .

She appeared unconvinced.

—Believe in romantic committed love a little longer, she urged me. Sabz nodded fervently, as if these words were for her. —Home wrecking's not as fun as it . . . doesn't look. Wait until you're certain it's already wrecked, and always, always knock first. And, Dimple, you have my word he'll never hear it from me — from *any* of us — but why would you risk everything you *have* for this?

All of them just stared at me.

—Look, I said. —It's not what you think. But even he knows it'll end at some point.

—He, Sangita echoed softly.

—Mystery man, Mallika supplied. —Did he say when?

—He said, I replied, with relief, honestly, —when the karmic circuit has been completed again.

They just shook their heads with pained sympathy. I felt their pain. It didn't sound so cosmic in this context.

—Look, Dimple, Sabz said now. —I know you have to follow your heart, and that's a complex thing. But believe me, don't let your crotch lead it around on a leash.

—I'm sorry I brought it up, I said. —Or, you did. We've just been exploring Bombay together. That's all.

This was kind of true?

—Yeah. Horizontally? Mallix queried.

That was kind of true, too. We'd started horizontal at the Star Chamber and just sprawled out from there. When I cast a glance in Sangita's direction now, she looked away. But Mallika leaned in, speaking earnestly:

—Dimple. Just remember. It's a fantasy — you're away from home. It's a parallel reality. You don't live with him, don't know his context.

—Is that so bad, not knowing? I challenged. —I've had enough reality. Isn't that why Bollywood films are so popular? The whole country's trying to escape!

—I thought you hated Bollywood films, Sabz said, looking wounded.

—What are you trying to escape from, darling? Mallika laughed. We were getting up to go now. —It's not like you're really part of this country.

For some reason, that almost hurt the most.

—I'm trying to be, I said quietly. She hesitated.

—Just be careful, Dimple, she said, a little more gently. —You might get hurt.

I'm already hurt! I wanted to scream. But I managed a smile.

—Don't worry, I said. —Point taken.

Kavita returned then, face salt printed, eyes shining. Sabz's own visage twisted with concern.

—Oh god! What'd she tell you?

This time when she reached for Kavita's hand, Kavita grabbed back.

—She told me, Kavita replied, tears now spilling onto upturning lips, and tongue telling truths that surely had not come from the face reader, —that I do, too.

Sabz leapt up, pulling Kavita into a eureka embrace and an unabashed kiss on the mouth.

—For Chrissake, Mallika sighed. —Get a room.

—We have one! Sabz smiled. —At your place!

—We have two! Kavita declared, nodding at me.

—And we have each other, Sabz said, very seriously now. She slid the geode off her finger — yet somehow it still remained on that finger, two rings wedged together where I'd seen one — and onto Kavita's.

*   *   *

Outside, to make her own conscientious-citizen Marlboro Lights contribution to Bombay's pollution level, Mallika lit up. I was probably contributing as well, with my mere sordid presence.

A couple ricks pulled up for that sordid presence and company. Kavita, Sabz, and Mallix nabbed one; they were going to pick up Kavita's stuff, then head to Mallika's, since there Kavs and Sabz could have their own room.

Mallika took one more long drag, chucked the stub of her smoke on the pavement, crushing it under her surreally skinny pothole-defying heel.

—Dimple? Sangita? Rick? she asked.

—We're going the other way. North, Sangita replied. —Can't have Mummy and Daddy thinking the whole flock's fled.

Then, to Kavita: —No issues. I'll tell them you're safe and sound with your NYU friends.

The trio zipped off. I stood with Sangita, I realized now, at the foot of the very landslide of slope where I'd entwined with a near stranger till I couldn't see straight just . . . hours ago?

I wanted to not see straight again. Life along the lines was too sharp, suffocating.

But why did it ache so much to curve, to bend?

I stood there, unsure of where I actually wanted to go.

—You can push off if you're late, Sangita. I'm not sure I'm going to Andheri tonight. I might need some time on my own.

—I figured as much, Sangita said quietly. —So I thought I'd get rid of the lot for you.

She hesitated.

—Dimple, she said. And then she asked the question no one else had pressed me on. —What about Karsh?

I felt the tears instantly rise.

—What about him? I said, and they shed. She lay her hand on my shoulder.

—Maybe call him? Talk it out?

—Isn't it a bit late for a spiritual person? I mean, don't they rise and set with the sun and all that?

—What are you talking about?

—He's not in Bombay, Sangita. He's on a . . . retreat. So there's not a lot of talking going on.

—Vipassana? Silent yoga?

—I don't know if he's vipping anything. He went to Matheran. Or Madurai. Where Krishna was born. To a Hare Krishna ashram.

—*Mathura*, she corrected me. —Probably Vrindavan, where Krishna spent his childhood, near Mathura, his birth city.

—*Hooray, hoo-oo-ray!* I sang and clapped Hare-Hare mantra style, sauf joylessly.

—Dimple. There's no need to mock the religion just because you're having difficulties with Karsh. It's a beautiful philosophy — all about love and devotion and surrendering to that beauty. The beauty of the blue-skinned god . . .

—Whatever. Blue balls is what I'm left with if I sit around. I'm just being open to options is all.

She paused.

—You can talk all you want, Dimple. And I understand life throws up confusing situations, things you weren't expecting. But in the end, you're deceiving the person you love. You're still together, right? I mean, you haven't broken up.

—Not in so many words, Sangita, but bloody hell — he's living at an *ashram*! He's given up all worldly *pleasures*! He's in search of *purity*!

—And he can't find that with you. . . .

Ouch! I didn't think she meant it that way, but still.

I did a little side-to-side, shrugged a little sadly. Shrugging made me think of the core dance move of bhangra, which made me think of Karsh. Thinking of Karsh made me sad, which made me shrug sadly again.

I was through with words. Aloud was overrated. When I spoke, it seemed like I was engaged in a sleazy, slimy, selfish, and very, very bad thing. I sounded like the victim: naïve, blind. Like he was a player.

But maybe I wanted to play? Wasn't play good? Especially for artists? And all those coincidences, that synchronicity —

didn't it add up to something? A negative of love if not the full-blown positive, a beforeimage if we weren't destined to have an afterimage?

It was the *after*-being-with-Cowboy part that was messing with my head. Did my lust have my love on a leash — or was my heart towing the rest of me along with it? Either way, it was pretty clear my crinkum-crankum and heart were Siamesically twinned, whichever one was calling the shots.

I guess I'd known everyone would tell me not to do this. Maybe I'd wanted them to. Because I was starting to feel something unstoppable in me — a dark sweet pull, a shaft of light and shadow-dance beneath a door ajar. It was a little scary watching from a corridor. But there was no fear inside that room.

Now, quietly, Sangita said, —It won't last forever. . . .

—I'm not looking for something to last, I choked up. —Nothing lasts!

It hit me then that maybe she meant the way I was feeling, or the way he was — that her words were perhaps a this-too-shall-pass to that sad shrug. Sangita was very still, and then suddenly busied herself with picking at a turquoise stain on her shirt. I felt a pang.

—I'm sorry, Sangita, I said, taking her hand. —I didn't mean you and Deepak. Honest.

—No issues, Dimple. Look, whatever way you cut it, a relationship's a wager. No guarantees. You decide to stick it out or you don't.

She squeezed my hand. —And don't worry. I'll never tell a soul, either. I know how sensitive these things are. Commitment. To what and whom . . . and whether to.

—That's a more poetic way to put it. The usual language is so awful, I said, grateful. —Maybe it's just . . . having a *connection*.

—Yes, Sangita nodded, voice hushed. —And that's something you have to figure out on your own. It's best to keep some things to yourself. Once your friends, family, society get involved . . .

—Um, having a wedding isn't really keeping something to your-self, Sangita, I said gently.

—No, it isn't. But it's still important to have something that's all yours.

Then, gently as well, still squeezing my hand: —Do you love him?

I hesitated, then nodded.

—You don't have to talk about it, she said softly. —But if you ever want to . . .

I didn't.

—Look, I said. —This whole . . . situation. Maybe it's some-thing I needed. For me. It's pushed me out of my comfort zone, made me ask questions — about dichotomies, dividing lines. It may even help me grow as an artist.

Sangita now examined me a slow moment, nodding.

—Then all I can say, Dimple, she finally replied, lifting my camera bag off the sidewalk where I'd set it between my feet and handing it to me, —is you better get to work.

*   *   *

It was out of the blue and into the black as my rick dithered south, hers north. And I only realized after she'd vanished com-pletely from sight that, when she'd said *you love him* — she hadn't specified whom, which one.

Did it even matter?

Was my heart big enough for both, for all of them?

CHAPTER 34

Breach

As soon as I got to my room, I pried off my peep-toes, took a breath, and sat down to work. I scrolled through the photos from Heptanesia and found they were royally frocked up, just like that day had by and large been: band shots all blurred, light straying to all the wrong spots, skinting on the right ones. Why had I felt so good about them when I'd taken them? Maybe I'd been moving too much to io's blues. I felt a slight pang at the thought that Mahesh had these photos from my flash drive, what he would make of me.

I hardly knew what to make of myself.

Out the window, across the waters: the noctiluca lights of Worli.

And then, abruptly, that seaface with its crest-and-crash insinuated skyline went dark: power out.

I panicked — could I find candle, flashlight in the hotel desk drawer? — before realizing nothing had happened Bandra-side. Here: a watted, wired midnight.

I hit the bathroom to wash up. Such a cold light: that blinding bright second bathrobe. I tore it from the hook, held it close. Then hid it under the bed and lay down upon the mattress, eyes wide with shock. Who was I?

What the hell was I doing?

* ※ *

I was still in the same position, eyes opening wide again with shock, in the morning. I knew nothing but this: I had to get as far from Bandra as possible, as if that would undo the incredible indelible goings-on of late, reset my slate.

When had my path gone awry?

That day I'd tried to go to Chor Bazaar, taken the blue.

I figured that was where I had to head now. Back to brown. A revised new beginning.

On autopilot, I showered, packed up my camera gear, and flung open the door . . . only to find Karsh standing in the hallway, hand poised to knock. I froze.

It felt like years since I'd seen him.

—I thought you left, I stammered.

—I've been in Juhu, at ISKCON. Gopal's father isn't doing so well, so we delayed, he explained, almost shyly. —We're aiming to leave Bombay tonight.

If laying eyes on Cowboy had been like viewing a projection, beholding Karsh felt like staring down a wraith. But that specter tilted a very real head at me now.

—I called you a couple times, but no one picked up.

—I was in a meeting, I said. He was averting his eyes, I noted during a nanosecond non-avert of my own.

—I got to thinking, he continued, still averting. —I. I wanted to make sure we visited Breach Candy. To photograph that rock. Where your parents . . . ? I already booked Laxman, that hotel driver; he's giving us a deal to keep him for the day.

—It's okay. I don't want to make you late or anything. . . .

But Karsh shook his head.

—No, Dimple, he said with surprising firmness. —Today was the day we'd planned on, and a promise is a promise. Come. He's waiting downstairs.

*　*　*

The elevator and lobby were smugly frenetic with the hormon-ally amped arrival of the Parsi Youth Congress. Outside, I switched my cell back on. In a moment, the missed calls from Karsh came in, as well as my parents' twice-nightly resend of their sweet-dreams-and-no-tuk-tuks text.

As we approached the Link, Laxman at the wheel, the network bar vanished from my phone, which I'd been gripping in my hand like a cliff edge. This disappearance filled me with irrational relief, as if Cowboy could clamber over the letters of his brief evocative texts and join us on the backseat hump if I got a signal.

I zipped the phone hastily into my bag, closed my eyes, and told myself it was all going to be all right. Karsh and I were together again — en route to Breach Candy, the site of my parents' first kiss. It would remind us of our history, our connection, allow us to begin anew.

Still, I felt like hurling.

—Sea Link bridge! Laxman announced, alert squirrel eyes in the rearview, Om symbol dangling off it, about where his mouth would have been. It was pretty evident we were on the bridge, given the sizable body of water below, and the fact we weren't wet. He indicated the sign by the toll as if to verify his own words, or ability to read.

—Beautiful! Karsh nodded encouragingly, as if we'd never seen it, and leaned forward to hand him the change.

We crossed the Link, cables overcrowding my viewfinder, as if closing us in. I kept the camera pressed to my face — and that face turned towards the window, staring between the slants at segmented silty blue sky.

—What's up, Dimple? You'd rather be in Bandra?

I panicked, turned.

—No! Of course not! I'd rather be in . . . Worli. Not! I mean, I *am* in Worli. Almost.

Karsh laughed, a little confused, and indicated my bloody Shy-gifted I'd Rather Be In Bandra T-shirt. Time for it to reincarnate into a dishrag.

—Oh, I said, sheepishly. He just smiled at me, shook his head.

We got off the bridge — or, rather, the slip road, as Sangita had correctly noted — following the sign indicating South Bombay to the left, but looping around right after a short stretch.

Going the wrong way in order to go the right way. Was that a metaphor for my behavior?

(A sign of . . . ?)

Thing was, it was one thing waxing all iambic and philosophical and French about your new freewheeling love life when, for example, you were engaged in a parallel existence with an almost-stranger in a Bombay suburb. But it was a wholly other thing to sit beside the very person you'd run over with that freewheel (whether he knew it or not) and truly face him for the first time.

The part that was hardest was the part that was softest: that old well-known face. It wasn't theoretical. It could be touched: The lids could be kissed while it slept, a fingertip tickle the tip of its nose; a hand could be held to its cheek. It could go places no other face had gone till recently. I knew: I'd kissed those lids, touched that cheek. I'd joyfully accompanied on those journeys.

Something about Karsh was a little weary, a little wounded, but I saw an old light ignite when those auriferous hot-honeyed eyes fell upon my own. So bright, an unblown birthday wish. I had to look away before my own guilt and gutlessness snuffed it out.

Haji Ali Road: through the window, that mosque floating in the sea, a luminous lifeboat, and the perpetually peopled pier leading up to it, coming to a standstill as traffic did as well. Laxman-ji leapt out of the car, carting a clear two-liter bottle of Coca-Cola I'd spotted on the front floor. He scurried ahead of the vehicle — was he abandoning us? in this state? — then threw open the hood and refilled the water, bounding back into the driver's seat with a second to spare as the traffic jam got quasi-moving again. Karsh gave me a smile.

—Funny, he said. —I was sure this car preferred Pepsi.

Looking at his mouth hurt; I could still feel it, the full lips, slightly fuzzed — but I tasted another mouth at the same time. As soon as I made eye contact (or eye-to-mouth contact) without the protective shield of the lens, I was done for, had to turn away again, stare fixedly out the window.

Of course this was precisely the moment traffic stalled once more, and an intrepid little girl who'd been weaving among the cars, carefully balancing a teetering tower of books and magazines, stepped into frame, eyes intently meeting mine. Coelho, Chopra, Follett popped up in my pane like toast as she flourished her wares. Laxman tried shooing her away, but she next held up a copy of *Asian Bride* magazine.

Karsh reached across me, buzzed down the window, and was trying to give the girl a one-hundred rupee note, gesturing that he didn't want anything in return.

She shook her head, refusing cash without the sale. She waggled the magazine, a little more emphatically — again, looking at me. I could see Karsh side-to-side capitulating; the girl accepted the payment, tendered the Asian bride.

—Don't do it! I cried, and with the urgency of a mother volleying herself in front of a freight train to propel a stroller out of harm's way, I rolled the pane back up before the magazine could be his. The girl jerked back in the nick of time.

The traffic jam lunged forward. As we pushed off, Karsh just stared at me.

—It was a bridal magazine, I explained weakly.

—So?

—I don't know if we should be supporting the institution of

marriage . . . especially in a country where so many girls are forced to marry. And dowries and stuff.

—I didn't think of it as supporting the institution of marriage, said Karsh slowly. —I kind of thought of it as supporting the girl. Maybe help her get khana, food. As she seems to be pretty much supporting *herself.*

Like I needed more guilt in my system.

—And what's wrong with marriage? Karsh asked. —Isn't that why you're here, on some level? That's a little killjoy, no, with Sangita's big day around the corner?

I opted for the adult thing, and chucked some culpability his way.

—I don't know. It's just . . . what does a piece of paper prove, anyway? That it's not . . . *illicit?*

—Wow. Romantic! Are you sure you want to do Breach Candy today?

—It was just a kiss, I said, although that kiss hadn't been just a kiss for my parents but a preamble to a lifelong ramble: a journey that would continue across years, continents, to this very moment. Still, I couldn't back down now. —A kiss doesn't necessarily mean anything, does it?

We were clearly having two different conversations. I was seeking absolution from the very victim of my wayward behavior . . . who looked like he wasn't sure how to react. Furthermore, my own kiss, on any level, had certainly not been just a kiss.

—Anyway, Karsh said finally. —It was just a few bucks. She could probably use it.

As we drove towards Breach Candy, Laxman pointed out the local sights. Former site of the US consulate. Ahead, thrusting a flagrant twenty-seven floors up, Antilia — Island of the Other, *Ilha das Sete Cidades* — the more-than-a-few-billion-bucks Ambani house (where it was rumored no one lived). I kept looking at Karsh's face reflected in my window; he kept glancing at me, as if he wanted to say something, then thought better of it.

Laxman's nonstop impassioned declarations fuzzed to a nearly comforting white noise, and when he pointed out the windshield — *Lata Mangeshkar house! You are hearing Lata Mangeshkar? Too much famous singer only!* — it even elicited a smile from Karsh in my direction.

—Your favorite, he whispered. Lata Mangeshkar was probably the last thing I'd put on my iPod, shortly after samples of fingernails dragging across chalkboards, children's cartoon character voices, and mewling peacocks.

I smiled back. This insideriness made me feel a little better, like time and memory were in our favor and I could just delete anything that wasn't.

Finally, Laxman-ji stopped on Bhulabhai Desai Road — or maybe it was Warden. I was so used to the endless waits in Bombay traffic that it took me a minute to realize he was, in fact, parking. We were across the street from the park access.

—Very seaside near. When ready, you send me missed call, he instructed us. —I wait exactly here.

We thanked him and got out. Somehow, it felt immediately awkward — despite the blare and buzz of the Bombay street — to now be alone with Karsh.

We entered by the iron gates. From the outside, it all looked the same. The park. Even us. We were both a little skinnier, tawnier, locks longer and wavier. But still, to any passerby who knew us, it was Karsh and Dimple, Dimple and Karsh, sound and vision, the beauty-and-beat four-eyed-and-eared beast back by popular demand, DKNY, KDNY, strolling amongst the other (skinnier, browner, wavier) lovers at Breach Candy.

We didn't say anything for a long time. Just walked, our steps scuffing up pebble and dust, offering the false comfort of old metronomy.

—So this is where it all happened, Karsh said at last.

—Where what happened? I said, defensive.

—Isn't this where they had their first kiss? Your parents?

—Oh! Yes. Yes, it is. I came here with my dad last time around, to see the famous rock. But we couldn't quite locate the exact spot.

—Still, Karsh said. —You'll never get closer than this.

He reached for my hand and squeezed. I squeezed back — and squeezed back tears at the same time. Holding hands with Karsh felt like a remnant of a distant past, whereas the memory of that few-years-old day with my dad seemed minutes ago . . . and his *own* memories on that day, the most present of all. My father's shy, slightly embarrassed smile, but an embarrassment of pleasure, of riches. *The rock may be gone,* he'd told me finally, after we'd concluded our futile search. *But the emotions remain.*

When I looked back at Karsh, I could see his eyes were watery as well. Reflecting the sea, or me, or his own private ache.

—I'll miss you, he said now.

—Will you? I blurted without thinking, planning. —I missed you before you left. Even now.

It came out bird throttle, a strangled sound. Our sliding glass back door back in Springfield; one clear summer day, a sparrow had sailed headlong into the pane and tumbled to its death, not recognizing a wall had risen, invisible but impermeable. There was something unspeakably sad about a winged creature downed like this, a song cut off mid-flow.

—What do you mean? Karsh was asking.

I hadn't meant to have a heart-to-heart; I wasn't sure where it would lead. But seemed my heart was not only in my mouth, but vocal cords as well.

—It's been lonely, Karsh. Even with you here.

If there's one thing a liar knows, it's the truth, and this was it.

I felt a goodbye underpinning my words, and didn't understand how it had arrived there. What was wrong with me? We had everything. We had friendship, (had had) loyalty, devotion, art, family, love angel music baby.

What was making me nearly exchange that . . . for . . . ?

—Yes, he replied quietly. —It was. It is.

Our hands had fallen apart. Not in an aggressive way, more matter of course. Which seemed worse. No struggle, no strain. I pocketed mine. Before us our shadows unwound from our ankles, stretched animal, mystical, as if they no longer belonged to us, would come untethered if we didn't keep moving.

We didn't keep moving.

—We're not so together, are we? I said now.

Sadly, he shook his head.

We stared through the fencing at the rock face tumbling seaward. Every visit, a little more of the beach had been blocked off. All open, wild, wave-swept in my parents' time, Scandal Point (as it was also known) had been unbound, only jaggedly and precariously defined, as seemed fitting for its legacy of shadowy liaisons. My mother had stepped gracefully out across rock tips in a swirling yellow sari and chappals, hooked only to the toes, her mane then a thick spill of squid-ink ebony to her hips; I doubted I could do that even in my jeans and sneaks and scrunchied hair without a bruising fall. Clearly, she'd had the gift of ocean-crossing even then.

The rocks were fewer these days; the park had leveled off a lot of them, even compared to my last visit to India. Now the division was defined: A rusty grille fence kept park park and seaface sea, a distinct border between the unruly and tamed. We came around the bend, towards the Children's Park, and looked over a low barrier down to the beach, flanked by buildings in the distance, hovering palms thrusting down from overhead, and the drop of the wall below us.

No one walked the beach, save a ragged little boy with a stick, picking his way through the rubble on some kind of private mission.

A patch of vibrant color; someone's shirts and sheets spread to dry by a small tarped enclosure. Someone's home.

How times had changed. My parents came here for their first kiss — first anything, with anyone, and then, tick, tick, tick, married, migrated, made me. I was here, with a boy I'd frocked and rocked and held so close yet couldn't get close enough. I'd slept with my hand in his boxer hem, the safest place, woken with his pillow crease on my cheek. His fingers hooked my back jeans pocket during New York–New Jersey sidetracks where it didn't matter where we'd go, everything meandering but our emotional atlas. We'd peed, pigged out in front of each other, our words underlain with unspoken promises. The future tense was as easily used as past and present, was, in fact, not tense at all.

We'd called each other daily. We'd called each other friend.

And now we were in India, of all places the very one that had first connected us, surrounded by other lovers linking, where a boy had once upon a time met a girl forever, my father shyly greeting my mother's song with his lips.

And no kiss to be had.

Just a girl. Just a boy. Just a beach.

On another beach, not so long ago, not so far away, awaiting his arrival with bated breath, I'd drawn a line from my heart to his, pointing seaward. Little had I known that, no matter my, his, best intentions, our innocent hopes, any line could become a border, a barrier waiting to happen.

There was so much to say that there was nothing to say. Full circle.

The waves broke. The laundry dried. The boy on the mission had vanished, the couples as well.

As we crossed back through the parking area, a new blue-jeaned child keened with disappointment, prematurely and parentally forced to dismount perhaps the same blindered pony I'd seen here that last time with my father, still being led in lethargic circles around the Marutis, the Tatas, the Hyundais. An Ambassador.

I sent the missed call.

Once we'd crossed over into Laxman's car, Karsh put on his headphones, leaned his head against the window. I slipped my shades off my own head and over my eyes, rested against my own pane, camera in my lap.

On the ride back, even Laxman was silent.

* CHAPTER 35 *

Heptanesia

Karsh had to head back to Juhu. I couldn't bear being in the car any longer — could I simply jump out with a Coca-Cola bottle and make a run for it, too? I was struggling to come up with an excuse to exit, when I realized no one was asking me to stay, and Laxman was already dropping me back at Lands End.

—Well, then, I said to Karsh, awkwardly. —Goodbye, I guess.

—I guess, he said, and he didn't look my way.

I stood by the Centauride entrance, the ever-attentive, yet obliviously smiling staff already opening the door to nod me in. I turned and walked away, back down the slope.

The image of that little girl blueprinted on a nearby Union Park portal possessed me then.

Somehow, it seemed, seeing once and for all whether that wee sea maiden was in fact drowning upon door frame might supply a kind of answer for me.

Often a photograph could serve as an entry point into a place, a space. But it could also freeze a moment, fetter it firmly to the past, ironically allow an amnesia for the total experience by containing it within a single frame.

Stop motion.

I decided to photograph her, free myself. From him? Me? In any case, in ten to fifteen minutes, I could be walking the edge, the frame, of Chuim Village. And step out of it — this time keeping my head above water. Both feet on the ground.

I was in a rick when I felt a slight tremor as my phone caught up to my whereabouts, no longer suspensing over water.

A missed call from Cowboy.

I'd leave him missed.

* * *

But, fourteen minutes later, when I approached that door, all thought of that little blue girl vanished. For that door was ajar.

And he was just stepping out of frame.

I stood very still, as if that would make him not see me. He saw me.

Then, as he had at the airport, he took a slightly stumbling step backwards, eyes still fixed on me.

I took one forward. Carried me over that threshold.

—I need to forget Unbombay, I told him, a quiet urgency.

—Amnesia, he said.

—And I need to remember, I added, —Bombay.

—Heptanesia.

And then we were in that room, and I couldn't remember what I needed to forget, only what I would never forget, and that was the space we were mapping, unmapping, he, we, reminding me.

* * *

Hours later, he explained that name to me. Heptanesia.

—It's what the ancient Greeks called the islands that became Bombay. A cluster of seven isles.

Seven steps to undock bedrock, unkey wedlock; a black horse *kala ghoda* loping away, no white horse nickering in. Blue roan, blue ruin — a consuming unclaiming oblivion was what that word evoked for me.

And now, in that afterglowed bungalow, in the aftermath of he plus me: a new low, a slow blue. I knew then it couldn't go on. I said

I had to go, and I meant it both immediately and indefinitely. He said he would drop me off. I said he couldn't, no. He didn't ask why, told me he'd take a quick shower, walk me to a rick.

He left, gathering his shadow with him.

I lay in its lack. Adrift, a dead man's float.

The room was bathed in blue.

And when I heard the bathroom door click . . . I photographed it. Lying on my back, Chica Tikka buoyed me, zoomed up to garner into her gaze the trio of white flowers entwined on the mast of this bed, the twilit shafts of azure and ochre of the street outside, viewed through that small grilled porthole.

The water was running down the hazy hall, surely from that spigot hosed to tiled wall. I slipped into the front room.

Jalousie here rendered the space dusky, dreamlike. I ran my finger along its sill, dust sinking behind index nail, steeping it slate. No maid, kamwali, came today? I took in the nooks, craning, felt I was searching for clues. Maybe as much to myself as to who this person was.

No pricey art gallery offerings or five-fixture separate-tub-and-showers or twenty-four-hour front desk — but all the better. A sofa that evoked the hitchka Dadaji used to sit on on the front porch of that first house in Powai, flat cushions tied together with triple bows, chimes hanging off the frame's underside. A compact collection of instruments in the room's right-hand corner: a banjo (bandurra?), bongo, and . . . bong. Oh.

I plucked a string, the bright sound bell clear.

Atop the surprisingly small-screen TV, on the right-hand shelves: an unlabeled, uncased cassette. CD: *Histoire de Melody Nelson*. Piled up beside a thick bound book, a smart dovetail shuffle of sundry business cards, topped with a single *Shanker Arora, Cinematographer*, address in microscopic print below, also Chuim Village. A neighbor, colleague?

Tome open to the tale of another *Cinématographe*: the Lumière brothers birthing cinema in India, a still shot of that train pulling up. A flyer for a blues night at the Blue Frog. Box of safety matches. I turned, nearly tripped over: burgundy throw pillows, thrown. Also, rather recklessly down there: a laptop with a frazzled Arsenal sticker on it. I longed to set it safely on the coffeetea table, but dared not touch.

Upon that table: notepad struck with doodles — the type you scrawl while feigning attention to someone on the phone. Near-empty bottle of Sula red, candle stuck in it, a slurp of wax southbound to tallowed table. Something sparkled there: a silver hoop earring, viridian baubles strung along it.

Only one. Earring.

My stomach clutched; I didn't want to know. Cowboy had had a life before me; I had, too. He had a life even *during* me — and I supposed I did as well. And who knew what lay ahead — if we even had a fate line at all?

I sure as frock didn't.

I pressed forth with my visual tour, and promptly felt better sighting, across the room, upper shelves housing many, mostly English language, books — A *Tale of Two Cities. Serenade. Calamity Jane's Letters to Her Daughter.* An entire series of Blueberry graphic novels. Several volumes on photographic, cinematographic — and cooking! — techniques. DVDs: *Persona. Manhattan. Double Vie de Véronique.*

And — *c'était possible?* Baudelaire's *Le Spleen de Paris.*

I was beginning to wonder if it was art that had truly linked us, bridged us, together. Had we been shooting our way towards each other all along? Straight from the hip? Shot in the dark?

A long shot no longer: My senior year at Lenne Lenape High, I'd read Plato's *Symposium*, where all these philosophers define love. I was most taken with Aristophanes's view that we were once all eight-limbed, globular beings, later split in half, destined to cartwheel the world in search of our missing hemispheres.

Was this how you landed up on that half-moon, once in a blue moon?

Here, a low end table, with what looked like a makeshift shrine upon it, but no Hindu deities to be found. Bust of a goddess, something Athena-esque, a pair of headphones slung around her neck. String of lapis lazuli. A rattle of keys hung off a shoelace. iPod dock. And a framed black-and-white of a saried woman, face down-dipped, hallowed with tenderness, gazing into the near-new-moon mien of an infant snugged in her arms, the tip of its nose just visible, swerving up wavelike from silk.

I lifted it up for a closer view. Baby Cowboy? Precursor to the screensaver child? She'd let her baby grow up to be . . . ?

Well, maybe so'd my mama. I set the photo down, lining it up exactly with the dust-free triangle that had held it.

How had I never seen any of these things? Had I been so wrapped up in my head, in him?

I reloaded. I knew the photos might be tricky to explain, but at least there was no one in them; anyway, I didn't have to share them. Maybe not even with myself.

The act was the record, the experience its grooves.

Water stopped.

I fled back to the bedroom, readying to pack my camera away. But not before I fell to my knees on the edge of the bed. Zoomed to the rippled sheet below me.

Where the truth lies: Click on a contour map of a half-imagined but all-real place. Face.

And then I tucked Chica Tikka away and lay on my back, gazing up at that flower-fret sky, learning it by heart just in case.

(His steps approaching . . .)

I figured I wouldn't ever be back here again, would never step in that eddying river twice. Thrice.

(. . . followed by that smile . . .)

* CHAPTER 36 *

Bridge Pose

The next day, I returned to Andheri to the great relief of my aunt and uncle. I couldn't risk any surprise visitors at the hotel after that whammy of finding Karsh at the door. Plus, Kavita had the key, and she and Sabz could be using it at the drop of a dupatta.

—Dimple, you're very quiet, my aunt remarked at dinner.

—No quieter than us, Sangita said quickly, meeting my eyes with the tiniest nod. —It's just that kind of day, I suppose.

—Sorry, Maasi, I replied. —I think the time difference is catching up to me.

—It takes the same number of days as time zones you travel across to catch up to yourself, Akasha informed me. —So you should be arriving any minute now.

To catch up to yourself. Like I had in that bungalow — only to wriggle out of my own grasp as soon as I got ahold of me. The one that got away.

My uncle and Sangita went for a walk afterward, around the gardens of the complex. I excused myself early to sleep. But sleep, as usual, excused itself from me.

Another missed call from my parents. Then I remembered: It was a day for celebrating, and I called to wish them a happy anniversary.

They were back at the hotel. Had seen the Taj, at sunrise and sunset, and Baby Taj, too, with a thick-spectacled tour guide sporting a huge red bindi that turned heart-shaped as he furrowed his brow over the course of the day.

In between oohs and aahs, my mother had apparently advised the grateful guide on how to better his relationship with his daughter-in-law, now a member of their joint family household (do *not* knock on their door first thing for your tea, and, baapray, let the couple go to bed early once in a while — arranged marriage; they're still figuring out how it works). My father just then returned from distributing the pain aux raisins purchased from the hotel's French patisserie to the street kids hawking postcards outside the gates, though they'd partaken not without a sale first: He was obstensibly now bearing a fat booklet of Fatehpur Sikri shots.

—But tomorrow we will be going there, my mother sighed, I supposed to both of us.

—For the first time since our honeymoon! my father added from close proximity, chewing on something, possibly a mille-feuille.

—The famous thread? I ventured. I could already picture them in that shrine, sankalping away in deep concentration. And since I'd currently taken up residence (gazing) in my navel, might as well go all the way: Surely they'd be wishing they hadn't spawned such a delinquent daughter.

We love-you'd and clicked off, and I slipped under the sheet, wondering how the hell people stayed together so long.

*   *   *

A soft breath upon my face, a scuffling beside me. The mattress sunk ever so slightly as a small weight deposited itself upon it.

I opened my eyes.

In the half-light, Akasha's wide wise irises drew into focus now, scrutinizing mine. They were overcast, bluescreened.

—Wait . . . don't blink, she whispered, eyes widening further. —I've never seen this before!

—What? What is it?

—Wow, Maasi, she exhaled, dropping back onto haunches and resting her hands on her knees. She shook her head, incredulous. —I see *zeros*. Your eyes are full of *zeros*!

*   *   *

Zero. A day for adieus. And so the next, my avast went ahoy. I gave my family the slip, took that last ship, akinship to Chuim Village. Left the banks of sense for the undercurrent. He beckoned, but I reckoned from some depth, I'd called.

Dip into the possibility . . .

Filibusting, but gut trusting; and then it's all in the now: He reaches for my hand; I forsake dry land, dive on into the squall.

Jumping ship, a little death.

I wait for regret; why doesn't it come?

Land legs are found, reached for, pulled on.

And just like that, in a breath, it was done. Out the flying fish door, blue girl drowned, lost to shore.

The we was gone.

*   *   *

Nightfell. Daybroke. And later, yet one more last backstroke — and, yes, something had changed. He'd hinted I couldn't come around here no more. Maybe my hesitation that time, this. The fact I was leaving soon. Or none of these things, it occurred to me, watching his profile in the driver's seat as we worked our way out through Union Park.

A seasick quease, sharp tumult in the belly like when you're just about to slip. Though I'd never been in this situation before, somehow I still knew this feeling.

Me and Cowboy, we had no proof, only projection. Maybe I'd been projecting this entire love story; maybe he'd been, too. But did it matter — as long as we'd shared the same projector?

—We can't go to the hotel, I said, and didn't say because that room was precisely the shape of Karsh's absence — and another pair of lovers was perhaps reuniting there even now. He didn't ask.

We couldn't go to that other side where he lived in theory though not always in reality.

—They need protection, was all he'd said, but somewhere inside, I'd already known there was someone at home for him, a someone or ones who meant enough that he didn't, couldn't, create that kind of superfluous pain.

Passing the scores of little shops and stalls, the tree-shade sleeper, the small boy swerving out of the way in the nick of time . . .

—And me? I'd asked, feeling petty and unevolved even as I did.

—You don't need protection, he smiled, steering back around the rushing child. Going where, this little creature? Why so fast? —And thank god for that.

I contemplated this, unable to identify how it made me feel. A just-detectable lift.

—And the bungalow . . . ? I asked.

—Shanker flies back tonight.

—Shanker?

—It's his place. I just have the keys — given my situation.

The name from that business card on the dusky shelf floated up into my mind. So that wasn't Cowboy's boat, the hull and hold we'd rocked so many hours in Chuim Village — but the cinematographer's place? All the connections I'd felt photographing those scattered objects of desire — the thin-skinned bandurra, a broken-consort pandora, album spines, book binds, undrunk wine . . . not *him*?

Was that my *(if you're reading this right now)* fucking soul mate? Shanker Arora?

—I think we'll always meet in unconventional spaces, Cowboy was saying now. Was a bungalow unconventional? A glimmer of coastline at road's end, an illusory horizon.

—I've got my life, you've got yours, he continued, as if talking to himself. —And this . . . this has been a gift, an extra — something that should propel us forward in those lives. You've got a lot of things to do; I want you to do them. And same goes for me. We're both at a beginning. . . .

What the frock? I bit back the question of whether we'd meet again. It felt against the rules we'd laid out that first day after the Star Chamber, and I'd be damned if I'd ask something so cliché.

—Will we meet again? I blurted immediately, damned.

Nearly past the strew of shops, a backwards ride, inevitable rewind.

—As Coelho says, if the desire is there, truly there, the universe conspires with you to realize it, he said slowly. —Because it's what you put out there to begin with — in the blueprint you wrote in the sky when you chose to come to earth. But it is you, in this human avatar you've willed yourself into, who must think it. Ink it.

Right. I'd note that on my calendar.

—So I'll take that as a definite maybe, I said. His phone rang. He didn't answer it, but that screensaver, that little boy. The irrational thought it was the same child whose life he'd just spared, rushing away down that road.

Catching up to himself?

He glanced at the message, set the cell down. It could have been him, such was the resemblance; I'd thought it was.

—I'm in a complicated situation. Thank you for taking me out of it for a little while.

—I am, too, I said, not adding: Now.

—I'm happy to be with you, he said. —But I'll be happy also when I'm not.

—You're one happy guy, I said glumly.

—That's not what I meant. I'll be happy about *us*. I'll always be happy there's an *us*.

Out of habit — how quickly they form! — I reached over to take his free, nonsteering hand. A rush of sad gratitude, a feeble attempt to hold on to something.

—Sorry, he said, removing it gently and glancing at me briefly, sidelong. —I need it to shift.

And that hand moved to the gears; mine, to my lap.

That small gesture — this gentle withdrawal — stung miles. I mean, the Beatles wrote a smash hit on the joys of hand holding. The aching gladdorious desire to do so.

A semi-epiphany (I was too worn out to have a full one):

Was that *song* why it hurt so much?

—I feel . . . sick . . . like someone just kicked me in the *gut*, I burst out.

—Can I tell you something? he asked now. —Without you getting upset?

I shrugged, nonchalant, already upset.

—You think too much about how you feel, Indie Girl.

I mulled that over.

—That doesn't make me *upset*. . . . I concluded.

Oh. I couldn't help but laugh then; he, too.

—The reservoir, he said now. —Run, run . . .

—It's just funny, I said finally. Not even a week. —That I'm the one who's leaving.

—You feel like it's me, na?

I nodded as we turned from Off Carter Road to Carter Road, Unbombay perhaps back to Bombay. Back on the map.

– But you forget, Indie Girl, he said quietly. —From the very beginning . . .

—I know, I know, I said. And despite what I knew, *Off* Off Carter Road — the ever-departing, always-arriving Arabian Sea blurring these unpaned windows — gave me hope that both places, spaces existed still, were part and parcel of the same mythical metropolis. —We were never here.

* * *

We passed Bandstand, where lovers paraded in public in order to be alone, leaned against one another, staring seaward, towards that bridge to everywhere and nowhere, or into the oceans of each other's unfathomable eyes. That bell would chime at the tidal rise, ring them out their reverie before the waters took them.

They say true love never dies, but it could kill you in an instant at high tide.

* * *

The hotel loomed majestically and somehow inappropriately in the near distance.

In Unbombay, Phoenix was no mill mall, but that firebird who after centuries ignites its nest, its home, so painstakingly built — casting all to ashes . . . from which another firebird eventually flies. The garuda, Vishnu's vahana — a sister creature? The avalerion: a legendary winged thing that drowns itself upon laying its eggs.

Back to zero. Double that zero. Tip into infinity.

—Doesn't this feel like a dream? I whispered now.

—Every day feels like a dream, he replied, smile soft in his voice. I dared take him in. So much affection in his eyes, my logical mind couldn't piece it together: this strangerlove, his fastidiously sustained distance with his easy proximity. How the closer we got, dragging in our respective tales and travails in a years-miles-long fishnet, the quicker we slipped through the holes and tears.

—Message me before you go, he said, pulling to a stop.

—Should I put it in a bottle? I inquired, stepping out.

When you cross, don't turn round. Save for that fateful day in Customs, he never had. But me, ever since, I'd always glanced unblinkingly back at him — neighless, all-yes — double-taking so gallopingly towards, so craningly far . . . it nearly became looking forward. No front and back to a circle, see.

Sea knees weak, a shaky landing. The Jeep swirled back round, single-footing, spun gone. And I saw:

I was truly at the beginning of Lands End.

And then I had to see what lay beneath. Past Castella de Aguada (which had done no good at keeping intruders at bay for me), the open-air amphitheater (where our story seemed middlelessly all beginning and end), beyond the tourists (who we were to each other), the locals (who we were to each other as well), and onto the palm-fronded path to where the world did indeed seem to end, in a swift headlong drop to the sea. A staggering return to dry land: I teetered down the steep steps, banked by rock face and brush. Passed a few men working wall-side, hauling chunks of rubble upwards — unclear whether something was being raised or razed.

Heartbreak or heartmake?

I felt an affection for them, surely unreciprocated, as I descended. Through palms below: a peak of sea, tarp roof, rubbish.

At rock's bottom: a low wall with a couple rust-blue wheelbarrows collapsed against it. Yellow buckets, trees flagged with plastic bags. And upon flattened gravel, a fleet of heat-defeating knurled banyans evoking a roofed space, a shaded gazebo with roots slung well beyond the flockering leaves.

Just ahead, gravel gave way to saffron sand, then to the black-cracked flat jut of sea rocks, jagging water between them, a waterworld version of the city's jigsaw pavement. A few fisherfolk squatted here or there, a child or two navigating the slippery surface with ice-skater ease. A hurl of blue netting. Beyond: a few scorched-sky red-edged boats.

Just past these tripled terrains, after a margin of seawater, a dark strip sanded ran, another besurfed stony turf under construction beyond it, a thin rivulet between these two fingers of land. Like a peace sign, a fork in the road — both? Roads not taken? Or two taken?

And raised aloft on sea-sunk piers, echoing the suspending slinks above: the bridge itself. That bridge that had been my soul's Pharos these days, suddenly no longer the sole highlight from this vantage point. Now there was also the fishing village, the Koliwada below it — which was always tucked out of sight viewed from a high-up hotel window or speeding crosswater taxi.

Viewed from this perspective, the Link was all bottom. Gazing under-bridge, cross-bay: tops lopped off the buildings Worli-side, my eyes flooding mostly with water. Above, the pylon mast and spans appeared a bit of wigwam, a brief curving up and off and away. Those sea-sunk pillars supporting the entire enterprise delved deep, elongated reflections joining cement reality to endow them with plummeting skyscraper dimensions, as if the real story were here — down, down to where they dove and clutched at ancient shifting sands.

The bottom of the deep blue me, we: All that running around, clubbing in Bandra, launching SoBo-ward from that slipdip road, clicking this town from either side, and it had never until today occurred to me to call upon this underlink, get wind of her side. All these untold stories — or at least untold to me.

And even the stories that seemed known: Cowboy. Karsh. Beneath the bridges we made to join each other, connect: Seashells screamed, doubloons dreamed. Sailors drowned, shit abounded. Currents hurtled, mermaids ungirdled, longed for land legs, then grieved the shedding of their scales. Sirens wooed the entire crew, seducing them to slip off sails.

The only way to let a place inside, a person inside, was to love it, I thought then. And no matter where these beings dispersed, dispelled to, whether we would meet again or not — throw each other a line from time to time — you couldn't lose what you let in. Just had to carry it across.

*　※　*

I crossed back now from water's edge, beneath the banyan and onto a shaded walkway. The Koliwada temple. In a small saffron mandir to the left: a Sai Baba with bell pepper flowers draped around him, single bulb filamenting an orb of light in the root-ropy haze.

The temple priest dozed in a chair to the side. I removed my shoes, moved past the crackled grey walls into the alcove beyond.

In that cavelike interior: bells, Oms; a wick-lit portrait of goddess Durga atop tiger. And center stage, a potholed, chunnied, and garlanded head, blazingly orange and raucously beautiful. Mouth agape (or perhaps nose, as it was bejeweled) in a sideways oval. Two huge-pupiled white eyes — an oddly rainbowless Iris; a third one in bindi position.

These irises didn't touch the tops, lending this vivid Technicolor goddesshead a nearly enraged look. She appeared nigh frilly, like babies in flouncy christening outfits, lolling there upon a little tapestry, accompanied by a feast of coconuts, bananas and blooms, and rupees, to which I added a note.

On a small low table before her: a pair of plaqued silver feet. Facing away from her.

When I turned my own feet back, I saw the whole of the banyan tree filled the Koliwada temple entrance. The bulb burning off the little yellow mandir seemed to glow brighter; day dropped a dab, a glimpse of dimming sea before I began my exit and ascent.

*　✳　*

As I retraced my steps upwards, pathward, I saw the workers were building, not breaking. Up higher and crowds now at the Castella de Aguada. Friends slung arms around one another, hanging out on the low wall, the more adventurous (or better shoed) venturing out onto the knobby terrain of rickety rocked sea edge, rendered minuscule against the backdrop of Coca-Cola billboard, luxury hotel, sea, and Link — now viewed from above again.

A half bridge that had been finished . . . and yet still remained half: abridged. Like that chimerically unspooling skyline I'd viewed upon first crossing. Incompletion. Don't tell me how the story ends.

One more shot with Chica Tikka.

The lights along the Link blurred in my lens, luciolian.

In my eyes, too. For bridges made me blue. But a beautiful blue. They were so magnificent, and yet so humble — so earnest and optimistic in their endeavoring. Reaching, stretching, spanning out to the other side, the Other. Lending an unwary hand, keeping both lands from falling off a flat map.

Keeping the faith. And always a sense of promise, potential upon crossing.

Sometimes bridges brought you closer. Sometimes they just took something away.

I reached for my phone. Changed the number: Cowboy to Unknown.

And went myaway.

✳ CHAPTER 37 ✳
Something Borrowed

Stowaway to a castaway past: Myaway turned out to be a rewind to my own road not taken. I was Chor Bazaar bound at last.

Truly alone at last, too. But, I thought, gazing down at my bag (third-, even fourth-eyed): both cameras accompanying, anchoring me in my adrift.

Once I realized that, I appreciated my solo state. And for a time-traveling return to zero, what better place to go than a *marché des antiquités?*

Plus, given the fact that such a significant part of my trip had been turning souvenir before my eyes, it seemed as good a time as any to pick up a few actual mementos for friends and family back home.

I'd scribbled a list of names on a scrap of paper, followed by eddying question marks as to what to get them . . . and was surprised at some of the ones that had flowed out:

Jimmy. Zara. Amanda.

But also: Gwyn? Karsh? Dadaji?

Every border: blurring.

* ✳ *

At Grant Road, I pocketed the paper, took a moment to get my bearings, then wandered into the heart of Muslim Bombay. Hand-painted store names declared (in English, Devanagari, and, I assumed, Urdu): *Ebrahim Esmail. Parda Manzil Shop.*

It also seemed the heart of meaty Mumbai (thank gods Karsh wasn't here, or we'd be exiting as we entered): Butcher Street towards

Mutton Street. The lanes grew carless, stallful — wares avalanching from shopfronts on either side, like they'd been jack-in-the-boxed out.

I'd come here with the intention of starting anew, clearing the slate — regaining my own balance, confidence, cool. But as I began to stumble around, pulling out Chica Tikka, I started to feel a little self-conscious. Exposed. And I wasn't sure if it was just me and the reaction I inspired, but there wasn't a whole lot of smiling going on here, like, say, at Crawford Market. Was this related to a fruit-heavy diet (at the latter) versus a meat-driven one?

Shallots?

Even the occasional female vendor I spotted on Mutton Street regarded me with the same look of mild suspicion. But I wasn't smiling anymore either, so I guess I wasn't really being the change I wanted to see in this world.

I unlidded Chica Tikka. That hijabed woman — the only other femina on the street now — was definitely giving me a reprimanding look.

Would anybody ever, ever love me again?

Or was it simply my big bolshy camera inspiring the demising of smiles?

Camera back in bag, I wondered if I was truly meant to be a photographer.

Walking around in public in India on my own, I couldn't shake this old knee-jerk tear-lurk sensation, out-of-the-blueing back to me today, of appearing somewhat . . . loose (as in sexually deviant, not relaxed) and . . . peripathetic — like I had strayed, diasporically speaking, to the other side and was now pleading for an in again. I didn't know if it was a sentiment left over from my Lee-jeaned and permed prior visits (before Bombay itself got Miss Sixty'd and keratin-haired). But something in me, the prodigirl daughter, always felt it was begging for India's approval, pardon even — and a hint of that feeling remained with me today. *Hey, Motherland! Like me, like me, like me! Please? With sugar on top?*

(Actually, you've got too much sugar on top.)

A couple generations ago, we used to be the cool ones: the Americans — the pioneers who dared go West, shipping dishwashers and TVs back to our less well-off relatives East, galloping around and returning now and again to visit this forsaken city by the sea, always arriving overfed and still hungry, clenching bottles of hand sanitizer like feeble weapons against what we once were.

That's how my parents described it, anyway. Though they still insisted on the hand sanitizer. But now, it felt the other way around: so many Western Heston boys and girls, expats, trust fund babies, NGO workers, transferred bankers, Fulbright scholars and Bombayologists — *Bombayologists!* — flocking to this town. We — this American-born compensation culture generation — were simply soliciting to come back, practically offering sexual favors in exchange for five-year visas, or the Holy Grail of the PIO card. But sadly for us, no one needed that 1975 dishwasher now (not when you could purchase one at Vijay Sales in pincode 400058 opposite the Maharashtra Bank, diagonally across from Bharat Petrol Pump from eleven A.M. to ten P.M. daily — or hire a 1995-born human one).

Or maybe it had always been the other way around on some level: Maybe staying in India was where it had always been at. Was living in a state of permanent homesickness a proof of that truth — my parents' for here, mine for who the hell knew where? A signal that one should never have up and left? Or was it a sign of a deeper discontent, an anywhere-*but*-hereness?

And by the way. Would anyone ever love me again?

My dizzying bout of circular thinking was interrupted by a tiny bleat. My gaze dropped and fell upon a lovely little brown-spotted white-ankled goat, bestowing upon me its beatific smile; its shadow resembled a small girl twisting, turning in a long ball gown.

The goat was tethered on a very short rope to a metal ring stick-ing out of the ground. I looked back up. This creature was my vahana — my divine vehicle, my godvan caravahana: for I'd been teleported to the nexus of Chor Bazaar, arriving dizzied, dusted, and amazed — literally, I was *in* a maze, a warren of sun-moted alleyways, riddled with stalls and stores peddling a mishmash of tan-talizing — and sometimes incomprehensible — wares.

I pulled out my list. Chandeliers; tea sets. For Catherine, tea-drinking queen. Projectors for a lumière unbrother; rotary dials, cell phones; missed calls. Missed. Goddesses, gods, Jesuses, Mary, medi-cine dolls for all-believing Gwyn. Old cameras, like Chica Tikka's foreclickers: a singular reflexing back to Dadaji. Stereo systems, 78 rpms, gramophone hi-fives and vinyl, vinyl, vinyl.

Karsh, Karsh, Karsh. My third eye, fourth, circled from LP to ship wheel, car spring to fish-eye lens, trays of jeweled undoored doorknobs, spinning a 360-degree love song. To him. To them. My lost-and-founds, and sometimes lost-agains.

As I seeked-and-hid, deep biddened into the heart of this hag-gling, dazzling helix, it began to feel what I sought was in fact what those objects collectively conjured up. The past fusing seamlessly with the present moment. A strain of an almost-forgotten refrain.

I know that we will meet again. Will you recognize me then?

*   *   *

The sun slued downward with all the velocity of a destringed marionette. I began to retrace my way out this labyrinth. Arjuna had whispered to his wife's womb the secret of the maze, and when his son Abhimanyu grew, so he made his way. I wondered what we'd been whispered in utero — the melodies, the myths we'd overheard, ingested — and how even now they were playing them-selves out.

Though the market was emptying, I could hear the dueling duet of deal-making before the sounds fragmented into words. It was a novice negotiation in progress, as the upwards tilt of the phrase endings suggested, and the smile in the voice, too. An English (American English?):

—Come *on*!

I rounded the bend to see — standing before a god-and-goddess-laden stall, blue eyes zeroing in on a brilliant blood orange Titwala Ganesha — the proprietress of this accent: a milkily gold-skinned salwar-kameezed woman browsing through mountains of deities.

A street away, evocative strains of the muezzin from the nearby mosque tugged the air with longing and faith so intermingled as to become a wish accompli as I trained my eyes on this girl.

It was Gwyn.

*   ✽   *

I zoomed in.

It wasn't Gwyn. But somehow I knew then, she'd been here, or was en route. She'd gone one way, West, and I'd thought her lost. But one-way West brought you East, was a circle, after all.

Ganesha: ally of origins. Shiva. Friend of ends.

When I exited the market, I had no knickknacks in hand. Nothing but that list of names.

They say whatever you lose you find at Chor Bazaar.

I hadn't found anything.

So perhaps that meant, it occurred to me as I flagged down a taxi on Sir Jamshedji Jeejeebhoy Road:

I hadn't lost anything?

*   ✽   *

And maybe it was time to be found as well.

—Andheri, I told the driver, —West.

I'd get one more girl back to my maasi and kaka at least.

I sank back into the seat, covered in a ruggy fuzz of blue blooms with sanguine heart centers.

The driver's eyes, a warm cinnamon, glanced at me from time to time in the rearview, looking like a separate entity, a severed stretch of face run astray from the upper back, wavy hair, broad shoulders resting against towel-twined headrest, like a visage trying to spin around, step back, and take a good look at itself.

I gave him the address. I asked him his name.

—Mehboob, he replied after a moment's hesitation. —I am Mussulman, madame.

I wondered why he felt the need to elaborate. Unless what he'd heard in my question was another query buried beneath, perhaps one he'd often been asked in his life, one that was maybe not always so buried beneath.

—Nice to meet you, Mehboob. Ji. I'm Dimple, I told him. It was the first time I'd spoken my name in what felt like a very long time.

—Dimple.

The floating eyes fixed on me. —You are Indian.

—From America, I replied, almost apologetically.

—You are still Indian. No matter where from.

I was relieved to be informed of this.

—And you? I asked him then. —Mehboob-ji?

He froze a moment, mirrored eyes stunned.

And then he uncorked the tale, told me how he had come from Uttar Pradesh many years ago. Where he had fallen in love with the wrong girl, but the rightest one for him: a Hindu girl, a young romance. Both families had banned the union, and the two, in the dead of night, had hitched a train and then a truck to Bombay, city of dreams, to lay their claim to live their own lives, together. And it had been a struggle: she doubling over into ragpicker, gathering plastic, glass, newspaper scraps from Bombay's streets, hours spent sorting them in sheds stinking of turned milk and dank cardboard; he posturing straighter, higher, hanging around the railway stations, scrambling to heft travelers' suitcases upon his head, to walk them, for a few rupees, a few paces to their destination, whether cab or abode. Forgiveness from their families had been eons in the making, and not everyone had accepted them even after all that; for many years, they weren't even welcome home — abandoned, orphaned by their own living parents.

So they made their home each other. It seemed in a heartbeat we were pulling up to Shoppers Stop. I thanked him, almost sorry to go.

—For a wonderful ride back, I told him. —For sharing your story.

His rearview eyes widened in disbelief.

—No, madame, I thank you! he exclaimed. —For wanting to *hear* my story. For speaking my name.

I couldn't speak now.

—And because, he added, —*you* are my god!

I was dumbstruck.

—Mehboob-ji, I whispered. —What do you mean?

And then he turned to face me, rearview eyes vanishing, coalescing upon, before me, for the very first time: a full face, lined with time, etched with experience — and attached to a whole body of an entire human being.

His was a kind countenance, eyes warm and underlain with a desperate optimism, a tidy beard only partly concealing a smile that made it possible for me to imagine his good-dream face, what he'd looked like as a boy on a day when all had gone well and one could never have imagined the struggles abounding, around, ahead.

—You are my god, he repeated quietly. —You hailed my taxi; you asked for this journey. And so it is thanks to you, madame, that I can feed my children, my wife. Keep a roof over our heads. It is thanks to *you*.

Something palpable between us, enveloping us, for that moment.

Love. Here, in this unexpected corner. Just when I thought I'd lost it.

Maybe it was always there, I thought, exiting that blue-flowered Fiat: incarnating in different faces, places, spaces all the time. Never lost, always found. If you could just see it . . . instead of looking so bloody hard for it.

CHAPTER 38

Something Blue

Amazingly, the next morning, I peeked out from my heavy-lidded room to a-boo no one home.

I sighed; it felt luxurious. Broke-yolk light dribbed in from the grilled bedroom window overlooking the shared courtyard, illuminating the T-shirts and dishcloths hanging to dry on nearly every bar.

I fell to a squat by the bedroom wall, the bug lights, and before I knew what I was doing, I'd tumbled upwards into headstand.

It was a finned movement, I realized, a winged one, too — swooping into a submarine view. Headstand, meditation: a kind of submersive ascent — a falling *up*, the way it felt in the suburban New Jersey aboveground swimming pools of school friends. That ever-expansive aqua: not smothering, rather, mothering, supporting, flight.

And, here, in Andheri — the poly-pincoded most populous Bombay suburb — I stilled, found myself buoyant in that flow, born out of the blue. Head clearing, crowning into the new.

Belle eau, beautiful water. The root of blue.

I felt . . . good. Even my own blues measured a whole note of joy; I could hear it now, see it. Blue sometimes meant sadness: blue Monday, the mood. But blue skies were often linked to optimism, happy days. In German, being blue meant being drunk. A Baudelairean, boozed-up blau.

And what was wrong with a spot of rain, a bit of inebriation? People cried happy tears, too, didn't they?

Wasn't the monsoon wonderful (if you weren't trying to drive in it)?

In my mind's eye, I focused on that hue now.

Iris: sea-to-sky-is-sea.

Literally. Sankalp: You're it. A riptide of the same dreamed oceanic shade caught my gaze, tealing out from beneath Sangita's borrowed (by me) bed, which I'd never been eye level with till now.

Bowled over by the possibility I'd imagined something into such being, I bowed down, thudded out the pose and crawled over to the bed frame, pulling that something out to investigate further. Like a magic trick, it unraveled: a sea scroll unwinding endlessly into my arms.

It was Sangita's wedding sari. Something about it looked different, but I couldn't quite place what. The ends, I saw, as they finally swept into my hands, were frayed, these scruffed threads a paler shade of cyan.

And once the sari silk had all flowed out from underbed, I caught a shock of yet another blue behind: electric — that überquote-covered container. I coaxed it out.

Zara's shoebox.

Inside: a couple flyers on which were written an address I nearly knew. A date: today.

And nothing else. No shoes.

Another root of blue, and this a part-Indo one: *bhel*. To shine, flash, burn. Also: to mix. And I was burning with a certitude: Sangita wasn't out running an errand, and certainly not a wedding one. And no way she was mixing, commingling with Deepak — not in those electrifying platforms.

Whatever music was moving her to dance, swinging her, saving her from her own breed of blues — I had to know. Had to go.

Hear it for myself.

* * *

I landed up in a very different Cuffe Parade. Entered a parallel universe World Trade Centre. No boats, buoys, or fisherboys.

I zoned out into that memory, but woke to find myself in a lobby with a ghost-town cineplex vibe, industrially deserted. What the frock was Sangita doing here? And where was everyone? I was contemplating hitting up the Causeway to pick up those souvenirs, when my attention was diverted by a bolt of color in the otherwise dim foyer.

A petite but inarguably postpubescent Indian chica with platinum dyed hair and a very Harajuku Girls outfit was sauntering in, accompanied by a pleasantly plump Indian boy with enormous pastel feet; he was attired in orange-and-black-print fabrics and periwinkle cravat with a fuzzy mop of hair — that he was currently yanking over his gelled crew cut. He looked familiar.

—Fred? I whispered as the pair passed before me.

—Meet Fred Flintstone! the boy yelped, then hummed the theme. He glanced at the girl for approval, but she appeared distinctly unimpressed. He took me in, skeptical. —You here for kummikum, too?

I did that side-to-side ambigu-nod to cover my bases, wondering if he was speaking Malayalam.

—The Comicon *Convention*, said platinum-blond brunette, clearly not fooled by my feigned ambiguity. *Comicon?!*

—Rikesh! Trupti!

Another Indian boy, a bit taller and getupped as Superman, landed up and high-fived the other two.

—Hey, Sanjay!

Sanjay turned to me, sticking out a hand. —Superman. Archnemesis: Apathy. Superpower —

—Dude, the girl interrupted. —We hate Superman. What kind of guy wears his underwear on the outside? I mean, no self-respect, ya!

She kind of looked like she liked Superman more than Rikesh/ Fred, though, as her gaze loitered on his thus dissed exteriorized undergarment.

—And all that time in phone booths, I added. —It's a little creepy.

Superman laughed good-naturedly. Actually, it could be it took a lot of self-esteem to wear your underwear on the outside.

Fred-ji glanced at my camera bag. —With the press?

I brandished my camera to verify the lie. The three now swooped into a big-grinned pose, except the girl, who was too cool to smile.

—What publication is this for? Superman-ji inquired politely.

—Uh. *Flash! Flash!* magazine.

Fred-ji *aacha'd.* —So you coming up, yaar?

Who knew where Sangita was anyway? Her phone was now switched off, direct to voice mail. I figured I might as well stick it out and secure some images. And I was also just curious to check out more brown people kitted out as non-brown superheros.

So I, yaar, Western Heston nodded.

—Wouldn't miss it.

Fred, Superman, and Harajuku Girl flew on through at the sign-in desk. I attempted the same breezy Bedrock stroll, but they stopped me — right below the high-flying neon banner declaring Comicon, with its comic girl heroine mascot etched upon it in all her bulbously breasted crevasse-cleavaged big-lidded red-and-blue kitted glory. Very Wonder Woman. Except carrying a basket of fish.

The spunky-looking sign-in female (i.e., with an entirely green face) glanced up at me.

—Excuse me, where are you from?

—I'm American, I single-reflexed, adding *Indian,* and too late realizing She-Hulk probably meant what press organization, given the cam (and that I was not, in fact, of that politically incorrectable origin either). I was contemplating playing the *Flash!* card again, or maybe saying I was dressed *up* as a *Flash!* photographer, when she threw out:

—Superpower?

I was at a loss. Was this loss my archnemesis?

She grinned at me, teeth appearing artificially whitened against the roaring forest of her face.

—Cowboys? she guessed, and gestured me on.

Before I stepped through, I photographed She-Hulk and, so he wouldn't feel left out, the random slobbish dude approaching her. Through my viewfinder: a kind of tan, long-haired hippie in Vegas tee, sunglasses, bathrobe, long boxer shorts . . . and Birks (envy!). Very *Big Lebowski*.

In fact . . .

Suddenly energized by the Dudeness of what had seemed mere dudity, I decided to case the joint. Indians of all shapes and sizes wandered around in their regalia: some of it costumes, some just appearing to be . . . Indian clothing. Several stalls were vending all things comique: tees, puzzles, books, stickers. And the most sizeable stall of all? One selling headbangers merch: Metallica, Iron Maiden. Clearly, heavy metal was alive and well in the Bay (after all, I supposed, in such a clangorous town, one had to make quite a lot of noise to be heard at all).

Behind the stalls was a stage area with a few folding chairs semi set up for something. A crew of Manga folk now besieged the platinum-blond brunette girl, a very passable sister-pair included, who were maybe from *Totoro*. A well-beyond-half-naked, sweet-faced Tarzan with three lovely moles constellating his right cheek hung out nonchalantly against a backdrop of Disney princesses; he was fig-leafed in a suede loincloth and looked like he'd used some excess fabric (of which there must have been hectares) to make a headband as well. X-Men, Princess Leia, and a host of people who didn't really look dressed up, just like they'd put on a stroke of face paint, milled about.

Harajuku Girl was smiling coyly at Superman now. He predictably got all cool and collected.

Everyone was with somebody, or about to be.

I got that lonely feeling again. I suddenly longed to discuss deep things with someone. Preferably someone I was having sex with.

Looking around at all this amped-up grinning youth, one thing was clear from their excitement at . . . themselves: Several of them would be getting laid tonight, pooling their hues and leaving confoundingly colored wig hair on each other's pillows come dawn.

I noticed a click of camera folk clearly on assignment, shooting some of the convention participants as an overly enthu journalisto fired questions their way:

—What superpower should a Mumbai superhero have?

A chorus of gung ho replies from the costumed posse:

—Teleportation! Traffic's a bitch in this city!

—The ability to turn dirt to nondirt! Shit to energy!

—An internal ice machine to stay cool! And keep your beer chilled!

—An anticorruption syringe to stick into the politicians!

—Handheld windmills to put an end to power cuts!

I'd give them that. But what about focaccia for all?

What about *making sure societies honored their women's inalienable rights to safety and total control of their own bodies?*

Forget Mumbai superheros: Couldn't we get some normal *sane* Bombay (or anywhere) people to successfully kick 375, 376, and 377 up the (illegally accessible) arse?

I suddenly felt exhausted. As I worked my way back to the entrance/exit, I returned fully to my navel.

And what about *me*? What about granting *me* a superpower to process all this what and who I'd obviously not been so careful I'd wished for? Or at least a god to lend a hand(s)?

Somehow the world had once seemed a tidier place, despite my couple-years-old angstful era of trying to find myself. I had been so confused back then — was I Indian, was I American? Loves me, loves me not? Those questions seemed touchingly green now. In a way, I found myself longing to be confused, about which side to choose — for it to be that simple: Draw a line from your heart to mine; I'd thought it done. But what if you were walking the line all that time? Tightrope and twine — tying, untying the knots?

Treading the hyphen, being the bridge — a space so illuminating with enigma, copious with ambiguity. I was mildly confused about why I *wasn't* confused.

I supposed an old kind of calm could overtake you, if you'd just immerse in that indefiniteness.

The entryway walls, which had seemed greyish, nondescript, were upon closer scrutiny a washed-out blue swirled with pale green tendrils. I lay a hand to one, which turned out to be peach-fuzzy. Comforting. I leaned against it, lifted Chica Tikka.

And when I lay eye to viewfinder, my assumption I'd be framing a bunch of brown people trying to be white was quashed, pronto. For, farther in the space, a flock of gods was thumping about the room now: a golden Laxmi, an elephant-headed Ganesha.

Sankalp? I did have a superpower: my third eye!

I peered deeper into that godland, filling it to the hilt.

My eyes whipped after a splash of cobalt lightning. An all-blue figure slinked, then winkingly vanished, into the comic cosmic crowd.

It was instantly imperative I photograph this deity, this slender stroke of azure energizing the space, weaving my own mood into the joyful stratosphere of the hue.

How could I have forgotten the gods in my immersion in blues?

Through the loudspeakers, a voice intoned, —Would all contestants please make themselves known? We are about to announce Best Costume.

Back inside, I peeked around to where the crowd had gathered vibrantly around the stage area.

—And the winner is . . .

A loaded hush.

—*Parag Patel!*

A chest-beating howl; this was toasty-toned Tarzan. Ironic and kind of cool that the contestant wearing the least fabric in the entire room had just snagged the prize.

I was edging back into the hullabaloo to see what he'd won, when I spotted again that splish of blue now heading *out*, past my furry wall, towards the elevator bank. Fred Flintstone bade it farewell, and She-Hulk high-fived it; clearly, everyone was down with their deities around here.

I once again turned entry to exit.

I followed my blue-skinned god.

—Excuse me! I called out. Even in this dimmed light, the creature glowed as if inner-lit — and froze.

For some reason, I felt shy, lowered my lens.

—Er, what's *your* superpower? I asked, heart pounding harder.

Shiva/Krishna/Vishnu turned to face me — and I at once saw this was no waiflike version of any of these gods.

In one hand, wrist wound with blue-crackled brown beads, was no Krishna's flute but a gilded brush, golden palette in the other. Shiva's snake, which I thought I'd spotted around the shoulders, was rather a thick plait of ebony hair wound around a neon neck. Second-skinning slender upper torso through upper thighs: a ring-a-bell gilt-stitched sun-spawned brocade (also swathed around elbows), a sheer silk waterfall dropping in a heavy shimmer from these quads to just past the surely blue-capped knees.

But the most startling element of all was the magnificent, magical skin: the deepest densest blue, a shade you could dive into like an unwavering iris, a tangible light. Every visible bit of it was drenched in this viscous liquid lapis lazuli Sunday best: lips, fingers dipped all the way to tips, nails blending into blue flesh.

Magnifishent: From the sea-sky of this face, two enormous eyes peered back at me, as if through a heavenly peephole, the all-seeing islands of this most elegant of goddesses.

I took her in, top to bottom. From swinging anchor earrings to blue-to-the-tips toes as well — which I could see just poking out from the ends of a pair of glitterwinged platforms.

From the back of the left shoe hung a diary key.

And what a secret it was unlocking.

I lowered Chica Tikka. Lidded her third eye. I forgot every yoga lesson ever given me and unequivocally did not exhale.

—*Sangita?* I whispered.

Sangita nodded.

*   *   *

Without a further word, we descended the World Trade (a few more costumed creatures bidding Sangita farewell by name) and stepped out into the blinding day to hit the Café Coffee inevitability a few paces up the road. A couple heads turned as we did so, but the scarlet-uniformed staff (who now seemed to be in costume to my comic-conned eyes) had clearly been caffeinating the pageant participants all day, for it was business as usual after that first curious glance.

We ordered drinks and chose a corner table, overlooking the street at Cuffe Parade.

—You look incredible, Sangita! I continued whispering. I wasn't sure why, since it was no secret we were here, or that she was, well, entirely blue. —Honestly, *you* should have won the costume contest.

—I didn't enter the contest.

—Why not?

—Because this doesn't feel like a costume.

I gave her a quizzical look.

—It feels like I've turned myself inside out and I'm wearing my guts on the outside, she explained quietly.

This had gone deep faster than I'd expected. I fumbled.

—Oh? Um. Wow. I had no idea you were part of this whole . . . comic scene.

—It's been my little secret. Anyway, I'm not exactly part of a *scene*. I was just wanting a full-body *experience*.

I considered her odd behavior and erratic hours, the fact she hadn't slept at home last night. Before I could stop myself, I asked, —Sangita. Are you . . . seeing a superhero?

Her eyes: the teeniest of upturns.

—I wish! she sighed. —Tarzan's pretty cute, isn't it?

—I know you've been out a lot lately.

I realized then I didn't want to ask any questions I wasn't prepared to answer myself, and fell silent.

—A full-body experience of *color*, Dimple. I've been going to art school; there was a place for me this term — not next. I'm working on a whole project on superheroines. And I have to thank *you* in part.

I was speechless. Me?

—Yes, you. I've been watching you, throwing yourself with such abandon into your work. And I got the sense there's a whole community out there of people like you, like me, who do that. Like Karsh. Kavita, too.

—Wow. Thank you, Sangita. I'm honored you feel that way, I finally uttered. —And . . . so . . . when are you going to tell Deepak? How serious you are about your art?

She did the ambigu-nod.

—In a way, he gets it, she said. —He doesn't want to work in his father's business any more than I want to decorate his house. But he simply cannot say no to his parents.

She absentmindedly tidied up a sugar spill, carefully depositing the swept crystals into her own saucer.

—This is what I want to do with my life, Dimple, she said. —I'm not in love with Deepak — well, not yet. Though I'm beginning to understand him better. Hopefully, I'll love someone enough one day, or, ideally, won't feel the need to choose, but for now, art is my first and only true love.

Such clarity, such firmness to her tone.

—Sangita, art clearly loves you back. You have to call off the wedding, tell Maasi and Kaka!

—I know. And soon. In fact, every day I wake up and think, today's the day. But as the date gets closer — despite the fact I've been dismantling the plans all along — part of me can't help feeling it's my duty to go through with it.

Dismantling. How she'd undone her wedding sari, I saw now, turned it into something new. The frayed ends of that underbed ensemble: It was the edge, the gilded border that had out-of-framed to become the main body of her azure avatar.

—Your duty is to be happy, Sangita.

—That's very modern-age modern-woman thinking, Dimple, she sighed. —Maybe smart, but a little . . . selfish?

—But you *are* a modern woman in the modern age. And maybe women should have started being selfish a lot earlier! I insisted. —Anyway, *is* it selfish? If you're unhappy, don't you just end up making everyone around you miserable, too?

She had that staring-out-to-sea look on her face.

—I never planned for it to turn out like this, she confided. —It's like life swept me up on a wave that grew tidal — and I landed on a shore I'd never intended to walk. Do you know what I mean?

—I think I do, Sangita. I really think I do.

—I think you do, too.

We stared at each other a long moment, a silent understanding passing between us. An understanding that had been there much, much longer than this moment.

—I guess somewhere inside, I've always known I was just going through the motions. It's just . . . it felt . . . with Kavita going away . . . and, well, other things about her . . . I just couldn't add more disappointment and pressure to Mummy and Daddy's plate. They need one quote good girl in the family. Even though I'm struggling with that role.

—Tell me about it, I nodded. —Anyway, *they* have two, Sangita. Two good girls. Maybe what's required is a redefining of *good?* No one wants to rock the boat. But sometimes you've got to rock it or drown. Good also means doing what's good for you. I know it's not always easy balancing that with what's good for the ones you love . . . but ultimately what's bad for you can't be good for them, you know?

I leaned in, threw all the justifications I'd mastered over the last days her way; they seemed purer in her context. —Your *dharma:* It's got to be to your heart first. What if this is the only chance we've got? And what if we have to relive whatever we do here, now, to eternity? You've got a gift — you have to be able to use it freely, without guilt or reservations.

Sangita looked up at me, watery-eyed.

—Sangita, I urged her, —it's your life. Your journey. You know what you want, what you love. That's a blessing, even if it comes with complications. Don't let it get away.

She reached across the table and lay her cobalt hand upon my own, which I realized now I simply considered brown.

—Oh, Dimple. How'd you get so wise?

—Believe me, I've been wrestling with the same issues . . . just in a different way. Knowing what you want. What you love.

Who. She laid her second hand on mine then.

—How's Karsh? she asked softly.

—I don't know, I said, even more softly. —I barely know how I am. But at least that I can work on. 'Cause I just can't seem to give me the slip. I'm just trying not to fight myself so hard anymore, I guess.

Her eyes danced a little, kindly.

—She used to be my archnemesis, too, she nodded.

—Who?

—Me.

And with that, abruptly, she rose. —Chalo, Dimple.

I jumped up, too, surprised. —Where are we going?

—Home.

—Andheri? I asked her, worried now. —You sure? How long does the paint stay on?

—I've been blue a long time, Sangita replied calmly. —A little longer can't hurt. I'm sick of being my own enemy.

—Yeah? I said, grabbing my bag and then her arm. —Me, too. So what's your superpower?

—You're about to see it, she said.

*　＊　*

We landed up at Ramzarukha. As we mounted the incline, I could see her deepening her breath, the flush of anxiety beneath the layers of paint. I took her hand.

—Sangz? I said. —I've seen a lot of blues lately. But I've never seen a blue so beautiful as you.

She began to smile, then stopped herself.

—What? Did I say something wrong?

—If I move too much, the paint cracks, she explained.

—Let it.

A beat. And then she grinned, so wide, uninhibitedly, her true blue skin splintering slightly to reveal rivulets of tawn beneath; blue meeting brown like an aerial shot of the earth. Of her world. I grinned back, big. At the elevator, we both looked at each other. Exhaled. Pushed.

Up. The only way.

CHAPTER 39

True Colors

We stepped through the magical mystery door, no time to even close it.

Meera Maasi and Dilip Kaka were at the table, settling down to an early dinner. Upon the sound of our entry, their eyes turned towards us, and, as if in slow motion, Kaka rose — the nearly served * chapati slipping from Meera Maasi's fingers to land with a soft *thwack* on his thali dish.

I hung back near the doorway. Sangita took a breath — and a giant step in. Everything around her seemed to fade to white, hush with the sheer hue and velocity of her will.

In the heart of the room she now stood, an avatar of her own creation: awash in azure, bannered in gold, paint crackled wherever she'd bent — an elbow, a knee, an ankle. Blue flecks like melancholic snow prismed her already dazzling platforms. And twin thin copper rills stuttered elliptically down her cheeks: tear tracks? I hadn't seen that descent.

Meera Maasi's mouth now dropped open completely, in pure astonishment.

—Sangita! What is this altoo faltoo? Please — go bathe immediately!

But Sangita held still, held her own.

—*This* is my mehendi party. And I'm not going anywhere, Mummy, she replied gently. —Not to Delhi. Not Mehrauli.

—Beta . . . my uncle said quietly. He looked more resigned than shocked, though. I moved in closer.

—Papaji. Mummy. You told me I had to survive once, Sangita

said now, visibly gathering strength. —When I was a baby, and born too soon, born blue. And now we must do it all over again.

A blue-skinned girl. A blue-skinned *goddess*.

—I have to live my life. And you have to survive that — and live yours.

The mere sound of Sangita's voice — so often so subdued — converged with the stunning visual to bow us down into speechlessness.

—All these years, I've tried to cause you no harm, no worry. Perhaps I always carried the knowledge of how my early birth created such distress, Mummy. And I knew your worries about... other people. I didn't want to add to them.

A quilted sound. It was Kavita, fidgeting in the doorway behind me, face straining with her sister's words, a shadowy figure just beyond her. Sangita looked quickly back towards her parents, took another breath.

—So I've been listening. Always — to you, to Papaji, to what everyone tells me is the right path. But I've also been looking... and somewhere along the way, I think we've stopped seeing the same thing.

Behind her, through the window: Gilbert Hill.

Sangita raised her gilded paintbrush, that golden palette. A faraway look, a near smile.

—I love art. I love painting. I love color. I can read a person from the slightest shift in the hue of their face, the time of day.

Amassing courage, she now turned back and gazed directly at Kavita: a soft but unwavering regard. Kavita seemed to unflush, unflinch a touch.

—And these last weeks, even the last couple of years, I've witnessed some of the people I love most doing what *they* love most. Kavita's choices — how proud I am of her! And Dimple. So I've come to tell you this: I'm going to choose my own palette now.

I've come to *show* you: They say a picture paints a thousand words? Well, I was born blue, and I've been blue for years. But I'm not going to live that way — not unless I choose the shade myself.

That shadowy figure still in the hall, Kavita inched forward to stand behind Sangita now, pride pigmenting her face, and an increasing bravery as well — as if she were absorbing the bright blue flame of her sister's volition. Gently, she squeezed Sangita's shoulder.

Sangita did not sway her stance, her gaze.

—And please make no mistake. I am *not marrying Deepak.*

That voice as steadily vivid as a strong stroke on startled canvas.

I watched my aunt going . . . slightly green.

Together they'd make turquoise, I thought. Kavita emerged from her sister's lengthening navy shadow. She raised her hand — like a surrender, a holdup, a stop-in-the-name-of-love.

—Um . . . ?

My aunt and uncle turned to her in near unison. Blueprinted, her palm, from where it had rested on Sangita's shoulder. She gestured that shadowy figure closer. And Sabz, in simple salwar kameez, now set down Kavita's knapsack, returning her home.

—Mummy? Papaji? Kavita tentatively began. —This is Sabina.

It was as good as announcing her own color.

My aunt turned, training all her pained fury on the bespectacled creature hovering at the threshold.

—Well, *Sabina,* she said icily, though I could sense a splintering not far off. —I am sorry to inform you: You came here for a wedding. And now, as you can see, it is off.

I'd never seen Sabz so still.

—So, my aunt concluded, —I suppose you can be on your way now.

And then, taking a breath, Sabz darted into the heart of the room with a force that could knock my aunt to the floor. Was she going to?

But at the last moment, she halted . . . and bent down in the gesture of ultimate respect to touch first my aunt's, then my uncle's feet.

As she rose, she met my aunt's eyes, and, barely louder than a whisper, replied, —I came here for a wedding, ji. Just not that one.

With a quick nod towards Kavita, she hurtled herself back out into the world again, closing the door thoroughly behind her.

Kavita and Sangita now gazed openly at each other, holding hands, Kavita exhilarated with nerves. My aunt was staring ceiling-ward, probably invoking the gods. My uncle's own regard: downcast, yogic. From the undulation of his chest, I could see he was smoothing out his breathing.

Before I knew what I was doing, despite my alliance with my sister-cousins, I'd stepped in nearer to my aunt. From the coffeetea table beside us, the glass-paned snapped-shot childhood irises of we three girls gazed up at our older selves, rapt.

My aunt had followed my eyes there, her own pooling with tears unblinkingly held in place.

And still, no sound. Even the traffic, construction, muezzin: finger to lips.

A creaking ruptured the silence. We all swiveled our heads doorward: Whose confession would be next?

In stepped the burtanwallah. And, like Mehboob's, for the first time I saw his full face when he lifted it . . . then froze, staring at the lot of us, immobilized around the pulsating blue beauty in the room.

Strong jaw, moon scar. He immediately ducked his head, bolted for the kitchen.

Taps on. Water rush.

My aunt fled the room.

*　*　*

They say Krishna, the blue-skinned god, held the universe in his mouth. Sangita, the blue-skinned goddess, had just revealed hers, and Kavita as well, letting their secrets at long last slip from tongue tips.

My own mouth held a forbidden kiss and, it seemed, endless tales untold. But I remained a goddess with no mouth. Or just a girl.

Until my own lips parted to see: My uncle, who'd automatically been following my aunt from the room, suddenly halted, turned, returned to his daughters, wrapping both in his arms.

A picture paints a thousand words. But I didn't even think to lift my camera.

This was a blue so ablaze, it would surely burn film.

My uncle then went to her, his wife, Kaka to Maasi. Passing the room, through their door ajar, I heard:

—It is those *shoes*, my aunt was sobbing. —We have been cursed by a hijra.

—Maybe, my uncle was saying, —we have been blessed.

CHAPTER 40

Pickle

I discovered my aunt alone in the kitchen later that night. She cut a lonely figure, ghostlike in a gauzy dressing gown, hair hanging long in a loose braid down her back, intent on the task of making tea.

She startled at my entry, and turned.

—Join you? I asked shyly. She nodded, gesturing automatically for me to sit and be served. But I shook my head, took the pan from her hands — she resisting at first, then surrendering with an almost audible sigh — and placed it on the two-plate gas burner.

As Meera Maasi mortar-and-pestled the cardamom, I grated the knob of ginger; it was a coup she allowed this, but clearly bigger battles had been endured lately. She poured the filtered water into the pot, and I measured out the tea, we two gliding in a silent but comfortable ballet, the only sound our padding feet, the hiss of lemongrass hitting hot water, and the slow-flowing glisten of sugar to pan.

—I cannot have my only niece working so hard, Maasi said when we were through, signaling for me to sit. She heaped my plate high with namak para — salty squares of fried dough leavened by the oomph of ajwain, oregano. Then she poured the tea, two cups grouped amicably together on the kitchen table, and moved to the cupboard. Inside, those rows of jars to rival Crawford Market's polished symmetry: lime pickle, chili pickle, carrot pickle, radish and hot chili pepper pickle — none labeled, all introduced by Meera Maasi as she opened each and held it just below my nostrils.

Her crowning glory was the top: a whole row of amber jars aglow with translucent strips of that fleshy drupe suspended in viscous liquid. There was something portentous about the weight and light, and strangely familiar, too.

—This, she said, —is my specialty. Chundo. Shredded mango pickle.

I stuck my nose in the proposed jar and inhaled. It was a heady smell, passionate to the point of irritation. It made sense, then, this belief some had around these parts about how ingesting onions was linked to an increase in a riled (when raw) or carnal (cooked) nature. Not that they made me angry, particularly, but the idea that food had an emotional existence in your body, and could feed or deplete your feelings, rang now olfactorily true.

I dipped my finger into the scoop of chundo now on my plate.

—Dimple! Maasi cried. —Do not touch your eyes! You'll be crying for hours.

When the pickle hit my mouth, I nearly felt like crying anyway. The taste was an explosion of conflict on the tongue: sweet cleaving to sour, so intertwined as to become a third substance — summoning for me a past I'd never known, yet longed for, never lived but clasped close, like a stranger's baby in my arms.

—It's amazing, I told her finally. —You made it yourself?

She smiled shyly, pleased.

—It's so . . . I went on. —Anything with mango, my mom says it makes her so homesick for India.

Maasi sighed.

—Funny, it makes me homesick, too. And I've never left India! Somehow I could understand that.

I nodded. —Well, me, too. And I've never really lived here.

I tried to think of an equivalent savor in the US. Candy apples at Halloween, radiant as sunny-day stained glass at Rice's Fruit Farm? That first summer watermelon, the sweetness at the tip of the triangular slice — the best bite of the lot, so prankishly pink.

These tastes were intertwined with Gwyn; my childhood palate and palette included every one of her hues.

But these same flavors and colors were so shiny and simple, in a way, the jellied jollities of a baby nation — they lacked the gravity of the past, seemed to bounce into the present with the gladdity, the insouciant joy of a beach ball.

And then there were the jars of mango pulp in our own kitchen cupboard, which my mother used on occasion to make kulfi and lassis. But my father's favorite was the pulp itself — mixed with ghee and cumin and served alongside the puris she used to fry at home.

Here, now, these seasonings returned that childhood kitchen to me, on one level brimming with life and an unshakeable sense of security. But in the corner of my child's-eye-view lurked this mysterious sussurating cupboard, incantory with tamarind paste and agarbathi, Mysore soap and sandalwood letter openers, vases shaped like peacocks (and for some reason, loads of triple A batteries), the darkness beyond these objects insinuating a depth, a desire, a portal to another place and time if I could only follow my nose. The trail of mango pulp, the amber jars — which I now realized had probably been sent by Maasi — had been like little flares along the way.

There were the zests of my American upbringing, and the relishes of my Indian roots. But no one ingredient embodied both. The closest connector so far as I could see was the ajwain on my tongue now — invoking India, this moment, this table . . . but also a midnight slice with a heavy sprinkling on Bleecker Street.

We sat in a comfortable silence, blowing at our tea. Meera Maasi poured a bit of hers into her saucer so it would cool faster — something, I recalled with a pang, Dadaji had always done.

—I learned from my own mother, Meera Maasi told me. —And your grandfather. He would take Shilpatai and me to the market to choose the mangoes ourselves. It was a special day. Together we'd chop up the fruit, mix the salt, pepper, sugar. Chili powder, cumin, clove. And the days we made pulp? We squeezed the mango with our hands so's not to lose a drop, jars upon jars. The entire kitchen smelled of it — as if we'd entered the fruit itself, the walls, floor, ceiling its skin.

—The skin's the best part!

—Oh, the skin! Shilpa and I would suck the peels to every last lick. We were inseparable then — very alike. People often asked if we were twins.

—Because you both had orange faces?

She laughed gently. —Aha! Perhaps that was why! The pickle was your Dadaji's favorite. Sweet and sour, he'd say — like Bombay itself. Life itself. Each taste on its own could be too much, or not enough — but if taken together turned into something new.

—Like love.

She didn't seem fazed by this hypothesis.

—Yes, like love. Often so bittersweet.

—But like the way two people together create a new taste, space — a new being in the room.

She nodded, smiling, but was looking out the grille now.

—Yes. Where there's mutual love. Otherwise, one tastes the bitter, the other the sweet.

She hesitated. Then added, —Perhaps when you try to push things together, something that might have worked falls apart.

I looked at her.

—Are you okay about Sangita's decision? I asked quietly.

She shrugged slowly, eyes woeful. —Kaka had warned me things might not go to plan.

—And Kavita's? Plans?

She closed her eyes, did the side-to-side nod.

—Did you know, Maasi? I whispered. —At all?

—I suppose we always know. We just don't want to know we know. People show us who they are all the time, whether they're trying to or not. They can't help it.

—But we don't see, I agreed, considering my own overactive projector, —if it doesn't fit with what we want to see. Sabz is a great person, Maasi. She's loyal, she's brave. She's the one who made Kavita come back — told her never to break the bond with her family.

Another side-to-side, this one slighter, eyes averted.

—Maybe, Maasi, it's like math. Sangita with Deepak created a negative space. Like subtraction — something got taken away from her. And maybe Kavita and Sabz together get better at being themselves? Maybe it's more about that equation than gender — being . . . straight, or crooked, or curious. . . .

We were all something to each other, whether or not we could stick to the roles we'd begun in, been directed towards, hoped for, sometimes. But now I wasn't thinking about Sangita, or Deepak, or Kavita, or Sabz.

—Maybe sometimes you've got room for . . . more.

Something about the taste on my buds and the intent, even sorrowfully kind look Maasi was giving me unbit my tongue. It was funny to find myself talking to her like this — she'd been like a stranger for many years. But maybe that was why it was possible as well.

I was good at strangers, it would appear.

—Do you think you can love more than one person, Maasi? Be in love with more than one person? Or with the wrong person?

Slowly, a nod. A pause. And an opening.

—I loved a man once, Dimple, she told me now. —More deeply than I thought my heart went. With a schoolgirl's abandon and a widow's grief.

I craned in, amazed at this revelation.

—Did he . . . die?

—No. It was grief for something that would never come to be. He loved someone else. And, funnily enough, I had begun to as well. But this didn't stop my heart from opening wider to fit him in. And hurting when that wasn't enough for me to work my way into his.

—Well, I said consolingly, —I can't see how someone would choose another woman over you. She'd have to be extra extra special to come anywhere close.

—Yes. She is. Your mother is extra extra special.

I froze.

—Wow! I cried. —And what did Mom think of the dude?

—She loved him back. With a schoolgirl's abandon and a widow's grief — but this grief like an advance grief. An imagining of one day, someday, losing the person she wanted to spend the rest of her life with. We all met at the same time, a picnic in Borivali. But they had eyes only for each other, and I grew invisible — more an echo than a twin of your mother. And that was that; they were inseparable from very early on. And I ran into the arms of the first taker — the other person I was beginning to care for: your uncle.

I was gobsmacked.

—I'm so sorry about how you felt, Maasi. But frock! Mom never told me. I thought she didn't have any boyfriends before Daddy?

Maasi smiled that sweet sorrowful smile.

—No, she replied. —She didn't.

I let that sink in a moment. Lots of jagged little pieces I'd always felt defined my aunt's sharp tongue and bitter actions suddenly fell together into the smooth image of an unhurt heart; those splintered fragments had once beat together as a whole.

—So your mother had the mad romance, my aunt summed up. —Was swept off her feet all the way to America. Wed, wandered, worked . . . and then was lucky enough to have you.

Something about the way she said it made it seem these events had happened yesterday, rather than roughly two decades ago.

—Well, it took them so long to have me, I replied, hoping to offer some comfort. —And you had Kavita and Sangita so easily. Maybe she thought you were the lucky one?

—Maybe. But it didn't feel like that in the beginning.

—Did Mom know how you felt? About . . . my dad?

—She knew how *she* felt. And — though I suppose I did blame her for a long time — can you really fault someone for this?

I related to Maasi on many levels. And I admired my mother in another way as well. It couldn't have been easy for her to follow her own heart when it would cause so much grief to someone she was so very close to.

—Maybe, I said, —the heart has more rooms, more *room* than we can fathom. And when you feel that connection, it doesn't matter whether the person is too young, too old, boy, girl, taken, not. Could be the heart is expansive enough to include all the pieces that don't fit. And love is . . . the glue?

A momentary silence.

—Then why, beta, my aunt asked me now, —does my own heart feel like it's breaking?

I reached across the table and took her hand.

—I think, Maasi, I replied, —it may just be *growing*.

She smiled then. And as soon as I'd said it, the truth of the sentiment struck me. Growing pains — is that what these were?

She spooned more chundo onto my plate, then handed me the utensil to lick.

I still had one last question.

—Maasi? Did Kaka know how you felt?

—He never said so much. But he is very, very wise. He knew I'd fallen in love with someone . . . but he also knew I might rise, stand up, land in love with him one day. He's a patient man.

She rose now to put away the jar. I caught her stifling a yawn, and gestured for her to go on and lie down; I'd tidy up. She hugged me.

—It's no coincidence, she said, —mangoes arrive just a moment before the monsoon.

And with that, Maasi retired to her bedroom. As the steel plates began to shine under the steady stream of water, I recalled those monsoon rains during childhood visits to India, night-dancing naked in torn sheets with Kavita and Sangita, exhilarated by the torrent of rain upon our young skin. Surely my mother and Meera Maasi had once joined in that dance before the complications of romantic love drew them apart on that soaked earthen dance floor.

Which reminded me of another midnight. The midnight my mother had received word that Dadaji had passed away. I'd been woken by the murmur of my father on the telephone, buried down a corridor of the house. His voice had been low, but something about its frequency and desolate calm roused me out of drowsing. I'd wandered from the dark of my bedroom — past the hallway in which he stood, hunched shadowly, nodding, phone pressed too hard to his cheek — to the lit kitchen. At the entrance, I'd halted.

At the table, my mother had been sitting, hair loose and wild down her back, eyes closed — a very similar jar of chundo open before her. She hadn't been eating any of it, just breathing deeply, inhaling. I'd been a little frightened by this odd action, but touched as well, watched as her tears dripped into the glassware, adding more salt to the sweet.

Somehow, without yet knowing the news about Dadaji, I knew — understood then that she was conjuring what was lost, filling her senses with its memory so as to piece together a sort of afterimage, submerge into an afterglow.

She missed her daddy.

I wanted to move closer, wrap my arms around her, or be wrapped by hers, but didn't want to break the spell. Time travel was a delicate thing, and from the tiny smile tugging the corner of her mouth, I knew she'd found just the right balance of sweet and salty, sour and spice.

I wondered now what her once-twin had been going through at that moment. The sister who'd had to call with the news from a mid-morning Bombay kitchen, wrapped in the arms of the man she'd made her life with, speaking quietly, urgently, to the man she'd longed for, who'd answered the phone at the American end. I wondered as well how Kavita and Sangita had coped — losing the grandfather they'd lived with. It had never occurred to me to wander into anyone else's grief; I'd never realized mourning could password you down a secret passageway into another person's heart. I had always seen it as a closed and emptied room.

I finished tidying up, stood for a moment at the sitting room window, watching Gilbert Hill rising valiantly up from the Andheri dust and construction, somehow resisting camouflage by the encroaching night.

Passing the bedroom, I saw Maasi sleeping with Akasha curled up in fetal position in her arms. They breathed in sync, the soft undulation of their bodies like gentle waves.

✳ CHAPTER 41 ✳

Gateway

A blessing — distraction from the mood of gloom — arrived the next day in the form of my parents, back from their second honeymoon.

The pair was chubbier, giddier — and louder — than I'd seen them in ages. My mother's Indian accent was also switched on to full, and they seemed to carry the aura of their travels with them. I was even pretty sure I could catch a whiff of jasmine oil clinging to their clothing from their stay in that Delhi five-star (or, four-star).

My aunt appeared ready to weep with relief when they entered — and to be honest, I felt that way, too. I raced towards them, yelling, —Mommy! Daddy!

My mother cast me a long look of suspicion tinged with pleasure. My father's smile was all happiness.

—You've lost too much weight, beta, she admonished me now. —Have you not been eating the Parsi eggs at the free breakfast?

—Um. Actually, I've been here a lot lately.

—Much to our delight! my uncle chimed in. My mother raised her brows quizzically at me, but let it go.

In fact, everyone seemed to be pretty keen to let everything go. For one, no mention of the herd of elephants in the room: the earth-quaking revelations that had taken place just yesterday. Then again, the three main characters involved in them had gotten gone ages ago; I was pretty sure Sangita, Kavita, and Sabz were shacked up at the hotel. Even Akasha was off squaring roots in a neighboring apartment, most likely teaching her tutor a thing or two.

As if to fill in these notable absences, my aunt and uncle commenced bombarding my parents with questions about their trip.

—I did not like Delhi, my mother announced grandly.

My father smiled good-naturedly.

—You didn't see Delhi, no? he pointed out, winking at me.

—She wouldn't leave the hotel.

—It was so lovely? my uncle inquired.

—It was too expensive only! my mother exclaimed. —I wanted to be sure to get our money's worth.

—I remember my own visit to Delhi, years ago, my aunt remarked. —It made me want to take a broom to this town. Why does it require the visit of a US president for anyone to clean up Bombay's act?

—It seemed a rich and interesting city, my father mused. —Deepak must be looking forward to the move.

An awkward silence.

—Where is Sangita? my mother asked now, as if just noticing.

—Working on her portfolio, my aunt sighed, finger-quoting the word, which I think roughly translated to: schmortfolio.

—And Kavita?

My aunt looked at my mother . . . and her eyes began watering.

—I'm . . . I'm sorry, she mumbled, coughing, embarrassed. —It must be . . .

—The chameli oil, my father said quietly, reaching quickly into his pocket and bestowing upon Maasi a compact Toblerone, clearly procured from the overly fragrant hotel's minibar.

My uncle's eyes were pained on my aunt's behalf. But my mother sprung into action.

—You know what, she said now. —I *did* catch a bug in Delhi. And I'd like to do something about it.

—Delhi belly? I ventured.

She smiled with forced cheerfulness. —The travel bug! What is all this sitting around the house? Come, Meera, just the girls! Let's go . . . shopping! For . . . pashminas!

My uncle nodded. —Superb idea. Go on, Meera. It will do you good. An outing is in order!

—And you come along with us, Dimple, my mother added, training her ESP eyes on me. I squirmed. —You look like you could use some air as well.

*　*　*

And so we three found ourselves heading steadily south, to Apollo Bunder.

Arvind instructed us to feign interest in the overpriced pashminas at this shop around the corner from the Taj so he could then park there for free for a couple hours while we wandered the area.

In the store, with its rainbow aaray of gauzy cashmere scarves, stoles, and shawls, twirling salesmen flounced and flaunted their fabrics like suicidal matadors. My aunt moved about like a zombie, though she did seem relieved to have my mother around again, sticking close to her.

My mother managed to bargain the hell out of the shop-keepers, and even swung a buy-five-get-one-free on a series of part-silk wraps.

—Gifts for all of us, she announced as we exited, unfurling three of them: a rani pink for my aunt, purple for herself, and turquoise for me.

—But why six? Maasi queried.

—We three, my mother said, pointedly avoiding my aunt's eyes. —And of course, Kavita, Sangita, and Sabina. For when they return from Bandra schmandra.

My aunt startled, but clearly chose not to ask how my mother knew this. And if she wasn't going to ask, I wasn't going to, either. Instead, we crossed over to the Gateway, which loomed suddenly, regally, deus ex machinally before us. I took a shot of the two of them from behind, draped in their new shawls, slightly out of the frame of the approaching enormous yellow basalt arch.

My aunt looked more out of place in this part of town than my mother, who was sweeping around as if she owned it. I wondered how long it had been since she'd done any sightseeing in her own city. Who ever did, really?

Past the balloon sellers, the hawkers, the gawkers, and closer to the slap of the Arabian Sea: I stood at the tip of Apollo Bunder, on the once fishermen's jetty, gazing at the Gateway. Built during the British Raj in honor of King George V and Queen Mary's 1911 visit (though they were only able to view a papier-mâché model of the structure at the time since it wasn't completed until sixteen years later). Where the governors and viceroys would land. Architectural harmony between the Muslim-style arch, the Hindu-design embellishments — but still the target of two terror attacks. The Gateway was the first thing those boating in to Bombay used to see, the entry point to the nation (and portal to colonialist rule) . . . and the fire exit for the last British troops upon India's independence.

Restored to tourist status again — a fitting final-days role to play, I supposed. The point of so many arrivals to Bombay — and me, finally here, a mere four days before my own departure.

I just wanted to keep arriving.

I photographed my mother and aunt, right through the Gateway. Then we roved the periphery, me shooting sightseers shooting the space.

Lining the promenade, the beautiful miserable horses of Apollo Bunder, pulling silver chariots for the tourists by day, legs bound by night. A constant whinnying struggle to simply stay standing. I'd stopped to snap the hooves of the closest ones, white-spoked carriage wheels trundling behind, when my aunt suddenly piped up:

—I cannot even say the last time I was in this part of Bombay. Shall we take a ride?

My mother and I both turned to her, surprised.

—Actually, I read these horses are kept in substandard stables, that the carriages may actually be phased out, I said, immediately regretting it upon seeing my aunt's disappointed expression. —Though if you really want to . . .

But my mother emphatically shook her head.

—What nonsense! Did you know at Columbus Circle, one of those horses ran wild, knocked a couple of tourists out of the seats — and then got hit by a car? No horse-drawn carriages for me, no, thank you.

—Baapray! They must attach the horses better! my aunt exclaimed.

—No, my mother disagreed. —They must *release* the horses better. Loosen the reins. Let them —

—Fly, I filled in, picturing *Horse in Motion*.

—I think I need to sit down, my aunt said weakly. And then she suggested her cure-all. —Chai?

—If I have one more cup of chai! my mother replied, perking up nonetheless. —A coffee? There is a Starbucks at the Taj Hotel now — the only luxury hotel in the world with a branch!

I laughed. —I thought you hated Starbucks!

—I was not suggesting we *go* there. It was simply a bit of information.

—How about LPQ? my aunt said now. —Kavita mentioned it. She loves the one in New York.

We took a cab all of two shakes to the Colaba branch of Le Pain Quotidien, located in an Art Deco former palace, and ordered our coffees. I roamed around photographing the café, thinking it could be interesting to shoot an LPQ in New York as well, see what was different and not so about the same space in two places.

As I full-circled back to the table, I caught part of their conversation.

—So you knew? my aunt was saying to my mother.

—About which one?

—Both.

My mother hesitated. Then nodded.

—Sangita called to tell us earlier when we were in Delhi, so we wouldn't feel a need to rush back to help out, she admitted now. —Although I then felt even more in a hurry to return. And Kavita . . . well, we've known about her for ages.

My aunt averted her gaze.

—And so have you, my mother added quietly.

Maasi was silent. And then, in a voice tinged with irony:

—Sabina Patel. The roommate who made Kavita's first year away from home bearable . . .

My mother nodded firmly. —Sabina. Without whom Kavita's days have apparently been unbearable.

My aunt digested this a moment, then spoke up.

—Baapray. This generation is so confused! Perhaps if we hadn't let her go to America . . .

—Every generation is so confused! America, India. You have one daughter in each. It is not the place, sister. Bol: What is it you are really afraid of?

—That it is not the place, my aunt replied slowly.

I dared rejoin now.

—I suppose love is untameable, I suggested, selfishly. Upon getting no reaction, I blurted, —The heart is not in control!

—What nonsense is this, Dimple? my mother scoffed. —The heart is in total control. We just must get our heads around it.

We paid, and my aunt rose to use the bathroom. But my mother wasn't done with me yet.

—What? I asked. —Do I have scone on my face?

She cut to the chase. —How's Karsh?

I couldn't speak, but shot her two thumbs-ups. My mother nodded down at my plate, where I'd unconsciously crumbled the entire scone into a mash-up mount of sultana-studded flour, back to its original elements. Busted.

She was narrowing her eyes at me as if to see me better.

—I don't know, I whispered. —He's on a retreat. From me.

—A retreat? Well, when in India, I suppose . . . Don't take it so personally, Dimple. Retreats are from everyone, not just you. Just think, beta. How hard it must be for him after what happened with his father.

—Oh, Ma, I sighed. —I know that. But I didn't realize just *how* hard it would be. It's like . . . we came here together, to the place that *brought* us together . . . and it all fell apart.

She didn't look as surprised as I felt.

—Dimple, she said. —This isn't the place that brought you together.

—Huh? We were destined to be together. But now I wonder if we're destined to be apart.

—You chose to be brought together. If you and Karsh are having problems, you can work on them . . . or not. It's a decision. Choices that make up your destiny.

We stood to go, leaving the scone to its own fate.

—And what you decide to do about it, she added. —Well, that's up to you. And I'm sure you'll do the right thing.

—Which is?

—Whatever you do, beta, my mother said, gently drawing my wrap closer around me.

*   *   *

Though nothing was resolved (or all was unresolved), a wave of relief washed over me. We stepped into the brilliant day, waiting for my aunt on the sidewalk. I laid my hand upon my mother's, there upon my shoulder.

—Ma, I'm so glad you're back. These last days here . . . I've never felt so alone in my life.

She turned to look at me, and I was surprised to find a grin on her face.

—What? What is it?

Laughing, she swept her arm majestically through the air, in a gesture that seemed to encompass not merely Chhatrapati Shivaji Maharaj Marg, where we stood, but all this city's hustle-bustle hurly-burly margs, roads, streets, circles, chowks — the whyways and becauseways, the little lanes, and even Harbour and Back Bay.

—In *Bombay*?

Sun ablaze in my eyes, I began to laugh, too.

She put her bag back down then, not even checking the side-walk for paan stains, and wrapped me up in a hug warmer than one hundred and one of the finest pashminas, an embrace that forgave me everything — to the extent there was nothing to forgive in the first place.

My aunt joined us.

—What's so funny? she asked.

—What isn't? my mother said, and pulled her into this hug as well.

CHAPTER 42

Our Ladies of the Mount

The next day, I finally had a (real!) meeting about my work: Mahesh passed a message to me via Flip that he urgently wanted to discuss a potential collaboration and I should meet him at his gallery that night. Flip suggested I swing by his place later so we could share a rick, and also hit up Shy's brainstorm session, texting me a typically landmark-intricate address in Khar West.

And of course it was also (one of) the day(s) when something old would have become something new, something borrowed, blue: Tonight would have been round about Sangita's wedding sangeet, her night of music and dance, if they'd taken the traditional route.

Or any route at all.

Not that I'd seen her since her colorful revelation. Kavita had been out all day yesterday, I imagined with Sabz, but had returned at night. Sangita, however, I guessed had opted to stay in the hotel until things cooled down.

Miraculously, my mother convinced my aunt, uncle, father, Akasha, Kavita, and *Sabz* to attend the latest Bollywood hit at Infiniti Mall: *Dil* something *Zindagi* whatever *Love* (Hey!). It was possible they all felt the same way about Bollywood, and common loathing could go a long way to bonding people.

I opted out and walked them down to Shoppers Stop, trying to figure out what to photograph in the hours I had till the meeting. Three days to find the real Bombay — ha! When I returned, I wasn't sure who, if anyone, would be behind the magical mystery door.

I entered — and discovered the bride-not-to-be back home, in the uncustomarily relaxed pose of reclining on the couch in her stained jeans and top.

In repose, Sangita appeared another, near-fluid creature. She seemed even to be emanating a bluish haze as the late afternoon light swam over her dreaming lids, which fluttered up at my entry. As did a plumed presence perched upon her fingertips: Zepploo, now scared, bolting back through the open door of the cage across the room.

—Sorry, Sangita, I whispered. Though she appeared peaceful, I felt tentative, not so sure her bravado was still in full force. —Go back to sleep. . . .

—No, it's okay. I wasn't sleeping. Just reflecting.

She took in Zepploo, shuddering in the cage. —Takes a while to get used to freedom, doesn't it?

I nodded, sat down on the arm of the couch.

—Well, it's good to see you, freebird. Asleep or awake, I said. —What you been up to?

—I've been working on my portfolio.

—At the hotel? Do you have a deadline?

She shrugged.

—All over. All hours. And I like to think of it as a lifeline.

—I'd love to see it. I guess I've been working on mine as well . . . but what I see seems to keep changing.

—Funny thing about seeing, that. Things never stay the same.

I nodded, appreciating this synchronicity with the family member I'd once thought I had the least in common with.

She tickled my knee. —Thanks for the Bandra base, by the way. That Parsi partying Congress keeps getting trashed and ringing the doorbell . . . but it's good for working late.

—No issues. How are you feeling?

—Can't you see? she laughed, indicating her extremities. I touched her arm. That was no imaginary bluish haze: A hint of tint still undertoned her skin.

—Man, you gots the blues, sister, I remarked.

—And they're a bitch to get off! The acrylic soaped off pretty easy, but I waited a little too long for the Holi powder. Several rounds of washing, and I'm still stained.

I smiled. —Well, you look good in blue. You know, Sangz, I came here figuring I'd be shooting the browns. But as this trip's gone on, blue's overruled. For me, too. Both in terms of how I feel and what I see . . .

She nodded. —You see what you feel. I get that. Me, I decided to wear my blues on the outside and get them out of my system that way. Or change the feel, the meaning. Even in sadness, you can find a little winged thing. You know?

I did. In fact, I was counting on it.

—The color suits you, I replied. —Like you were doing a female take on Krishna? Shiva?

She fingered the string of beads around her neck, mahogany still tinged in parts.

—Well, Shiva did have the blues — after an erotic meditation spilled out of him as a tear. This tear grew into a rudraksha tree.

She went on to explain the seeds wore up to 108 faces. Though brown-black when dried, when ripe with life, they were shelled in brilliant blue: blueberry beads. This blue wasn't a pigment, but a structural color — like sky, blue eye, beetle carapace, butterfly wing, bird feather, fish scale. Mother-of-pearl. Goddess Iris's iridescence begotten by interference effects: parallel lines, layers scoring the material, sometimes scattering light of shorter wavelengths to the forefront.

My blues felt structural as well, belying the brown pigment of my skin. And they'd certainly been catalyzed by interference effects of another kind: I was scored with the lines, the grooves, the waves of life, love, loss, longing — Bombay itself rubbing up against me. A long-play record.

—Although, she concluded now, —my first inspiration to go blue is, of course, a woman.

I scanned my zeroic knowledge of the blue-hued goddess pantheon and came up blank.

—At Mount Mary. The Basilica in Bandra? Please don't tell me you haven't seen her yet.

—Someone told me the story, I whispered now, and it ached a little.

Not far, a hilltop chapel. Our Lady of the Mount, marred — right hand riven by goldrushing raiders. Our Lady of Navigators, holding her place. How she'd arrived before arriving — in a Koli reverie — and then, one long-ago day, washed up on those waves. An inundated virgin, thought gone to the grave. A stunned fisherman netting her in: Mot Mauli, mother-of-pearl amongst the sweltering sows. The priests, the Perreiras.

To me dreaming now.

I felt I knew the story so intimately — because of the teller — and was surprised to realize only now I'd never visited the actual setting, though it must have been only moments away from that Chuim Village bungalow. But Chuim felt long gone too far.

—I've never been, I said finally.

Sangita took my hand, yanked herself up with me, then me up with her.

—Well, no better time to visit her than *l'heure bleu* . . .

—You have time?

—Of course. What else have we got? she replied, reaching around for her bag. Then she turned to me. —Why didn't you tell me you wanted to explore the blues? You've come to the right girl.

*　*　*

This time, with Sangita as my guide, we found the correct slope. The day I'd visited the underlink, I'd passed another uphill entry to the left, before which a cartload of little pink wax body parts was being sold. I'd thought it was the mount to Mary's, but turned out it was the access to an ashram.

Here we stood at the base, somewhere near Bullock and Cart Road. Steeplechasing the sky upwards: a set of long pink-edged steps, creating over their ascending span a mosaical whimsical portrait of an enormous kidface in profile, pointing up. The only way.

—Our mothers came here, you know, Sangita said, easing into my thoughts as we climbed. —For Bandra Fair, in September. When they were children.

I just remember being very small, I remembered my mother saying. *And looking up, up, so far up I couldn't see a down.*

Gazing up up the steps to the mounting hill beyond, I wondered if this was that very view — me, we standing in the very place she, they'd stood.

Their own mother had been born to my then-sixteen-year-old great-grandmother in a kitchen in Vile Parle East, guided by a midwife. Whenever that tale had been told to me, the laboring household in that once-jungle had seemed the other end of the earth . . . but it had probably been only about twenty minutes from where we were now.

—It's hard to imagine our moms doing so much together when they were kids, I said, though I'd caught a glimpse of this childhood yesterday at the Gateway.

—Maybe they just have to remember when they were children? Sangita mused. —And they'll find that space again.

An idea tremored in the back of my mind then, though it was a different kind of ascent I was imagining. I tucked it away for future reference.

Dust dredged in tic-tac-toe crevices, the steps celestine as they tipped summitward. A stone wall bordering the left was splotched in this shade, too, as if the firmament had loosened its grip and spilled, splattering it.

We hadn't even gotten to the top, and already the blues had begun.

As we continued our Mary mounting (me clicking) of the now-paved and surprisingly peaceful hill, it occurred to me that the biggest blues were perhaps being worn by Sangita's jilted fiancé.

—Sangita. I hope you don't mind my asking, but how is Deepak doing with all this news?

—Deepak? He's been my greatest ally. I told him about my reservations a while back. We spent the majority of our time together, me trying to get him to understand. And eventually, he did — once he could get over what all the familial reactions would be.

Zoom on a dahi wada vendor manning his round table, a couple of motorcycles parked under tarp.

—Baby steps, she began. —We didn't want to traumatize the ones we loved. . . .

She explained to me how, just as she'd dismantled her wedding sari, she'd undone the wedding itself.

—For starters, we bribed the astrologer to superdelay the auspicious date, then fixed up a computer readout to match. Pared things down to make it a much less complicated event — kept it all in-house, so to speak. And Mallix was right; we managed to cancel in time to get back at least some of our deposits on the venue, the caterers.

Was that where she and Deepak had shot off to that night at LHB?

Cresting in my lens, upon the tip-top hillock, the cusp of Mount Mary's basilica was just visible.

—You're quite a team, then, aren't you? I considered aloud. —What about all the people who'd have gotten you gifts?

—Well, we pruned the wedding to immediate family and a few close friends; strictly no-gifts policy, and usually they do cash anyways. So nothing lost — in fact, something saved for them! And if anyone bought us anything, we'll return it to them.

By the entry gate, wax figures for sale for the wing-and-a-prayer churchgoers. Laid out on berylline cloth, mostly white casts of small humans, limbs, legs, arms — perhaps to heal illness and injury. For more modern expectations: a little magenta car, and a few mini multilevel buildings in splotchy orange.

—So all those wedding errands you were doing . . .

—. . . were in fact to undo the wedding. And in the end, I just told Daddy and he became our accomplice.

I spun around, caught her smug sneaky grin in my lens.

—*What?* Kaka?

—What do you think all that deep breathing's about? He's at it twice a day now. He's a very enlightened man, Dimple.

—As is Deepak, clearly. What else does he know? That you're already in art school?

—Deepak was the first person I told, Sangita affirmed with a smile. —In fact, even before, his gift of my eye surgery was to support my . . . artistic aspirations — he was tired of my paint-splattered glasses, thought it would help me have clearer vision. But neither of us was ready to tell our parents the real reason at the time. Easier to let them think it was other types of aesthetics that inspired it.

Before us, a waxy white block with the word HOTEL printed across it, next to another labeled TOWER, a disproportionate tallowed human of the same height (or giant) leaning against it. To the side, a tiny blue baby figure. I filled my frame with this infant, snapped Sangita's hand cradling it.

—Deepak understands more than he lets on. He knows what it's like to be forced into a role you're not ready for, or maybe don't even want. Forget Delhi: He wanted to go abroad, to New York, actually — get involved in a start-up with friends out there. But his parents set him on the path: education, career, marriage, mortgage, kids. I don't know if he can stop that machine from turning.

—What do you mean? You think he'll look for another wife now?

—I don't know. Maybe. Unless he finds a way to buy more time.

One stall over: wooden crosses, painted angels in soaring postures, bars strung with rosaries of every color.

—It's funny, but I'd be a little sad if he were to get engaged again too quickly, Sangita said softly. —For him — and even for me.

—Sangita. Do you actually *like* like Deepak?

—I do like Deepak. And *like* matters a lot — it's a little less conditional than love can be, na? We've been through so much together, undoing this wedding, isn't it?

She smiled mischievously now. —Plus, he's got certain . . . skills.

—Such as?

—Dimple! Read between the sheets!

I gasped.

—Sangita! What the frock? You've been tessellating your—

—Yes, *fiancé*. How scandalous!

—Where?

—During our wedding errands, sometimes, she giggled. —When his folks are in Delhi. Sometimes . . . even at the studio at J.J. And, by the way: Thanks again for the last five-star luxury shag.

She looked at me slyly. —Sorry, Dimple. Also, I nicked a couple of your condoms. Been meaning to tell you. I'd run out and no way I could be seen around Shoppers Stop or my paint supplies haunts — or anywhere! — scoring those.

This was perhaps the biggest whammy of all.

—You did *what*? When?

—Just maybe . . . two? That first day.

So Karsh *hadn't* taken them? They'd been missing since before he'd even arrived. It was true: You see what's in your head.

—Deepak's got a case of blue balls at the moment — literally! she went on. —And . . . figuratively! Serves him right for getting down with a blue girl.

I grinned.

—Frock, Sangita! You like him. You lust him. So why not marry him?

She paused telepathically now so I could photograph the view through the entry gates, the basilica exuding a dusky hue in this bluest hour.

—If he can't stand up for what he wants to do now, it's not a good start, she said finally. —But I have faith he'll figure it out in his own time. Anyway, all that pent-up angst sure makes him . . . energetic, let's just say.

—So you haven't broken up?

—Considering we were never technically going out — just engaged — I don't think there's any way of really breaking up. Just breaking off the engagement. Which we did between the two of us pretty soon after you got here.

—Frock. That man can keep a secret.

—And so can I, she said gently, gazing into my eyes. I got the feeling she didn't mean her own, but who knew what else the evidently innately suspicious perspective from inside my own head was skewing?

In any case, I didn't say anything.

She didn't ask.

—And so can *she*, murmured Sangita. And through the gate, ever closer to Mary, we stepped.

*   *   *

Outside, before the bright blued portal: Nikes, chappals, sandals, Crocs. We added our own to the mass — stepping past a buttress erected by a Mr. Fernandes and family from . . . Chuim Village — and entered.

—Between you and me, Sangita confided now, —I think

Mummy was afraid of what might be happening . . . but was more afraid your mother wouldn't come if she knew. But I'll make up the flight tickets to all of you one day, promise.

—Are you kidding? I don't regret coming here. I doubt my parents do either. We were all just looking for an excuse — though now I wonder why we needed an excuse to come home.

But I knew the answer. The fear of not finding it where it was supposed to be. That despite a journey of miles after miles, years upon years, it would have inched just out of reach yet again when we got here.

It was the time, not the place, my mother had once sighed to me, that they were seeking.

The anxiety at discovering: Home is not a place.

*　*　*

Stone and wood, teak and glass. A nave into which panes over the four side entrances poured light like slaking water. Breathtaking windows: a central flower composed of eight circling blooms in alternating gold and blue, glass peacocking to the sides.

Our eyes ascended a seven-stepped marble altar to land upon a halo-up radiating Mary with gildingly giddy toddler Jesus. I tipped my head back; this view of the ceiling sanctuary arches was astonishingly like that supine one of the Star Chamber.

Another mural'd Mary, appearing very high-melanin to my NR eyes. Peeking out from below her gold-trim robe, brown chappaled feet tread gingerly across the caption *Joseph discovers Mary's pregnancy.* Below that, a much longer Devanagari script I imagined said the same thing . . . but one could never be too sure one was saying the same thing. Na?

—She looks Indian, I whispered. —Or at least, Anglo-Indian. Parsi?

A row ahead of us a woman knelt, head wrapped in a sari powdered blue, bleeding orange.

—I never thought of it before. But you're right.

—Even baby Jesus looks Indian, or at least of multicultural diasporic origin. Like, Latino.

—Well, everyone comes to Mount Mary, Sangita hush-toned back. —Every religion, even those without. In fact, this church also has darshan, almost every day.

She nodded upwards. Above the marble pulpit, on a stone arch splitting nave from sanctuary, an oceanic canvas of orbed Mary and Jesus, sea of saints surrounding them:

ALL GENERATIONS SHALL CALL ME BLESSED.

We sat in silence then. Something about the church looked inside out, like it had widened its cathedral belly, quaffed a loch of rain, a dose of dust, a mellowed wield of light, wood, wind, a paned stained-glass garden rainbowing up from this heady masala.

The confession booth, I saw now, was totally exposed. In fact, no booth, to speak of (or in), curtainless; just a wooden barrier with latticed window.

An open-air secret.

Sangita's eyes were on the sanctum sanctorum before us.

—She's beautiful, I said now.

—She is, Sangita replied. —But she's not the one I meant.

*　*　*

Outside, we shod up. And I noticed then the sign just above the teeming footgear:

ENTER WITH YOUR FOOTWEAR ON. DON'T LEAVE YOUR FOOTWEAR AT THE ENTRANCE.

All I did, anyone did here, it seemed, was break the rules. And break them long enough, a new (dis)order's in place.

Across the wide way Sangita led me, past the Road Cross center street, the nave's baby here incarnated in an older petal-strung thread-spun cross-hung Jesus slung off peeling painted wood. We continued past farther flying Christs, nosegiggling garlands, to yet more steps mounting still higher upon hillock, blue-titled with ascending-descending words: *prayer penance meditation. Peace, rosary, reparation. Sacrifice.*

At their apex, an open-air chapel. Exposure, no enclosure: Our Lady of Fatima. Shoeless clusters gathered before this mistily celestial blue marie, a dreaming beauty in vertical glass box. Flaming wicks burned directly onto coals in lieu of candles. The fence before her supporting block was strung with blooms and missives, rosaries and rudrakshas, diminutive images of Jesus — and even Hindu gods. Chica Tikka snapped: the bared soles of this praying public caught in a private moment, blossoms crushed below toes, some pedicured, one hangnailed, sari ends skimming the ground, skinny jeans just missing it. The wicks unspurled smoke signals to the cirrus.

—During my more challenging moments, I'd just park here at night, and look up to the chapel, emptying my mind, Sangita told me.

She pointed. This way: Mahim Creek. That way: Sharukh Khan's house.

But I knew another set of landmarks, other places, other stories that had unfolded — were unfolding — not so far from where we were now. And at last, here on Mary Hill, by the doubled sky of these double blue-girl goddesses, I felt I'd finally found the place for a full confession. It was also a prayer, and a thank-you, and a wish you were here, and a wish I am, too.

O sisters who art in Bandra, understand me, whether I sink or swim:

I *wasn't* sorry. Until eternity, I would do it all again.

* CHAPTER 43 *

The Swimming Cities
of Bandrissima

Back at Bandstand, Flip texted me the maid had arrived late and he was still on a Skype call, so I should catch up with him at his place a little later. Sangita was hailing a rick from the brood swarming the foot of the hilled drive leading up to the hotel.

—Andheri bound? I asked her. —I have a meeting tonight in Bandra and have to pick up Flip in Khar West in an hour.

But my sister-cousin wasn't done with the tone tour quite yet.

—No issues. I can drop you near your meeting after, she told me as we got into a tuk-tuk. —But if you've got an hour — you did say you wanted to see my portfolio, na?

—Did you bring it? I asked her, confused. She just smiled at me.

—It's on the way. Waroda Road, she told the driver, which I guessed was where her studio was. —Chappal Road. Amitabh Bachchan landmark.

Chappal Road was in fact Chapel Road, and was not a street lined with toe-hook-sandal sellers by Linking Road as I'd originally thought. Nor, when we quit rick and walked a little ways, was Amitabh Bachchan pacing the street waiting, live bait, for our arrival.

He was, however, glowering down at us off a time-traveling wall, his younger and several-times-more-gigantesque self starbursting forth from a pinwheel of teal and saffron rays, thumbs hooked through belt loops of rugged blue jeans.

A worn-around-the-edges, old-time Bollywood poster? But no: The Man himself was painted directly onto the wall. Sangita, leaning now against his King Kong groin, appeared a lewd Lilliputian as I gathered the pair in frame.

—An artist named Ranjit painted this, she told me. —His work's a great bridge in bringing awareness of street art to the masses, especially those who find graffiti less palatable.

That made sense. After all, classic Bollywood icons spoke to the older generation as well as the young.

—Tour of the neighborhood as we go? she suggested. Out of film, I swapped to my digital. She nodded at it. —I think she'll like it, too.

Who were we to resist?

Sangita led me through the twisty tangling village lane. It soon became clear, as the street itself transformed into kaleidoscopic canvas, that we weren't going to any studio. This tour was to photograph the gaga glorious stretches splashed upon the walls and doorways, from the shutters to the gutters, of this art chapel road.

A wallow of dwelling veneered with a blue-robed girl, back to us, a matching heart-shaped balloon sweeping off into the distance, turning wall to window with its fluttering impression of depth. Rainbow-striped shuttergate rolled down to street edge, peace sign pigmented upon it. Just beyond: a chubby bumblebee, bubble-beaming *Make someone smile.*

Upper half of next low building: a faded sepia. But lower half: green as neon just-hatched primordial slime. Before the house: a Kinetic Honda, dollhouse-size crosses with teeny Jes-i. Sangita hovered, pointing to a paint splosh on an unpotholed patch of pavement here — which turned out to be, upon closer lens look, a series of funny funky little fish with swooping butterfly-blue wings. They were stupefyingly near-real, however miniature, as if freshly flung from a fisherwoman's basket. A couple of the sleek sea creatures even appeared to be gasping for breath.

—Rawas, Sangita informed me. —The Indian salmon.

—Awe-salmon, I replied, unable to help myself. —The English raw-awesome.

The uneven gritgrime of the surroundings made it appear these paintings had been unearthed, that the true story lay beneath the surface — yet this was a time-torsioning archaeology, a something old excavating a something new.

Sangita paused by another dribble, all the way downwall to pool at the bottom, where carefully crafted merpeople congregated, winged as those other fish, slipping right onto pavement, one even bending where the wall caught it. No serendipitous spill, this. Nothing was an accident, a mistake, when examined closely.

—The smooth patches are best for miniatures, and the bylanes if you're working by day. They're narrow, stay shaded longer so you don't dehydrate as fast.

I dropped to a squat to snap the mermaids' peregrination.

—Pouring off the wall onto the road like that, I breathed. —Like a bridge between the real and unreal . . .

—As mermaids always are.

Next vision: Fatma Villa. Triple Optics. A wall visaged with a stunned sweat-beaded bespectacled man caught in fiery concentric rings — a spec over a literal third eye in bindi position, this one looking the other way.

—Poch Rock, I believe. They're from France.

Bulging kidlike letters spelling out *BAN/DRA*, split into dual balloon syllables on grey wall. Another fish, very different from the mini winged ones we'd seen: big, bold, multihued, and toothy, skimming the painted pink-swathed head of an enormous-eyed girl who resembled the child face in profile on Mount Mary's steps.

—Seth's work, Sangita told me as I focused. —He paints the world over with characters who look like the native people. He's from France as well. Miss Van, too. How I long to go there one day — it's my dream!

—Me, too! I said. —Cartier-Bresson. Sophie Calle. Rimbaud, Baudelaire . . .

—*Paris Spleen*, she roosed. —You know, everyone hoped, believed mine were wedding dreams. But me, I'm dreaming different reds, blues, hues. I want to go to Amsterdam, see the streets there. ROA's horses in the UK. And Blu's work — around Bethlehem, an image tearing down the watchtower, the border. Ride Swoon's *Swimming Cities* wherever the tide takes us . . .

Here: a faceless cop. There: a sunglassed dude with smoke-spurl hair and a squiggle of a figure, like ink had merely dripped in a bodily direction. —And Os Gemeos, these break-dancing twins from Brazil. They were even invited to paint the trains! They did this spot near the Police Gymkhana on Marine Drive, but it was whited out.

By a chana and puri shop, a squatting sulkish fair-skinned kid multiple times bigger than we passersby. And just around a bend, hovering at eye level, zoom-viewable: a halo of interlinked mermaids. I gestured Sangita over.

Street art, the art of the street; borders blurred. It was as if we'd stepped into the painting itself, the world a canvas, we like wee brushes tagging out our way: cartoonish pineapples rolling off an open cart. A juice center strung with triple lime garlands. Walls, windows began to disappear, the art upon them overriding them, as if in some kind of bristling hallucination, all these graphically splendid creatures were wandering along with us. Our little dance had shifted along the way, fin-seeking, wing-fishing. Another cluster of turquoise salt swimmers. These were fast becoming my favorites, like the spilt clues on a treasure hunt — to what, I wasn't sure. Did they lead to the sea?

—We've got Ranjit, who freestyles; Tyler, who stencils. Guru from Hyderabad. All superb, Sangita told me. —But here's my favorite Bombay street artist —

We stood now, past a little iron-pressing stall, before a black-and-white spiral-splash of tubes helixing the wall before us.

—JAS. She also did the *Horn Not OK Please* by the Bagel Shop; ten-hour job minimum. Enamel. This one looks like it must've taken at least eight to ten hours. Latex, quick dry.

Sangita nodded at the helix. —The longest journey is the journey inward.

I guessed this was the title. But it was our story as well. We moved in unison now, without a word or glance pausing as we fell upon these brave new whirls of mergirls. Scattered across walls and window panels, the catch uncaught: fish after flying fish, some star studded as constellations, others invoked in the saris of wee Koli women. So real as to be ethereal, rising off the hard stretches of street, the surrounding sketched ships and fisherfolk slashes and swirls of rainbow abstraction. As if the fish-eye view were the real — all else a Piscean dream.

Just out of frame, Sangita was examining the ragged edge of one of these mercreatures, expertly teasing it smooth with her fingernail.

This treasure hunt led . . . to this treasure hunt. This was no roundabout route to Sangita's studio, her portfolio. For we were walking within her without studio, immersed in, even *part of*, her portfolio.

—We began that way, didn't we? I said now, wondering why she hadn't just said it. —Gilled, underwater. Learning to breathe.

—Sometimes remembering to breathe *out* of water's the challenge, Sangita laughed softly. She rose up again, prying the bits of paint out from under her refining finger. —You know, in French, *t'as le spleen* means to have the blues. . . .

Bombay Spleen; Bombay blues. But *spleen* also meant *guts.* Maybe guts like your insides — the way all of Bombay seemed spleen-skinningly turned inside out, so much life laid out before you, and death, too. But perhaps as well guts as in: courage.

—The blues. But that's not the same as sadness, na? I replied, considering it. —Melancholy has a beauty, an energy to it. It's not enervating, not static.

—Yes. There's movement. Depth. And that's what I love about street art. It's the weather, the hour; constantly changing, interacting with the passersby, the passerviewers, the neighborhood . . . transforming as it disintegrates. Like all of us, fading, altering with time. And inviting everyone in — democratic as cloud spotting. It's a dialogue with the city we live in. A collaboration.

We looked at each other, and what we knew was clear. Not a confession so much as a declaration.

—Before I accepted the scholarship, Sangita said, —I thought: Well, even if I can't go to school, no one can stop me from painting. This — street art — was my statement, I suppose. But once I made it, I realized no one could stop me from going to art school, either. It gave me strength to have a secret — albeit a rather public one.

I could understand that, though my secret wasn't quite so audience-friendly.

—I feel so out of touch with this city I live in, in so many ways. And marriage right now feels like something that would just take me farther away — and not only in terms of the move.

—Maybe you just wanted to touch it, I said. I could understand that, too. —This place. Bombay.

—Yes. Actually touch it. I know it's a small thing, in a small way. But I guess I was looking for a way in . . . by getting out *into* it.

—How'd you even know where to begin? I asked her.

—I started with the Wall Project, on Tulsi Pipe Road. Government commissioned; pretty much anyone can turn up and paint. But I like being on my own more. I believe street art should maintain its punk approach.

Did Sangita just say . . . *punk*?

A smearing on stone. A torrent of half-goddess half-girl half-sea-soul shoal. Saraswati in sneakers, veena plugged into amp with a mertail cable beside it. Laxmi in Mallix-style stilettos, flashing credit cards in finned fingers. She-vahanas with longboard limbs, rick-tipped toes, scootering shoes, surfboard wings. All with that same tag: LGB(t).

—I was waiting so long for a wall, she told me now. —For someone to make room for me. Then I realized I could make room for myself.

—You realized you could build a window.

I shot every bit of merflesh we fell upon as she recounted to me how she'd sometimes come alone, sometimes with Deepak night-driving her. Genuflecting in her alfresco chapel, her utterly outdoor sanctum sanctorum, by the light of a flashlight, valise of tools in tow — a reverse Cinderella shredding her old saris to paint-rag tatters, a little mermaid opting for fins *and* feet . . . she'd take these deadened spaces and into them pour paintblood.

We walked a long, long way before we fell into a speaking silence.

We turned down another bungalowed bylane, stood by a street vendor, where Sangita bought one Classic Milds.

—A few more are here, she said, indicating a minuscule paint patch to the side of the stall. A starfish, each tip swirling with fins, in the center a whirl of cerulean girls, angel lips curving together in kisses. —These were for Kavita. And Sabz now, too.

—So . . . you knew? Even before the rainbow mugs?

She nodded.

—LGBT, I said aloud now, realizing.

—Little Girl Blue, Sangita explained. —True. And yes, the acronym was also a reference to Kavita's sexuality . . . which I didn't realize until I'd acronymized my blue girl herself. Anyway, true colors are always in view. It's just we look and we listen, maybe . . . but we don't see, don't hear. Till we spell it out for ourselves.

Spoken like her mother's daughter. And it sounded a lot like me and Karsh, come to think of it. Or like me and me.

—I suppose it was my way of coming out with her. Declaring it on the street — little knowing we'd come out together off the street, in our home one day. I'll bring her here. With Sabz. Soon.

I was going to ask her why she hadn't told anyone about her tag, her true identity, but I knew the answer, and she spoke it.

—Nothing is a secret, she said. —Not if you know it. Though it still feels nice to keep it. To have something to yourself. But — and it would have to be the right time and place — I'm beginning to feel I can share this now, and still keep it to myself. Do you know what I mean? That no one can take away what you give away.

Lens to eye now; something very familiar about the doorway, that bungalow across the way . . .

Breathe through the eyes.

Zoom. That tiny depiction of a waterwound blue Mary, intertwining fisherman.

But this Mary had fins. And wings. How had I missed this? In that submerged experience of the out-of-frame, this entire village — even the portal to my own experience — I'd dodged as I'd burned.

Sangita had followed my gaze. My throat went dry, but I reeled up the words:

—That fisherman's dream?

—That was my starting point. For this entire Piscis Volans — flying fish — series: imagining what that dream might have been, and the moment that statue of Mary was conjured up by the tides.

—But why . . . this house?

She shrugged. —I don't know. Something drew me here. I knocked to ask if it was okay, but no one was in. Or no one answered, in any case.

I'd felt that pull as well. The swimming cities of Bandrissima. I'd been swept along, even compelled the current to this very place, collecting debris, trash, treasure, along the way, souveniring as I steered, reveniring now.

I missed him. Would I always?

—But then I imagined, Sangita continued, —what if *Mary* had had the dream? What if she was the one floating on fins, then flying on wings, who saved the fisherman . . . or simply herself?

I would, always. And Mary: As the waters seamed over her head, I knew what she'd felt, for I'd felt, too: that flip of fear onto its belly, a surfer's soul arch into the wild blue — and, lungs returning to their gilled infant state, a sudden sense of levity under liquid sky. She'd found herself floating, body learning a new way to breathe, lips shipping bubbles far deep wide — a greeting to the lands that lay ahead.

A dream within a dream. Mary saved the fisherman by dreaming the fisherman — not the other way around. She dreamed herself into being found. The streets swam with flying fish. Little Girl Blue was none other than the blue-skinned goddess beside me. We had always been awash in clues.

My heart skipped a beat, or maybe my head. I could see now that that door I'd once, twice, infinite times poured myself through was ever so slightly ajar.

Who knew who was inside? Whether it was him or that mysterious cinematographer. Or no one at all. A wind at the door; no more port of call.

It didn't seem to make a difference.

I decided then to *keep* missing him.

A merMary. I would swim.

Sangita crushed out her cigarette. I hooked my arm in hers.

—This would have been the day of your sangeet, I said. She smiled a little ruefully, perhaps awaiting some kind, but unwelcome, sympathy.

—Well, I guess, then, what better place to have been than a chapel, or a church with seven steps?

—But, Sangita, I said, an idea abrew in my head, —I beg to differ. A sangeet is a dance and music event. So what better place to be than Manhole tonight? We can go after my meeting. Come along?

—Thanks, Dimple. But I think I've got to do another song and dance — go home, keep trying to break down that wall with Mummy.

Dripdrop by brushstroke, I knew she would eventually do it: find the skylight in that wall by, ironically, filling it in, as she'd done with her flying fish.

Time to face the music. She walked me to the Samudra hotel, first landmark on Flip's address.

But before we parted ways, she touched my arm and removed that string of beads from around her neck, placed them around my own.

—The tears of Shiva, the god of destruction, without whom there can be no creation. Whatever you've lost, Dimple, is not lost. It is simply reincarnating.

And she was gone. But not really gone.

* CHAPTER 44 *

Home Is Not a Place

When I got to the right street, I wandered up and down seeking the address, finally phoning Flip.

—Lala, he saluted on first ring.

—Pinto. Niño. Santa Mario. Methinks I'm getting warmer but can't tell.

—Landmark? What do you see?

—I see . . . brown people, I whispered.

—Ha! You're in the right *country*, then. Passed the Hanuman mandir?

—Passed the Sai Baba mandir.

—That *is* the Hanuman mandir. See a couple little vendors just down the way? Head towards them. . . .

—There, I confirmed. —I mean, here.

—Great. Okay. Now . . . ever so slowly approach the stall. . . .

I did so, feeling engaged in an unlikely round of Mother May I.

—Lean in towards the vendor . . .

Mother May I. Yes, I did.

—. . . and pick me up a couple of Gudang Garams?

I should've known.

—Slacker! Why don't you come down and get 'em yourself?

—I'm in a meeting.

—Yeah, right. I'm in that one, too.

—Dude, he pleaded, laughing back, busted. So I tried to get him the bads from the first stall, which looked exactly like the second one, but the mustached vendor pointed to that latter stand, with a world weariness that made it seem his entire day was spent correcting this particular error.

Flip must have heard me close the deal, for he proceeded to give me another set of directions that included walking back to where I'd been to begin with.

There seemed to be a disproportionate number of signs for dentists around here. I could discern a rhythmic thump and the overwhelmingly plaintive pitch of a lone voice warbling in what I can only describe as an ancient way. I turned to discover it emitting from a significantly less ancient-looking man leading a horn-painted cow up the road and beating a drum, choli tote strung off his shoulder.

—Landmark: singing beggar, I informed Flip.

—Dimple. Did you know the difference between a mendicant and a beggar is a mendicant makes music for money?

—Okay, so landmark: busker with nandi. *Nandicant*, I clarified, digging out some rupage for this street musician, wondering now how Flip seemed to possess this psychic compass for my whereabouts . . . and why the mendicant's melody was hitting me in stereo, from the phone as well as the street. I glanced up to find my man waving at me from a window out which he'd surely overseen all this circling smokes-purchasing nandicant-donating activity of mine. He already had a Gudang Garam in hand.

—Why didn't you just say to follow the smoke? I called up to him now, clicking off.

—Third floor, Lala, he said with a grin, indicating I should enter by a building society side passage. As I did, I crossed paths with a petite industrious-looking woman in a sari, who gave off a lovely stomach-rumbling odor of tarka.

Every floor up, my eyes splashed with street art again — or stairwell art. Ground floor: a painted panel depicting Mary, flowers sunbursting in her heart space, Sai Baba waving a foot away. First floor: a skinny-boy Ganesha stickered to the wall, faded swastikas painted directly onto the humidity-hacked patch beside him. Second floor: Jesus hanging off a cross . . . a Guru Nanak by his side.

No wonder there seemed to be little resistance to street art here: People had been painting the walls and ground (rangoli) — and even the cows — for eons. And what was Holi but a massive paint-gun party?

Third floor: Flip stood in a flexing, levitating X in his doorway, as if he were single (well, double) handed-and-footedly keeping the frame from caving.

—Good day, Lala?

He slid the few inches down, nabbed the smokes with one hand, high-fiving me with the other. It was on the tip of my tongue to fill him in on Sangita's street art secret, but I kept it there, and simply nodded.

—Sorry, I couldn't leave till the maid came and went. She makes a killer mung dahl.

The maid was a cook? I kicked off my sneaks and stepped in. The apartment was redolent of this famous dahl — was, in fact, redolent of that industrious woman I'd just crossed.

—Nice to finally meet an Indian in Bandra who eats Indian food, I commented, pulling out my camera and snapping his Clairefontaine, open on the mattress behind him. —You ever put that thing away?

—Do you? he countered, striking a pose so cheesy, I nearly offered him a cracker to lay it on.

—Touché.

And then I couldn't resist.

—How's that profile going? I asked tentatively. I didn't know how much he knew about my situation with Karsh.

—It's going. Though could be going *faster* if I could only track down some of my subjects. I figure I'll catch a few tonight. Shy for sure.

I now accepted the ceremoniously presented shot of Flip's ever-present Old Monk. A gulpable, not clickable, one. It burned and I let out a fire-breathing sigh of relief.

—Okay. I'm officially in a meeting now, I rasped. Flip smiled, lidded the Monk, and slid it in his messenger bag, followed by the Clairefontaine.

—Actually, you *are* supposed to be officially in an actual meeting about now, he pointed out. —Chalo. I don't want you to be too late. Just IST late.

Pinto hath spoketh: We had to make like a lentil and split.

—Is it ten to fifteen minutes away? I asked, a little worried now. He sighed. —Are we *in* Bandra? And heading *to* Bandra?

He after-you'd me out the door, then slapped a friendly hand on my back as we headed down the deified stairwell.

—Lala — only, what, three more days in Bombay? Bol: Will you ever understand where you are?

I slung an arm around him.

—I hope not, Pinto, I replied. —'Cause then I wouldn't be there anymore.

* * *

Bandra was buzzing tonight. As we jumped in a rick, Flip's friend Slinky messaged to say he was DJing a really cool art opening near Pali Village Café if we wanted to join. Kavita and Sabz were off to some kind of AntiValentine's event, probably linked with AzBaaz, on Ambedkar Road. Flip mentioned that io was maybe doing an acoustic set in Pali Naka at Mrigmeg's, which I guessed was either a venue or a human. And Mahesh had texted me directions to his place by now — involving landmarking IMPPA, the Indian Motion Picture Producers' Association (acronym making it sound like funding was secured via the devious work of gnomes) — with a PS that he hoped I'd stick around for afters.

Although I was booked for that meeting with him and then Shy's ponderfest, I recited all our options to Flip, who was with incredible grace managing to slug his Old Monk in the cantering rick.

—And there's something on at Mesh's place again later. We could hit it after Shy's, I concluded. Flip gave me a *duh* look.

We alit in Pali Village before a lovely little balustraded bungalow, half obscured by a peepul (or neem? or tamarind? *Gulmohar*, Flip sighed) tree, scaled up to a swoozily pink balcony, and stepped in and onto a stoked-yolk floor paved with manhole lids. Circular skylights echoed each one, scadding day-end rays throughout and illuminating the mellow-yellow brick road leading from entry room down a long corridor that branched into a couple spaces on either side and at the end.

Double take: Those skylights were bulbed, not paned. The buttery walls and high-raftered paper lanterns and hanging plants ringleting everywhere amplified this feeling of natural light.

As did the circular windows drawn upon the walls.

This space was rolling in zeros.

Camera out, I nearly bumped into a sign reading MANHOLE: DROP IN & DROP OUT.

—Welcome to every event you've been going on about for the last ten to fifteen minutes, Flip smirked.

Mahesh's place turned out to be . . . Manhole. As did Mrigmeg's. Pali Village, Pali Naka. Landmarks Pali Village Café, Ambedkar Road, IMPPA all pointed here.

—It doesn't feel like an art opening, I commented, considering Slinky's message.

Flip shrugged. —There's art, and it's open. That's more the way Mesh runs things. He wanted to create a space where people connect more to the artists, not the frames. Hence none here, or if at all, circular ones. To invite people in rather than boxing them out.

—It feels like a home.

—It *is* a home.

Most of the entry room was taken up by a table covered with coffee dispensers smelling of chai, as well as a few bottles of white wine. Mrigmeg, of the how-do-you 'do, stood solemnly beating a bongo in the corner, then noted me eyeing the bar and swiftly reincarnated into a bartendress (first female server I'd seen in the Bay), pouring me a plastic cup of the disquietingly fizzing vino.

—Happy AntiValentine's, she greeted, presenting me with not only the drink but a surprisingly perky perished rose.

The warmth of the space was heartening, unlike the stark white walls of umpteen galleries I'd been to. Somehow this — probably coupled with the fact hardly anyone was here yet — made it feel there was less pressure to buy something. Which would maybe make it easier to enjoy the art itself, some of which I glimpsed a little farther down the hall.

—Have a look around, Flip told me, parking by the minibar to avail himself of his own Old Monk. I moved into the corridor, unframed fine line drawings sweeping across the walls: anatomical renderings of the heart, the four chambers filled with tiny cartoonish figures (by none other than Pozy). The floor was lined with ripped paper hearts, still more being scattered now by Mrigmeg, along with dried rose petals and empty chocolate foils.

To the left: an office space, brilliantly muraled; someone with dreads hunched over a laptop there. To the right, a topsy-turvy room that made me bleary at first glance. The furniture — a couple chairs and tables — was painted the same rainbow arcs as floor and walls, creating a wonky world for happy little bluebirds to fly.

At the far end, the passage tributaried into a larger room from which low-key beats and a soft swell of conversation hummed. I was about to head down there, but the dreadlocked dude in the office now swiveled around, caught sight of me, and gestured me in.

It was a turbanless Mesh.

—Mahesh! I smiled. —It's beauteous.

He grinned back. —Glad you like.

He gestured me around to face his laptop, and with a mouse click a photo slide show kicked in.

It took me a moment to recognize what it was.

Those io shots, from Heptanesia. As Mesh scrolled through them, he filled me in. Apparently, i and o had been gone on the pics. Furthermore, all the (to my eyes) errors, the accidental in them, were what they loved most. The way their heads blurred decapitatingly into little lights, whizzed together while they played. The sprayglazings from my flash hitting too hard, rendering microphone a sharded blast of a mouth on the girlthing's face. Plugs evanescing into the ether. Guitar strings rippling like the neon aftermath of a fireworks display through the boy's whirring fingers.

Out in the hall, I could hear the murmur of people arriving, but I couldn't take my eyes off my own work.

—I think everything unintentionally blurred, I confessed now.

—Because I was unintentionally dancing along with them.

—Well, some kind of capital-I Intention was at work nonetheless. They said your photos perfectly conjure the third absent presence they make and melt into together whenever they create music.

It occurred to me some of this fortuitous stray light, mistakes turned takes, may have come about from our flashes colliding. Conspiring.

Me and Mahesh.

—They're doing an album launch at the next Crosstreet, he confided now. —Mum's the word; news isn't supposed to leak who the mystery artists are till the night. But they wanted to see about using your images for it. If it's cool by you, we can also show them here for some acoustic sets they'll be doing after.

—It's more than cool by me! I exclaimed. —But I thought they launched at Heptanesia the other night?

—They launch pretty often, Mesh laughed. —Whenever they feel like it, in fact.

—That's all great, Mesh. But I'm a little confused. Don't you do their art?

—My stuff's much more realistic — whatever that means. They wanted less local. So I suppose you're the ether, and I'm the real. A continuum.

He looked at me . . . and for a moment he looked faraway, or we did.

—I'd be honored, Mahesh, I said quietly. It felt like a promise, and he nodded.

—And I loved your shots of Karsh, he added now. —A few of them slipped onto your flash drive. His site looks great, too.

—I haven't been online this trip. But I thought *your* shots of Karsh were on his site now?

—As well. But mostly yours. Room for all, after all.

He nodded towards the corridor. The beats had notched up in the back, but not so much as the conversational tide. —And all are in that room now. I'm going to wrap up some work. Why don't you go brainstorm?

*　❋　*

That room had indeed filled up during our meeting. I slipped directly into the side shadows, a perfect vantage point for my I-spy.

The vibe was like a happening, even though I'd never been to one: circlings, no rows. People lounging on gaddas, slumped knee-hunched against walls, and some impressively erect freestanding (or sitting) lotus positioners (well, the white guy from your Iyengar class . . . and was that *Gopi?*). A skinny twinlike pair of silhouettes sidled into the shadows by the grille leading out to the balcony, so adumbrally blended, they conjured a two-headed creature with what appeared a swaddling babe across their conjoined laps. And just viewable through that window, a few tenebrous figures, mostly obscured by smoke, some bitter, some sweet: clearly the Gudang Garam (and hash, and possibly hookah) section. I could make out a shining shaved head amongst them, likely artist/DJ Pozy's, amidst a bevy of longer-locked folk. Light pooled upon that scalp. Halohead.

A bare-bones console was set up: a laptop piped into speakers on a rainbow desk that must have been moved here from the *away above the chimney tops* room. Everyone was swaying to the tuneage — something très (diasporically) '97 was on now; that state-of-grace flight song from Talvin Singh's *Anokha*? Shy held a little control panel and sat at the front of the circle, if a circle had a front.

—. . . so any of you up for joining the protest to bring back Bombay's nightlife, meet as Pooja's explained at Carter Road in a week's time. Lucky for us, The Fifth Room's been brave enough to take on the next Crosstreet party —

A familiar voice struck out then.

—I just think it's fucked up. Partying in the heart of the Koliwada — a gaonthan.

It was none other than Sabz, cross-leggedly knee-bumping Kavita beside her. —It's like . . . slum tourism. Crashing someone's house and you don't even invite the owners!

—Are you suggesting we ask along the fishermen? Flip laughed with Old Monkish abandon.

—The fisher*people*! Sabz corrected him. —What, you think the women just sit around on the beach descaling the catch for your entertainment? Anyway, we should be careful about partaking in this . . . homogenized brand of cool that's cold to its surroundings. Upper-middle-class cash cold.

—Cash cold? someone inquired now, sounding hopeful for some reason.

—I mean, in New York, lots of spots you can mingle with more of a range, Sabz expounded. —Even at HotPot — all sorts of tax brackets throwing it down to the same beat.

I caught her eye from the sidelines — or rather, she caught me snapping her with my digicam — and smiled.

—But the gap between blue collar and white isn't so pronounced there as it is here, right, Sabz? Shy suggested. —Maybe that's why the same kind of mix doesn't occur.

—So it *is* about money! Sabz yelped accusingly. —Check Shy's soundtrack right now. *Anokha*, if I'm not mistaken? South Asian music in '97 was a political and cultural statement as well as a musical one. State of Bengal. Outcaste Records. Asian Dub Foundation. Anjali. In New York, we had, *still* have, Basement Bhangra, and, just as groundbreaking for the second gen, was Mutiny at the Cooler. These were the sounds of a subculture becoming culture, a people gaining critical momentum — carrying the debate and the diaspora to the dance floor. I mean, can anyone tell me the sound of Bombay *today*? How much non-English music do you hear here in the equivalent — the *hip* — venues? And isn't the term *indie* an oxymoron when this music scene is so infiltrated by Bollywood, ads, corporate sponsorship? This tuneage isn't creating a new language, a new hybrid sound. It isn't the sound of a *people*, a *moment*.

A pause for reflection (or inhalation). But perhaps it was something much simpler, I thought then — a grass-is-greener kind of thing. Kids of the diaspora were looking for a sound to bring their scattered hemispheres together — to wed their motherland with their homeland. Isn't it?

Even those question-mark-ending statements by American desis: Wasn't the true query buried beneath *Do we really have the right to impose a Western framework on a non-Western culture or is this a continuation of the legacy of colonialism?* really, on one level, or all (like my feeling at Chor Bazaar), basically a Secret Admirer valentine, a conversation candy heart to India: *Could you/Be mine/ Please say yes/Marry me?*

Kavita was gazing at Sabz with that pride of old, mixed with a good measure of bemusement.

—But you can't impose a Western diasporic framework on India, can you? Shy was asking patiently. —This was the sound for that particular cultural and historical moment. And once it's been done in '97, the terrain's changed. How can you do it again . . . and why would you need to?

I was surprised to hear her say that, given her love of that particular year in South Asian music out of the UK. But then, perhaps this was her testament to that love — the firm belief that that sound was unique and had already done its inimitable work.

—But could you tell me which music you mean specifically is *not* the sound of a people, a moment here in Bombay? Flip asked Sabz now.

—Of course not, Sabz scoffed. —I don't *listen* to it. I'm just offering a critique.

Well, what could you really say to that? But Flip had Clairefontaine out and gridding to go.

—Shy. And according to *you*: What *is* the sound of this tribe?

—Any sound any of the tribe makes. Whether in Bombay or not, over here or over there, Shy replied with a hippie chillness that belied the bossy, overly generalizing, and perhaps correct nature of her statement. She was a little in love with the sound of her own voice in that spoken-word-artist way — as was pretty much everyone else. It *was* a very nice voice, I had to give her that. Like, from the diaphragm.

—But we from *over there* made it possible for you to come back *here* and branch out from being quote Indian, Sabz pulpiteered, rather cavalierly now that she'd hooked Kavita's look. —We even made it possible for you to work your Indianness in India, Shy. How many chicas *from* here can get away with that? What I'm saying's just: You're coasting on globalization. People here don't seem to know the *history.*

—That's somewhat true, Slinky joined in. He was in a beret, booting up his own laptop near the console. —One thing I love about being in Bombay's I get to relive my UK youth, watch a new generation discover DJ culture. What's been going on for decades there's just beginning here: people going out *for* the music, not music as background noise. Organizations like SlumGods and Tiny Drops are bridging economic and social gaps in the music scene. And that scene itself is expanding into a wider variety of genres. We had psy-trance, Goan trance. Then dubstep. Imminently, subgenres will appear — are already appearing — and we'll see the development of cultural mash styles. Culture here isn't mixed in the same way as in the UK, but it's mixed in a whole other way. . . .

Halohead's soft-spoken, perhaps smoke-muffled voice, piped in from the balcony, —And Bombay's youth will actually *live* through this evolution and have the real experience, not do the iPhone jump. You know, going from no phones to cell phones with no in-between. So they'll learn the history by living it. And they'll make it that way, too.

I slid to the floor, back against the wall.

—Maybe India's had enough history, needs a break, at least in some spaces? I considered aloud now. I didn't know if it was all these nights of not sleeping, but at the moment, even the thought of my own history exhausted me, and I hardly had one.

—Dimple, how can you possibly suggest breaking free of history? Sabz was sighing despondently.

—Well, *we* have, Kavita said quietly, laying a hand on Sabz's knee now. —Sometimes you have to just move on. Begin again. Not take it all so personally.

—But the personal and political are the same thing! Sabz

contended, laying her own hand upon Kavita's. If she was correct, that made me for one ragingly political, considering how personally I usually took everything. —I don't mean I have no regrets. Personally. Or politically. But you can't erase the past. History. You have to own up to it. And I do.

She trailed off. This *I do* was an apology, loud and clear; it was a commitment, too. No one in the room seemed jarred, though; for a moment, I couldn't recall why we'd even gathered here today in the first place. Kavita was silent, but interlaced her fingers to church-steeple-see-all-the-people meshiness with Sabz's, leaned on her shoulder.

—Dimple. Would you break free of your own history? the terrace guy piped up suddenly, halohead tilting.

I heard two layers to this question as well, though I was probably the only one who did. But I didn't have to brainstorm long: *amor fati,* loving what is necessary — that one must live in such a manner they'd wholeheartedly relive any moment to eternity. At the very least, or even most, it was a handy way to banish useless guilt and regret and general negative vibing in your daily life. The line you needed to draw wasn't a rupture so much as a seam between your then and now — a peppy willingness to do it all again (though a gratitude not to have to).

By embracing all that came before, you liberated yourself of it.

—I wouldn't change a thing, I replied, considering it, meaning it.

My heart was bruised, but it wasn't broken, not really, and even the bruising was somehow an accustomed feeling, an ancient evocation — perhaps even a residue from the way we came from nothing into something, and would one day dissolve into nothingness again. Always coming and going. A cycle.

I mean, it also kind of sucked. But what was I going to do about it?

A shindigging twang: The Siamese twinlike formation by the window wall lifted the swaddling babe, which turned out to be an acoustic guitar, and one half of the duo began to strum, the other to hum.

—Not a thing? Halohead asked again.

I vigorously shook my own, highly unhaloed, head.

—And that's what frees you of your history, I concluded. —I guess . . . history's not always linear. The yellow brick road begins with a swirl. There's no place like home, because home is *not* a place.

A silence into which the strumming, the humming expanded. I was pretty sure I heard my own words echoing out the humming mouth: *Home is not a place.*

—Home is about harmony. It's about finding a way to coexist, Shy said now, calmly reining the conversation back in. —And that's precisely what we'd like to do at The Fifth Room, what Crosstreet's about: being local and global. My dream for this party is one day it's not bound to a physical location. We find our tribe all over the world, an open invitation. I mean, where's everybody in here from, for example?

In this space, no one got touchy about the question. A few people offered up their backgrounds: Delhi (met with a couple sympathetic clucks), DC, Shillong, Kenya, Toronto, even Espírito Santo.

—You know, the next generation this conversation will be over, said the white yoga guy (currently residing in Goregaon East). —Kaput. No one will know where anyone's from. Or even bother to ask.

—No more cultural confusion that fills our days and nights and NYU debates, Kavita added pensively.

—And then maybe, finally, a person can love someone from anywhere, said Sabz. —Any country, city, socioeconomic status. Any gender.

I chewed on that. I thought about my-not-my cowboy from nowhere, in an Unbombay that had become palpably perspiringly real, tangible as a shattered hourglass. And Karsh from a solid somewhere that had dissolved before my very eyes, slip-upped through my fingers.

No matter where we were, we each carried around a universe inside us, slid it into our lens, our headphones, and all that we saw, heard, experienced was colored from that viewpoint.

A map was every map you'd ever known, was written in your skin. We were many places, many people at once. Reincarnation at all times.

An idea for the Crosstreet flyers occurred to me then: an image of paths that never physically crossed, yet intertwined in spirit, were inextricably linked on the emotional, psychological, experiential level: 14th Street greeting 14th Road. Gansevort gliding into mantra Grant. Rivington rocking up to Rebello Road. Malcolm X Boulevard to Mahatma Gandhi Marg.

Catch you at the curve of Union Square and Union Park.

—I'll dance to that, Shy was beaming. Slinky had stepped seamlessly to the decks and was now playing a joyful blend of funk and fizz. And, hesitatinglessly, the who-knows-where-from cross-leggers, lotus-ites, shadow skulkers third-dimensioned upwards and began to dance their this-conversation-will-be-over consensus to his life-affirming beats, Flip's Old Monk an oceanic message in a bottle, a pass-it-on making rounds of the swilling swaying room.

Shy was packing away her own laptop, and I walked up to her now.

—The Fifth Room. Maybe there are other ways as well, to find that harmony, I said, for her ears only. —Not just about sound, but vision.

—Yes! she smiled. —Mesh told me you'd be here, and I'm so glad. I was going to tell you, Dimple. We'd love to use your work at the next Crosstreet. Your art, their music. Those io shots were amazing.

But I had a different idea.

—Take the io shots. But I'm not your mystery artist, I replied. Then: —Have you considered using a painter?

She tilted her head. I went on: —Even . . . a street artist?

—We *are* looking at painting The Fifth Room, if that's what you mean. Maybe even the outside.

—Well, I just may know, I told her, —someone who was waiting so long for a wall. . . .

CHAPTER 45 ·

Photo Finish

That tribe danced every inch of that room to multilimbed life.

When the plug was finally pulled, Kavita and Sabz told me they were heading back home. Meaning: Andheri.

—We don't want to worry your parents, Sabz said, nodding to Kavita. —Especially if we want them to be . . . one day, however long it takes . . . mine, too.

A question in her gaze. But Kavita's entire open-armed self exuded an unequivocal yes. And with that, the perhaps most diehard romantic pair of the lot was off in rickshaw number one.

As the last straggle of stormy-brained revelers was gently kicked out of the Manhole, Mahesh materialized, taking it upon himself to organize the transport to the inevitable after-party. One by one, he gestured over the lurk of circling ricks and expertly performed the late-night arithmetuk-tuk of dividing everyone into groups of three.

—Moving right along . . . okay, Flip, India, Shubhra . . . Pokie, Pooja Sound System, Iza Viola . . . Dimple . . .

I hesitated but was thrown into the next rick in line, then wedged in by:

—Gokulanandini . . .

Gopi girl flung her sweaty Hare Krishna mantra'd Manhole-dancera'd arms around me and planted a kiss on my cheek that was, if I was not mistaken, heavily perfumed with eau de ye monk of olde.

—We need one more for this rick. Go in and scout out the after-partiers! Mesh called out to a random hipsterite lingering on the balcony. She indolently walked back into Manhole . . . and then — with military precision and surprising violence — ejected another clump of carousers onto the sidewalk.

From that clump, the head-glow halo boy was shoved into the remaining space in our tuk-tuk. I leaned over to say hello . . . and found a strangely familiar-looking creature before me.

More than familiar.

It was Karsh. Minus the goatee, the headful of wavy hair, and, more notably, any kind of smile whatsoever.

He looked at me.

I looked at him.

Mahesh patted the rick to move along. But not before Gokulanandini crawled over us and ejected herself back onto the sidewalk.

—Never mind. I live in Bandra now, she explained sweetly. —Why go all the way to fucking Versova just to come back here?

As we pulled away, she stuck her evidently third-principle-flouting grin back in the window. —And don't forget, guys — the world on the outside is so much bigger than the inside!

The rick swiveled around.

Me and Karsh sitting in it.

We had a scant moment to register this reality — the two of us together in the more-than-chummy confines of a tuk-tuk — before it lurched off, following, I imagined, Mesh's directions.

I swallowed hard. Karsh was looking for space not in the Krishna-historic hills . . . but *in* Bombay? My hunch had been right: He'd been looking for space from me.

I trained my eyes on the PLEASE DO NOT TOUCH ME sign on the driver's meter—which he'd actually slotted down to zero without our asking. Proof that we'd finally arrived? I was no longer a tourist in my own motherland?

But thing was, being with Karsh made me feel like a tourist in my own life. So much had happened — so much I could never tell him, probably, and perhaps his own journey had been one he couldn't take me along on either. My head roiled with all the things said and unsaid. I considered chanting Om, but what came out was:

—Um . . .

—Oh . . . he replied.

A Pavlovian lovelorn dog, my body nevertheless began to stretch towards him of its own accord, as it would have in recent days of old — to drape a leg over his knee, lay a cheek on his shoulder, interwine his hand and pluck gently on his pinky nail, plectrum like.

But the fact that my body knew that map — the terrain of Karsh's body — belied the fact it had so intimately, so barely learned another, too. And that magnetism of old wasn't quite the same; Karsh felt more estranged brother to me than once boyfriend. Maybe I could only be attracted to one person at a time (or was forcing myself to be); did that make me not a two-timer?

In any case, where to lean, to touch, was not up to us; the rick bounced us relentlessly on and off each other as it navigated Bandra's potholed streets.

All I could manage, weakly, was a vague imitation of Gokulanandini's comment:

—So . . . do you want to go to frocking Versova?

—Still sarcastic, I see, he replied coolly. —Well, good to know some things never change.

It was a needling comment, yet no rancor in his voice.

—I'm not being sarcastic. I'm quoting.

He just glanced at me, and it was a weary regard. He looked the same but different — like when you see a waitress from your local diner on the N/R and you can't quite place how you know her, but know her, you know you do. Karsh looked a lot like somebody that I used to know, as the song went. Or more like someone I still knew and had to act like I didn't know.

—Well, in reply to your wonderfully phrased question, he said, turning to gaze out the front windshield, —I wouldn't mind calling it a night, no.

—I wouldn't either, I admitted. Suddenly hiding under a bedsheet, willing myself into a coma seemed like the best party in town.

—Back into Bandra?

I nodded. He leaned forward and told the driver to turn around.

—You're in Bandra, too? I asked him.

—Staying with a friend, he said, not meeting my eyes. I didn't ask, but wondered if this was connected to Gopi girl's move to this suburb. —I'll drop you off first. Where to?

—I'm still deciding.

—Deciding where you're staying?

—I might . . . go for a walk, I said. —You go ahead and get out first. I'm not a baby, Karsh. I can drop you off and go on myself.

—What does that have to do with being a baby?

—I mean, maybe if I weren't so *protected* all the time . . .

—Look. I get it. You go your way. I go mine. Sharing the rick is a technicality. Boss —

He was speaking to the driver again, and now uttered something completely confounding though the coal-fire eyes in the rearview blinked not twice.

—. . . 29th Road, next to Grand Hotel, near Tava Restaurant, on Turner Road, near Basilico, on Pali Naka, by Eat Around the Corner . . .

—That made no sense, I informed Karsh when he'd completed this incomprehensible set of directions. —Are you staying with a friend — or ten friends? In twenty places?

—That was all one place. What, you're a Bandra specialist now?

—West not East, I replied. —It's just . . . you can't be on Pali Naka *and* 29th Road *and* Turner Road at the same time.

—We'll see about that. So where are *you* staying?

—Um. Ambedkar Road, Khar West . . . near Hanuman Mandir near Hotel Samudra by lots of dentists and brown people and an undercover cigarette vendor next to Chuim Village, I replied, simultaneously realizing, without Flip, I had no keys.

—Right. *That's* straightforward. Anyway, why aren't you at the hotel? It's still paid up.

Because even though you're gone, they keep leaving two bathrobes for us, and it makes my heart climb my throat and nest there, sob-swallowing like a forsaken choking chaklee?

—The Parsi Youth Congress is making too much noise. They trashed the seventeenth floor. Plus, they think I'm one of them.

—Still having trouble sleeping? he asked, with a moment's old-school concern. But he caught himself and turned away.

—Not that there's anything wrong with being Parsi, I added now, to ease the pain of that turnaway.

It was all wrong. The conversation felt so stilted, the pauses abyssed with ditches, hairpin curves. We used to be able to talk without speaking, silence just another form of communication, connection. Now it slid down between us.

The tuk-tuk bopped over potholes, the motor's judder skiddering up my legs, sometimes knocking us a bit hip to hip. I wedged my camera bag between us, knapsack between my feet. I couldn't bring myself to look at Karsh, but in peripheral vision could see his profile going stop motion with the rick's jerks.

We were retracing our route, repassing Manhole.

And then, so quietly I nearly missed it:

—So. You really wouldn't change a thing?

—No, I wouldn't, I replied, just as softly. For a moment, he looked like I'd slapped him.

—Well, I'm glad things are working out for you, Dimple.

—That's not what I meant, I began, but stopped short. How could I explain it? I couldn't wish to undo what I, we'd done, could I? Because wouldn't that undo the beautiful parts that had come before, too — ending us up with list of opening credits and no story to tell?

—Well, what about you? I asked defensively. —Would you change everything?

—Yes, he said, adamant. —I know how you are about trying to banish regret. Nietzsche. All that. But I don't think lack of regret means you're more evolved. Sometimes you need to feel it to realize you've learned something, to make change. And there are a lot of things I'm changing now. But I guess what's done is done.

—It's not just what's done is done. If we changed any of it, *all* of it would change, wouldn't it? Even the stuff you'd want to stay the same?

I would rather have gotten to be with you and go through this pain now, I thought but did not say, *than not have had the great fortune of knowing someone like you, of being with you at all.*

He said nothing. How could we — *we!* — have nothing to say?

So I said, —It's strange . . . having nothing to say to each other. Isn't it?

He shrugged. I tried again.

—I mean . . . it's like I don't even know you anymore. . . .

—It happens, Dimple.

—What does?

—People move on. They do what they have to do.

At that precise moment, I almost wished I'd never come to India, taken this trip — that I could have stopped time when all was still good between us. But if this growing apart was writ in our destiny — mightn't it have happened anywhere? In New York, too?

Or was destiny geographically specific, I wondered as the rick nicely missed a little lobo-like canine by about an inch, tuttering down Waterfield Road.

—Maybe our time was just up, Karsh was saying now.

Ouch.

—If you say so, I told him. I kept my focus fixed forward; if our eyes met, I'd surely see blurry in an instant.

The streets were relatively empty at this hour, except for a taxi pulling up to a red at the intersection of Waterfield and Turner roads. I gazed at our own signal, willing it to stay green so our rick could just hurry up and separate us physically — to match the psychic split that had evidently already taken place.

It did. Stay green. But the taxi didn't slow for its red —

And the rick didn't brake at our green —

Someone's got to stop, I thought.

The taxi continuing to jet forward across our path, the rick lunging straight for it —

The rest must have happened in a couple seconds. But we undertowed into the time warp: My body tensed for the collision that was surely, incredibly about to occur.

This? I thought. *This is how it ends? In a rickshaw in Bandra? I mean, bloody hell!*

Followed by: *My parents will kill me. I love my parents.*

And then: *Save Karsh. Save me —*

Oh god oh god oh please oh please oh hare hare . . .

Karsh screamed *Noooooo!* — or maybe he'd been screaming all along.

BANG! Cartoon slam; taxi wham. The entire rick jumped. But time'd tongued a tab, gone all helixy, spiraling in and out of itself, longest journey inwarding out, and a nanosecond before that bang, Karsh flung his arm out to protect me. Almost simultaneously, I threw mine across him, result being we whacked each other, he catching my right shoulder, me thugging his chin. Our bodies catapulted forward against the half partition, knees slamming into this dividing wall.

And the driver — for whom I'd had no prayer — was launched in the air and out the rickshaw.

I think I howled. My mouth was open — but the sound seemed to be swirling at us, from the world into it, rather than the other way around.

The rick, driverless, continued to pitch forward. The driver was hanging on to tuk-tuk bottom for dear life. I had no clue what to do. I wanted to reach down and haul him up but couldn't unsink my grip on the partition. Everything was too fast, too fuzzy.

Approaching: a bank of curbside ricks.

And, with a far less violent thump, our own rick now whomped a parked tuk-tuk . . . and finally walloped to a stop.

Freeze-frame after what felt like an overcranking fast-catch slow-playback eternal split-second unreeling of a year, a decade, a forever in the life — though it must have been a snip of a minute, all that. Time seizured back out into linearity.

Hole in the record; hole in the camera: Karsh and I exchanged glances, every facial aperture open to hinge-bust — eyes, mouth, panting nostrils. And then, like magic, about fifteen men emerged from their sleeping vehicles — rick drivers, soon clustering round our little trio, gasping, shouting *Bhanchod!* and pointing towards where the taxi had hit and run. Warmly concerned faces, incendiary expressions, outraged and comforting voices, all organically familiar — as if we'd all been in it together at some point before.

I thought: Not only do we carry our pasts forward with us into the future — baggage, memories, habits, dreams towed along in that wake — but the future also flows back to us, dippering up present and past in this tidal embrace. Our own hereafter had nearly been cut adrift, short. But our present had propelled me and Karsh: nettingly swooped it up and, with the weight of the gravitational past to pull against, hauled it safely over that threshold into port.

In other words: We got lucky. Out my open door I could see, a few feet away, the driver supine in the street.

I fell out of the rick, miraculously to my feet, followed by Karsh, who immediately fell to his knees by the driver's side.

A couple other rickwallahs squatted down there beside them. Our driver attempted with great difficulty to heave himself up on an elbow, wobbling slightly as his rescue team gripped him underarm and helped him rise.

He collapsed against his battered rick, and in that instant, I saw his battered heart as well: The entire front windshield had shattered, the muzzle of the tuk-tuk smashed in. Had the driver not been thrown, he'd likely be dead.

Had the timing been a split second off, and the taxi hit a few inches farther back, we could have all been dead.

Dead dead dead. The word made me feel insurgently, almost self-indulgently, alive.

—Paani? one driver offered.

Another: —Chai?

—I think we're okay, Karsh replied, appreciatively side-to-siding. —Nahi, bhai. Thank you.

I shook my head, too. The driver was finally upright, his weight on the wounded vehicle. Karsh leaned in to him. Automatic transmission: I knew he was asking if he was all right.

In fact, weirdly, I understood everything everyone was saying at this moment, meaning and intent superceding language itself. Or maybe they were speaking English; it all sounded the same.

The driver rolled his body against the rick, like he wanted to merge with it. For a moment, he was still. Then, taking a deep breath, he steadied himself, turning towards us with those coal-burning eyes.

—Boss? he whispered, gazing soulfully at Karsh, and even at me. He then let flow a long phrase ending upwards in a question . . . and my mouth fell open, comprehending.

—Wow, Karsh said under his breath. Laying a hand on the driver's shoulder, he shook his head, jerking it towards the road behind us. Then he dug into his pocket and pulled out a couple hundred rupee notes. Now the driver shook his head, a simple strong gesture, but Karsh gently tucked the money in his upper pocket and patted it.

Karsh turned to me with the most earnest eyes — strikingly similar to those of the driver, I saw now. He put an arm gently around me, and started walking us off, away from that clustering throng of concern. Glancing back, I saw the men tending to our man; even the parked ricks appeared to be huddling to comfort the stunned damaged sister-vehicle in their midst.

—Wow, Karsh said again, shaking his head.

—What? What happened, Karsh? What was he saying? I asked now, though I was sure I knew. Karsh stopped, turned to stare at me.

—He stood up. Looked at us. And said: I'm very sorry, sir. Madame. Would you like me to get you another rickshaw?

Yes. That.

—I told him we'd go on by foot, Karsh went on. —It's not far to where I'm staying. Then we can get you home safe. You okay to walk?

I nodded. Oddly, I felt no physical pain. But Karsh's arm stayed around me, mine around him. No loverly hug. But, after a ride that had been all wrong, it felt just right.

* CHAPTER 46 *
Please (Do Not) Touch Me

In a matter of moments, Karsh stopped by a building.

—Ravi's place, he explained now, as the night watchman nodded us in. He punched the button. As we rode up, leaning against the elevator walls, I turned to him.

—Why didn't you just say you were staying at Ravi's?

—I know you're not such a big fan.

—Oh, I said, feeling a little guilty. —It's not that I'm not a *fan.* . . .

—Yeah, right! Karsh laughed. First smile all night. —But, you know, he really bailed me out, despite the fact those gigs didn't quite work out. See, I never left Bombay. Gopal's father took a turn for the worse. . . .

He hesitated. —He didn't make it. We were at the hospital right until the end.

—Oh god, Karsh. I'm so sorry. . . .

—It was a tough time. But it was cathartic for me in a way, being with him until nearly his last hour — something I never got to do with my own dad.

He closed his eyes now.

—And after he passed on, with Gopal going as well, the idea of ashram life felt a little lonely. Gopal was the one who told me to reach out to my old friends, make peace, try again. And Ravi, bless him, threw his doors wide open, no questions asked.

I wondered why he hadn't called me. But then, I hadn't called him either.

—In fact, we've just started working on a track together, Karsh told me, lids lifting. —I never knew it, but Ravi's dream's to produce. We're looking for a lyric, but the rest's coming together nicely.

He got a distant look on his face.

—Ravi and I connected on so many levels — much more than just music. He's really my brother now.

The two had become that close?

—They're probably asleep, he whispered as the elevator creaked to a stop.

—They?

—The family. His daughter's home from Japalouppe this week — horseback riding camp. And his wife's back, too.

I let that sink in.

—I haven't heard from Mallika in a while, I whispered then.

—She's gone back already, Karsh said, and the entire love story we weren't speaking, between the two of them, rang, reverbed. —To New York. She kind of didn't want to be here for this part, you know?

He glanced mischievously at me now.

—Anyway, I'm sure they won't mind you're here. Ravi even told me to feel free to bring women up if I met any worthy ones.

—And? Did you? I asked before I could help myself.

—First worthy one I've met, he replied as we arrived.

* * *

The elevator opened right up into Ravi's apartment. And that abode could have been a Greenwich, Connecticut, manor, such was the sense of space it evoked in this congested suburb: a generous open-plan kitchen with island bar, feeding off into a cushy living area with lots of brightly embroidered gaddas and swoodgy sofas, lights on dim. To the left a corridor disappeared, I supposed, towards the bedrooms and more.

We stepped in — and I immediately knee-buckled, a quick shock of pain zapping up my leg.

—Oh, man, Karsh said, reaching out to support me, faltering a little on his own knee as he did. —I guess we *did* get a little banged up.

He flicked a set of wall switches, notched up the track lighting. We doddered over to the kitchen, supporting each other like an elderly couple still deeply in love, crazy after all these years.

I'd always thought I'd grow old with Karsh. But then, maybe I just had.

—Ice? he asked, ducking into the freezer. —And something to go with?

He handed me several cubes wrapped in a napkin for my knees, then fixed us up a couple of three-cube stiff drinks. Clinking glasses, we moved past the laptopped table; one looked like Karsh's outdated (but updated by him) seventeen-inch. Reams of papers and files covered that surface as well.

—Looks like he's been burning that candle. He's been working on the *Indian Idol* deal all hours, trying to close it, Karsh said, pushing open a sliding glass door. —You sure you feel okay?

—Better than okay, I said. We stepped out to the balcony running the length of the apartment, sat on the ledge by the railing. The air was a balm, and I relaxed against the bars.

Karsh reached into his pocket — then pulled out a ziplock containing a little roll-up giving off a familiar Silly Putty whiff. I burst out laughing.

—Manali in pocket? Now you're a true Bandra-ite.

—It might help us wind down after our . . . adventure, he smiled, lighting up.

—Do the devotees know? I inquired cheekily, feeling a happy nostalgic inner twirl at that sweet sick smell. —How's that working out for you?

—I make it a point, he exhaled now, handing me the joint, —not to light up during darshan.

—So you quit the Hare Krishnas? Godhead?

—I didn't *quit* them, he said as I, with neither faithlessness nor further ado, merged with Dopehead. —I just didn't quit anything else, either. ISKCON really helped me, you know? I mean, I'm not doing the four thirty screening so much lately. But I needed it for a start. To tie myself to the mast.

Our ice-packed knees bumped as we sat hunched on the terrace ledge.

I nodded.

—I know what you mean. Me, I needed to bring down the whole ship — and inundate a little shore for good measure.

—I was on a sinking one to begin with. It was a complete mind-fuck to come here, to India, you know? I thought I'd feel more at home in the place where my father had lived. But I didn't find anything I was looking for.

He looked as confused as I felt about how any of this could have happened, and not happened. To us. Not to us.

—Me neither, I admitted. I recalled our toast in Tompkins Square. —But I found a lot of other things, I guess. And you did, too.

—I did. I found that I can't be one thing, for one.

—Indian American, American Indian? I asked him, though that dilemma seemed to be from a past life (so I did have one!). I wasn't so surprised when he shook his head.

—I tried to swap music for spirituality, take a clean path, purge, purify, find my silence. But the spiritual path led me full circle back to music — I mean, what drew me most to ISKCON in the first place was the singing, the dance. And the connection with the divine — I caught a glimpse of it, and it's a beautiful space to be.

—You've always had that, though, I pointed out.

—I guess I see that now. And I see that I need all of those things, all of those sides. You know? At the same time, even — not in some kind of evolution that takes me down a straight path.

—There's no straight path. In Bombay, anyway.

—The sacred, the secular, the purity, the grime. I need the saints, and I need the sinners.

—Here I am! I waved a little cheerlessly.

—You're no sinner.

—I'm no saint, I replied quietly. A beat; our eyes met. Nobody asked.

—But you know what? Karsh said finally, such kindness in his voice. —You're, we're . . . we're all of those people, you know?

—A walking — or hobbling? — contradiction?

—I'm not sure it's a contradiction.

—Maybe not, I said, with a little forced levity. —The sacred cow; the burger at Rock and A Hard Place. You, my dear, are both vaca and lunch.

—Fucking eloquent, said Karsh, and grinned. —And damn deep.

—Or very superficial, I said, considering it. —All you have to do's look at a Bombay street — all those jigsaw pieces missing or broken or sticking out of the pavement. They still make a road, a path. Albeit a road that can really trip you up, make you fall on your face. But it's like . . . if you see just a few random parts of a puzzle, it looks like they don't fit — but if you could view the entire image, they've all got their place. Maybe we just go along amassing the pieces, the pavers in life — and one day, you get a sense of the bigger picture. Of a path . . . *paths* . . .

He was nodding thoughtfully, mulling it over.

—And for whatever it's worth, I said softly now, —I'm glad ours crossed.

—We did more than just cross paths, Dimple, he replied, even more softly. I nodded.

We'd also spent so much time diverging during this trip — but it seemed we'd been running parallel all along, crescenting, even, life companions bound to brighten and bend, join forces to reunite tonight, in a near-not-miss.

—So, he said now. —You fly in a couple days?

Day after day after. But thank gods there *was* a day after.

—I fly, I said. And then, hesitating, —You?

He shook his head.

—I'm staying on, he said gently. For some reason that made me picture the entire Jet Airways return flight pilotlessly empty, save for me.

—Vrindavan at last? I asked, a little sadly. He shook his head again.

—Bombay, he told me. —We've got that track to finish. And a couple gigs seem to be falling into place, finally, thanks to Ravi — and Shailly, too. We're even talking about taking Crosstreet to New York one day . . . and maybe bringing Adda here!

Running parallel. A circle, more like. —And I'm looking into working with Tiny Drops, SlumGods; I want to find a way to give something to this city instead of just seeing what it can give me. There's always tech work if that doesn't pan out; I can do a lot remotely.

Good old *the hardware*.

—Funny, I said. —Not so long ago, you couldn't wait to leave this place.

—I know. But I feel I'm just about ready to have my India experience *now*, you know? I didn't realize there'd be so much to work through to get to this point to begin with: grieving, soul searching. I thought it'd be hit the ground running. All about the music.

—That's all still part of the music. At least the way you do music.

—Thank you, he said sincerely. —That means a lot.

He looked down now. —You know, it's funny. I thought all I had to do to get here was arrive.

—Yeah. I know what you mean.

—You always do.

Our hands were inches apart on the terrace ledge. Summer. HotPot. Bartop. How our fingers had wrangled against magnet tips, an elemental desire to interlace. No such pull tonight, but no repel, either.

—We never did everything, I said now, considering all those places we'd meant to visit during this trip. —Banganga . . .

—Actually, I went, Karsh admitted. —With Ravi. But we never hit Linking Road to buy our future children future toys.

A pregnant pause.

—They'd probably break within the hour, so maybe that's a good thing, I said finally. —Elephanta Island —

—And that incredible vinyl dealer in that chawl, near Mohammed Ali Road. Still haven't gone. Those hip-hop boys in Dharavi. But Chor Bazaar —

—Um, I went, I confessed. —These beautiful Victrolas you'd have adored, Karsh. Phonographs for miles —

—Actually, I went, too. But all I could see were cameras, old photographs forever.

We digested this.

Neither of us mentioned Breach Candy.

As far as that list, though, I supposed we'd done many of the things we'd meant to do. Just not together. It was as if we'd ripped it in half: *You cover the top; I'll do the rest.*

In a weird way, we were still a team. Just in new positions.

—Mazagaon, he was saying quietly. —We never made it to Mazagaon.

His father's last home. A small silence.

—But I don't think I want to see it, he said finally. —I mean, part of me does. But the other part knows: Closure happens in your head. Nowhere else. And you can't wait for someone, something — someplace — to give it to you. You have to close that loop yourself. Maybe if there were two of me . . .

That crumpled pink paper I'd smoothed, confused.

—But we saw many, many things we never guessed we'd see, Karsh said now, trying a smile. —And that counts for something.

Inside, a child calling out in her sleep. For a strange moment, I thought it was ours. Padded footsteps, door creak, a murmur of a voice — at first I couldn't tell whether it was mother, father, ayah — lulling her back to slumber with a song that traveled to us in fragments across the flat.

It was father. Through the sliding door, I could see Ravi now, backlit, gently rocking the sleeping girl in his arms, all baby face and gangly limbs. A muted lullaby.

He lifted his face just then, caught sight of us on the terrace, and nodded.

My ice-packed-knee hand touched the edge of Karsh's. Our fingertips linked in passing the last embers of the joint.

The desire to hold, to hold on; I wasn't so sure anymore that could be done. Wings molted at different speeds. People slipped your grip, flew the coop when you least expected it — even you yourself. Coup.

He was gazing down at our hands as well. Then he picked mine up, turning it palm up as he'd done at HotPot, reading himself into my future that summer evening we'd once-upon'd.

He squinted now, straining into its network of forks and intersects, sideswipes and parallels, shortcuts and long and winding roads, then finally sat back with an *Aha!* look.

—Well?

—It would appear to me, he concluded, —that it's most certainly . . . fucked up.

He grinned, and we both burst out laughing. My ice pack flumped off my knee, and he pushed it back into place.

—I'm not sure what happened, he said, smiling a little sadly. And I knew he wasn't talking about the accident, but the accidental:

the love we hadn't intended to handle with such indelicacy. The love we hadn't made. And the love we had made, too.

—I'm not sure either, I said. —But I guess bright side is . . . anything's possible?

He kept smiling, rueful but appreciating my attempt to leaven the situation. Ravi had vanished back down the hallway, surely to tuck in his daughter.

I gave Karsh my arm, helped him rise with me. Our knees buckled simultaneously, and we caught each other, tipped against the railing a moment. I looked at him.

We were ancient. I was seeing the boy I'd loved at seventeen, eighteen, nineteen . . . for a hundred and one years. Like when you look at baby pictures of someone you've known only older — parents, grandparents — and in that young flesh behold the features of the person they would many years and experiences later incarnate: as if they were prehistoric babies, wizened children. This was the spleen of that feeling: Somehow I was seeing Karsh now, yet aged, elegant — and in his accumulation of years, still beholding the boy — that beautiful boy I'd so loved my whole life.

He was standing here now. It was the closest I'd ever come to seeing what seemed to be the soul. That special something that flowed through the time-and-space-bound body, defying geography and metronomy and chronology. If we could see the light of stars millions of years after they'd died, didn't it mean we could maybe also see the light of objects, of people, of actions — actual *destinies* — millions of years *before* their birth . . . perhaps whether they'd be born or not? Did they meet in that transit? That cosmic Link in the sky, so to speak?

The ether?

All I knew was: I loved Karsh with every ounce of my being. I missed him with every ounce as well, although he was right here beside me. I had a feeling I always would — and neither his company nor his absence would alleviate this. A nostalgia steeped even this present moment with him, an anticipation even for what had already passed.

We were bigger than boyfriend-girlfriend, ex-boyfriend-ex-girlfriend, even than friend. In fact, we were bigger than the both of us.

Was that what Cowboy had meant about meeting in unconventional spaces?

Whatever he'd meant, or that I'd projected onto what he'd meant, I was getting the distinct and highly non-frocked-up impression, the surefire sense of what that most unconventional shifting morphing space of all was, in fact:

Home.

*　*　*

Ravi's silhouette, back in the kitchen. Karsh entered ahead of me to explain what had happened.

Tentatively, I approached Ravi, stuck out my hand.

—Dimple, I said.

—I know who you are, Dimple, Ravi said, and his eyes were bright with genuine worry. —Man, that's messed up, what happened to you two. You sure you don't want to go to a hospital or anything? I can take you both.

—We didn't bump our heads, I replied, touched. —I think it's fine. Just a little limp.

—You can stay here tonight if you need?

—Oh . . . no, thank you. I better get back.

—Where?

Suddenly, there was nowhere I wanted to be more than Ramzarukha, surrounded by the elders and the younger, my sister-cousin equals, and even the wallahs. Most of all, I wanted my mommy and daddy.

—Andheri, I replied. —West.

—Are you sure, Dimple? Well, there's no way you're taking a rick tonight, said Karsh. —I'll call a Meru.

He accompanied me down. In the lobby, we stood a second longer staring at each other, words failing. But this was very different from the strained tuk-tuk silence earlier this evening. The one in the Children's Park. Now there was so much felt that nothing needed to be said at all.

And our goodbye no longer felt like one — given the fact we could have had our final one tonight. That arm that used to wrap around me every day, that hand I'd once held and could no longer hold the same way: It was still the arm that threw itself protectively in front of me before the collision, by pure instinct pushing me back from the barrier, the border, to this side of life. It was still the hand I knew, attached to the boy I'd always know — even if now that boy and I were at a crossroads, for maybe a little, maybe a long while.

A moment could last forever, as it had in the instant leading up to the crash. And conversely, forever was a rip, a pothole, if you will, on the road of time — eternal while it lasted but could be over in the blink of an eye. Yet a kalpa whirling-dervished a trillion times — a kind of kalpa — in that blink. For forever, whether a minute, a month, a sigh, a century, was simply this: immersion. A circle. No beginning; no end. No front; back.

No sides. You could never really lose a person you loved — even if that person up and got gone. As long as you didn't lose the love. And there was a lot of comfort in that thought.

—We almost died tonight, he said now.

—But we completely lived, I replied. And I took his hand. That hand. I buried my face in his palm, and kissed it — those mysterious lifelines and lovelines encrypting our tale, each and every one still including us no matter where the story went from here. Then I lifted my face, folded his fingers over that kiss, sealing it there, squeezing his fist tightly closured with both hands now.

—Dimple, he whispered.

—I always will, I said. And I would.

—I never stopped, he said. And he hadn't.

There were tears in his eyes now, or maybe in mine. The Meru pulled up. With my last glance, I glimpsed Karsh raising that held kiss to his heart, like a pledge of allegiance to some new borderless nation.

—And I wouldn't change that for the world, he said quietly.

* CHAPTER 47 *

Perspective

A fitful sleep, not really a sleep, but an agitated wake, aweep. A few hours tears-twisted, calf-shin-knee athrob — arm flung out before me, arm flung out before *we* — half dreaming a heartbroken rickshaw.

My lost-not-lost love: the closeness of Karsh, despite it all. And I knew the only bridge to closerness could be my camera, my portal back into a landscape where so much had changed: all the old markers shifting, the usual wayposts waywarded, waylaid.

As the waters enveloped me, I felt the underbelly of this unrest — a something slowfrom to be savored. Like negative to positive, destruction to creation, a pulsing sense of a seedlinged sadness, an insuppressible flowering from the heart of something blue.

All you could get was close. I left a note saying I was out working and, camera in hand, was about to gimp out of the still sleeping house, when I found Sangita observing me from the bedroom door, her face twisted in concern. I guessed I really *was* weak in the knees.

—Too much dancing? she whispered after me into the corridor. She'd explain away my absence, I knew. I would conjure my cure.

—Too little, I replied.

*   *   *

Fingering those blue-brown beads as I headed down the drive and out to Shoppers Stop to hail a taxi — the sight of any rick now investing me with a new anxiety — an idea began to form, broken bits stringing together.

I knew then what I was going to shoot today, and raised my hand.

When a rickshaw pulled up before the taxi I'd set eyes on, I took a breath. And ran into that room. Got back on that horse.

*   *   *

Dismount. New haunt. I escorted my ears, followed my nose. Soft sifting sounds. Breathe through the eyes: somewhere, a most wonderful sight. Smelled-before-seen — an open flour mill. Inside, all was enveloped in a fog of the thin winnowed stuff in the midst of which a white-tanked worker, bran-brown limbs besprinkled in the fleur de farine, sat cross-legged on burlap, diligently cleaning grains for a ghostly grinding.

Deep inhale. A gusting dream wedged in the midst of the streetskin's tannery of hues. Like Karsh's tabla-ready palms, talc'd for the duggi, dusting the dayan.

Listen — and to the imagined rhythm, walk on.

In my thoughts, I talked to him the whole time:

A mere stone's throw from Mallika-posh Malabar Hill, gazing down at the arrow-struck waters of Banganga, ancient tank, its rectangle banked on all sides by steps. Karsh, they say Ram came here in search of Sita when she'd been abducted, and Laxman bowed a baan into the ground, that sibling archery freeing these sweet spring-fed waters, so sea-close, to slake his thirsting brother. My eyes keening to hear: an excellent silence in these elevated tank-perimeter-running pedestrian streets, punctuated by the slap of laundry in the little dhobi ghat; the creaking wheels of the vegetable cart; a bee-drone below-hum from the temple homes of the Brahmin families living upon its banks, amongst the shrines of Advaita gurus, the crematorium where all would one day ash countuppingly to zero once more.

The submerged roar of Colaba Causeway, once a bridge linking two islands. Wandering past stalls dealing gods, tees, bangles, squirt guns, SJ, a boy from Bihar, draws up beside me. Looks fifteen though possibly twice that. Do you hear him whisper his own mantra: Coca, Manali, what you like? He runs parallel beside me the causeway's whole length, finally indicating the alley behind the train-ticket-Internet-café shopfront leading to his den of intoxicating goods. I shake my head no; he just nods, moves on to his next dazed and dazzled expat, stained teeth stoking his sweet-boy smile. Life had been hard and he'd had to battle, batter it into a shape that would make space for him. This boy made man too soon, he casts a strong shadow, Karsh, reminds me once again that mine, ours, was, is but one little story in a city of many, many beating cheating bleeding fighting lighting hearts. That we were, we are, so very lucky. That no matter how bad it can get sometimes . . . it's really not that bad.

So many tales. On the NGMA sidewalk, just past the charcoal portrait artist, his sketches of Ash stuck up to the wall behind him, implying the Bollywood star sat and posed for him numerous times on this very patch . . . Listen: the slivered whisper of names writ on a single grain of rice by the man with the handlebar mustache just beyond. Here, the rice writer — turning literal the saying that every grain you intake has your name upon it. With magnifying glass and thin-tipped brushes, he appellates the basmati, enclosing each one in a tiny hyperbolizing water-filled capsule to render it legible. Zoom on the sheet of paper by his tools: a list of names, many paired, painstakingly spelled out so he makes no mistake. On that ink-swirled sheet, I hear a love song, Karsh — not ours, but theirs . . . though perhaps all love songs are still ours, even if we're not in love anymore.

Are we?

I can even hear what I won't see. That little ways down the road day, as you accompany your own eyes, follow your own nose: near Fountain Akbar Ally, Saint Thomas Cathedral, a thick sweet scent of bread just baked kneading your stomach-rumbling path thataway.

Flip's favorite bakery, once a wartime Japanese bank, walls flexed with vintage pictures of Parsi bodybuilders . . .

—Imagine, Dimple — me eating so much in Bombay! Each bite of butter-limned brun maska a panacea, each sip of sweet lime juice elixoreal, of Irani milk tea, ambrosiac. Thus baked Zarathrustra by day; rafters reverberating with dreaming bakers by night: a Parsi café begun by a father in 1951, run by three brothers and a son . . .

And, today, frequented by two new friends, breaking bread as one. And that evening, that midnight, you're with this friend, our friend, on your wary to Dharavi.

—First rick since our night, Dimple. After you go back. Back to our other city.

Your feet padding down dusty paths, a scent of something burning . . .

—. . . to an upper-floor kitchen converted to a cramped rehearsal, recording space . . . and here's what I know your eyes would fall upon first: that South Indian newspaper upon which their laptop sits, faucet dripping into nowhere, a perilous inch away.

Yes, Karsh. And in that space: one mic stand, three boys, baseball capped, wide-midnight-eyed, rapping in Tamil, Hindi, English about their block, this hood. Is this electronica?

—Excuse me, Dimple, but it's actually an electro-experimental-dubstep-hip-hop crew. Dimple, are you laughing?

Yes. That's so like you! Like us. A relief.

—Dimple, I'll think of you on the walk out when I see, wedged between two slum homes, and atop a mountainous rubbish pile, a dog of scrawn and scruff scrooning a silhouetted serenade to that crescent moon. . . .

I'll see that same moon, Karsh. From a Manhattan street. And I also know you'll wander around Kala Ghoda, near Dhobi Talao Market, slip into Furtados — selling wares part religious, part musical.

—Same thing.

You're tuning a guitar?

—From a rack of electric Gibsons tippling on each other in holy spirit camaraderie, and — a mere shelf above — flocks of angels, beseeching Jesuses, and an errant digital tuner beside a munificent Mary. But the part you'll love most? The cracked glass on that huge portrait of Mother Teresa by a brilliant red fire extinguisher. You'll photograph it as if the sheer force of her's star-splintered that border.

And you'll go to that chawl they told us about that first night, Karsh? That simply dressed, shadow-bearded man in the tenement house in Pydhonie — "a place where feet are bathed" — the tiny flat expanding with the grooved shooting radii of vinyl, vinyl everywhere. A house made of music.

—Yes. Flip will take me. I'll even take the train. Then a taxi. Then a short walk, stepping from brilliant day into corridor night. A moment for our pupils to widen: cracked pista-hued wood on the hallway ceiling, long sodden pink walls. We'll take off our shoes, leave them by a table at the threshold; the flat's so small, the vendor's wife, smiling eyes peering out from burka, will step out to allow us in. And in that minuscule room, a shirt hanging to dry by the fridge (vinyl above it), wall smoldering with sockets (vinyl below them), kitchen cupboards ajar (vinyl inside them), he'll offer us water.

You're drinking it, Karsh? Bombay immersion at last? No more hypochondria? I hear a whirring?

—Two fans, Dimple. He'll turn one on only when we enter; it spins its own tune. Above, a pink painted loft. I know you'd be up there right away — he'd let you, too — shooting the vinyl stacked in that loft sky, snapping down to the flat flower-fabric bed, oscillating with vinyl, too, Flip and me poring over the stuff. The mother lode.

Aloft. Like you at HotPot, in that balconied booth. Encircled by music, gazing down at all of us, immersed in your spinning below.

—And we're immersed here, too, Dimple —we'll sit six hours with

this most patient, sweetly shy man. So reserved, he, for the noise com-
ing off these LPs, even unplayed. He'd been warned by family, the
community not to collect music, see, but kept on from his youth for
the love of it. And now, with vinyl vanishing from so many places, he
has — lives in — a total sonic treasure trove! Bollywood soundtracks,
Indian classical. An LP, in its entirety, covered in Amitabh Bachchan
images. Watch him whirl —

　Like a wall on Chapel Road.
　—Where?
　Waroda? Never mind. Go on. I'm listening.
　—So many records — look! But *also:* Top Instrumental Hits
with "We Are the World," "Hello" . . . Little Shop of Horrors. Fame.
Motown.

　But that's not what I hear playing. . . .
　—No, Dimple. What you hear is that song my father so loved,
"Light Years." I found it. Here. In this chawl, in Pydhonie — so many
miles from where he first played it to me. On an LP of blazing burning
blue, blood-red round spindle hole. I can't leave without it. And he'll
wrap the parcel so carefully, in today's news, twine winding around it.
And keep it a secret, Dimple: It's for you. Dimple — are you still there?

　I'm here. I'm . . . so happy. You know, all this time I thought it was
a Punjabi song you were seeking. Thank you. And funny thing is, I'll
be in New York that day, Karsh. Just landed. Standing on a manhole
in the East Village and seeing, like a vision, the Made In India lid
whirling into a blue spinning disc.
　—I know, Dimple. I see you.

　And I hear you. Even in the din of all my Broadway, your Bombay
traffic. As I turn into Tompkins Square, read that sign for the first
time — just behind our bench, remember? Where we'd been, all
along. And also, where for over two reveling hours that exhilarated
day — well before our births or even our families' arrivals to this starred

and striped land from that of spinning blue-godded consciousness — so
many others, beneath the girthier of these two trees, had song-and-
dancingly birthed an entire movement to a tambourine beat.

—Allen Ginsberg included. That's no trashfetti below your feet,
Dimple . . . rather, raining from its garlanded trunk, crushed petals —

Like a thrown bridal bouquet. No tambourine today. But that
twelve-string busker, still here. As if he never went home.

—Maybe he is home. Petals on the bedspread. For a moment, I'll
hear him rise up off the vinyl: Minutes seem like hours and hours
seem like days *. . . "The Celebrated Walkin' Blues." We'll leave then.*
And when I bend to put my shoes back on, I'll see that that chawl hall
table is in fact no table . . . but beneath the cornflowered fabric, a
stack of still more music.

So the world on the outside's made of music, too, Karsh.

—Yes. Same as the in.

✴ ❋ ✴

The first strains of the muezzin. I was near Mohammed Ali
Road, so close to the musical abode Karsh would visit in this amal-
gamating future. Before me, Hasanabad: marble mausoleum tipped
with blue domes, as if the very sky had seeped into them to make
way for eventide.

There was one more place I had to see — for Karsh. His own
eyes couldn't yet bear it, so mine would bare it for them.

That pale pink paper zipped into the outer pocket of my camera case.

Unsure of my way, I found myself near Byculla Station. Followed
Love Lane, Gunpowder Lane. And then a helix of bylanes, into the
village of Matharpacady.

A dreamer sleeping below peepul tree . . .

Direct step into a time gone by. Off the heaving main roads, away from the encircling high-rises, street din dimmed into a sworn silence, as if even a whisper would break the reverie, the entire village delicate and defined as a reflection that could reverb into ever-widening circles, rumor and dissipate with the merest stone skip of a sound.

The warren wound, uphill-down, with many-altared passages, Jesus-and-Marys lodestarring the tapered way.

And houses — oh! No two alike. Houses with names: *Sacred Heart Chummery; Keep Sake*. Houses that immediately, inarguably, felt like homes.

These houses breathed; I nearly felt their breath, a must-sweet exhalation of history, memory. Bygone souls, these homes: sloping roofs, teak-hatted, a modest beckoning — not quite on the coy side of quaint. Dream-lidded eyes insinuated in awnings fawning over doors, windows, balconies. Dwelling skins wearing weathered wood well, sapphire and scarlet shuttered extremities felicitously applauding their panes, some gussied up in stained glass. Double-storied, stairwayed bodies, with trellising expressions. Bloom-brooched and fern-fanned, mouthed with sublimely magnetic verandahs, upon a few of which neighbors gathered — elderly, not so, and a child, too, silhouetted against a glowing open door.

Inviting. And as I rambled through this slope-shadowed, petal-flecked, trashfetti-speckled landscape, I came upon one that unquestionably invited me most. One look at this place, in shades similar to the blue domes I'd just seen, and — before even laying eyes upon its name — I knew.

I ventured towards that house of longing. Through that wrought gate, up the potted-plant path, to the double front doors: latched. But beside them: a luminous, white-barred rectangle of window drew me mothlike. Its curtain blew askance, allowing a sneak peek into a cozy room: paintings of places, photographs of people, both clearly loved, framed upon the walls. Teakwood floor; grandfather clock;

end tables with voluptuously shaded lamps. A statue of Mary; a brindled horse. Rocking chair piled with folded blankets. Near it, a round table enticed with a tea service. Set for two.

By the far wall: a piano, sheet music fluttering slightly, as if a phantom were page-flicking. Something pinkish upon the instrument's top.

Suddenly, a face peered back at my own, inquisitive but calm. An elderly woman with a finely lined, heart-shaped visage. She wore a blossom-pink nightgown, her long hair silver from the roots nearly to the ends, which hued gradually to black, a youth spent measurably behind her in inches of tresses.

Her skin was a honey hue in the light of the room she stood in. She could have been from anywhere.

—I'm . . . sorry, I whispered.

—Are you lost, daughter? she asked me.

—I'm not sure, I replied, though I was quite sure I wasn't. Around her neck, a small gold cross, like the one that had been mailed to Karsh. I showed her the address on the envelope then, and after a moment's hesitation, the note within: *He left this.*

She stared at me a long moment, mouth set, eyes sparking.

—But this is the one, she said softly. Despite my gut hunch, I was mystified; I didn't know what I'd expected to see here — him? Yes, in fact, what I'd awaited: him. Tucked away in an auricle-like pouch off the heart, sidestepping the time-space grid, still alive, still possible. And so I asked an absurd question.

—But are you sure *you* live here?

The old woman didn't appear startled by this query. One day, I thought, I'd be old, too, and probably wouldn't consider this so.

—I was born in this home. More than eighty-five years ago, eighty-six soon. The house is still older. A century, nearly.

As she spoke, from somewhere within its previous walls, the deafening wail of a mother, her mother. The firm reassuring voice of the midwife. The singing, the sweets, the clamoring communal joy of the neighbors.

—Did only your family live here? I asked. —Blood family?

—Blood family, bone family. Blood's relative, after all, she said, and now her eyes went woeful. —Someone did live here for a time. A young person. Too young.

I had no idea how Karsh's father had stumbled upon this home, the one he would make his last in this world. A wrong turn off Love Lane, Gunpowder Lane? A drawing towards the light? Eyes dilated by a kind of faith in the blue domes — or blinded by the neon lure of that other nearby red-lit district?

Had he come upon this door just as I had, seeking someone lost?

The woman stepped slightly to the side now, drawing the curtain with her. A rounder view: The room was bathed in pink light. And the clock, the photographs, the piano were still there. Except the clocks were counterclocking, the photos unfading, the piano keys slipping in a dip-jut dance . . .

My camera was frocking with me. Except. I wasn't holding my camera.

In that other camera, kamra, chamber: chimera. I saw now a young girl, entire ringleted head of ebony, wasp waist whooshed in a very different sort of dress — rose with blue love knots, many of which had been snipped off, shipped off — singing to a savior, a homeland, a lost soul, hands floating over the keys. As she sang, a hymn of birth turned dirge, an oratory of silver to black (or perhaps black to silver) . . . and back again. The song was a familiar one, though I was sure at the same time that I didn't know it.

That melody Karsh had called out, sung out, in that child voice?

The story fell into place as the vision of the girl at the piano aged before my eyes, growing ever closer to that of the old woman in this opening.

I knew then how he'd happened upon her: a night in nearby

Kamathipura, the brothel district, set up in the ninteenth century to glut the lust of British troops during the Raj. The bordellos of White Lane. The Devadasis, those servant-of-god girls from the South in their red and white beads — poor children illegally wedded off to Yellamma, goddess of fertility, destined to never marry a mortal, but to serve her by, traditionally, vending their virginity to the highest bidder.

Inside, in preparation for their night's clients, the girls had bleached their skin, combed their hair, donned their saris. Outside, they stood on offer, upon a street littered with condom boxes, beedi stubs, drunken drugged men in search of a quenchless sating.

But it was another sort of compulsion that had overtaken him. Nearly nothing left to his name, he bet on luck one last time, found himself doused in an evening of gambling on Falkland Road. Swollen with shame and self-loathing, he'd been unable to stop, to kick the addiction that had cost him over time his very home, his very family.

That night, it had all skewed horribly wrong. Die gone demonic, though he'd managed to buy some time. When he'd emerged, quietly fearful, shakily resigned, from the den of his disquietude, all lost but for the clothes on his back and a something swirling and sea-drunk in his arms — the one object he would not wager away, the symbol of the last spurl of his fast diminishing faith, desire to *be* — the cacaphony of the red light district quelled as his ears had keened to this same song: the melody I'd heard just now, on that ghostly piano. Ringing as the midnight masses once sung on these bylanes, his ear strangely, bionically attuned, as when one hears the voice of the gods.

But he was agnostic at best, Karsh's father, and what he heard was, in fact, the voices of another hearing the voice of God. He realized he wanted his final exit to be wombed in this aura of love, of faith. The aura he'd inhabited only once, his newborn son's baby toes tickling his treasuring hands, two decades ago.

He realized this might be the closest he'd ever get to something divine again.

And all we can get is close.

Stinking of blue ruin, he exited Kamathipura, stalking that sound. It was the sound of something longed for, and he filled his ears till all that hummed within, without, was this seashell song swellingly telling of another place, a shore hopefully within reach — and for him, a boy across that ocean, and the mother of that boy as well.

As if possessed, like me tonight, Karsh's father found himself, suddenly but not suddenly in the little bylanes of Matharpacady.

Silhouette of a pani puri vendor pushing his precious pram of snacks up an incline; the yellowing alcove of the brightly blue-doored mochi shop, cobbler seated on the floor, soling a slipper. In the pink pearled light of his own laden arms, he trailed his haze towards the Holy Cross Oratory, built long ago when Bombay was hit by bubonic plague. After praying to Saint Roque for protection, it was said no resident of this village fell ill. But for Karsh's father, the plague began on the inside, not the out, and even a saint couldn't enter that space.

It would have to be a person. At least for a little while.

Carefully clutching that moonstrike of spiraling pink dusk, he made his way down another incline, fell upon this home.

It was one woman, this chorus. She, Catarina Henriqueta, had been singing, a voice spherical with the so many she'd lost.

Like my own face tonight, his had appeared in this window. A mendicant of sorts, he'd begun to hum along.

Something about him — his boyish self light-yeared beneath the grizzle and grief, the childlike treble of his humming — had reminded her of the ones who had not come, the children who would have been about and beyond his age by now.

The two called and responded through these bars, past the song itself.

—Lightning struck us to the ground . . . and now I'm waiting for the sound . . . to catch up and come around, he'd sung.

—So many years of hanging on . . . how could we know they were long gone . . . all the stars we wished upon, she'd sung back. The doors unlatched, and he was inside — and then they were both dancing in that unchronicled room: thawed by connection, together out of time, conjuring a fifth chamber to the heart, a fifth element where all that had been lost to them perhaps still beat on.

For the woman, it had been the unborn daughters, sons. Heirs.

For Karsh's father, it had been Karsh.

The pink light seemed to emit from atop the piano. And upon that piano, I saw now, a split second before this age-old woman bird-queried her head at me, blocking it inadvertently from view: a conch shell? A spiraling dizziness. The concha in the auricle, its deepest depression, leading sound out the ear canal to the world. I was hearing Karsh's story from angles perhaps even he did not know.

For I was an oracle today, akashwani — voice from the ether, sky. And I was loving him from angles maybe he didn't know as well.

Abruptly, I could see Sangita at this moment. Breathe through the ear:

Dimple. Something bold, something true; I woke and I knew. An image within spilling forth in a rush —to flesh out from my fingers, the finest hairs of the brush.

No notepads, no sketch for the final — never — likeness. Crystalline in my mind, how I must unwind it. My sojourning suitcase packed with magic tint tricks (replenished near Jude's, by Pali Market). Sari rags — half a length, my old ones ravished, used up. For blending, a few simple takeaway cups. A couple liters acrylic, outdoor, artist paints — much richer, dries quick, on these streets named for saints.

This would be small-scale stuff. Brushes bathed, not too rough. (Pray stay wet for the night.) And stainers seeking my blues —

easing just the true hues — (and perhaps other shades, too; breaking news!) — into being from white.

Bylanes, smooth patches, like the back of my hand. In this goddess-harvest moon — skin still steeped in sky swoon — brushes whirling of their own irrepressible command.

Iris. Iridescence. Seashell. Magnifishence. Goddess of the rainbow, sky, and the sea. Wed to the wind. Sandals, like Zara's, wing-finned. An eye that encompasses god and human. Arco iris: a spiraling to the heartland.

Oft I dream of a shady street, a piece of breeze to ward off the heat. In the fevered day, they stand just at bay, ask do I get paid; if not why on earth do I bother to paint? Offer water, chai, sometimes a chair. Linger, loiter.

Stare.

But now it's night on Chapel, in Chuim. A couple bystanders pause, perplexed, then move on. Here comes the drunkard who likes to art-direct — giving me tips on how to do my work best.

—Why so much blue? he asks, full of rue.

—Because it's my truth. My birthingest hue.

No police, blue meanies on this scene do tread (though I've got a fake go-ahead on Deepak's dad's letterhead). The locals don't know, and if they stop me, I say: Of course I have permission; I'd just name a name. I used to name others, fictitious ones. But today I'll say I've Sangita's volition.

They will meet me, Kavita and her beloved, too. I'll tell them, my sisters: These are for you. (It will strengthen them for what they know they want to do.) Their happiness true, one will tender:

—So . . . you do?

And the other will reply, —I have. And I will. And forever will do.

I'll be here a few hours, then make my getaway. When it's all over: a main road chance (stencil and spray).

Approaching day.

And when dawn washes over these inlets of streets, they'll swirl clockwise in concha . . . rainbows ringing round shankhas . . .

Every color we've won:

Spiraling lovers complete.

The rock of a chair, in time with Sangita's cycling hand. My aunt in Dadaji's Andheri seat, Akasha sprawled across her lap, asleep. Gazing down at her and seeing her own once-little girls incarnating there, limbs eventually outgrowing her well-intentioned embrace. Widening it, trying to encircle, if not contain them.

I felt the full force of Karsh's father's love as well, likewise circling him close, yet spiraling him loose. Letting him go.

Upon the pink paper in my hand, a love letter of sorts, that address, the words: *He kept it.*

And I couldn't be sure, so brief had been my profound glimpse through the grille: But it appeared this conch, this shankha, swirled left.

Beat scupped. For I knew then the truth of the matter: that Karsh's father had not fallen from that train. That one day, he'd put ear to shell and heard not the song he sought — only white noise.

He'd always known he wouldn't stay long in this home, in this world. No way to pay up. No other out. No other direction without that old tune to follow. So he would create a manhole, an exit of his own. He'd just needed to feel a little love first.

And when later, at the station, the mounting sound from the inside of that undone shankha matched the roar of the world outside him as it pitched along the tracks, and sensing a burning light, a bruising orb rushing towards him, he'd plunged into it and danced his own dark raga onto, off the rails.

They were leading him nowhere — so he'd take them with him. When I understood he had jumped, I understood in the same breath something unnameable but tangible as the leathery hand of the woman I was now laying my own upon as she reached through the bars towards me. It was about Karsh.

Karsh lying in fetal position on the dorm room floor that morning, unable to rise. The nightmares, the sweats. The shakes, the constant seeking.

I understood that Karsh had understood this as well. A low keening. And when the curtain blew again in the zephyr of the slow rotating fan, upon the piano mantel: no conch. Now: gramophone.

Shiva, god of destruction, was Karsh's deity. Atop his NYU desk this Nataraj could be found, his dancing god. His blacks were denser than I'd known, or had wanted to know. And I knew then, too, that when it came to Karsh, once my lover, now my brother, always my friend: My blues would be unending as the way the baby blue of this bungalow pooled seamlessly into the now indigo night, and that this — his drive to create, his desire to self-destruct — was the smudgy rubbed-out border, *morbidezza*, where we two would meet again one day.

The old woman was nodding, but she was no longer looking at me.

—It was his time. But I will always be grateful. He gave me a moment with an unknown unborn son when he felt he'd lost his own.

I nodded back, unable to speak.

—Come back sometime, child, the old woman said, and her eyes were wet. —I am not prepared for guests now.

Her voice was kind but firm. There was a love story here, and the mourning of one as well.

Before she let the curtain drop, finally, between us, I saw that avatar of the concha, this gramophone now in place, swirled clockwise, the direction of life. Karsh would lean that way as long as he could hear some kind of music.

This I knew, as I turned and walked away: Some of the greatest love stories would always remain unspoken, but would reincarnate in different people, places, songs eternally.

When we told our own, we told every single one.

*   *   *

One day I would do something, I resolved then. I didn't know what it was yet, but it had to do with all this. It had to do with my lens, a new multi-eared and -eyed perspective.

And for now, and always, I knew: Love had to be allowed in wherever, whenever, and in whatever form it took. We didn't have to shrink to fit it, box it to casket. And even then, when we found it dying, could opt for ashing down rather than burial, scatter it to all five corners of the earth and ether.

Whatever could be celebrated must be celebrated.

I was an oracle today but still had a long way to go. I was an oracle today but still would arrive always here:

Love could be. Must be.

CHAPTER 48

Brown Girls in the Ring

I'd wandered wide, and didn't return to Andheri till nighttide, to find voices conspiring there. I followed these undertones to fall upon Kavita and Sangita and Sabz, cross-legged on the floor by a cartoonishly snoring Akasha in my bed, all in a secretive huddle, like when we were girls reading Famous Five books by flashlight. I hovered just outside the door.

—It's going to be difficult tomorrow, Sangita was sighing. —It was supposed to be an auspicious day for a wedding, after all.

A silence.

—It still could be, Sabz replied slowly.

Another silence, but this one weighted with a kind of understanding.

—I thought you said marriage was just for people acting straight, Kavita whispered.

—I know I did. But then I realized . . .

Akasha suddenly rose up on an elbow, a dreams eavesdropper. They all glanced up as I stepped into the room as well, and it was both surprising and not that we were seeing the same number imbuing the room.

A zero could double, tip into infinity: a compass, encompass everybody — even those not in the room, no longer even amongst us.

—They can also be for people, Akasha murmured.

—Making a circle, I said. And my mind completed an idea so obvious, that had been always before our eyes, forming over days, hours, these nigh-three incredible weeks. It was high time to announce it to the world. Our world. —And I know just the place.

*   *   *

The next morning, on what would have been the main day of Sangita's wedding, a heaviness inundated the Andheri apartment as if it had a weather of its own. All the wallahs had been canceled for the big-now-unbig day, so even the jingle of the mystery door couldn't cut through the thick haze of guilt, disappointment, despair — AKA, fear for the future — clouding our climate.

It was also the anniversary of Dadaji's passing. And my own last full day in Bombay. I was blue. But I now knew you had to follow a color all the way through.

The only sign of life was Akasha, who crouched, wrapped in a furl of flowery fabric in Zepploo's corner, engaged in some kind of eye-reading session with the tiny twitterer, who under her tender loving care had gone from a flicker of life to full-flamed Passeriforme in the last days. Zep cocked his tiny head in stop-motion movements as if truly digesting, keening in on what Akasha was confiding.

My uncle and father drank their tea side by side on the zigzaggy couch, then did a few rounds of deep breathing, my father sneak-peeking at Kaka to measure his own progress. That accomplished, they decided to take a stroll on Juhu Beach.

Moments later, Akasha cast me a look and slipped out the door per plan, carrying an unplanned package swathed in the fabric she'd just been wearing. Had that been a wedding present? To be transferred?

My aunt had busied herself rewashing thalis in the kitchen, my mother reorganizing the pickle cupboard, lingering over the jars of chundo.

As for Kavita and Sangita, the duo appeared lost in their laptops — but when I passed the dining table, I noticed they were chatting with each other, online boxes agitated with emoticons and exclamation points. Today, finally, Kavita had dressed as she usually did in the USA — that is, like an Indian (well, my old view of what an Indian dressed like): She and Sabz wore matching blue-green salwar kameezes with dupattas that looked suspiciously like the left-over fabric from Sangita's wedding sari.

On Kavita's finger, that bit of sparkling celestite. On Sabz's, its matching yet inverse puzzle piece. And on their feet, the red, white, and blue checkered Vans they'd bought together in the Village back in the day.

Sangita, the unbride to be, stood by the grille, staring out over Andheri. Her shoulders tensed slightly.

—Not having second thoughts, are you? I whispered.

—Not at all. I just really miss Dadaji today. More than usual.

—I do, too. But I don't think it would make him happy to see you like this. I don't think it's *making* him happy. And after all, he's most certainly the Best Man today.

So I smacked my hands together, then addressed them all.

—Women, your attention! We can't sit around like it's a day of mourning.

—But we are back to zero, Dimple! my aunt retorted, emerging from the kitchen with my mother at her heels.

—Um. Okay. But back to zero — isn't that the same as a fresh start? I insisted. Sangita, Sabz, and Kavita knowingly met my eyes, the latter two a little eagerly. —As in Shiva. Destruction as a precursor to creation?

I had my mother and Maasi's attention. I wasn't going to waste it.

—Listen. I know we were going to honor Dadaji today, too. Well, he most certainly wouldn't approve of our focusing on what was lost; his spirit's still here, in the people and places he loved. Just like in Sangita's painting.

Kavita and Sabz were fervently nodding.

—Further, it's supposed to be an auspicious day for a union, no?

—Yes. Sangita's and *Deepak's*, my aunt replied stiffly.

—Those are just details. The point is: Good energy's in the air.

Who says we can't pick up other people's auspicious vibes and put them to good use?

—What are you saying, Dimple? my mother asked impatiently.

—I'm saying: *We* should unite. No reason for there to be an iota of rancor, resentment, resistance in this room: This is a space, an address so full of love, if we could just get past our expectations of what everyone else in it should be, do . . . and who they should be with. We still have much to celebrate — even if it's not what we thought we were going to be celebrating.

They were all not only staring at me now, but leaning slightly in as well . . . even those (all, save the elders) who *knew*.

—So let's get to that part, I said. —Move past the bitter and on to the sweet.

Akasha bounded back into the room then, box-free. As planned, she'd just filled Arvind in on our day's destination.

—There's no time for fussing and fighting, she now declared, strummer fretting the air.

—Yes, I agreed. —For example: You once were the most kindred of spirits, when you were little girls, right, Ma? Maasi?

Both sisters nodded in twinlike unison, looking a little puzzled as well. And as my parents had once advised me, during my rift with Gwyn that seventeenth summer, and Sangita so recently as we mounted to Mary, I told them now: —Then be little girls again. In fact, let's all be.

—I wouldn't mind clearing the air, Sangita concurred. —Getting to the bottom of it once and for all.

I glanced out that epic window, then back to this beloved room.

—Or, I said slowly, grinning, —to the *top*.

And so on the day where once had been a wedding planned, we found ourselves embarking on our own pilgrimage — ascending towards our own reunion.

CHAPTER 49

Landing Up

Gilbert Hill wasn't far from Andheri station. Not that we were going to take the train, of course. Arvind had insisted he not only drive but also ascend with us since he wasn't sure "what type of people" we'd find on top.

We couldn't all fit in the car, which had occurred to me last night. So Kavita and Sabz were going to meet us there — and score some alone time at this significant setting. They announced now they'd head down to Shoppers Stop and catch a rick.

—How will you ever find us? my aunt worried. —You must go through a *slum* to get there.

—Don't worry, ji, Sabz reassured her. —I've been to Gilbert Hill before.

—You have? Maasi exclaimed. I was surprised as well; Sabz hadn't mentioned that detail when I told them my idea. —So how is it that *we* have not? You've spent less time in India than any of us!

Sabz grinned. —That's probably why, ji. I mean, I've never been to the Statue of Liberty, but was born and raised in Jersey.

So about twenty minutes before us, the pair headed arm in arm down the incline of Ramzarukha. Down to go up.

As if we were about to ascend Ansel Adams's mountainous muse, El Capitan, my aunt was tucked away in the kitchen, busily packing up bottles of filtered water and Horlicks biscuits and fried puris, even unlocking that Fort Knox fridge to slip yet another plastic-boxed load into the bag after all that. My mother added several sugar-rushing packages of mithai she'd purchased earlier for the wedding.

Maasi gave her a pained look.

—That was for . . .

Her voice trailed off. My mother shrugged.

—Why let it go to waste, Meera?

Sangita reappeared now in jeans and unusually unstained flowing shirt, looking a good measure happier than moments before . . . and a good half foot taller.

Upon her feet were Zara's magic slippers.

My aunt demurred, —Beta, I don't think this is practical footwear to climb up a mountain.

—It's not a mountain, Mummy. It's a hill.

—Actually, it's not even a hill, Akasha piped up. —It's a freestanding basalt monolith ejected from the earth during the Mesozoic era — Cretaceous-Tertiary, in fact — in the same event that killed off the *dinosaurs*. Remember?

—But you are already going to go so high up, my aunt insisted, ignoring this piece of prehistoric trivia. —Why do you need to be higher?

—If Dimple's willing to limp up this freestanding monolith, Sangita countered, —then I'm okay to platform it.

—I'm fine, I jumped in. I still hadn't told anyone about the accident, had blamed my wobble on a pothole slip. —No need for you to twist an ankle on my behalf.

My aunt dropped with effort to her haunches to examine the heels, as if they were perhaps removable. But Sangita held fast.

—These were Dimple's gift to me, she said. —She had them especially made for my wedding day, and it's still that day — just minus the wedding.

My aunt sighed. My mother leaned down alongside her to check out the shoes.

—They'll hold up, she concluded. —Zara Thrustra makes a damn tough heel. And in any case, it doesn't look like your dikree has any intention of removing them.

—Stubborn as nails, Meera Maasi said, shaking her head at Sangita. My mother smiled át her sister.

—It takes one to know one.

—Yes, Shilpa, my aunt agreed, turning to my mother. —It *does*.

The two met eyes . . . and laughed. I awaited a continuation of the diatribe, but Meera Maasi surprised me.

—Such beautiful shoes —I've never laid eyes upon anything like them. Thank you, Dimple. For making the effort. For always making the effort.

*   *   *

When we descended to the car — totteringly, limpingly, hobblingly, yet still excitedly — for a moment I wasn't sure who the sweet-faced bare-noggined man in the driver's seat was. Another halohead?

I stood there a moment, hand off door handle. Was this the right Maruti?

—Dimple! laughed Sangita, catching up. —It's Arvind. He's just been to Tirupati, that's all.

Aha. Another pilgrimage — this to the foothills of the Eastern Ghats, as Akasha did not hesitate to share. Another shaved head.

It was a squeeze: my mother in front, and Sangita, Maasi, and me behind. Akasha curled up on my lap, in the middle-hump zone. Upon her own she held that large square sheathed thing, which she'd apparently left with Arvind.

I could have sworn I heard a tiny chirping sound.

—Akasha, that's not . . . ?

But it had to be. I realized now, as we'd exited, I'd noted in peripheral vision that Zepploo's space by the threshold had been cleared out.

—It's time, Maasi, Akasha replied solemnly, as if she were the elder.

I supposed it was.

And to the tune of that most recognized song in the English language — that world's-your-oyster-and-you-be-the-pearl, make-a-wish ditty penned by two near-party-pitch-perfect near-pitch-skinned Kentucky sisters over a century ago, including a *third* Patty Smith (Hill) — Arvind reversed out of the parking space.

We crossed S.V. Road and turned into Cama Lane.

We slurred upslope, a winding road a-tumult with shops and stalls and people, peopling, steepling.

Window view: an egg vendor, the dizzyingly white orbs throbbing in turquoise and tangerine stacks. Another stall blocked by a bevy of haggling women, heads brightly clad against the near midday sun, bangled fists plunked on hips as some item was weighed on a silvery scale. Parked motorcycles beneath teepeeing tarp, in-motion motorcycles that *appeared* parked since zero momentum could be gained on this crowdydow market street. Laundry hanging to dry, buildings the hue of tea-stained teeth, corroded poles, a ruffle of ravaged trees. Schoolkids mucked about in dirthills the opulent shade of saffron.

And so we rose, inching our way up beyond the spirited village until the glorious edge of Gilbert Hill manifested itself in the near distance. In a funny way, it was like spotting a celebrity on a New York City sidewalk, so long had this jig of upthrust earth been viewed from window frame, a distance, memory.

It was stunning. Shocking, nearly. A profile regal enough to emboss on a gold coin.

Arvind parked and leapt out with us, even lighter on his feet without his hair. We spilled out into a resounding riot of color: the bloom-bling of a phoolwallah stand in the midst of another pile of saffron dirt. The wallah stood stringing garlands of mogra and marigold, filling small wicker baskets with blossoms and baubles, sun-dunked chunnis and sundry sweets from the laden table.

My mother and aunt set about purchasing a few of these baskets to offer to the goddess atop the hill. We clasped them like bouquets, a motley procession of bridesmaids approaching the steps that would lead us to Durga's sky-high abode.

Those steps commenced just past a low building in a clearing — which wasn't clear but beautifully wreckaged with luminous plants in broken pots, more dirt piles, stacks of folded chairs, and one other parked car that looked as if it had been there as long as the sixty-five-million-year-old monolith.

From so close up, it was difficult to see the hilltop itself, only the stairs, which mounted like a crooking ladder up one of its craggy sides.

An unhill.

My aunt and mother gazed skeptically up. We halted just before the climb began, in front of a massive sign, its top half Devanagari, bottom a reprint of an English-language *New York Times* article.

—Gilbert Hill has appeared in *Sholay*, Akasha reported. —And one of the US versions of this type of monolith — only three in the world, two in America — in *Close Encounters of the Third Kind*.

—You don't have to translate, I pointed out. —The English is just below.

—I'm *reading* the English. The Hindi says nothing of the sort.

I wondered if every dual-lingo sign I'd viewed in India through my NR eyes had in fact been conveying two different pieces of information. After all, so many people were a minimum of bilingual in this city; perhaps it made sense signs wouldn't waste time and precious space repeating themselves.

—Should we wait for Kavita and Sabina? my aunt asked.

—They'll text when they're here, I beige-lied, buying them time just in case. —So let's just go up? They may overtake us in any case.

I took a step towards the steps — and buckled at the knee on my more tuk-tuk tizzied side.

—Are you sure you want to do this, Dimple? my aunt asked anxiously. —You'll be okay, beta?

I rubbed my ankle. —I'm sure.

—Well, you lead the way, then, my mother instructed me. —That way, if you fall, we can catch you.

—And if *you* fall?

—What kind of altoo faltoo comment is that? Do I look like a woman who falls? my mother said with her end-of-discussion look. She took her sister's arm. —Chalo, ya. I don't have all day for enlightenment, you lot.

Sangita joined me, impressively steady in those platforms on pockmarked earth.

—Okay, people, I announced, foot to rung-like step. —The only way is up.

And so I led the weird unwedding procession — well, that is, after Akasha, who was scampering upwards with a downhiller's ease, and Arvind, who'd gone ahead with the cheeping flower-fabric box to check out the Durga demographic (and get a sense of how far off we were from the summit).

—Let me carry the mithai, my mother was saying to my aunt, trying to extract the bag from her arms. —I'm stronger physically.

—Stronger! my aunt scoffed, hanging on to it with surprising might. —From all that fast American food? Well, I'm stronger *mentally*.

—What nonsense! What, from all that —

And here, my mother did an exaggerated (no easy feat) rendition of kapalabhati breathing. Actually, it was more like the sound of a water buffalo blowing its nose.

—*Mom!* I cried, horrified. The two were now practically engaged in a wrestling match — not advisable on such a steep climb — over the package of sweets. Sangita turned around and nabbed the bag.

—For god's sake, I'll carry the bloody thing. You'll both fall to your deaths.

—But —! they both protested. Sangita held up a warning finger. And it worked.

Arvind was back, and herded the squabbling sisters protectively from behind. With a guilty look, our moms now wordlessly followed us up. I reached back to lend a hand a couple times, but despite their suppressed panting (or single-nostril breathing), I was ignored, now that they were trying to prove their fortitude to each other.

A few more steps and they were ventilating enough to have desisted arguing completely.

Gilbert Hill felt like a living thing, as if we were clambering upon a munificent giant's back. The steep stairway chiseled right from the volcanic colonnade teetered skyward, the scant blue-and-white angling rail along one side offering little in the way of assurance; it looked like it was hanging on for dear life itself. But this was about faith, people!

The grey steps were bordered in pink and pistachio; as we climbed, I photographed the crimson markings running up their centers.

—Dimple! Stop walking with camera face! my mother called out from behind me. —You are going to fall — and then what kind of photographs will *those* be?

I lowered my camera, turned to Sangita.

—Paan? I inquired, nodding down at the red marks.

—Dimple! Not on a pilgrimage route. This is kumkum — you know, tikka, bindi powder. The way devotees bless the path.

—Shouldn't we do that, too? I asked her. Blessing one's path seemed a pretty good idea, come to think of it; I wondered how it would go down in Manhattan. Sangita delved into her bumpack. I expected a travel-size container of acrylic paint or stainer to emerge, but she now presented me with a tube of swish lipstick.

—A little pricey, I laughed. —I'm sure Durga wouldn't want you to squander MAC. Laxmi, maybe.

—It's almost finished. I'll just do a couple strokes — a symbolic gesture.

To either side of the tikka'd (and now lipsticked) stairs: a slab-dashery of rock, sienna dirt, that ubiquitous trashfetti. Burnt-looking brush and bramble and crackle-dry hibiscus trees jutted out at random slants, as if someone had just stuck them into the side of the hill in a haphazard rush.

About halfway up, the stairway veered sharply at a slipshod landing, bordered by a jumble of landslid-like, paint-dappled rocks. We paused to discreetly allow our mothers to catch up.

A group of hoop-earringed and nose-ringed schoolgirls were descending towards us, holding hands — perhaps for balance, perhaps the way so many same-sex friends did in this city. The girls' braids were looped up like Princess Leia, chunnis dropping on their chests in a V, ends trailing off their backs like dark double bridal trains.

They held perfectly still, surprisingly sweatless — and then I realized they were patiently awaiting Chica Tikka. I smiled back: Click.

As the girls passed us, my mother commented:

—Something about them reminds me of us.

—They are from the *slums*, my aunt protested, but her eyes had softened.

Akasha — who'd already several times run to the top and back to join us, in ever-shortening laps — reappeared.

—It's *so* amazing up there! I can't believe all this time it was just in our backyard!

—But I keep getting this feeling of déjà vu, my mother said now. —Not just with the schoolgirls. Nahi, Meeroo? That we have been here before . . .

—In a past life? I wondered aloud.

—Yes. I know what you mean, my aunt concurred. —Each step up takes me back to this feeling.

I laughed now. —Frock! Are you two actually agreeing for once?

—It is too hot to argue, my mother said defensively.

—It is not too hot, it is too *steep*, my aunt retorted.

Nearly there. At the top, we could now just see the mandir, a beckoning wedding-cake white. A yelp of vertiginous steps to the right . . . and suddenly, a final set expanded and flattened, slipping its confines to pool up into temple pavilion.

Arvind, evidently satisfied we were in no danger, now 180ed back down, with a mild look of resigned confusion following Maasi's instructions to keep an eye out for Kavita and Sabina.

—Ta-da! Akasha exclaimed. —Feels pretty cool standing on something sixty-five million years old, doesn't it?

Our eyes flooded with the blinding white of the temple, so open-arched it seemed carved *out* of sky — the marble secondary, the way you could imagine stars as pinpricks in a vast throw of black velvet, a glimpse to a geodetically radiant land behind.

Here, a couple hundred feet in the air, turned out the top of this primeval protrusion was absolutely shockingly pancake . . . no, chapati . . . chowpatty . . . *flat*. Most of the plateau was made up of the temple, fronted by that shining pavilion, and ringed by an ironed-looking lawn fenced in, just barely, from the sheer drop.

We took a moment, some among us catching our breaths. No crowd here as at Prabhadevi, Mumbadevi, ISKCON. No gatekeeper, bouncer; no corralling queues.

—It's like Durga *knew*, I marveled now. —Like this whole experience is just for us!

Sangita rolled her eyes.

—Dimple, don't flatter yourself. It's because it's eleven A.M. and we're the only idiots climbing a zillion steps in this heat.

My mother and aunt, carrying their twin offerings for Durga, for Dadaji, stood staring at the temple now, tilting their heads like little chaklees. Akasha, who'd already run to the railing for the view, gestured us over. We climbed the last few steps, crossed the pavilion to join her.

—You become more spiritual when you're higher, my mother now claimed with great authority. —Altitude ushers out your inner divinity.

—That's because there's less traffic when you're this far up, Sangita commented.

—No, it's not just that. It's as if you are literally closer to God, my aunt said. —And when you look down, you see how insignificant our little lives are.

—Or how significant they are? I countered. —How we are, in fact, in it together? I mean: Why is *up* closer? What makes us think the divine isn't viewable from any, every angle?

Rising higher than high-rise, than Sagar City's steep-fee swags (and surely delving deeper), the hues of the hill merged, taupes and tawns melding back down into the baked landscape, itself visually slaked by the azureous tarps, glowing like slam-dunks of swimming-pool water, of the tenuous surrounding slums (here, the doodhwallah's home, Akasha informed us, the burtanwallah soon to be shifting to the redevelopment building, left).

Far below, in one of the recycling centers: cardboard stacks camouflaged between brush and branch, and a pale blue door to nowhere, supine in the sea of undulating brown.

Akasha leaned over the railing to point out some sights.

—The Arabian Sea. Airport. Lokhandwala. Madh Island, Jogeshwari. Juhu. Those high-rises over there? Powai.

Powai Lake, the site of my youngest visits to Dadaji, before he'd relocated to the Andheri apartment. Now many of these place-names held memories for me — some bringing to mind a very different map not so long ago not-only-fingerprinted into my skin.

—And there. Ramzarukha. Our home.

How tiny it appeared from here, this building that housed the flat that had been a beacon for me these past days as I sank, floated, then swam.

Flow. A love-illumined lighthouse as real as Sunk Rock, Dolphin Rock, Prong's . . . and from whose sitting room I'd gazed to this summit where we now at last stood as my trip drew to a close.

Return to zero: the source. I recalled the funeral that day we'd arrived, the white-swathed throng of mourners sitting quietly to the side of the parking area. There would have been no sight of them from this vantage point. And for the denizens of that building: no peak of us, here, now.

And tomorrow? From the plane? What would I see — what would I know about this city, these people I'd compassed and encompassed myself?

We fell into a silence, our eyes drinking in the world we were in.

This view *was* the prayer, the blessing.

Rani. One day we will walk there, to the summit, you and I. And you will see, truly see, where you are.

—What is it, beta? my mother asked now, pulling up close beside me.

—This, I said, indicating the vista. —All this time. This is where I've, we've, been.

—Yes. This is where we *are.*

—And we *have* been here before, my aunt added, joining us. —How lush the view during the rainy season . . . Remember, Tai, the wet earth smelled so good, we even tried to eat it as children?

—Yes, my mother said slowly. —That Diwali we came to the base to see all the lights wound around the hill like a Christmas tree . . .

—Remember that man who wrote our names on those grains of rice at the top one day? Yours on mine, mine on yours —

—I do. How could we have forgotten?

—Too incredible, this amnesia. As if it were another life-time only.

—Perhaps it was, my mother said now. *Heptanesia*, I did not say. They looked at each other.

— Sitting with Dadaji on the edge, perhaps just here, Tai. Plane spotting. Imagining the places we'd one day go . . .

—I suppose I imagined extra hard, my mother said quietly. —And that's why I went.

My aunt's voice was rife with rivulets. —I always wished I'd left, too. Oh, how I couldn't believe it when you were gone.

My mother took her sister's hands in both her own.

—And I couldn't believe it when *you* were gone from my new world, she confessed. —Oh, Meeroo, I always wondered what would have happened if I'd stayed back. It's as if I've never been able to have a fixed sense of home since then. How I envied your rooted-ness. And perhaps still do.

—And I your freedom. I suppose the grass is greener on the other side.

I was so moved, considering those two little girls who once couldn't have envisaged life one without the other . . . eventually making their homes eight thousand miles apart.

—Actually, my mother laughed, pointing down, around, to the parched panorama. —It *is* greener.

Home was certainly not a place. That's why there was no place like it. I wasn't even sure it was a noun — more a verb, a direction. A movement, horse in motion, towards a *feeling*.

Of sanctuary. Which you might find in a place. In a person. A song. Sight.

—Home is not a place, I confirmed aloud.

—Dimple Maasi! You're so deep, Akasha commended me.

—Of course home is a place, my aunt interjected. —Beta, I think you may be dehydrated.

—It is not dehydration. She hasn't *slept*, my mother begged to differ. —Home is a *time*. And that is why, whenever I return to India, I cannot find it.

I nodded.

—Exactly. What I mean is, I explained, figuring it out as I did, —It's always elsewhere and here. In transit, like us. When I'm in Bombay, home's New York. From New York, sometimes it's Jersey.

And I wasn't sure why, but I was welling up then.

—It's like . . . I'm only at home under unfamiliar skies, I said with difficulty.

—But, beta. Every sky is familiar, Maasi said gently, tipping my chin. —Just look at it.

I did. And it *was* familiar, this sky. Yet something looked, felt different as well, though I couldn't quite put my finger on it.

Another jet plane. The same day-moon Dadaji and I had watched, wished upon over the years and miles.

—Shall we? my mother suggested. And we moved towards the temple, to honor this man who was in part the reason we were here: today upon this unhill, and every day, on this planet.

*   *   *

We passed the unusual figureheads of this shrine-ship (two sculpted mustached maharajahs flanking the entry, prompting my mother to grumble, *What is this? Air India? Out of 330 million gods, this was the best they could come up with?*). As she kvetched on in, my eyes saw what my mind knew:

We weren't the only ones here.

Through the arch, a flash of a snowy-haired man dozing in a plastic chair — the temple priest? Why did *he* look so familiar?

By this entry: Akasha's box, which she now gathered into her arms, disappearing off to the temple side . . .

Revealing, on the pavilion: two pairs of checkered Vans.

No one seemed to see but me. We stepped in, which, save for the few degrees drop, was sort of still out, given all the open arches here. Even a sprightly tree grew up through the roof, rooted in a tiny temple within the temple.

Still, not a soul, save the sleeping priest. Where were they? A bell hung from high ceiling; a couple of speakers lodged in the rafters. Durga's digs were a small step down into a chandeliered alcove: This Gaondevi reminded me of the Koliwada Durga, of Mumba, in her sheer volume of color. The deity's body was just insinuated by a blare of coruscating cloth draped around the main feature at hand: her bijou-bindied, crimson-lipped, crowned goddesshead.

Her implied chest burgeoned with flowers, perhaps from the same downhill phoolwallah. Before her, a table laden with coconuts, sacred threads, dishes of kumkum powder, a smatter of rice grains — and those Styrofoamy sweets (thermocol; pang).

We de-chappaled, wiped our feet on a red mat at the threshold, then entered. My mother and aunt quietly added their baskets to the table, bent their heads in prayer.

I bent mine to Chica Tikka.

I wish you were here, Dadaji, I thought to myself. *I know you are here. Before me. Beside me. I will find you.*

As usual, I had trouble keeping my eyes closed. As always, it was joint family living in this Hindu shrine: Behind this central goddess, a Panthera-piggybacking Durga giddyupped to the right, a Ganesha to the left, both on raised platforms.

To the side, a cupboard with elaborate latch bulged with bolts of mirrored fabric, wires, *more* speakers. As if on cue, now: music. And here, just risen, the DJ: the familiar-looking priest, tending to the goddess now. He set our coconut before her, refreshed her garland with our own. Finally, bridally ringing bells through the temple, our prayers relayed, he offered us prasad.

As he bequeathed me the blessed sugar cubes, I saw that he looked just like Dadaji. It was startlingly . . . the most natural thing in the world. A white fuzz of hair haloed his otherwise bald head. Saffron pants; rudraksha'd neck. From his plain white short-sleeved shirt, his dark arms flowed, wrists riddled with threads. A stroke of scarlet ash between his brows, which were now rising over his intent amber eyes in what I deemed recognition.

Sankalp again: *Wish you were here.*

You Are Here.

The priest nodded to my camera, stood very still. I gathered him into my lens and clicked — an incredibly whole front-and-side circular sensation of Dadaji conjured up beside and before me, on *both* sides of the lens this time.

*　*　*

As we exited the Durgamata temple within the temple, we passed that other shrine within the shrine: the mini monkey-god mandir from whose roof rose that sprawling tree — jutting into the space that must have led to one of the temple turrets.

Upon a ledge by a low-slung branch: a vial of rosewater. And before the mini mandir, bordered on either side by orange and pink donation boxes, two offerings had been made: baskets just like our own, petals alert, fragrance ticklish.

I had more than an inkling of who they came from . . . yet still, no sight of the pair. Inside the alcove, Hanuman perched, by his feet a lick of ghee, scat of blooms, little lamp burning. Also before him, lest his appetite kick in, a bit of roti, steel cup of water.

—Normally, only men do the Hanuman pooja, my aunt informed me now as I squatted to photograph the shrine.

—Why is that?

—Because Hanuman is celibate: brahmachari, she explained. Then, lowering her voice, —*Temptation.*

—How did he resist Sita, then? I asked, not lowering mine. Hanuman had offered to liberate her, Ram's wife — fly her out of the Garden of Ashoka in the Ramayana (rather more benevolent than Oz's Dorothy-abducting flying monkeys).

—Dimple! Do not speak of Hanuman that way! my aunt chastised.

—Do not speak of *Sita* that way! my mother added.

It occurred to me the offerings to this Hanuman had surely been the seditious idea of a certain bespectacled NYU Gender Studies post-colonialist (g)angster.

By the tree: a woklike wish-making wick-dish, agarbathi ashing down its blessings.

—We should wish for something, too, I proposed. And this time, I had a simple and pertinent one to make. Sangita produced a lighter from her bag.

—Why are you having a lighter in your bag? my aunt asked, eyes narrowing.

—Power cuts? Sangita suggested. She lit the tallest stick of incense, a swirl of mogra smoke circling upwards.

As we made our way towards that arched slice of blue sky at the temple's back, I intentioned my wish: that what we were about to witness would be accepted — *blessed* — by all in good faith.

Once my sankalp had been sent, I stepped out from behind the pillar. Outside, I saw a little stone house, possibly that of the priest. A caretaker's cottage.

I also saw two figures, luminous in the midday sun. The bearers of the Vans deposited at temple entry . . . but here, uncheckered, feet bare.

By the edge of the world when the world was flat, just at the rim of the stark drop down Gilbert Hill's jigjagging face: Kavita and Sabz shimmered through a slow dreamlike dance. They were circling a patch of grass, eyes fixed on each other, Sabz moving backwards with surprising precision. With each step, they held still a moment, hands clasped together, unheard words exchanged through lips curving up in matching smiles. An unhurried waltz with slight pauses, ringing around a wowza of wildflowers . . . and when that circle had been completed, it was repeated — in the other direction. No follower; no leader. Or both. Both.

A slow exhalation upon my shoulder, someone drawing up: Sangita, then my mother. In the relative silence, Akasha's voice rose, engaged in prattling chatter somewhere beyond the perimeter. But we three stood silently, watching the two engage in their sacred-secular-sexular spindling revolution.

I knew they'd been looking for some way to avow their love, if only for each other. And here, freestanding, now landing on this national monument and heritage site, sixty-five million years in the making, one hundred sixty-five steps in the sky (as counted by Akasha) — they'd found the place to promise their love would grow old, renew as well.

A sharp *inhale*. I turned to find Meera Maasi behind me, breathless, brows stunned . . . but eyes recognizing something.

—It's the one hundred sixty-five steps, I whispered gently, referring to her huff-puffing. But my aunt shook her head, eyes never leaving her daughter and Sabz.

—Seven, she whispered back. —It's the seven steps.

Seven steps. Heptasteps. Seven islands connected through zero after zero, summoning infinities through this threading dance. And then, at last, a stillstand, though their eyes tangoed on, tripped the light fantastic.

—What happened to those little girls? my aunt sighed now. My mother touched her shoulder.

—Nothing happened. They just got a little bigger. And we have to hold our arms wider to fit them now. That's all.

To encircle, if not contain. Sabz and Kavita, hands still linked, fingers so entwined as to unite the split celestite into unbroken sky, glanced over, discovered their audience.

I expected my aunt to lunge forth, break this union — or at least interrupt it. But now my maasi took the *eighth* step — perhaps the bravest of all: She stepped *towards* them. Kavita and Sabz stood very still, as if to not wake from this dream, pierce the veil. When my aunt reached the two, an arm fell around Kavita's shoulder. Tentatively, the other hovered, poised to handshake Sabz.

And Sabz grabbed this hand, wrapped it around her own waist, and drew Maasi close between the two of them.

I watched the three, backs now to us, gazing over the drop of Gilbert Hill.

Sangita and my mother and I were standing in mirror formation, my mom between us.

—It always felt strange, the idea of having a wedding without Dadaji's presence, Sangita said now. —Which is why we'd chosen this day. And how perfect to be here . . .

—His favorite place in Bombay, my mother concurred, stirred. Sangita squeezed her hand, and smiled.

—Though it never occurred to me to suggest this venue to Deepak's family!

—Some unions you can't pay off an astrologer, or count on an algorithm, to bless, I added, realizing now that Sangita probably hadn't done either, had most likely chosen this perhaps-at-first-truth-turned-to-fiction date herself.

For some unions, you had to read your own stars. Or write them.

Akasha appeared and unswathed the cage she'd so painstakingly brought up here, then unlatched the little grilled door. The sparrow perched very still for a moment, eyes darting into ours, as if verifying we were for real. Then Zep briskly yet assiduously examined the opening, and took a tiny clawed step onto Akasha's fingers. Akasha rose, gently cupping this chidiya, this chaklee, in her hands.

—Time to let go! she asserted, just barely restraining great emotion. The only other audible sound was an overhead jet, astonishingly visible — windows even — from this vantage point. Coming or going, I wasn't sure. I felt a fleeting tightness in my chest; I'd soon be on one as well. I followed the jet's now ever ascending path until it was swallowed up by an improbably cloudless sky.

Despite the drone, I was certain I could just make out Zep's sweet song warbling his own assent, a flutter of a harmony from so many miles below.

And then I realized what it was — that element of difference I couldn't quite put a finger on, what I was seeing for the very first time during this monumental and microscopic trip to Bombay.

Headstandup there: the sea above the clouds, the smog, the crowds. Above me, all around we. A first-time searing, soaring, however illusory, hue.

A true blue sky.

Into which, leaping off the edge of the world, now flew a little winged thing, in fine feather enough for his freedom at last. I'd feared the chaklee would fall when Akasha uncupped her hands and with a whispered kiss released him. But of course, for the free ones — the winged ones (often, the ones who winged it): The only way was up.

My aunt, with Sabz and Kavita, walked towards us now, a twist on a father giving away a bride. Instead, here was a mother embracing two daughters — an old and a new.

—Well, she said now, trying a smile, —I suppose, why waste an auspicious day for a union?

—I now pronounce us . . . us, I declared.

And then we were all there, together watching this little bird's flight. Zepploo dipped and swooped, became a dancing brown speck in the distance, then followed a color all the way through, consumed by pure blue — or perhaps, ethereeling, drank the very sky into his being.

—We love you, Zeppelin! Akasha cried, waving out into the world.

I turned to her, breaking out of my reverie.

—*Zeppelin?* As in —?

She grinned. —Of course. "Stairway to Heaven." Finest rock band in history.

✳   ✳   ✳

We were an unlikely un-unwedding party on our way down. Which, it turned out, was far more challenging than the going up, as gravity tugged us beyond our desired speed towards its heart, not to mention vertigo, to every hinge and pivot.

Akasha, as usual immune to the laws of physics, led the way, skipping downhill with her cage (bird-free now but stacked with the empty phoolwallah baskets), and circling back up to us every time she hit bottom, to check on our wary progress. My mother and aunt followed, aiding each other on the steeper steps, hand in hand — as in times past they must have been as they zipped up and down. But Sabz, better off in Vans (fitter pilgrimage footwear) wasn't convinced, eased her way in between them to lend both arms, and shoulders, too.

Next down the aisle, another set of sisters: Kavita and Sangita, chattering excitedly between themselves.

I'd gestured for them all to go ahead, took my time photographing the backs of this precious posse.

At the little landing where the stairs angled, twisted abruptly, then dropped, I glanced down at the paint-smattered rocks I'd noted on the way up. But now, pulling them into my lens, I saw that these — as on Chapel, Waroda, in Chuim — were no random smatterings. Specks and splashes of color twirled on rock face, spelling out the spilled ardor of Gilbert Hill romantics in names and hearts, a precipitous calculus of love. Forgoing all fear, some amorous souls had even brushstroked their soft spots onto the most dizzying unfootholdable juts and slabs: *Teeny + Sunil, Sam + Shona*. Half stories: *Mere Jaan. Dinky Hearts Naveen*. And now, unwritten perhaps but still a story in the making: *Kavita + Sabz*. A total in and of itself.

I recalled my doubled heart in the Juhu sand, single letter left within. Perhaps inhabiting it had been just as daring, life-at-staking as these scrawled sums before me.

I photographed these moments, lives etched onto Gilbert Hill, so many love stories surrounding, abounding on this glorious mount marry day. Then looked up: passing me now, a wonderfully wizened woman with silvery braid swum to saried sacrum. She was as crooked as the stairs themselves, but smiling most peaceably as she hunch-backed over fallen flowers, rock, rubble, her bare feet jingling with thick silver anklets.

A Linking Road hallucination? Flashback? She looked like a female version of the temple priest. She looked like my grandmother. And now she looked at me — another pair of omniscient amber eyes — letting a petal fall from fingers onto a paint-splashed stone bordering the landing by my feet.

I glanced down to watch my footing as I continued my descent, and saw, splotched on that stone, something I swear hadn't been there a moment before. I put camera to eye, zooming in for verifica-tion. Froze.

Was I dreaming? No. Down to the right, the recycling area. Ahead, the low building with the dual-language sign where we'd parked.

And here, one tiny word etched across brown stone in chalky blue, just dusting my fingertip.

Rani.

＊　＊　＊

And so we found ourselves. Not falling. Nor flying. But between the two: on this last full day in Bombay, landing card complete.

When we got to the bottom, we were greeted by two eager faces. Dilip Kaka and my father pulled Kavita and Sabz into a tight squeeze. A taxi idled behind in the near distance.

—Abhinandan, my uncle said to the newly wed pair.

—Congratulations, my father said, this time, translation surely the same.

—Enough altoo faltoo, Meera Maasi broke in now, that old sternness in her tone. —I don't know about you, but I've worked up quite an appetite. Anyone?

And she presented that plastic box, opened it now: the lovingly prepared and padlocked pieces of kanavla. The rows of painstakingly rolled ear-shaped sweets cradled each other, seemed to be intently listening. She distributed them ceremoniously now, offering lobe-first the fattest centerpiece last: into her own sister's mouth.

—Nothing bitter on such a day, na, Tai? she said, smiling at my mother.

＊　＊　＊

We got out at Ramzarukha.

A blue supine door leading nowhere led everywhere.

A curving half staircase by the Juhu sea, too.

A half bridge could carry you over the threshold.

And my limp was gone.

CHAPTER 50

Reception

The more fallen off the map, the better, Shy told me when we later spoke of the evening ahead.

Gods know I'd fallen off it long ago.

For all I knew, he was mere minutes from me now. For all I knew, these were counted in light-years.

*   *   *

Like this trip — an eternal blink. A moment of forever. And so the day of Sangita's unwedding derobed to the evening of what would have been her reception . . . and my last night in Bombay.

It was a good thing Gilbert Hill had cured my weak-in-the-knees-ness, for it was also the night of the most overground underground party in Bombay: Shy's Crosstreet fiesta — tonight to be held at The Fifth Room in Worli, a venue so off the beaten track, she insisted I ride over with a local.

That local was Sangita, with whom I now swapped tuk-tuk for taxi at Bandstand, so we could cross the Link together.

The Fifth Room was, in fact, a family home, Sangita explained to me now: an evacuee property, part of a post-Partition land swap between Muslim families and Hindu ones.

Also, since it was a home, that meant less overhead.

Which, more important, meant cheaper beer.

Jitters of ricks sloped up left towards S.V. Road as we hit the Link. Despite my imminent departure, Shy'd made me promise to come down — and I wouldn't have missed it. I was pretty clued in as to who tonight's mystery DJ was: my favorite in the world, whether he was spinning or still. And tonight's mystery artist — well, she was sitting just beside me, ear-to-earing like a kid.

For this day of her unlocked wedlock would be the night of her artistic unveiling. Via my photographs.

I also figured it was my last opportunity to say so long to the Bandra bunch before I headed back to the States — a sprawling piece of map that seemed quasi-mythical to me now, as India had gotten under my skin. Despite my oft fumbling foothold here, I felt a resonant pang at the idea of leaving — a pang I had a hunch I was just going to have to live with, no matter where or with whom I was — though the edges of it shimmered with the light of my old longed-for skyline.

I hoped to make a quick detour to Worli Fort while I was on that side, affording the one proper view of the Link I hadn't yet had (having ridden it, viewed it aerially from a seventeenth-floor window, and subterraneanly from the Bandra Koliwada). A last shot.

The party had shifted up to six, free entry till eight, as there was to be a scheduled patrol that night which meant shutdown at roughly the pumpkin hour. At five, Sangita and I were already en route.

—You hang on to the purchy just in case, she instructed me, passing over the toll receipt. —Round trip. Deepak's coming later and can give me a lift. I don't know how late we're staying — and I know you might want to party till the patrol. Just don't miss that flight!

Then she squeezed my shoulder.

—Or . . . do!

—Whatever you say, l'artista, I grinned. —Your big night.

—Yours, too! They're your photos; we could hardly have moved the walls themselves here.

—I don't know about that. I get the feeling your Piscis Volans might be able to fly off them and land where they like.

Where we like. Where I so loved now: below us, Mahim Bay; beyond, the Arabian Sea. Ages ago during the tsunami, an urban legend had circulated that a mermaid carcass had washed up on the Chennai shore. Later, the story was deemed to be a hoax. But that didn't mean mermaids didn't exist, did it?

Unicorns?

The unknown existed whether we knew it or not. The unknown number could still ring your cell phone; out of habit, I gripped mine in hand, though no call was expected at this point, perhaps never had been.

Ahoy, Cowboy, avast. I wasn't over him; I wasn't under him. My solace was simply knowing he was just . . . around. Crossing that bridge now, a visceral feeling that I was nearing him. Somewhere on this side, that space he was so fiercely loyal to, even in his possible infidelity. I felt a loyalty to it as well, and the people it housed: a place I'd possibly never set foot in, people I'd perhaps never meet. Or perhaps already had met? Who knew?

Bandra-Worli. Over here. You?

Back in Jersey, when I was small(er), an elderly man, surely retired, would wander the school playground after hours with a metal detector like a grippy golf club. He let me try it once, and that feeling, *ah* — when slight suction occurred under sand: voilà! A long-lost spoon from the cafeteria would emerge, scintillating as a doubloon. The yearn of metal upon metal, as magnet sidling fridgeward to pin up a photograph, echoed in me now: anticipation.

Strangely, the draw towards Worli I felt from Bandra swapped around as soon as we got off the Link. Now, an emptiness filled me, and I got the distinct feeling that what I was seeking was back in Bandra. Always on the other side. It was only on the bridge itself that I felt I was where I was supposed to be, and he was at just the correct distance. Not far enough to create pain, just a pull, not close enough to make me hectic, just quietly happy.

I seemed to have a penchant for finding stability in transit. We met in Arrivals, re-met the moment I'd makeshifted a home in a train station. We'd connected by shifting ships in the Cuffe Parade sea — then parted ways by a bridge. Even that room in Chuim — sinkingly linking in a home that was neither mine nor his — we'd claimed with kisses, sold for a sigh.

But tonight, I thought, smiling at my beautiful cousin, was about another kind of homecoming. For tonight was an evening for sisters and brothers, lovers, ex-lovers; for dreamers, possibilities teeming; for drunken moonbeamers, dance delirious screamers, poets and preeners.

For our coconspiriting team. (And hopefully heart healers.)

Left off the Link. And tonight, no whirling back round. First (Flip) landmark: turning off at the last cigarette vendor. Past tarped shacks, mewling cats, supine pipes, cosmopolitan trash. Second: the cement-stack-surrounded COAST GUARD HEADQUARTERS sign. We squeezed up the narrow road, just beyond a lot hubbubbed with kaput cars, to a squat rambling bungalow.

It kind of fit in, and it kind of didn't, this shack. Abstract art tagged a rippling number 5 across one wall.

This must be the place.

Onto the dirt path; a lone fisherman made his way down it, and a couple of saried women carrying totes aflow with cilantro, stalked with lemongrass.

—Do you think they know? I whispered.

—Know what?

—I don't know. It just seems weird there's going to be a party going on right here. In their village. Pronto.

For some reason, I was embarrassed in front of the Kolifolk, and waited for them to pass before opening the door and slipping in with Sangita.

—Yes, well, said Sangita, —I guess off the map is still *some-one's* map.

We stepped on in. The decor in room one of The Fifth Room was a mash-up — trattoria meets opium den meets knickknack-paddywhack attack. Red-and-white-checked tablecloths on the pizzeria-round tables, cushions stitched with elephants on the wooden chairs. A pudgy jovial man whose silvering hair surprised his baby face, and a black crochet skullcapped creature with back (and swan-ning nape) to me were seated at one table, deep in discussion.

The wall behind them was hot pink, rani pink, graffitied to the hilt with neon streaks. The adjoining walls were pista green, mustard yellow. Mesmerizing metallic dashes flocked in every nook and swoop, these glints schools, shoals, aggregates of fish — some Matsya-like (god-headed, human-headed, animal-limbed), others asteroidal (sea star, brittle star, basket star), all framelessly floating in circular backdrops upon the bungalow walls, winging their unwav-ering way out of the insinuated circumferences.

Unsinkable. I seized Sangita's hand, unable to withhold a gasp.

—Damn beautiful, she whispered. —If I, we, must say so ourselves.

Sangita's images finned the space, made it feel for a moment like we were underwater — but it was a different inundation from that floating Union Park elixir of a bar, less sinking than Chuim. Here, a sea-sky: that aloft feeling.

—We must, I averred. —Oh, Sangita, your first-ever exhibition!

The skully flipped around, revealed it cappingly contained Shailly — already kitted out in full party dress: fluorescent man-beater tank tucked into a multiply belted, sequined maxiskirt, hitched up on one side to reveal leg warmers and biker boots.

—The projections look incredible, don't they? Shy enthused. She indicated the jovial man, who bumbled up and clapped his hands in delight. —Sangita, Bobby here loved them so much they're thinking of making them permanent fixtures — or hiring you to paint directly on the walls! Perfect starting point for honoring the Kolis *and* the art scene.

—What? Sangita stammered. Shy hopped over to us, taking us each by an arm.

—Bobby, this is the artist!

Bobby half bowed towards Sangita.

—And *this* is Dimple, Shailly continued.

—Ah! The photographer.

I was finally *the* photographer? Not the DJ's girlfriend, not the ABCD photographer? It felt like a coup. Now *I* was grinning like a kid.

—Shall we take a look around and see if you're happy with the placement? he asked now, addressing us both.

—Go on, I nodded to them, tapping my camera. I'd leave her to her moment. —I'll case the joint.

Aquarium: Sangita's fishes lured me farther into the space, a few pitching light onto a bottled wall running the entire length of the room. The bar, complete with a lone boozer: Flip, scribbling as usual in his Clairefontaine notebook — nearly on the last page. I decided not to disturb his reverie — his writerie — just yet.

Above the bar, a filamented word: JALA.

A matryoshka collection ran the upper echelons of the room on a long lining shelf. On a facing wall, a set of bookshelves crowned with a massive Buddha head, and carefully cluttered with items perhaps left over from the home's former incarnation as a bric-a-brac shop (which hadn't gone down so well in a city that seemed composed of bric-a-brac): a silver tea service, ceramic rabbit collection, Moroccan tagine, wicker basket of polished stones, and on the bottom, stacks of board games. Scrabble and Monopoly. Taboo. Connect Four. Life.

Fresh flowers injected olfactory swank here and there. Hitchka-type sofas scattered with pillows like in our living room back home. A vase of peacock feathers. A thick book of Mario Miranda's original drawings of the Jazz Yatras. *Taj Mahal Foxtrot.*

Other portals — minus doors, but swing-glimming with beads — beckoned. But so did someone else.

Flip had finally looked up and was saluting me . . . with an Oberoi Hotel pen.

—Pinto.

—Lala.

I photographed him now.

—You ever put that thing away? he said with a smile, echoing my recent words to him.

—And you? I said, snapping that epic gridded notebook. —Last night in the Bay. Might as well shoot it.

—Don't remind me, Lala, Flip sighed. —Let's drown that sorrow. What's your poison?

—I'll have what you're having.

He nodded to the bartender, who was already pouring out his potion: Old Monk. Three cubes.

—A shot here's the cost of an entire bottle, Flip now informed me.

—Where *is* your bouteille?

—Bottom's up. But no issues; Bobby's given me open-bar privileges, seeing how I'm mentioning this spot in my piece.

Still, we tried to sip slowly.

—And where's your subject? I asked him, glancing around, a little nervously.

—Funny you should say that. I asked him how he'd transitioned from tablas to turntable, and he thought about it, then said he'd move from the decks to the drums tonight and show me in reverse. He headed back Bandra-side to pick them up.

—Yeah? I said, relieved to hear that busted-wheel trolley might be rolled open at long last. —How's that article going anyway? Any takers yet?

—I may have some very good news. You know *DJ Magazine*'s launching here? I talked to some cats who sounded interested in picking it up for the inaugural issue.

—Wow! Congrats, Flip! I said, slapping him on the back so hard, he spit out one of his three cubes, which now drippled down his übertee: *And those who were dancing were believed mad by those who could not hear the music.*

He'd been wearing the same one at L'Heure Bleu. Mingling with my thrill for Sangita, worry wicked through me for Karsh, hope and anxiety creating a turbulent brew. I prayed tonight wouldn't be an experience in that same irony (no one dancing *despite* hearing the music).

—I was thinking of using some of your pics, too. If cool by you.

I tried to smile, swirled my shrinking cubes around the glass.

—What? You don't look so happy.

—Look, Flip, I said. —Just remember: Karsh is a human being who's been going through his own . . . journey. So I understand you have to do your writerly duty. But just be gentle about it, okay?

—About what?

—His, you know. Bombing that night at LHB.

—Bombing? Flip grinned. —He *was* the bomb! I thought you knew me better than that. You think a fellow punk would view that brazen in-your-facing a failure? Dude, it took guts to play LHB first after those crackdowns — and to play what he wanted to play. Not only that, but to do something as subversive as bring trad-gone-rad Indian music back to India when it was essentially against the rules. Yo!

I stopped swirling.

—You saw that as subversive?

—Incorporating history? The past? You bet. He was a total fucking captain brave-art. And I'm sure as hell spinning it that way. You know, very few people here are clued in to the roots of the music scene. And wasn't it you who once said history's not always linear, homelands aren't always in their actual location?

—That'd be me.

—Well. I'm calling it "Future Past: Musical Mutiny on the Bombay Bowery." And you're mentioned, too, of course —

I guess he hadn't heard we were no longer together together.

—Um. Listen, Flip. Me and Karsh, well —

—. . . as a cutting-edge photographer from the New York music scene who shoots on film. That's pretty Future Past, too. I also quoted some of that wisdom you've been spewing along the way.

I raised my glass.

—Well, here's to the Bowery, then, I said.

—Not to the dowry, he quipped. —She okay?

He nodded at Sangita, now tour-guiding her own art expo with Bobby and Shy like a pro.

—More than. You do your thing, Pinto. I'm going to do mine.

I wanted to click the five rooms of the venue before they were (fingers, toes, eyes crossed) too dance-packed to see, and left him now.

I was two rooms in, if that first foyer area counted; where were the other three? I looked towards the bead-strung portals, one marked AGNI, the other BHŪMI.

Eeny meeny into BHŪMI. Vestibule, then two unmarked doors before me. I opened one.

The toilets, complete with hot-pink hose and drain scattered with those massive tic-tac bug-quashers. Shockingly: no toilet attendant.

No lady-in-waiting.

The other room? A bedroom. With a bed.

It was early. I figured I would just sit a moment.

There's a mare black and shining with yellow hair . . .
And found the jugular. A ladder; stair.
I woke up to the beat. A beat I knew by heart.

✳   ✱   ✳

What a greeting as I moved from auricle to atrium:
A torrent of *hi hi's!*

And when I slipped through ante into afterchamber, I could have been anywhere. Even New York — which was where these ancient Punjabi beats immediately transported me.

A resounding chorus of *ho ho's!* Shadow strutters chiaroscuroed in a disco-ball glow. Streamers rippled in the fish-swum flecked-wall candy-foil light. Behind-stage screen echoing back the crowd before it: a perfect circle.

And though the space was filled to the gills with these *gur nalon isqh mitha* uncorrallable, choralling boys and girls, my eyes at once landed upon one, only one, all the way on the other side.

Up at the decks, a beautiful boy in a HotPot double-dhol tee same as me spun out his heart. A boy I used to know and always would, and I felt an overwhelming gratitude for this. But I could barely catch a glimpse of him, so elbow-bump jam-packed shimmy-smacked was the crowd he was playing to — hands in the air and down, screwing the lightbulb on and on and on, hello-good-bying in sweatastic sync. They wattled and daubed, pugged and pined. Through the roof: bhangra gone edgy in a venue on the edge.

Playing upon the halo boy's angel lips, in a room swum with angelfish: an old smile I hadn't seen in a long, long while.

For he'd made a call to dance. And this time, they'd heard him.

* CHAPTER 51 *

L'Inde of 1001 Dances

It was one space now, warehouse style. The hippie dripping beads serving as doors ribboned to the sides, tables and chairs stacked away, every inch rendered danceable.

No longer walled. No floor, no ceiling. Dwelling swelling — a rumpus room, rafters gone rapture, timber to timbre, lumber to limber, mainstayed entirely by burnished flesh, the crackling energy of adrena-skin, boom tone, pheromoans.

Promise: It was busting its bounds with what was, could be, is.

I had found it. The quinta-space. For the fifth room was this: the space we made together when all the bulwarks, the barriers, came ashing down. A fortressed undress.

The fifth element, literally the *quintessential*: Ether. Akasha. Aether — son of Erebus and Nyx. What souls were of — god breath. Fifth chakra (Vishuddha): blue throat; inner voice. The nothing that was something, Shiva spiraling into Ganesha. The stuff used to delineate the universe, unaffected by the other elements. The medium through which sound moved, song of a conch shell. The sky, the space. The one without a body.

A blue-black shining.

I walked into the heart of this hearing . . . and saw boy meets girl meets boy, boy meets boy, girl meets girl. Meets world.

Sabz remeeting Kavita, synchronized once more. Once I sank into the music, the lens, all I'd been battling flew out the window as well. Yes, there was an abundance of graphic-print tees here — but so what? A high-on-the-hipster scene — I mean, as soon as you made something an antiparty, you were part of the party — but even hipsters were human, and why not just bring it all together?

And Shailly — she *was* a cultural conduit! And a hootchuit as well, as I watched her — maxiskirt pulled up underarm and overchest to turn sequined tube dress, leg warmers as sleeves, hair turbaned up into fluorescent tank, secured by a hissen of snake belts — threading her way through the heaving crowd, funneling shots into their upraised baby bird beaks.

Moonshine. Even the brawlers were harmonic tonight. Twirling on the dark drenched dance floor, I spun them all into frame: Heptanesiac. We joined our seven islands, our seven hundred, reclaimed on the packed canvas of a family home in this six-hundred-year-old fishing village, the land of a thousand and one dances — that light-year sound, catching up to come around — and I loved them all. I didn't know them all that well, but that didn't matter, did it, when we each contained a fifth chamber, an extra room in the heart that could adore unchangingly, that was all the other rooms together and more.

Breathe through the eyes: I spun till their faces roundabout merged, a cul-de-sac come crossroads, crosstreeting to circle again.

And like these Piscis Volans pirouetting off the paintings, finning out of frame, merwomen and mermen, we. In a country of one-point-three billion, you didn't need everyone to love you. You needed to love someone, or something. You *were* what you loved. And he loved. I loved. We loved. Did it matter what or whom or how or for how long — or if it was requited? Not tonight. Not applicable, unaccountable. It was ether.

And now the lifting of the unbridal veil: Through the mic, Shailly was announcing:

—Little Girl Blue — true!

Unbridled: a roaring reception, as for royalty. Sangita's slow-mo wade through the crowd to stand by Shy, her own shy yet graceful bow, our eyes currenting together across that submarine space, a circuit of pride, warmth, sisterhood.

Tonight, these were my people, this was my sound. At least here and now; all we had, after all. Here for the love of the dance.

Toda, tab bhi bola. And though apart, Karsh and me, me and him, *when broke it still spoke,* a jittery jugalbandi: yes, still a team. His four-eyed sound and my four-eared vision *blue, blue, electric blue,* fated to coincide, collaborate this night of the flying fish. He who Shailly was introducing now:

—And give it up for our fabulous DJ . . . Karsh!

No Jammin'. No Redshift. Blue. Just Karsh. A return to ourselves. Flip and I strained to see him, but it was near impossible in this mad circumgyrating crowd. But we could hear the hoof hurdling of his headless horseman loud and clear, as he unabashedly declared:

—*Let's take each other on a journey!*

Karsh kept the *ho ho's* and *hi hi's* running, the crowd whooping along. But they were mixing, melding with another word — a she-vocal stretching the *ho ho's* into *home homes. . . .*

And then Karsh was one with io, screen beaming my shots from Heptanesia, Mesh's as well. Onstage now, the Martian boy slithering his strings, the swampthing spacegirl up there singing:

—*Home is not a place that we can hold on to . . . still I thought I saw it in your eyes . . . could you light the way 'cause I keep trying to . . . seems I'm only at home under unfamiliar skies. . . .*

Home. Flight. My own approached, and I was diving into my Train Dance, my goodbye to them. But when Flip walked over now and tapped my watch, I couldn't say it.

—Lala. You can't go yet. I mean, did you even find the real Bombay?

—Work in progress, I said. —Besides, I've come to the conclusion it's not in Bombay.

He forced a smile onto his sadness.

—Yeah. Screw Bombay! he said fervidly. Then, trouper that he was, —There's always Chennai. . . .

He glanced down.

—Chandigarh . ... he said softly.

—I love you, Pinto, I told him, and it was true. —It meant the world to me to have a fellow philosopunk in Bombay.

Not even an aphorism from my favorite punkosophe. Flip just looked at me now and said nothing. *I love you, too* was what I heard him not say, bell clear — that's often how it was said, after all — and I gave him a hug to last till we'd meet again.

It's what none of us was saying; it was what all of us were saying.

And up there was the one I wasn't saying it to the loudest: my little boy blue. Gokulanandini grinningly absconded with Flip now, who cast me a mock terrorized back glance. And I squeezed forward for a better look.

On deck, Karsh was visible for a moment again, head just shadowing with hair, goatee just beginning to grow back. He passed a nod to Shy to take over. And now the *home homes* were melding, marrying another word soaring off vinyl, as the io girl stepped off the mic and let the LP speak: an urgent impassioned call to ride that racked me with an astounding sense of déjà vu, though it sounded alien in this context.

Karsh dipped from view, adieu. Vocals arrivederci'd out, followed by the strings bis-balding, annyeonging guitar, sayonara sitar, the see-you didgeridoo. Bass palaam-na next, then drum kit do-svidaniya, until all that was left was a shivery shuddery tribal beat — *dha dhin dhin dha* — a sound soaked in sweat and concentration to the point I knew it had to be happening now, live.

Aloha, halohead: I pushed forth to find Karsh sitting cross-legged on the raised platform, baby talc at the ready to flour-mill his palms, drumming out his doubled heart on those stretched skins. He seemed to be levitating. Not a drop in the dance energy, though now the crowd's movements went duggi-shruggy-drugged, like everyone was immersed in some primordial ritual their bodies had never forgotten, turntablist table-turning in a tablatastic twist.

... *dha dhin dhin dha/dha dhin dhin dha/na tin tin ta/ta dhin dhin dha* ...

Scuddering thuds thundered up to join Karsh's conjurist talc-swift hands, drawing song from goatskin, as he'd done in other ways so many times from my own. The higher-pitched baby drum, the larger bass reunited: dayan with bayan, leaping into the tala, strokes outlining the circle of rhythm: three claps, one wave in teentaal, sixteen beats split 4/4 — a hot-blood smooth-gait pace. Reveling in revaal, the four-beat footing of a Marwari horse.

Tali/khali: *Clap clap wave clap*. He glanced up, scanned the room. I knew for whom. I moved closer still.

And that vinyl vocal rising, riding, leaping off the beat.

I knew that voice. And when I heard the word, if there'd been any doubt, I also knew: This was for me.

Patti Smith. *Hi hi's ho ho's* gone *home homes* gone *ommms* come horses. *Horses. Horses.* And as the word clarified, the multilimbed gods and goddesses of the room began chanting along:

—*Horses! Horses!*

Immaculate reception. Karsh caught my eye then; I caught his sound. I was saying a sort of farewell, and he held my gaze steady, then slowly, surely lowered his lids and opened his eyes into mine again.

Clap clap. Wave. It was an aarti, an embrace, a blessing. A heart thump from him; one from me, too. A *We Are Good.*

Clap. If I stayed till the end, there would be an end. So I had to leave then. No goodbyes to be uttered. For any of them.

I didn't need to see this night through. I could see it already: The party would wind down, they'd throng around Karsh, show him the love, stoking the faith. Pull out their litigous John Terry smokes, their pocketful of Manali. Longboarding plans would be made: drum circle meets on Carter Road, browsing around the Farmers' Market. Road trip to Nashik. Those with evening alibis would squirt drops in their eyes, blink flutterbye wide. They'd bundle into cars — chauffeured ones, hired-for-the-nights, taxis, a few own-owned — cross that bridge, then split up into ricks. A few would sneak into their parents' homes; others would fumble for keys to shared apartments from Santa Cruz to Khar to Versova, tumbling over each other's bodies in late-night-euphoria hookups that would lead to dodged eyes in broad daylight, sometimes full-on love touchdowns.

A new commissioner would come to town and hopefully bring back the night. It was here now, whether he did or didn't.

Some might not be here the next time I came. One tying another kind of knot, a self-lassoing slip through a circle aswung in a no-room-for-all Bandra flat gone pool bottom. The catch: unMeshed — a quest for reinvention dead-ending so he'd close the circuit, flow out of the manhole, leaving behind the very first, and empty, ebbing origami wallet. In fact from by-then-tearful Toronto, still a Bandra boy through, through. Was that why he'd looped me in before he'd gone? Even into channeling along?

A creative soul moved on. And a destroyer's as well. A boy attired in designer tee and AK-47 who'd bloodbathed the masses would go the way of that flesh, give up the ghost through a noose.

Vamoose: Thackeray pass on. Six thousand Darjeeling guitars strum "Imagine" for a much-missed girl gone too brutally, too young, so many miles from home. A dreamer's dying declaration (echoing from the New York Dakota pavement): Would we someday live as one?

But others here, now: visas expired, jobs calling from Singapore, Dubai. London and the laylines at Portobello, Lancaster. NYU acceptances. Those tagged walls, the rainbow-ribalded streets of Bandra. By next time, the flying fish might be faded, flecked — painted over. And these landmarks, they'd all have changed — a creakling around Amitabh's fingertips and furious smile — or gone forever.

Pages petering out from photocopied magazines sold by a hungry little girl on Haji Ali Road. The flour mill, Dadaji's hill — oldest bulge of Bombay. The welcoming bungalows of Matharpacady.

And nearby Worli Fort, a 1675 tourist-less laundry-ramparted blue ruin, embanked by the fishindigens and built by the British to keep an eye out for moonshone Mahim Bay marauders. Atop this fort, perplexingly, tonight: stacks of pavers, city streets broke down into their individual units. Jesus. A beached dinghy with prowed garland, surreally stranded upon the edifice itself. And within a starklit opening in this alluring wreck: the concrete walls and floor of a bodybuilding gym. (A vyayamshala — largely bench-pressing fisherfolk.)

With a temple in it.

A national heritage site nonexistent on a current Existing Land Use Plan.

If numbered, their days: How high could we count?

And the landmark cow? Hopefully, she'd still be there — the traffic-stopping sacred — on the street.

Karsh was still playing, but our eyes remained locked . . . then loosened. I lifted my hand in a little wave. A beat, or 4/4, and Karsh now raised a palm towards mine. And then it fell, his eyes back on bayan and dayan. Though they remained downcast, the nod he gave was a nod for me.

Tonight, I was a woozy-maned Rapunzel, hair flying up, not down, a just-past-limping two-bootlegging Cinderella, no lost slipper, an unsleeping insomniac Beauty. A brown-blue-skinned girl, maybe goddess — who knew? But what I did know: Your happily-ever-after *is* a once-upon-a-time.

We end where we begin.

And once upon a time, I'd climbed a ladder to deliver a lost sneaker to a downtown diaspora prince. I had danced towards him, his beats had reined me in. But today, they were letting me go. Tonight, they were propelling me lovingly, happily ever afterly away.

On this day of an unwedding, no groomsman riding in, no horse-drawn carriage — rather, a drum-skinned stallion accompanying me out of this unhitched space, my departure disguised as a dance.

Or my dance as an até-a-vista. To door. Through vestibule.

All that was left in the sonic mix: my breath. Sign over exit: PAVAN. Air. I stepped from the actual four rooms of this house-party home, the four chambers of my heart, the crowd call of *Horses!* galloping along with me — into the true fifth.

Rumor had it unicorns were around. And I sure as hell could ride my blue mare now.

Giddyup. And giddily out.

CHAPTER 52

Union Circle

Outside Crosstreet, nada but me. No chauffeurs, valets. Not a fisher-person to be found

I wasn't one for goodbyes. And there was one more person I had to not say it to. Nigh the pumpkin hour, and my horse drew up in the body of a Meru taxicab, dropping off another set of revelers to alight in love with Karsh.

I was just getting into it when my phone beeped: sankalp. Message in a bottle.

A return from Unknown:

Bandra. Over there. You.

Well, only one way to join here to there, as I'd learned. And I was already digging out the purchy, crossing that bridge, my horse not scaring, merely looking to land, Karsh on the other side of where I was headed, Cowboy mirror-shoring where I'd just been, me barebacking that hyphen, no lady-in-waiting but a cowgirl fate-gaiting, skippering, too, car lights sliding the many-cabled sails of this splurge of a surge of a bridge, as if it were sensuously blinking up and down, knowing if I were to bait it with my photo-graphic tackle, snap it from this fast-speed pane, all I'd get'd be black backdrop skirred with neon squidges, skywriting hiero-glyphically hippocamping, a neo-mythic X-ray lightning bugged with birds drugged, flying fish glug, zeppelins unplugged . . . now gazing into another set of rearview driver eyes (mappleblack, piquant), my re-return message to him, that bay-roving bucka-roo, (sub)urban picaroon, just capriolistically hop-skipping-sent as that steeded sea-riding gangplanking swanimal of a finished yet incomplete — or was it unfinished yet complete? — bridge wiped out my signal, his.

Link.

✳ ✳ ✳

I thought about how it had all come to pass, all the way from 14th Street to 14th Road, Union Square to Union Park. Out of the blue and into my life, I'd dropped the map and found him by my side. And what we'd inhabited, incarnated, had been so out of bounds on any other hitherto charted terrain . . . yet turned out to be somehow still so very within reach. All those streets named for saints hadn't kept me in line. But I suppose I'd never been trying for a straight line, after all.

We'd come together, and I'd fallen apart a little. As had many aspects of my life as I'd known it. But what a relief it was still beating, my heart. Harder and stronger, huger and steadier than ever. And now I'd be leaving, but cupping that spark in my hand, that little thing we'd ignited into a great blue flame. Smoke signals: Maybe it would always be just that tiny sparkler I'd pinch between two fingers; maybe it would never be his hand again in mine. No fixer, for if we held too tight, crushed those scant luminous wings as Caravaggio had done to light up his own darkness, we'd lose even that.

What you caught you can't keep: a strange situation. We stood there, the two of us, at Lands End. *There is no l'Inde.* Bombay was water punctuated by islands, I thought then, not islands surrounded by sea. Cowboy didn't need me, not the way Karsh had, maybe even still did — but maybe that's what I'd needed. He couldn't deceive me, because there had never been any specific boxed-in thing he'd let me believe. All that had been true were the moments spent, and whatever we'd trusted those to be. And even that — those meanings — could transform, even transcend the moment itself, with time.

With Karsh, it was geography and history: everything said, shared that had built up our connection. With Cowboy, biology, metronomy: all we hadn't said, wouldn't have time to say. In a way, the two bridged each other — as if they were continuations of the same being.

Actually, I realized, it wasn't either of them. It was me. My shift. Perhaps I was both sides but also the link that could turn fraught waters into a smooth sail, ride the past and future together on the wave of the now. And I was going to need space to figure that one out.

A sole double-hearted *D* on tiding Juhu sand . . .

Cowboy was humming now.

—*Busted flat in Baton Rouge . . .*

—*Waitin' for a train*, I serenaded back. But I was singing Janis; he was singing Kris.

—The blues, he said quietly. —You sort out yours, I'll sort mine. And we will meet again. In a new space and time.

It wasn't a lyric, or now it was.

—This life or the next, I added.

—Same thing, we replied. I guess he had no need for a traditional way to stay in touch. But then again, I supposed I didn't either. I just didn't stop surprising myself — and the most surprising thing of all was the calm that accompanied these revelations. I didn't feel a certain kind of sorrow when it was called for, it seemed, nor guilt when it was most required — or when I *supposed* it was. My melancholy so piercing it released a sort of joy from that pinprick. I was getting better at happiness, though. And ambiguity.

I guess.

Mostly, I felt, in myself — as I'd sensed throughout this trip, perhaps even before: that island beneath, making itself known. A little breeze carrying meward a scent from somewhere else, foreign hues.

And now that scent clarified itself, that shade: my own skin.

I pinched it.

I looked towards that bridge.

Cowboy followed my gaze.

—I'm not good at goodbyes, he said softly. —Are you?

—I don't know, I replied truthfully. —I haven't had to say too many.

Bom Bahia. Good-bay. Mum-bye. Bye-bye. He didn't say anything then. The silence filled with the chugging swirl of approaching ricks.

—Well, then, I said, trying to sound cheerful. —Hello?

I stuck out my hand. My name was on my lips . . . but I left it there.

His own lips parted . . . and then he said it:

—Hello.

Things got a little blurry then, but: There was a squeeze that was long but not so long to crush, and a kiss on the head that was too tender to take (yet too quick to heartbreak), a deeper one on lips that returned the mouths we'd exchanged in Chuim back to their rightful faces — *goddess with a* by the time we broke the bond, but secured the connection. An unweaving of hands, and a turning from those eyes . . .

It would never be enough. The unfinished, even unbegun, nature of our business left me a-tumult with desire. But maybe that was okay; longing for something could be beautiful, too, couldn't it? It was a pull and a momentum, a propulsion towards the heart.

A rick pulled up then, and I got in. But just before I drew my foot off ground and into the tuk-tuk — the signal to the highly-engrossed-in-us driver to hit the sputtering gas — I dipped my head down and looked back up at him.

—Cowboy?

—Indie Girl? he said, almost a whisper. I was in, I was out.

—We'll always have Unbombay, I said, and managed a true smile. And then I gathered my one foot up off the ground of Lands End, and was in. He smiled back, eyes softer than I'd ever seen them, but a steely resolve, too, nodding.

The driver pulled the lever down on the meter.

Back to zero.

*　*　*

Horse in motion: *And they're off!* I wanted to keep that last smile in my mind's eye, the perfect arc of a mouth I already missed.

This time, I didn't look back.

I looked towards Juhu, Andheri.

I looked towards New York.

✻ CHAPTER 53 ✻

Lighthouse

Andheri, the wee hours. Illumined as Diwali, darkness bayed at our windows, entire household up, chai a-brewing, and a simmer to the air as on the dawn of an auspicious event.

I guess any day could be. You had to live it to know it, had to know it to auspicate it. Sabz was over as well, was staying next door at Vipin Uncle and Vinanti Aunty's (who hopefully weren't growing too optimistic for their Silicon Valley son).

At the table, my aunt and uncle were teary-eyed. Meera Maasi was organizing the stainless steel thali before her: valiant wick, tiny silver pot, marigold petals.

—Are you sure you don't want company for the ride, beta? my uncle asked again. I'd insisted I leave with Arvind alone, for I knew how weeped up it would get the closer we got to the airport. We were just that kind of family, separation anxiety even when someone hit the loo. After much hesitation and debate, they'd finally agreed.

—Thank you, Kaka, I said. —But no need. You're all up so early, this way you can get some sleep and make the most of the rest of your day.

—Are you sure you'll be okay? my aunt asked anxiously.

—She'll be with Arvind, Kavita sighed. My uncle nodded.

—After all, he conceded, —I suppose Dimple seems to get around this town more than any of us.

You could say that again.

—Beta, be sure you come see us again soon, he added. —The house felt so lovely with you in it.

My aunt nodded, too fervently.

—The entire *city* felt lovelier, she said.

I heard a sudden stifled snort, and turned to take in my father, burying face in handkerchief.

—Daddy! We'll be together again in a couple of weeks!

My parents had decided to extend their stay; my mother wanted to be around for her sister and, after having taken so long to get *here*, felt it made no sense to be in such a rush to get *there*.

—Obviously, we know our own flight details, my mother scoffed, but she looked a touch quiverlipped as well.

I'd see Sabz and Kavita in a matter of days, too — and Sangita and her own parents had promised to visit us, perhaps by this time next year. So why was I getting so emotional? Could I still blame it on jet lag?

Or was it because of how an eternity could be over in the blink of an eye?

Well then, I supposed it was best not to blink. Perhaps that's why I'd sleeplessly kept all apertures open, shrinking and expanding, all these days.

—But when will we all be together *here* again? my mother whispered now. I wrapped an arm around her, on one side of me, and my aunt on the other. I knew this anxiety was a remnant of a lost but still lingering time. In Dadaji's last years, he'd murmur a similar pained query upon our exit: *Who knows if I will ever see you again?*

Those visits had required the comfort of the same-moon philosophy to be able to leave at all.

And then, of course, one of those times, my Dadaji had been right. And I didn't see him again.

Or at least not a bodily him. He'd been present with me this entire trip, permeated my Bombay life through and through — although, I was only mildly surprised to realize now, no more present than he was with me in my American life as well.

After all, they were the same life, these lives.

My aunt was preparing a cluster of sugar crystals on the plate now.

—To sweeten your journey back home, she explained.

Sangita passed me a secretive smile. Earlier, I'd offered her something in private, to sweeten her own homecoming. Replenish her fruit basket, so to speak.

She'd stared at the Condomania pack in disbelief.

Dimple! she'd whispered, mock indignantly. And then, impishly: *I promise they won't go to waste.*

My aunt lit the flame. She thrice swirled the thali plate before me, clockwise, then sprinkled a pinch of sugar upon my tongue, me openmouthed as a baby Zepploo.

As I crunched, I reached over and offered her a pinch as well. Her eyes searched me, confused.

—And to sweeten your journey . . . for when you come visit us, I translated. She side-to-side smiled, accepting. And then the *drrring* of the magical mystery door: Arvind had arrived.

Amidst the embraces, the inevitable to-do list:

—Dimple, beta, be sure to stop by the post office and pick up the mail, my father requested politely, averting his sentimental gaze. —The medical journals must be piling up.

—And *Architectural Digest.* You have the keys, na? my mother jumped in, putting on her best businesslike voice. —Please water the plants. And speak to them as you do so. In mellifluous tones, ya.

I side-to-sided now, grinned, —Ya na.

—Telephone us as soon as you arrive? my uncle asked.

—And even after, my aunt added.

—See you in a heartbeat, Kavita smiled.

—See you in my heart, Sangita affirmed. We three sisters group-hugged.

But it was Akasha, still sleepily pajama'd, who joined now and held me longest of all. When we separated, she was gazing with love, and then surprise, into my eyes, her own pupils nearly iris-wide.

She never told me what she saw.

Arvind took my bags, and as we stepped over the threshold, my aunt suddenly lunged forward, plunging the thali plate at me in a move that made me wonder if she'd ever fenced.

—Wait! she cried. —The bindi!

She dipped a finger in the silver pot now, pressing the vermilion powder between my brows. A few flecks fell into my eyes, freeing a couple captive tears.

—The kumkum our mother, your grandmother, pressed between the brows of your own mother the morning she left for America, Meera Maasi explained with great emotion.

—That's funny . . . I said. My mother supposedly had the same bindi powder back in New Jersey.

My mother turned to face her sister, now voicing this fact.

—But *I* have that tikka powder, she objected, a touch defiantly. —In the temple at home.

My aunt smiled a sly smile.

—I swapped them when you weren't looking, she revealed now, triumphantly. —All those years ago. With the kumkum Ma used for my wedding. After all, they were matching containers.

My mother's mouth fell open in indignation.

—How could you?

How quickly we fell back into our old dynamics.

—Ah, Tai. To keep a little bit of you with me when you left, my aunt said, all slyness slipping away. —And to send a little bit of me with you.

The two were now hugging each other as if *they* were the ones leaving for distant shores. Transference. A good moment to descend with Arvind.

But just before I did, I glanced down at the threshold. Where that little winged thing had greeted us upon our arrival nearly three weeks ago.

I photographed the empty birdcage, little latch door ajar.

∗ ✳ ∗

Down the *only way is up* elevator. I touched Arvind's shoulder, nodded at my camera. He nodded back. But when I clicked, it was he who said:

—Smile!

I tried. As we made our way to the car, through the pre-dawn dark, a lurch of loneliness slammed me from an unsuspected angle. This time, I'd be traveling alone. But, I considered self-consolingly as Arvind loaded up the trunk, wasn't this the natural state of the human being? I slid into the backseat. Born alone into the world, destined to exit it solo as well — and in between, life a solitary journey during which one had to, on her own, figure out how to navigate the twists and turns, the ups and downs, the meandering course of —

—Dimple! a chorus of voices cried out.

I turned to find my mother and father, and uncle and aunt, rushing up to join us. They'd clearly taken the stairs.

Okay. Maybe my own life was more a family journey.

And I wouldn't have had it any other way. Maasi reached over, tucked the marigold behind my ear.

It all felt a little like the dramatic see-off after a wedding, the bride's family bidding her farewell forever. Except with no groom. But I could muck out my own stable, thank you. (And muck up as well, but hay.)

—What altoo faltoo! my mother scoffed, squeezing in next to me. My father got in on my other side. —Not seeing our very own daughter off? We are not like these Western Hestons . . . nahi, Meeratai?

—No, Tai, my aunt agreed. She smiled, shutting the door behind her sister, my uncle behind my father. —We most certainly are not.

And to the tune of "Happy Birthday to You," my aunt and uncle turned teenier and teenier in the head-tail-light-lit not-quite-broke-yet day, waving until we'd disappeared down the drive of Ramzarukha.

* ❋ *

Chhatrapati Shivaji airport, and my parents' anxiety grew palpable again.

—Call us when you get there, my mother reminded me.

—Call us even when you don't get there, my father added.

—What nonsense! my mother snapped at him. —Of course she will get there.

—I meant *before* she gets there, my father clarified mildly. —From the airport.

—JFK? I asked, nodding.

—And this airport, too? he appealed shyly. —So we know you have been allowed through the border?

—I'll call, I told them, with a double hug for the runway, the road. —From both sides.

I returned to the car, where Arvind idled by the trunk, not wanting to interfere in a family moment. And before he knew what had hit him, I gave him a hug, too.

Before I left them, I turned back a moment, took them in: Arvind still glowing . . . and the cherished two huddling a little ways before him, faces vibrant with hope and wist so enmeshed as to be another sentiment altogether.

—And, Mom, Daddy? I added. —I hope you get your wish.

—What wish? my mother asked, puzzled.

—The one you went to tie the thread for? At Fatehpur Sikri?

—Dimple, my father laughed, —we went to *untie* a thread.

I stared at them, befuddled. My mother nodded.

—To say thank you for being granted the wish we made so many years ago. On our honeymoon, she elaborated.

—Oh? I said, dumbfounded. —You did?

—When we wished, my father smiled gently, —for *you*.

A circle: so many years ago, a young newlywed couple following a guide into an inner shrine, that space a tapestry of desire, a magic carpet room. The bride treading carefully in brand-new sari, groom taking care of her, her arm held with pride. Together choosing the saffron thread and interweaving fingers, willing the same wish — sankalp! — no need to voice it.

Forward to two and a half decades later, that much older bride, strolling carefree in Ann Taylor slacks and Banana Republic top, taking the arm of her still senior groom to aid with his one aching knee, and together entering that same space . . . to choose a symbolic thread to unknot together.

From tying the knot to unknotting the tie. And out into the brilliant sunshine, to be greeted by a medley of seated musicians in the temple courtyard, introduced as celebrities by the — son? grandson? — of the original tour guide of that family business:

—They are having success!

Applause, and then music.

Now, an eye-opening desire to rush towards them and join that huddle. But my mother, clearly feeling the same way, was — like Karsh's love-struck beats — ushering me away, tears filling her own eyes.

—And now that we found you, she said, tapping her watch, —get lost.

The flight wasn't full. Three seats, my mother's, my father's, my window: all mine today. Across the aisle, another empty seat. Karsh's?

Nonetheless, I could nearly see them there. I countrounded on my rudraksha. And as we swam dirigibly up, crowning from this wild blue yonder into that still indigo hour — star-flecked above as artificially lit metropolis below, city-sky-sea a perfect flickering circle — I could nevertheless nearly see as well, swerving on the very curvature of the earth below me, in that many-browned-and-blued land:

Roundabout Nandini, that sweet-toothed Indo-Iris, throwing face back, plane spotting. Rising higher, and that panorama of tarp rooftops. Higher still: upon the stark stoic lighthouse of Gilbert Hill, oh, minuscule temple priest, my alter-altar Dadaji, nodding to me from its crest . . .

And somewhere out there, both far and near, in a sea linked to this shining sea: Lady Liberty, once penny bright now verdigris. A brown-skinned girl gone blue like me. Still carrying that torch.

No, there was no place like home. But that's because home was surely not a place.

Still. I was getting there.

Bombay Browns

Sienna, swarthy, saffron, tan. Sorrel, suede. Cinnaman.
Almond, ginger, copper, brick. Rust. Ditch. Match: flick.
Bronze, russet, cumin. Buff. Cream of wheat. Racecourse. Snuff.
Ochre, umber, ecru, down. Seahorse gold. Saddle brown.
Braun; bran; brawn; tawn. Cowhat band. Fan. Fawn.
Sari flab. Coco(a)nut. Dun-drab. Doeskin, husk.
Wicket-goal: chappal sole. Old World monkey:
    Old Monk world.

Toda, tab bhi bola; bay. Terracotta. Mahogany.

Khaki, coffee, toffee smack. Backpack. Bottla Jack.
Arjuna's bow. Holy cow. Mr Chow's paneer kung pao.
Gilbert Hill: cretaceous crust. Rupee bills. Brindled chestnut.
Subscriber Trunk Dialing phone. Sultana scone. Toblerone.
Horse in Motion. Sunsunk ocean. Bahut construction!
    Two-elm devotion.
Hazel, brew. Hanuman. Honey, ghee. Tarzan.
Karsh's eyes. 995. Mangul sutra. Focaccias rise.

Dust. Grit. Sweat. Spit. Dung. Wet. Armpit.

Yolk broke. Paan stain. Lager-lipped beer brain.
Banyan bark. Dog pelt. Pony lash. Pothole welt.
Teak clock (tick tock). Birkenstock. Missing rock.
Tarka swish; frying fish. Mutton marg's brac-a-bric.

Shorn porn. Unicorn horn. Monsoon morn. *Asian Bride* torn.
Bell clap. Brown line train. Stained map. Sugarcane.
Mamallapuram Lighthouse stamp. Cymbal, pedal, Furtados amp.

Mop mope. Antelope. Raw dope. Taupe rope.

Lands End. Moon scar. Lonestar buckle. Twelve-blues bar.
Head-tail-light. Glass-glued kite. Flail: head lice! Trophy wife.
Moonshine swill; rilled dirthill. Jon Bon Jovi's rapunzels.
Soot; root; boot; glut. Cockroach (underfoot).
High noon dune. Mahim Creek. Topaz moon. Henna streak.
Bike spoke. Well choke. Cowpat; chowpat. Cola-Coke.
(Amul) buttered toast (in chai). Singhdana roast. Drivers' eyes.

Hay; clay; neigh. Boar. Hood. Gateway. Mangrove wood.

Psyched dick: Horlicks. Girled slick: burning wick.
Bum; rum; spat gum. Sucked thumb. Rotten plum.
Hip flip! Loo; screw. Tobacco chew. Sinew.
No diggity: jaggery-pokery; gur — *nalon* slur. Manali blur.
Stipple nipple: firecracked. *This old man* unknicker-knackered my
    off-whack (knick)knack.
Gurus-gods for abishek. Multilimbed goddess(es) sex.
Sex! Sex! (Sex please?) Vyayamshala flex. (Moldy cheese.)

Tiffin whiff. Skiff; spliff; *sneeze* . . .

Cobra flash. Aamras. Brun maska. Sun rash.
Bowed stern. Auburn. Butter churn. Fishergirl gurn.
Worn leather. Inclement whether. Untethered nether.
    Yaktail feather.

Gymkhana, pyjama, bandana; dinghy. Ablution. Pollution.
     Malkit Singh(ing).
Hoof; woof. Mangalore-tile roof. Manhole fleur: kaput.
     Gaonthan route.
Beige lie. Kulfi malai. Parch of sea, peel of sky.
Camel hump. Beedi stump. Bayan, dayan . . .

Tabla thump:

HORSES!!!!!

dha — dhin — dhin — dha —
dha- dhin- dhin- dha-
dha dhin dhin dha
dha dhin dhin dha/dha dhin dhin dha/na tin tin ta/
ta dhin dhin dha!

Landslide! Nandi hide. Lion pride. Low tide.
Guru, gargle, roti. Goat. Beached boat. Shopping tote.
Brunette; barrette; Bollywood. Guitar fret. Sandalwood.
Earth up-dug. Baccha-labored rug. Chin slug-thug. Lightning bug.
Bamboo; bacchoo; laddoos; Juhu: sand-sketched heart.
     Mehendi art.
Shiva's tears. Khadi wheel. Chutney smears. Kiwi peel.
Chickpea. Buckled knee. Market (flea). Room key.

Stray cat. Cricket bat. Diwali, thali aftermath.

Inexplicablewallahs. Kanavla(Lalas). Garam masala. Japa mala.
     (Third unprincipled winceable *Patrón Reposado* . . .)
Bungalow. Dungaree. Jodhpur, jungle, panch. Puri.

Shoeshine. Knots of twine. Palms aligned. Gollup of brine.
Coffeetea table; sable; broom. Kamwali; Koli; kam(r)arooned.
Land legs. Sula dregs. Gopi's dreads. Sacred thread.
Mulch; muck. Soiled frock. Stirrup, syrup. Tata truck.

Mustard pop! Mochi shop. Pavers' jigsaw interlock.

Sleeping beasts at Bandra station . . . !
Mud-muddled years of Reclamation . . . !
Bronze that Catherine would have been
(As was lady-in-waiting, Enlightening).
Sparrow wing. Zeppelin. Brown girl in the rain and ring.
Unrein my hand; unbridaling: l'Inde. Land. Land*ing*.
Sheen of le spleen. The skin we're in.
And now out on a limb, yet still agrin:

Tone in: A brown girl of bluesings . . .

Bombay Blues

Jazzswing; muezzin ring.
The breast-beat of mourners; bawl of newborners.
The once-weres, yet-to-bes
(real as those present, like the light of stars deadened)
Or those near hereupon. An illusion of dawn.

Blueberry beads ripening. Silt-swirl surf tidening.
Blau and Braun twinning. Pydhonie song spinning.
Cornflower; peri-twinkle. Maya; midnight van winkle.
Samudri Ghoda pool glide. Eventide centauride.
Peacock's cosmic blush. Fiat flyover rush.
Oil drum; soap scum; mendicant's mappled cow horn . . .
Blue water lily. Nilgiri hilly.

Linking Road toys (unrealized little blue girls and boys).
Supari prophylac-strip. Our own (lacked) hip to hip.
And hip to hop beatbox. Devotee b-vox.
Candyfloss stand. Tinge of hand slips from hand.
Aarti wish blown: This Kingfisher has flown.
Sea legs. Robin's egg. Agate. Tilted 8 . . .
A monk's funk big band. The reel teal of headstand.

Hair ribboned in cyan; a shoulder to sigh on.
Rainbow's fifth (or third) hue. Dew of déjà vu.
Universe roused with weed. Ring round the rosary.
Phosphorescent fish scale. Dadaji's heGaventh airmail:

"Light Years" within ears (far to near). Shifting gears (far is here).
Vue aérienne of world. Ghetto's billiard (blue) balls.
    Bangles bojangle thrall . . .
Washed out World Trade wall.

Blue Maniac jolt: Watch us as we molt!
Celestite sky — splits open: third eye.
Bombay sapphire — a bawdy desire.
Wedding sari unravels; the pigment of travel.
Black and blue knees. Rickshaws' moonlit frieze.
Blue-black Kali; stick-on bindi; longboard graffiti;
    Koli-cobalt-boat belly . . .
Wheelbarrow sheen. Mulshi lake green.

Electric destinations at a queen-appelled station.
An outliar's (dis)orientation: Harbour Line vacation.
Baby of wax. Drone of a shankha sax.
Man on the tracks. What we can't get back.
Star Chamber ceiling; more than a feeling.
Unstranger's gaze-haze; tilts hat of suede.
    (No need to persuade. Wanna be waylaid!)
Blue is the fire of desire held at bay.

Pashmina swooze. Three (whee! hee!) ice cubes.
Seaman Avenue heels. A gift, you can't steal.
Ultra(bucket)marine: glean in fisherman's mien.
Scrolls of fishnetting. Hept(unease): unforgetting.
Seaface flickers out. Palette: hope. Habit: doubt.
Catherine's love-me-knottings. Begotten: besotten.
    (Can't touch the bottom!)
The profound flush of faith in what you're living without.

Indigo nights. Luciole fireflights.
Lapis Lazuli. Unicorn's azure sight.
A question mark in Parel: an unending why . . .
    (?????)
Temple bell drone. Hasanabad domes.
Sloe undertone of alone. Unknown Number on phone.
Imbrue of the brew that you do till you're blau
    (der blaue angel bedeviled and reveling now . . .)
Slippery chroma of home.

Off Off Carter Road. A fingerspun globe.
Double bathrobe. Blue Frog's boogied strobe.
Encroaching cement: Steel keels hellbent.
    (Yet something still bends, something still mends.)
Street sign to Chuim. Chim(er)arooned.
Tint of a turban. Wave-glint off urban. Blueprint of your skin . . .
Cradle or tomb? *(Yet something still blooms.)*

Blue jeans beshed. Horizonless bed.
The blue moon we voodoo'd. From ash: Phoenix we grew.
    (Some'd say: *Screw loose.* Well, shooby doo doo!)
A circle-back Jeep. Avast! We're in deep.
Days without sleep (no count muttonous sheep).
Laundry rock-strewn; io's boon-croon; we three steeped in
    monsoon . . .
    Bye-bye balloon. Half-remembered tune:

. . . *bhoolegi woh barsaat ki raat* . . .
Poker chip stash. Confetti trash.
Astrologer aftercast. Tummy on fast.
Amor fati: Love your fate start to last.
Dhobi-pressed kameez. Gwyn's port-passing ease.

CBGB's sweet sleaze. (*Oh my frocking. . . . GEEZ!*) Freeze:
Held breath; little death. Bleu celeste; amethyst.
    Untelled, us-spelled, endless kiss . . .
Hi hi, ho ho — hc. Blues in my cuntry.

Breaking (heart) news! The US blues interlude of a resident refugee:

    Beached bottle missive. Sketched twinvitation.
    Gerberas effloresce in glad chlorination.
    Red white blue Va(hana)s; the flag of that nation.
    Athens paper cup. Golf's New York–Jersey cruise.
    Coffee-on-denim drops. Tompkins Square busker blues.
    Bharat Natyam duds: blue-trunk-unbuckled muse.
    The shade of all maps. Of leaving your lap.
        (Spin of a halo: a glim of wingflap . . .)
    Blue polish cracks: Create and then scrap.

*Ain't Nothing But The; Lady Sings The; Tangled Up In; You Look
Good In; Linger On Your; Celebrated Walkin'* . . .

Fibble-Ow!!!!!

        Splee spill-y-a dop-um boop-um-koo
    A seep-um, beep-um, ool-ya keep-um sop-um-hoo
  A sock-a meena, bop-a-spleen-a spoolia-dop-um-kop-a-queen-a
    Sploop-um, doop-um, ill-y-a kloop-um hue-a-blu . . . hue-a-blu!

You lose you bruise. Joni: *Songs are like tattoos.*
Bungalow low: chiaroscuro.
Woe-be-gone high: *where the truth lies.*
Viridian earring; souvenir-steering; unreveniring (no same river twice).
Trois Couleurs: Bleu. Clues not to you.

Blue roan; blue ruin. Begin with an undoing:
Befriending an ending's akin to beginning.
Blueshift; a contraction — but birthing may follow.
Universe in your mouth (but be sure not to swallow).
Unending manhole: *l'heure bleu*; the blue hour.
Ether-breath of the soul. Cure-all Curaçao.
    (The *where-are-you-now*-er?)
Thread yester- and to- with arras of tomorrows.

Basilica view: Lady of the Mount woo.
Blue-hulled pantheon. Value of slowfrom.
A porthole to nowhere to everywhere hearkens —
A swimming MerMary; a portal that sparkens —
A swish and a swash of a buoy and a boat.
Chapel's acrylic slick stain; grids of Clairefontaine.
    Love Lane's swell conch shell strain . . .
Neelkanth: a blue throat. Intone yourself afloat.

Mazagaon house palings. A plunger's tale derailing.
Meditating brain. The one that got awaying.
A bucket of paint blending sinner and saint:
Landmarks gone seadarks: Distill tincture from taint.
Royal; navy; coast guard. Boy Blue reclaimed.
Comicomplexion; Banganga reflection. Genuflect of all questions.
    (*Home is a direction . . .*)
Backseat blossoms aflame: a driver with a name.

Sea Link iridescence. Cama Peak's magni*fish*ence.
Fifth room of the heart: the quintessential part.
The palate of together even when we're apart.
Iris of Shy. Bowie's blue eye.

Glow of hello; dye of goodbye.
Supine door. Marble floor. Sam Adams spills to distant shore . . .
Where happy little chaklees fly.

A city of *belle eau* bellowed by land.
Unbury that treasure: Unclasp your hands.
Dupatta unfurls: (un)veiled birth: Blue Girl!
Liberty's verdigris when she's green-lit to breathe.
Untie the knots: all winged things released.
The canvas of free. The easel of ease.
A stairway to impossibly possible seas . . .

Observe: in the blue hour, a hyacinth cast.
Remember this first: that nothing can last.
Airport avast: Yet nothing is last!
Airport ahoy! My own bridle hue:
All things grow old . . . yet all things renew.
All things borrowed — like you. All treasured: (True) Blue.
Angel-finned-winged; ghostwritten: *Rani*. We *do*. . . .

And this saturation, with melancholic fascination . . .
Borders are blurring (it's akin to elation!).
For as we submerge in this city, streets aquamarine,
Le Spleen wines, dines, and weans: seen and unseen seams:
What we have and have been. What we'll reverie into being.
Where we are, where we'll be — but carry-on where we've been:
　　(Somehow you always still know what I mean. . . .)

Indefinite Stay: Saudade's bright flame.
Leave to Remain: the love that refrains.
For the ones we have christened, and for those still unnamed.

(Haven of Peace: Half-bridge always complete.)
Yes, yes! Encore again!
We will meet, we'll crosstreet! Unabashed! Unashamed!
Nil-neel: ethereal. An eternal bluescreen . . .

Nineteen days in Bombay. A cerulean dream.

Author's Note

Over the course of February 2011 to March 2012 I spent time in Bombay for this project. Though not specified as such, much of the temporal setting of the novel as a result refers to this period, up through the end of 2012, when I was in the heart of the writing process. One notable exception is the inclusion of the discussion of Section 377 in the book. Though this recriminalization of homosexuality occurred later, it felt like too critical a topic to omit completely from a story that for me was and is an opportunity to explore the import and necessity of freedom of expression as well as the many wondrous and wonderful and bigger-than-boxable-or-beatable forms love takes.

It, and we, cannot be contained.

Acknowledgments

Thank you, Bernard, my lighthouse, my closest friend. For putting *Writer* on my landing card all those years ago (and always landing with me). And many mercis, my most treasured mergirls, Lecla Marie and Zoé Rani, for much-appreciated perspective. Home is where you are.

My beloved brother, Rajiv. For the reservoir.

David Levithan, how wonderful to be reunited. Thank you for the big heart, and the love you've always shown these characters, from when they were just a twinkle in my eyes.

Christy Fletcher, for your care, forthrightness, and insight on this project. And Sylvie Greenberg, for your fresh, attentive (and very speedy!) eyes.

Thank you to my dear family in Pune and Andheri, especially my sis, Trupti (Teeny) Patel.

Extra-sparkly bleeps to Kenneth Lobo, my on-the-ground and in-the-heart coconspirator. Here's to the Star Chamber!

Special thanks to Ali Sachedina, for throwing out an arm. For the neon, and the new town. We completely lived.

Thank you, dear Jon Faddis, for writing the original scat section (page 547, in itals) for the "Bombay Blues" coda (splee!).

Also, much appreciation to: Naresh Fernandes, for the unremitting spark of your company and your inimitable point of view. Kainaz Amaria, Sarita Khurana, Smriti Mundhra, Nisha Sondhe (for visual fodder, you gifted photographers/filmmakers, all). Atul Ohri, Uri Solanki (for sonic information and inspiration). Jas Charanjiva (last-minute muse who shifted the course of a character's life). Dave Sharma (tablatastic consultant). And for their great hospitality, thank you, Sameer and Shona Bulchandani, and Bindiya Chawla. Also thanks to: Emmanuelle de Decker, Rahul Guha, Minal Hajratwala, Hanna Ingber, Amit Keswani, Vanisha Kumar, Dan Reed, Sree Sreenivasan, as well as Sout Dandy Squad, for that private midnight gig in Dharavi.

Blue Marie mercis to Karen Essex, cerulean sister. Tchin-tchin to that endless candle.

Big love to Adam Patro/Atom Fellows and Marie Tueje, my musical (and more) brother and sister, for musical (and more) sustenance during this project (and more).

Double-hearts to Arvind Devalia for his alwaysness.

A resounding Room 212 shout-out to Rekha Malhotra for the party that started it all.

Within the text, the characters make reference to a number of the songs and artists that inspired me while writing the book. Thank you to Patti Smith, Malkit Singh, Taj Mahal, Boney M., Iggy Pop (and the Stooges), the B-52s, Patty Smyth, Serge Gainsbourg, Arcade Fire, Bob Dylan, Bon Jovi, The Knock-Knocks, The Beatles, Kris Kristofferson (and Janis Joplin), Joni Mitchell, David Bowie, and PJ Harvey (as well as to "Mammas Don't Let Your Babies Grow Up to be Cowboys," "Over the Rainbow," and two of my parents' favorite classics, "Roop Tera Mastana" and "Zindagi Bhar Nahin Bhoolegi Woh Barsaat Ki Raat") for sharing their musical spark with both me and my characters. The original scat section (page 547, in itals) for the "Bombay Blues" coda was written by my friend Jon Faddis (also the composer of "The Fibble-Ow Blues" referred to in that same section). All other lyrics are my own, composed for the album of original songs based on this novel, which can be found at www.ThisIsTanuja.com.

And for providing the key notes to musing my blues, thank you, seven once-islands, for your knowns and unknowns, the friends who grew wonderfully strange and the strangers who turned suddenly friends during this immense, intense adventure of my 38 days in Bombay: so very glad to have shared a moment or forever of the path with you.

And last, but also a first: Thank you to my enormously appreciated *Born Confused* readers for all the Dimple love, and for continuing to ask me what happened next. I think I know now.

✳   ✳   ✳

In loving memory of:

Odette-ji Hidier
Joyce K. Muldrew
and Papy Jean-Jean-ji Hidier.

I know you're in the fifth room.

For more information on the author, please visit
www.ThisIsTanuja.com